AVERY THORN

Tied To The Sea

THE NAMELESS SYREN SERIES

THE NAMELESS SYREN SERIES BOOK 2

This is a work of fiction. Names, characters, businesses, places, events, and incidents are either the products of the author's imagination or used in a fictitious manner. Any resemblance to actual persons, living or dead, or actual events is purely coincidental— or used with permission.

Tied To The Sea (The Nameless Syren Series Volume 2)© 2019 by Jennifer Natoli.
All rights reserved.

ISBN: 978-0-578-61438-0

Edited By Emilee Robins and Jennifer Natoli
Cover Design by Jay Aheer

TIED TO THE SEA

For all the people being eaten away by the shadows of their mind
Always keep fighting

Table of Contents

Chapter One 6
Chapter Two 18
Chapter Three 37
Chapter Four 47
Chapter Five 65
Chapter Six 85
Chapter Seven 102
Chapter Eight 120
Chapter Nine 144
Chapter Ten 157
Chapter Eleven 165
Chapter Twelve 175
Chapter Thirteen 199
Chapter Fourteen 218
Chapter Fifteen 237
Chapter Sixteen 255
Chapter Seventeen 268
Chapter Eighteen 282
Chapter Nineteen 295
Chapter Twenty 310
Chapter Twenty-One 319
Chapter Twenty-Two 324
Chapter Twenty-Three 343
Chapter Twenty-Four 364
Chapter Twenty-Five 383
Epilogue 397

TIED TO THE SEA

Afterword **403**
About The Author **406**

Chapter One

JASON

I tapped my fingers nervously on the steering wheel as I pulled onto my street. Fuck if I wasn't jumping out of my skin and hoping I was someone else at that very moment; there's no telling how my parents would react to the news about Atalanta.

I had called them an hour ago to tell them I was finally coming home and that I had news. They were relieved to get answers as to my whereabouts the last two weeks and said they were on their way back from the university.

Pulling into the driveway, my stomach sunk when I saw their car. It wasn't that I was afraid to tell them what was going on. If there was anyone I could trust with this, it was my parents. But recounting what happened that night still made guilt flair in my chest, and I honestly was too exhausted to handle the storm of emotions that I was about to deal with.

I took a deep breath in and parked the car. "It's okay."

Climbing out of the driver's seat, I stretched my stiff muscles and walked up the driveway. I didn't even get halfway up to the door when it burst open and my mom came darting out, her long tresses of auburn hair bouncing wildly as she flung her arms around me.

"Oh, my baby boy! Are you okay? Of course you're not okay, look at you! You've clearly lost weight, and Gods, the bags under your eyes could go over the airport weight limit! Are you injured?" She asked as she pulled away and began to pat me down.

I gave her a reassuring smile. "Yeah, Mom. I'm okay. A bit tired, but okay."

"That's good," she smiled, and then proceeded to smack me across the head." What in the hell were you doing running off like that?! Your father and I were worried sick!"

"Ow!" I winced and covered my head as she continued to try and hit me. "I told you I was fine!"

She looked into my eyes, and I could see hers swimming with tears. "And you think that was good enough? A few vague phone calls? The random text message? Wouldn't even tell us where you were!"

"The situation was a bit...precarious."

"Jason Aurelius Thatcher Monroe, what did you get yourself into!?" She scowled as she pointed her finger accusingly in my face.

"Let's go inside, and I'll tell you."

With my hand on her shoulder, I guided my still fuming mother back towards the house. My father stood in the doorway, trying to look like the calm, cool, and collected one, but I knew better. He was probably freaking out internally more than my mother was externally. He just had the tendency to let my mother be the emotional one. He once said that if they were both the irrational ones, it wouldn't help anybody.

When I got through the door, my father pulled me into a fierce hug.

"I'm glad you're safe," he whispered as he squeezed me just a bit too tight.

I hugged him back tighter.

I felt a furious scratching at my foot. Looking down, I saw the white eight pounds of fluff that was Rocket, hitting me with his little paws, trying to get my attention.

I picked him up and cuddled him close to me." I guess you missed me too, buddy?"

His little nose twitched as he took in all the foreign scents that were probably on me before he began to diligently rub his face against my shirt. I couldn't help but chuckle. He was trying to cover up all the other smells with his own, putting his little rabbit claim back on me.

With Rocket in my arms, I walked into the living room and flopped down, exhausted, on the big couch. My parents, who were studying me expectantly, sat down on the smaller couch next to me, on the edge of the cushions.

"So, out with it," Mom demanded.

I sighed." I don't really know where to start."

"Start with the worst part," My father offered as he took my mother's hand into his own.

That was something I had always found interesting. Often, people said,' start from the beginning. 'But my father believed that if you started from the section most difficult to tell, then you've gotten through the worst of it and it would be easier to tell the rest of the story.

I wondered this time if telling the worst part would make it any easier.

"I was stupid. I let my anger get the best of me, and it ruined a family. Because of me, someone is dead, another person is in the hospital, and..." I paused and took a deep breath. "I turned someone."

My mother gasped, her hands flying up to cover her mouth, and I could see that her eyes were already filling with tears again.

She was about to fly into questions when my father put his free hand on her arm and said. "Not yet."

Looking over to me, my father added, "Okay. Now, start from the beginning."

So, I told them about Atalanta. I had mentioned her in passing to them a couple of times, as this girl I was interested in, but now I told them everything. How

9

from the very moment of meeting her, she had been suspicious of what I was. Of course, that had been my fault. I had been careless when I refilled my bottle with salt, and she'd caught me red-handed.

Despite her suspicions, the two of us had grown closer and started a somewhat awkward romance. At first, I had hoped she would have dropped the whole issue, but she had just turned to asking other people around town.

"Why didn't you tell us?" Dad asked.

"I thought I was handling it."

I didn't mention that I was afraid they would have told me to stay away from her.

"Well, clearly you weren't," Mom chided.

"Amy," My father scolded." Jason is an adult. If he felt that he needed our help, he's smart enough to ask for it. That being said, I do think you should have come to us."

I looked down at Rocket, whom I was holding like a baby. His belly was exposed to me, little nose twitching. I knew my father was right. Yet, thinking back, I didn't think I would have changed a thing leading up to…to what I had said. That, I would change if I could. Everything that happened afterwards was my fault.

TIED TO THE SEA

"Mistakes were made, and now I must lay with them," I muttered, quoting Ajax from all those weeks ago.

My mother, having calmed down from her rage, softly asked for me to continue. So I told them about Atalanta finding me napping at the bottom of the pool, us getting into a fight, and her going out on the boat.

"Do you remember that storm from a couple weeks ago?" I asked. They both nodded. "Well, Atalanta and her family were out in that storm. When I realized that it was coming in, Percy, who I was with at the time, realized she was in danger. So me and several others went out to go find her."

"Percival was with you? There were others?" my father asked.

I nodded. "Yes, but I'll get to that later. So we went out..." I recounted going out into the storm and finding the North family hanging on for dear life, Atalanta and her sister falling overboard and their father hitting his head and slipping into a coma.

"When we got there, Atalanta wasn't breathing." My breath hitched as I remembered holding her dying body. "We couldn't get her to breathe on her own, so I did the only thing I could think of."

My voice croaked when I added, "It was my fault she was out on that boat. I couldn't just let her die."

My mother was off the couch, rushing towards me with the intention to sweep me into her arms and provide that motherly comfort, but I held up my hand. She halted. Thankfully, instead of hugging me, she sat down next to me and put her hand on my knee.

I would keep it together. I reminded myself that I was just tired and took several deep breaths in before I continued.

"We weren't able to find her sister, but Atalanta made it through her transition. It was rough, but she finally woke up the day before yesterday and is back at her house recovering."

My shoulders slumped, and I sat back further into the couch. My hands were trembling. I honestly couldn't remember the last time I had a decent meal or a full night of sleep. That was probably why my head wouldn't stop pounding.

My parents were silent, watching me. I didn't mind. I could wait for their inevitable questions while I tried to pull myself together.

Maybe close my eyes for a moment.

I wondered how Atalanta was doing. When I left, she had been asleep. She'd slept a lot in the last few days. If she was awake now, I could only assume she was crying or eating, as it seemed that was almost all she was capable of doing at the moment. I couldn't blame her. However, if she was crying, I wanted to be there for her. At least knowing that Percy was there with her brought me some peace.

TIED TO THE SEA

Yet, there was this nagging in the back of my brain, similar to when I felt a storm coming. There was no storm, at least not today. It would rain on and off for a few hours, and that was about it.

What was this feeling, then?

I was jolted out of my daze when something cool was pressed to my face. Opening my eyes, I saw my mother staring down at me with a warm smile.

"My poor, foolish boy. You shouldn't be separated from your mate so soon."

"My mate?" I shook my head. "She's not my mate."

"Did you think that changing someone wouldn't forge some sort of connection between the two of you? You have feelings for her and changed her. As far as your instincts are concerned, she's yours."

My frown deepened. I didn't understand what she was talking about. From what I was told, mates chose each other and only formed a mating bond after performing a ceremony. Though, when I thought about it, all of the changed Mer I had met were mated to the Mer that had turned them.

"I bet you don't feel so hot right now." She felt my forehead with the back of her hand.

I nodded. I was exhausted and hadn't realized how feverish I felt until she placed the cool rag on my forehead.

13

"Your body is protesting your separation. It's in our very DNA to protect those we've turned, similar to the deep sea Mer ability to create bonds. Except that nagging feeling will only get worse the longer you're apart. It probably doesn't help that you clearly haven't been sleeping. It's harder, the separation, when one of you isn't well."

"Is that why you and Dad are always so close to each other?" I asked.

My father, who had still been sitting on the couch when I opened my eyes, stood and walked over to us. Taking Mom into his arms, he said. "Well, we've been around a long time. At this point, it's just love."

The two of them shared an adoring look.

I knew their story. Many years ago my mother washed ashore, coming to the surface for the first time after an argument with her family. My father was a scholar who was exploring this region, studying the sea life. Imagine his luck when he stumbled upon a real-life mythical sea creature. He didn't know that, of course; he had thought he found a nut job who couldn't speak a lick of English walking up and down the beach butt-naked.

Just like in The Little Mermaid, my dad took her in and got to know her despite the communication barrier. It wasn't a cliffside castle, and my father wasn't a prince, but they still fell in love. Eventually, he figured out what she was and he took the risk by asking her to turn him.

It almost destroyed the relationship they built, and after much argument, he stopped asking. They were good for a while until he got sick, and my mother decided she could either let him die from consumption or try and save him. Merfolk don't suffer from the same illnesses as humans, so she knew that if she was successful, his newly altered immune system could quickly kill off the bacteria.

It was successful, and they have been happily mated for the last hundred and fifty years.

I was snapped out of my musings when my parents had begun to get all lovey-dovey with each other, something I was used to at this point and was at least grateful I had parents that got along. However, when Dad began to put his hands up Mom's shirt, I gagged.

"Gods, guys, stop! I'm right here!" I shouted and covered my eyes.

My mom chuckled." Sorry, honey."

"No, you're not," I grumbled back.

I stood from the couch, ignoring the light-headed feeling that came over me, and walked into the kitchen to grab some water. Taking a sip of the cool tap water, I scrunched my nose. It was missing something. Reaching into the cupboard, I snagged the salt and dumped its contents into the water before taking another sip.

I sighed. "Better."

"You should take your mate swimming later. I bet it will help her recover faster," Mom suggested as she came into the kitchen and pulled a slice of cake out of the fridge.

There was cake?

I opened the fridge, and when I didn't see any, I looked up to my mom, who was happily biting down on her slice, and pouted.

"This is my slice. Get your own," she said, pulling the plate closer to her.

"I would, but I don't see any more."

"Too bad, then," she mocked.

I scowled and shut the door to the fridge. I shot my glare over to my father when I heard him chuckling softly. I bet he knew where she hid the cake. One look told me he wouldn't tell me though, especially when Mom shared a bite of her slice with him.

Traitor.

"She's not my mate," I grumbled, getting back on track would help distract me from the cake. My poor cake.

"You can deny it, but like I said, your instincts will say otherwise. You're jittery, burning up, and I bet two dollars you can't stop worrying about her. Like a drug addict going through withdrawal." She took another bite and said around a mouthful of cake. "Actually, I'm surprised you were even able to stay separated from her for this long. The first few weeks are the worst. I could hardly go to the bathroom alone without feeling nauseous."

I couldn't meet her eyes. She wasn't wrong. That little nagging at the back of my brain was there, making me wonder if Atalanta was okay. I had a feeling the answer to her second statement had something to do with the other guys.

"It's complicated," I muttered.

"Often, things aren't as complicated as we make them seem," Dad said.

"I know," I replied. I didn't think I could tell them about the others yet.

"Regardless," Mom pointed her fork at me." Take her for a swim tonight, and tomorrow you should bring her around for dinner."

I looked down at the glass of salt water in my hand. It wasn't a bad idea.

"I'll see if Atalanta's up for a swim tonight, but I can't guarantee about tomorrow night. We are going to go visit her father in the hospital tomorrow, and I don't know if she will be okay to socialize with strangers."

That, and I didn't want her around my parents until we sorted out that file we found. The last couple of days, we had been letting Atalanta recover before we went about asking why she had a file for a fake identity and who she really was. One thing at a time, Percy had said.

I felt a buzz in my back pocket and pulled out my phone to read the text on the screen.

My brow furrowed." Hey, something's come up. I have to go."

"Is everything alright?" Dad asked, concern etched in his voice.

"Yeah, Davie needs my help starting his car," I lied as I put down my glass and hurried towards the door. I stopped to hug my parents and scratch the top of Rocket's head before jogging to my car.

I looked at my phone and reread the message.

Ajax:

"Taking Atalanta to the hospital."

"Fuck!" I growled as I screeched out of the driveway.

Chapter Two

ATALANTA

"Who's Clint?" Ajax murmured as we stood as still as possible next to the door to the cabin. Right outside was a man wearing a dark tailored suit, his hands on his hips as he waited impatiently.

I gulped.

Clint was my family's handler. I couldn't tell them that though, so I threw out the first thing we were taught to say: random family member.

"Clint's my cousin, and he is not a federal agent. He just, umm...he just likes suits," I whispered, praying they would believe the lie that someone as dark as me would be related to someone as white as him. If they questioned it, I would just need to say he was from my mom's side and hoped they bought it.

I watched through the peephole as Clint leaned forward and knocked on the door again. Any second, he would be getting suspicious and trying to look through the window to see past the curtains.

I looked down at my scaly body. While most of it was hidden by clothes, scales still adorned my cheeks and mutant-like hands. I knew Clint couldn't see me like this. As quietly as I could, I scrambled back into my father's room, taking Percy and Ajax with me.

"Do you think if we just ignore him, he will go away?" Percy asked. His body was tense, almost as if he were ready to spring out and attack Clint at any second.

I shook my head. "Not likely. He's probably here because he couldn't get ahold of my father."

Clint would sooner pull out his gun and bash his way in to check if we were dead than just leave.

Percy and Ajax shared a look before Percy straightened and walked back into the living room towards the door.

"What are you doing?" I hissed.

"I'm going to answer the door. Stay in the back with Ajax. I'll tell him you're not home."

Shit! I didn't know what to do. If we didn't answer the door, Clint would storm in, guns blazing. But if Percy answered the door, who knew what would happen?

I bit my lip and nodded, deciding to take the chance where the boys were less likely to be shot.

Ajax gently took my hand and guided me into the bathroom. I huddled down next to the toilet, against the tub, while Ajax stood by the door waiting. When I heard the front door open, that slow creak of the rusted hinges, I strained my ears to listen in. Surprisingly, I didn't have to strain that hard. I guess my new DNA came with the enhanced senses package. Too bad the scales were nonrefundable.

"Hi, can I help you?" Percy asked.

"Um...my apologies. This is 876 Arcadian Lane, correct?"

"That's right."

My heart raced in my chest. I could just see Clint now, hands at his hips and his jacket concealing the standard issued 45 not an inch away from his gun hand. Ready to pull it out and gun down Percy if he suspected for even one second he was in danger.

"I'm looking for the North family. This was the address they gave me."

"Yup, this is their place, who's asking?" There was something different in Percy's tone. Usually, he acted cool and proper, but right then he sounded like the twenty-something year old that he looked like. It was weird.

"I'm Titus 'brother. I haven't heard from him or his daughters in a while. I got worried and came over to check on them."

I winced. Brother? Fuck. Really, Clint? We really should have decided what he would be the last time he checked in. If the guys weren't suspicious before, they would be now.

"Cool, guess you didn't hear—"

"Hear what? Are they okay?"

"There was an accident. Titus is in the hospital." Percy explained.

Clint swore." What about the girls? Are my nieces okay?"

I had to hand it to him, at least. Clint was a good actor. I could actually hear the worry in his voice. Though, perhaps he was genuinely worried. I couldn't believe it was about us, as more than likely he was going to get in trouble with his bosses.

"Atalanta was pretty banged up, and Cal…Well, why don't I take you there? I'll give you the rundown on the way."

"…Okay. Yeah, I would be very grateful."

"Let me just grab my shoes and keys."

I heard hurried, light footsteps heading our way, and I tensed until I saw Percy poke his head into the bathroom. "I'm going to tell him you were discharged a couple days ago and that we are your friends watching over you. Cover up your scales with bandages and head to the hospital as fast as you can."

And like that, he was gone, walking back to the front door, his tone chill as he said, "I'm Percy, Atalanta's friend. Just stopped by to pick up the place while Atalanta is with her dad."

"Oh, I'm Clint."

"Nice to meet ya, Clint."

All right, now I didn't know who should win the Oscar as their voices faded and I heard the sound of a car driving off.

Slowly, I stood from my spot on the floor and looked at Ajax. "We should go get me dolled up to play the injured victim."

"You were injured. But not a victim," He corrected as he hurried out of the room, quickly coming back with our sizable first aid kit.

I nodded, conceding his point. This time, I wasn't a victim.

He gestured for me to sit down on the toilet before kneeling down in front of me. "Your cousin-uncle smelled like gun powder."

I tensed and looked up at him, honestly surprised he could smell that on Clint. Trying to play it off, I chuckled." Yeah, Clint's a bit gun obsessed. Goes to the range all the time."

"I'm sure he does," he said, his tone skeptical, but his facial expression giving nothing away.

We sat in uncomfortable silence for a few moments as Ajax used the large bandages from the first aid kit to cover the scales on my face and the eye which was no longer brown, while I wrapped a few bandages up my arms.

I always wore long sleeves regardless, and was usually careful about keeping them from riding up, but while scars were one thing for someone's brain to brush off, scales were probably hard to miss. I looked at my webbed, clawed hands. I needed mittens.

As soon as we were done, I shot up, scrambled into my room, and began to rifle through the boxes. Grabbing the first mitten looking thing I saw, I rushed out the door with Ajax by my side.

His dark green truck was parked off to the side of the cabin. Walking ahead of me, Ajax opened the door and helped me up into the high seats. When he hopped into the driver's seat, he pulled out his phone.

"I'll tell the others."

"I don't want to pull them away for this," I insisted, not wanting more people there making this situation more complicated than it already was.

"They would want to know."

I sighed and slumped into the seat. This was a disaster. Granted, what in my life wasn't a disaster right now?

I looked down at my lap and stared at the mittens I held in my freaky mutant hands. The pink material was soft, its wool worn and little fuzz balls pilled up all over the place. These weren't mine. They must have been Cal's, and somehow they had gotten mixed up with my stuff.

"I'll have to give these back to her when I see her," I mumbled.

"Give what back to who?" Ajax asked.

"The mittens, they're Cal's. She'll need them more than me," I replied, holding up the mittens for him to see.

"Atalanta..."

I looked over at him, his face full of concern.

"What's wrong?"

"Cal's gone," he said slowly.

My brow furrowed in confusion until I remembered. My eyes slowly moved back down to the mittens, and I croaked. "Oh...right."

How could I have forgotten about my sister's death? It just didn't feel real to me, I guess. As the younger sibling, I had never lived without my sister. And even if I had, with how close we are...were...could the average person truly imagine what it was like to lose a sibling unless they had experienced it themselves?

Slowly, I pulled the mittens over my hands. I would need to be careful not to let my claws poke through the fuzzy fabric. Just the idea of destroying Cal's mittens filled me with such loss and hopelessness I felt tears begin to well up.

A warm palm rested on the top of my head, a comforting pat. Ajax was watching me out of the corner of his eye as he drove down the mountain.

I embraced the small amount of comfort he was trying to provide. Taking a deep breath, I shoved down that welling emotion that told me I was about to start crying. I needed to be strong in this moment. We were on our way to the hospital, and I would need to make sure that Clint and the guys didn't make the situation any worse by unraveling things that either party couldn't know.

We made it to the hospital a good five minutes before Percy arrived with Clint. I could only guess Percy purposely took the long way. Surprisingly, the hospital staff we'd run into weren't suspicious in the least when the two of us came rushing through the door and asking for passes to my father's room.

I mentally prepared to act like a horribly injured girl. Beyond being pretty damaged emotionally and having an extreme level of exhaustion, I was fine. Better than fine, in fact. The few moments I didn't feel like taking a month-long nap, I felt like I could lift a bus or run like an Olympic gold medalist. My body felt like it could be strong and capable when it wasn't weighed down. A small part of me, perhaps 2 percent of my subconscious was excited to see what I could do, while the other 98 percent of my being was still a scared little trash pile.

For the betterment of my performance, this was one of those moments my body decided that a nap was better than walking, and my legs gave out from under me as we made our way down the hallway.

Agile as a jaguar, Ajax scooped me up and into his arms before I even hit the ground.

"This might be too much for you." He muttered into my hair, holding me close.

"I haven't even done anything yet. I just walked down the hallway."

"Too much excitement." Ajax gave me a small smile.

I huffed." At least I won't have to pretend to be the poor recovering victim now."

"You are recovering." He pointed out.

I shrugged. "Then just make sure I don't fall asleep."

He grunted. "No promises."

"Were you this exhausted after you were turned?" I asked.

His eyes glazed over as he thought back. It was the same look people often got when they remembered an extremely old memory, but it couldn't have been that old. He didn't look much older than Percy.

He shook his head. "No, I wasn't as bad as you. But I…I was turned under different circumstances."

I wanted to push and to know more, but something told me to drop it.

We made it to the second floor of the hospital without incident. The fact that no one questioned why a bear of a man was carrying around a small bandaged woman made me wonder at the capability of the hospital staff.

We stopped in front of one of the doors and Ajax gently put me down. "This is his room."

I slowly opened the door and stepped into the room. He looked so small on that bed, hooked up to the machines.

I stumbled over to the visitor's chair next to my father's bed and slowly lowered myself into it, my eyes never moving from him. "You always see your parents as these indomitable creatures until something like this happens. Have the doctors said anything new? About when he might wake up?"

After I had woken up, Ajax informed me that my father had sustained a pretty bad head injury. Since he was the one to bring my father in, and with Cal and I missing, the hospital made Ajax my father's medical contact.

"He had extensive swelling in his brain. It's gone down, but they don't feel safe to take him out of the coma just yet."

I just nodded and continued to stare at my father. Before I knew it, I started speaking again, "I remember this time when I was eight. We were at this little carnival that was set up in a parking lot. I was on that ride, you know the one with the swings that would spin you around in circles super fast? My cousin and I were fooling around, swinging the chairs back and forth till we were bumping into each other while the ride was going.

I chuckled and reached over to grip my father's hand. It was a little cold to the touch. "He thought my cousin had kicked me in the head. He was so worried I was hurt, he strong-armed the guy to stop the ride. Security was called on him, but he wouldn't even talk to them until he checked on me. Stubborn bastard."

My voice hitched, and I held his hand tighter.

I felt Ajax moving closer, and I saw him crouch down next to me out of the corner of my eye.

"It's okay to cry, you know."

I shook my head vigorously. "I'm not going to cry. I've done enough crying over the past few days."

Despite my words, I felt the tears coming on again. Damn it!

Ajax reached over and brushed the back of his fingers against my cheek, and I felt that overwhelming pool of sadness seep out of me, leaving only warmth. I watched as his shoulders slumped and his mouth turned into a deep frown for a moment before he shook it off and gave me a weary smile.

I narrowed my eyes at him. I had felt this before.

Just as I opened my mouth to say something, Clint and Percy strolled through the door.

"We will talk about this later," I hissed at Ajax and slowly stood to give an attempted warm smile to Clint. "Hey, Uncle Clint."

"Hey, Sport! How are you feeling?" He seemed to be about to reach for a hug but thought better of it.

I tilted my head and shrugged. "I've seen better days."

"Looks like it," He looked over at Percy and Ajax. "Can I have a few moments alone with my niece?"

They nodded, and Percy said, "Of course," before he stepped closer and hummed. "I'll leave you alone with your cousin."

When he pulled away, I had never seen a more cocky look on his face. I felt the blush rise up on my cheeks so fast it almost made me dizzy. Oh, I was in so much trouble. I watched those two swagger off through the door, the biggest smiles on their faces. Dicks.

As soon as they were out of sight, Clint's friendly, loving smile turned sour.

He stepped super close into my personal space and hissed, "What the hell happened?"

Eyes wide, I stepped back and almost tripped backward."Didn't Percy tell you?"

"He told me three of you were out on a boat and got caught in a storm, and now your dad is in a coma, you look like you were thrown into a meat grinder and your sister is dead. I want to know the real story. Were you found?"

I flinched, feeling like he had slapped me in the face. "We weren't found. There actually was a boat accident."

"Why didn't you contact us?"

"I've been unconscious. I only just woke up the other day," I snapped back.

He pointed a perfectly manicured finger in my face. "You know the rules. As soon as you woke up, you should have contacted us."

"And It's been two weeks, and you are only showing up now!" I shot back before taking in a deep breath and holding my hands out. "Clint, we need to calm down."

"Calm down? You know how much trouble I'm in? One of my charges is dead, and the other is in a coma! The only one left just had to be you!"

I bit my lip to stop it from trembling. "What the hell is wrong with you, Clint? I get that we are technically just your job, but seriously? I thought you were better than that."

Clint stared down at me and his face fell. "I'm sorry. You're right. I've been so worried about you guys that I haven't slept, and seeing you two here like this and finding out about your sister, I just snapped."

I crossed my arms over my chest, feeling really awkward. I studied Clint, around six feet tall with an olive Italian complexion and warm brown eyes. Though, beyond his looks, I didn't know too much about him. He was in his late twenties, maybe early thirties? And utterly devoted to his job. I think he had a son.

Wanting to break the silence, I asked, "Why did it take you so long to check in on us?"

"Your check-in was only a few days ago, and I flew right over after your father didn't come to meet me."

"Oh," I rubbed my temple." Sorry, my days are a little mixed up."

He smiled." Can't blame you for that."

We heard a commotion out in the hallway and went to check it out. Clint's hand hovered over his hip and he made sure to poke his head out before I could. When I saw his shoulders relax, I poked my head out behind him.

All five of the guys were standing out in the hall. Jason, Hip, and Theseus were gesturing wildly to Percy and Ajax.

"If she's as okay as you say, why won't you let us go in and see her?" Jason growled.

"I thought we were going to wait until tomorrow to bring her here." Theseus muttered, looking around nervously.

Hip was waving his phone in the air. "What the fuck was with the text, Ajax? 'Taking Atalanta to the hospital'? If she was fine, did you need to sound so vague and ominous?"

"It's my friends," I said to Clint, walking around him out into the open.

All of the boys went silent when they saw me.

"OH MY G—" Jason started before Percy elbowed him in the ribs and quickly whispered while signing to Theseus that they were bandages to cover the scales.

Super hearing was pretty beneficial, so far.

"I mean," Jason coughed and came closer." Oh, my God, it's so good to see you up and walking around. How are you feeling?"

I couldn't help but giggle. I smiled up at him." I'm doing okay."

He reached out and took my hands in his. When our skin touched, a tingling sensation spread from my palms throughout my body. It felt good. This need for him I hadn't realized was there, settled. It was like getting a hit from a drug I was suddenly addicted to.

I looked into his eyes, curious if he was feeling the same thing I was. The smile that was on his face grew wider, telling me he was. I wondered if it had something to do with the whole him-changing-me thing.

Suddenly I was surrounded by large bodies, the other guys coming close and either patting me on the head or kissing my cheek with murmurs of 'I'm glad you're okay,' 'good to see you up and about 'as if they hadn't spent the last three days hovering around me while I recovered. They were just putting on a show.

"Want to introduce me to your friends, Atty?" Clint asked from outside my circle of man muscle.

My smile fell as the sting of him using Cal's nickname for me pricked me right in the heart. As the guys parted from me, I stuck the smile back on my face and let go of Jason's hands.

"Guys, this is my uncle, Clint. When he hadn't heard from my dad in a while, he got worried and had to come check on us. Clint, these are my…friends!" I began to point to each of them as I said their names. "That's Theseus, Hip, Percy, who you've met, Ajax, and this is Jason."

"Oh, wow, it's so nice to know that this little squirt is finally making some friends," Clint teased as he not so subtly tugged me away from the others and put his arm around my shoulder.

I glanced up at him, taken aback by his behavior. If I didn't know any better, I would have thought he was being possessive. He must have just felt protective of his only up and walking charge. To him, the guys were strangers, and not the men who saved my life.

"Clint, these men were the ones who saved us that night…" I hesitated before making up a little white lie. "They had been caught in the storm, too. When they saw our boat, they pulled us to shore. Because their boat was bigger, it held up against the waves better than ours did."

Clint's eyebrows shot up. "Oh. Then I guess I should be thanking you. Though, if you don't mind, I'm going to be taking my niece home. She's probably had a long day, and I'm sure just wants to rest."

I felt my heart sink into my stomach.

"No!" I shouted without thinking.

The guys stepped closer to us reactively, but I held up my hand for them to stop.

I turned to Clint." I'm sorry. I…um, I'm not ready to leave Dad yet. Can I stay here for a while longer?"

Clint looked confused but nodded anyway." Uh, sure. We can stay a little longer."

I looked to the others, who only stood there awkwardly until Percy took action. With a broad smile on his face — a smile that freaked me out, to be honest — he pulled Clint aside and began asking him, in that friendly tone he had been using, where Clint was staying and how he would be happy to set him up at the local inn. Clint didn't seem too happy about the idea.

I stepped back into my father's room and sat back down in the chair, already exhausted again. The others followed me in, Ajax and Theseus standing in the large doorway like a privacy wall.

I sighed." What are we going to do? He can't come and stay with me, at least not while I'm still scaly."

"Do you know when he'll leave?" Jason asked, coming over and sitting precariously on the arm of the chair.

I shook my head." We haven't talked about it yet, but I have a feeling he will stay until they wake my dad."

Hip sat carefully on the edge of my father's bed, facing me, our knees knocking together. "We could make something up. Like you're staying with one of us while you're recovering and there isn't enough room to add another."

"He would just insist on staying with me in the cabin."

"Why not just have Theseus compel him?" Ajax suggested with a grunt.

My eyes shot to the tall ginger in the doorway. "Compel him?"

When he didn't react, Ajax poked him in the side and nodded towards us. Theseus rubbed the back of his head, a wry smile on his face. "I'll be honest. I can't see what you guys are talking about."

"Sorry," Hip and Jason said at the same time and angled themselves so they were facing the doorway.

I leaned around Jason so Theseus could see me better. "Ajax was saying you could compel Clint?"

His eyebrows rose and he nodded. "Oh, yeah. We could do that."

"But what do they mean by compel?" I asked.

"You've pointed it out before. That weird mind thing I do with my voice. How did you describe it? Your 'brain being filled with cotton.'" He said, wiggling his fingers at his head.

I blinked and searched my memory for what he was talking about until I was able to grab ahold of a faint memory. "That's you compelling someone? You mean like Dracula?"

"Kind of. I have the ability to…" he waved his hand around, looking for the right word. "…persuade others to do things."

"He's being modest. He can make anyone do or believe just about anything when he tries," Hip grinned.

My brows furrowed as I caught another memory. "Wait, is he how you got me out of trouble for injuring those girls?"

Hip nodded." He owed me a favor."

I turned back to Theseus. "But you were surprised by what happened."

He shrugged. "Well, Hip never told me why I was erasing their memories of what happened, and I didn't ask. I put two and two together when I saw you the next day."

I didn't know how I felt about this proclaimed ability, but if it bought us time, I would have to deal with it.

"It won't hurt Clint, will it? Like, his mind won't get scrambled by you messing with it?"

"A simple suggestion like this? No," Theseus reassured me, shaking his head.

I blanched at the idea that there were suggestions that could fry someone's brain and then nodded. "Okay. Do it."

With a smile, Theseus gave a slight bow and then walked out of the room.

"So is he the only one with this ability?" I asked, remembering that Theseus wasn't the only one my brain had gone all cotton ball for.

I was staring at Jason when I asked, and I watched as a small blush reddened his cheeks.

"Most of us have a bit of what we call 'syren voice', though we can't do much with it unless there's a lot of emotion in the suggestion. Plus, humans kind of become immune to our voices over time," Jason answered.

So that was why Jason's voice hadn't drawn me nearly as much since that first day.

Hip picked up a lock of my now long hair and twirled it between his fingers. "I personally stink at syren voice. Never been able to convince anyone of anything."

"I don't know about that, you little trickster," I grinned.

"Hush," He replied, gently tugging on the lock of hair.

Percy and Theseus came back into the room. Clint wasn't with them.

"I persuaded your uncle that staying at the inn was better than with you. He was a hard one. Wanted to make sure you were okay before he left. I told him he could see you tomorrow." Theseus said, his tone relaxed as if he hadn't just manipulated someone's mind.

"Alright." I relaxed, sinking into the chair, my tired eyes sliding over to my father. "You're sleeping more than me, old man. You better wake up soon."

The guys didn't say anything as I watched my father's chest rise and fall for a long time. They sort of settled in around me. Jason perched himself on the arm of my chair while Hip actually sat down at my feet and rested his head against my knee. The other three stood against the wall next to us.

The silence didn't feel awkward. There were a lot of things we had to settle, Clint being a big one, but at that moment everything was relatively peaceful. Before I knew it, my eyes were drifting closed.

Chapter Three

AJAX

I felt as Atalanta drifted off to sleep. The underlying torrent of torment that was her signature settled. The others in the room were completely aware of her every movement, and relaxed when they too realized she had slipped into dreamland.

Jason sighed and leaned down to kiss Atalanta's head. "My parents suggested we take her down to the beach tonight. Said it would help her recovery."

"That doesn't sound like a half bad idea." Hip agreed.

I cocked an eyebrow at him. Hip, agreeing with Jason?

Hip, seeing my expression, shrugged and mouthed 'what?'.

I shook my head. I hoped this was the olive branch for the two of them. I was getting tired of the hostility between them.

Granted —

I looked over to Percy and Theseus, who, though standing next to each other, were about as far apart as two people could be. The tension was almost palpable, even for those without my ability.

"I think we could all use a swim," I threw out.

The others looked at me, confused. I didn't want to have to spell it out to them. We were all just as tired as Atalanta was, and with us having been preoccupied with her care, the cravings were hitting us hard. Or perhaps their confusion stemmed from my active participants today? I suppose I had spoken more than the average...

"He's right," Theseus said.

Percy nodded. "All right. Let us get the little princess back to the cabin and then head out for a swim."

Hip and Jason slowly stood and stared each other down, their hands up. I thought they were about to attack each other, their emotions brimming with the anger between them. Just before I was about to intervene, they began shaking their fists and then opening them. One paper, one scissors.

I snorted.

Rock paper scissors?

Jason had been the one to lose. I was confused at why they had played such a childish game until the triumphant Hip slowly moved to pick up Atalanta.

That was one way to not fight over her. I couldn't help but smile. Progress. These last two weeks, stepping around each other hadn't been a total waste.

That smile fell and turned into an eye-roll when Hip smirked pompously at Jason, who responded by sticking his tongue out at him. I empathized with the spark of jealousy Jason felt at seeing Hip's arms around her, as I longed to hold her as well. My skin still felt warm from when I had carried her to the room.

The five of us, plus our cargo, made our way out of the hospital. I made a point to stop by the nurse's station to see if Dr. Charles, Titus' doctor, had left any notes with his nurse. He hadn't, but the nurse said Titus' vitals seemed better today, so that was good at least.

In the parking lot, we decided Hip would ride with me. As he carefully climbed into my passenger seat with his precious package, I lifted his motorcycle into the back of my truck next to a few of the paint buckets.

The drive back to the cabin was more peaceful than when we left. Hip wasn't the type to feel the need to fill the silence beyond a soft humming, which I didn't mind as he seemed a decent singer. His emotional signature was also lighter than the others. A little mischievous, but not constantly filled with the darkness like the others. It was nice.

Our little caravan filled up almost all of the available space on the cleared cliffside that the cabin sat on.

"Come on, Speedy, it's time to wake up." Hip crooned as he poked the tip of Atalanta's nose.

I thought for a moment that she wouldn't wake up, but her uncovered eye fluttered open.

"Hey, Sleeping Beauty. Have a good nap?" Hip asked.

I felt his adoration flare for her as he stared down at her beautiful face.

"I'm sorry. I didn't mean to fall asleep." She looked around." We're back at the cabin?"

She was disappointed. She probably wanted to stay with her father longer.

"We can visit him again tomorrow," I said, pulling her attention to me.

She brightened up at that, and wiggled herself around in Hip's lap as she tried to open the door and get out of the truck.

I chuckled when Hip groaned softly, and I felt his desire flare.

If she heard him, Atalanta ignored the groan, and successfully hopped out of the truck.

"It should be safe enough to take these off, right?" She called, gesturing to the bandages.

"It should be safe. We will have to get more of the adhesive ones until you learn to control your shift," Percy replied, as he walked up to her and gently removed the one over her eye.

Atalanta slowly unwrapped the bandages on her hands and wrists, being careful not to let her sleeves slide up. "I would prefer to do that sooner than later. So I believe it's time for a lesson while I can still keep my eyes open."

"I talked to my parents, and they suggested us going for a swim tonight," Jason called to us from the steps.

"In the ocean?" She asked, stiffening.

I felt a small wave of apprehension from her. Stepping closer, I placed my hand on her shoulder and said, "It's okay. We will all be there with you this time."

"I'm not scared," She insisted, putting on a brave face.

"It's okay if you are. The ocean can be a scary place," Theseus smiled." But Ajax is right. With us there with you, you should be fine."

She bit her lip, then nodded." Okay."

"Time for a lesson, then!" Hip exclaimed.

We all made our way inside the cabin and set up in the living room. The others spent the next hour trying to teach her how to retract her partially shifted form, i.e. the claws, fangs, webbing between her toes and fingers, and her scales. They weren't having much success.

"You just need to relax." Theseus encouraged with a smile.

Atalanta, who was extremely frustrated at this point, literally stomped her foot. "I have never been more relaxed in my life!"

Everyone laughed at that, much to her exasperation. She crossed her arms over her chest and scowled at all of us.

She grumbled." Well, I was. You guys are just horrible teachers."

We were sitting on the floor now, the five of us in a slack circle with Atalanta standing in the center.

Percy, who had been looking pensive, slid his eyes over to me. I met his gaze and smirked. I knew what was coming.

"Ajax," Percy began, drawing out my name." why don't you end our misery and teach Atalanta what she needs to know."

I shrugged." Okay."

Atalanta turned and looked at me skeptically. "What? Do you know some secret that they don't?"

I nodded." Of course."

Jason snorted. "Care to share with the rest of the class?"

I stood and sauntered up to Atalanta. I took her clawed hands in mine and gently tugged her close to me. I tried to ignore the desire that began to burn from her body being this close to mine. It was lesson time.

However, that reminder didn't stop the images of devouring her mouth and tasting her from running rampant in my mind.

I glanced at the others before saying, "They weren't made like we were. Their problem is that they are trying to explain something they were born with."

"Oh." Her faced morphed into one of understanding.

I grinned. "Exactly."

"Now they're just making fun of us." Hip mumbled.

Atalanta tilted her head and smiled at Hip over my shoulder. "He's saying it would be like trying to explain how we breathe to someone who never has. You wouldn't really know how to, beyond the mechanics. Whereas he had to learn when he was turned, therefore has had a different experience."

Jason, Theseus, and Hip grumbled and got all pouty while Percy kept with his quiet contemplation.

Slowly, I moved my hands from hers and slid them down to her hips. I mentally reminded my hands not to move from that spot while I explained.

"Picture it like a new muscle. While you can relax, it doesn't mean that particular muscle will."

"Like when you're standing and you're relaxed but your leg muscles are still working?" she asked.

I nodded. "So picture this form like a new muscle, a subconscious one. Our scales emerge when we are stressed or upset. It's a defense mechanism. If it makes it easier, imagine it as a single muscle, or perhaps like a little ball in your gut."

I thought to mention how Mer can also phase while they're extremely aroused, but seeing as it was actually really difficult to reach that level of self control, I kept quiet for my own future amusement.

She closed her eyes, picturing the muscle.

After a few moments, I asked her. "Can you see it?"

Keeping her eyes closed, she nodded and replied, "I see it as a little ball in my chest."

I chuckled. "You don't need to tell us how you see it," I leaned in and brushed my lips against her ear. "Okay, now release the tension in that little ball."

She shivered, and I resisted the urge to nip the tip of her ear. I backed away from her, knowing that getting her excited wouldn't help anything, and watched as the claws and scales on her hands receded back under her skin. Her hands looked human again after quite a while. She wiggled her little fingers as if she felt the change there.

I couldn't tell how much of her scales receded with all of the clothing she wore, but the small scales on her cheeks remained.

When she opened her eyes, she looked down at her hands and smiled. "I did it!"

She lifted up the hem of her shirt, her smile turning into a frown when she saw that the scales that rode up her hips and framed her cute little belly button were still present.

She pursed her lips. "Are these the ones I won't be able to get rid of?"

I shrugged. "Probably not."

I knew it took me a couple weeks before I got a hold of my shift. My mind went back to those days, Aria laughing at me as I struggled just as Atalanta was doing. A pang of sadness rung in my chest as the faded memory of her laughter sang in my head.

Atalanta huffed and squirmed out of my grasp, pulling me back to the present. I blinked and saw that she was pulling off her shoes to discover that her feet were still webbed.

"Damn." She mumbled.

"I say it's good for your first time," Jason said, popping up from his spot and walking over to kiss her on the cheek. "Good job."

Theseus joined them and hugged her gently from behind. "What he said."

Atalanta continued to pout as the two of them tried to cheer her up. I glanced over to Percy, who met my gaze and nodded approvingly before getting up to join the other three. From there, my eyes bounced over to Hip, who was still sitting, watching us, his eyes distant. I wondered what was bothering him. For a moment I considered asking, but I mentally shrugged it off. It wasn't my concern.

"You guys want to watch movies until nightfall? You can continue to practice while we chill, Atalanta," Jason suggested.

The others all nodded, seeming to really like the idea. I did as well, relaxing and watching some mindless film, not having to worry.

Atalanta snorted." With what T.V.?"

We all looked around at the bare cabin awkwardly. I was once again filled with the need I had felt over the last two weeks. To fill the damn empty space.

I shared a look with Jason. We would be filling this cabin with comfortable furniture if it was the last thing we did.

Until then, I sighed. "We can go to my cabin. It's not far."

"Your cabin?" Hip asked, finally joining in on the conversation.

Percy readjusted his glasses and commented. "I don't believe I have ever been to your home, Ajax."

"Me neither." Theseus joined in.

"I have," Atalanta grinned.

They all looked at her, and I could see the little giggle that was working its way up in her chest. The little bit of joy flaring inside her warmed my insides, and I felt better about offering for them to all come to my cabin. I knew it was a bit of a mess, but I had a very nice stereo system and flat screen. It was better than the alternative of someone grabbing their laptop and all of us crowding on top of the air mattress.

Hip and Theseus, now acting like eager little puppies, headed out of the cabin with the four of us following after them.

In an uncharacteristic move, Percy scooped Atalanta into his arms and carried her through the woods with us, snuggling her close to his chest. Their calm faces couldn't fool me. I felt an interesting swash of emotions coming from the two of them. Atalanta radiated excitement mixed with trepidation, while Percy felt a little embarrassed along with the usual protectiveness he gave off.

I heard him mutter something about her being tired and wanting to protect her feet, but I knew it was just an excuse.

Curious, I flicked my eyes over to Jason, who walked beside me, behind the rest. He watched Percy and Atalanta with an unreadable expression, yet he radiated loneliness. I knew what he would be feeling. The made Mer wouldn't experience the mating urges like someone who was born, especially the males. For us, its a much duller sensation, but I still remembered Aria telling me how being away from me, not being able to touch me when she wanted, was extremely unpleasant, like going through withdrawal.

I made a mental reminder to make sure Atalanta sat with him during the movie.

Chapter Four

ATALANTA

Ajax's cabin really was cozy and very tidy. Not what I would have suspected from the often paint-covered Ajax. Simple, dark furniture contrasted with the light wood of the walls. It was warm and shined with a unique quality that made me love it instantly.

The moment we got there, all of us had been nosier than was polite, wandering around the rooms and asking all sorts of questions. At one point, I learned that Ajax had built the place himself, which made me look at the beautiful kitchen with its long marble-topped counters and dark cabinets with near adoration. Even if I could be out-cooked by a toddler, this kitchen made me want to be the best chef I could be.

Now, after getting our fill of being horrible snoops, the five of us marveled over his entertainment system. Theseus won rock paper scissors for movie pick and decided we would watch the next superhero movie on my required watch list. After fiddling with turning the captions on, we settled on and around Ajax's large black couch and began watching The Dark Knight Returns.

I was snuggled with my back against Jason's side while my legs were sprawled in Percy's lap. Being between the two of them like this made my heart race.

It didn't help when images of the last time I was on a couch with Jason flashed into my mind.

My eyes went to Ajax, who had chosen to sit on the Lazy Boy instead of the floor in front of me where Theseus and Hip were. His multicolored gaze flickered to me and then to the two men on either side of me. I could have sworn I saw a flare of smugness on that ruggedly handsome face of his. He had totally planned this. The meddler.

I would like to say that I watched the movie, and I did watch some of it, but my mind kept wandering. With every move and shift, I was reminded of how close I was to the four guys around me. My body hyper aware of their innocent touches. It got to the point where fantasies of them began to run through my mind. In one of them, they were all together.

I was riding Theseus, his head tilted back in pleasure as Jason and Percy worshiped my breasts and neck from behind. Hip was in front of me, whispering in my ear as he stroked my clit. Ajax, his bulky frame too large to fit on the bed, watched from the sidelines eagerly, his hand stroking his erection. All of it was driving me crazy!

I blinked and shifted, hoping that they couldn't smell my arousal. By the way Ajax stared at me, he certainly knew what was running through my brain. The smile he gave me was inviting, daring me to act.

I seriously was not ready for something like that though, so to distract myself from them, I kept practicing on relaxing the little ball inside my chest that I designated my Mer form. It was extremely difficult, probably because my arousal kept pushing my scales to the surface, but I kept trying.

I was excited when after about ten minutes I succeeded on getting my feet to return to normal, but then there was a massive explosion in the movie which startled me, making that little ball tighten all over again, and I was back to having webbed hands and feet.

The ones who heard my squeak of surprise and then groan of frustration began laughing. Much to my embarrassment.

When the movie finished, I nominated a movie with less action.

"Two bets she wants to watch one of those romantic comedies," Percy said, his brown eyes sparkling.

"In fact, I do," I challenged.

Hip shifted around to look at us better. "I don't mind. I kind of like chick flicks."

Theseus, who I had tapped when I put out my request, shrugged." I guess, if that's what she wants."

I turned back to Percy, quirking a brow at him, challenging him to tell me no.

He met my stare with one of his own, and we were in our showdown for a solid minute before he broke.

"Fine," he grunted and pulled my legs, which had fallen, back into his lap.

TIED TO THE SEA

Curious about his silence, I tilted my head back to look at Jason. His eyes were closed and breathing even. He was asleep?

I looked back to the others, who were studying Jason as well.

"He fell asleep during the climax of the last movie." Ajax confirmed.

I was surprised he could sleep through the explosive ending, but I couldn't really blame him. He appeared more exhausted than the others. I had known that during my two week long nap Jason had barely left my side, hardly sleeping or eating, and it showed. I don't think it helped when I finally woke up either. I felt horrible being responsible for his exhaustion.

Quietly, I pointed to the blanket which had been draped across the back of Ajax's chair, and he tossed it over to me. With Hip's help, we swaddled Jason in the blanket; he didn't even stir.

Having won my battle for a rom-com, we found one on Netflix and relaxed back for a much calmer movie, making a point to keep the volume lower this time. Carefully, I snuggled myself closer to Jason's warmth, and about halfway through the movie, I joined him in dreamland.

When I woke up next, I was laying entirely across the couch, Percy, Ajax, and Theseus were gone. As I shifted, I realized that I, too, was now wrapped up in the blanket cocoon with Jason spooning me, still fast asleep.

Careful not to wake Jason, I loosened our cocoon and looked around. Hip was now in the lazy-boy watching some show on the television. I spied Percy wandering around the kitchen behind him, but I didn't see either Ajax or Theseus.

At my movement, Hip looked away from the screen and gave me a smile. "Hey there, Speedy. If you keep sleeping so much, I might need to call you Droopy."

"Droopy?" I asked sleepily. "Is that one of the seven dwarves?"

"No, you're thinking of Dopey. I'm talking about that little white cartoon dog who was always tired."

"That's a really vague reference." I smiled and asked, "Do you like cartoons, Hip?"

He rested his chin on his knuckles and grinned. "And if I did?"

"Hey, no judge," I yawned. At Hip's cocky look, I added. "A girl needs her beauty sleep."

His eyes, which looked green at the moment, studied my face. "I think you're good."

I ignored his comment and asked, "Where are Theseus and Ajax?"

"They are in Ajax's studio, I think."

A studio? Was that the second smaller building I had seen next to the cabin? Curious, I slowly began to untangle myself from Jason and our cocoon. A difficult process, as Jason was wrapped around me like a snake. He was definitely one of those people who liked to sleep cuddle. Just as I was free, a relaxed arm wrapped over me from behind and pulled me back against a hard chest.

Jason had pulled me closer in his sleep and was nuzzling my hair, making my heart swell and then immediately begin to gallop and spread a warmth through my body as my ass was being prodded by some morning wood.

The wide smile I had didn't last, though, as I looked back to Hip, who was scowling. My smile fell, and I felt terrible for letting Jason wrap himself around me like this, in such an intimate moment, in front of Hip.

Reluctantly, I pushed Jason's arms off me and got off the couch before he could sleepily pull me back. Looking down at him, I could see that in his sleepy state, he was not happy about me leaving. His hand searched around for me, his face scrunched up in an adorable pout.

I giggled and reached down to snatch up one of the little decorative pillows we had shoved to the floor and placed it in the way of his searching hand. When his palm brushed against it, he grasped it and pulled it close to him.

Suddenly, there was a flash. Looking up, I saw Hip standing next to me with his phone out, snapping photos.

"Mr. Perfect cuddling a pillow. The perfect beginning to my new photo album, if only it were a stuffed animal." He chuckled.

I cocked an eyebrow at him. "And exactly what is going into this album?"

"Photos of the others looking stupid, of course." Hip grinned cheekily, holding up his phone with a mischievous grin on his face.

"I'm sure you cuddle pillows in your sleep, too."

"Oh, of course I do, but I wouldn't dare get caught doing it." He chuckled before snapping another photo.

I leaned over his shoulder to study the photo. "We will see about that."

I left Hip with his blackmail photos and wandered over to Percy, who was watching a sizzling skillet with a calm intensity. His gaze didn't even waver from whatever was in the pan as I approached.

"Whatcha cooking?" I whispered.

"I am searing us up some salmon. I don't want to burn it."

I crinkled my nose in disgust. If I was being honest, I really didn't like fish all that much. Most certainly not as much as all the boys seemed to. Though, knowing what I knew now, their love of fish made much more sense.

"Oh!" I gasped and beamed, excitedly. "Now that I know, you guys don't have a reason to not tell me about the water bottles."

"The water bottles?" Percy asked.

I crossed my arms over my chest. "You know. The water bottles I've seen everybody carrying around. The ones you all pour freaking salt into."

"Ah, yes. I was told about your first meeting with Jason." He carefully flipped the fish in the skillet. "While our kind can walk on two legs and pretend to be human, we are not. We are creatures of the sea, and we must always return to the sea. Staying away from the water for too long causes us immense discomfort and pain. Drinking salt water stems those cravings, though they are a temporary fix."

I tilted my head back, my mouth open in an 'o'.

That made sense. Thinking about it, it also explained why a town who could hardly afford to keep its buildings up to code would spend thousands of dollars maintaining such a large saltwater filtered pool. They must feel more comfortable swimming in it than standard chlorine.

My brow furrowed when I remembered something. "I haven't seen you toting around a water bottle."

Percy let out a slow hum which sounded very much like a sigh." Unlike Mr. Monroe, I don't deprive that part of myself. There is a path behind the library which leads to the beach. I regularly take walks during my lunch breaks to go for a swim."

I tilted my head and thoughtfully said," I haven't really felt any cravings like that yet."

"It will probably take you much longer than those of us who were born Mer. You weren't born in the ocean, so it isn't as much a part of you as it is us."

I nodded, unsure if that particular information bothered me or not. The way he was painting it made me feel like I had a foot stuck in both worlds. If I learned anything from reading urban fantasy, it was that being stuck in the middle of two species was a pain in the ass.

Percy scooped the cooked fish filets out of the pan and placed them neatly down on a large plate. "I am almost done with dinner."

"Are you making anything else?" I asked, hoping I didn't sound too obvious.

Percy's eyes flicked over to me, seeing right through me in an instant. "You don't have to eat it. But I am betting you'll find it much more appealing now than you did two weeks ago."

"If you say so," I grumbled.

He put the plate of salmon in the microwave to keep warm before pulling out a package of green beans from the fridge. "There are also potatoes roasting in the oven and some salad I tossed up in the fridge if it turns out you don't like it."

A warmth spread inside my chest. "Thank you."

"You're welcome. Do you mind finding Theseus and Ajax and telling them to finish up with whatever they are doing?" He asked.

"Sure," I replied, making my way out of the kitchen and back into the living room where Hip had gone back to watching T.V. and Jason still slept on the couch.

I wondered why Percy referred to the two of them so formally while calling Theseus and Ajax by their first names. It was something I made a mental note to ask him later.

I strode to the door, my bare feet making a soft clacking sound on the hardwood floor. Noticing it was different from the usual squeaky-thud sound I often heard and drowned out, I looked down. My feet were still scaly with wide webbing between the toes. Curious, I lifted my foot and studied the pads. There were scales there as well.

Why hadn't I noticed them before? You would think something like that would have been noticeable before now.

I pushed the thoughts away and made my way out of the cabin. It was snowing outside, pretty heavily, actually. The little flakes of cold swirled around violently.

I pulled back, instantly thinking about grabbing a coat only to realize that despite having the door open I didn't feel the chill air hit my skin as harshly as it should have. I had thought perhaps I hadn't been bothered by the cold when we trekked to Ajax's cabin because it had grown much warmer in my two weeks of unconsciousness, and Percy's body was like my own personal space heater.

Tentatively, I stepped out of the cabin, my feet crunching into the pile of snow which had already accumulated on the porch. My toes should have been icicles, but instead, the snow felt no colder to me than perhaps the inside of a fridge.

"Well, that's useful. I guess I won't be needing a new coat any time soon." I muttered to myself.

Stepping barefoot through the snow, I trudged over to the second, smaller cabin Ajax had, in nothing more than a thin, long sleeved top and old yoga pants.

Hopping up the steps, I knocked on the door and waited. When a minute or so passed with no answer, I knocked again and called," Ajax! Theseus! Dinner is almost ready!"

Again, no answer.

With a huff, I tugged at the door's handle and grunted as the hinges, which looked rusted, protested me trying to open the door. Eventually I got it moving, the door slowly creaking open.

TIED TO THE SEA

Inside was a vast, extremely large, cluttered room. The first thing I noticed in all of the chaos were canvases upon canvases propped against one another. Some of them were blank while others were filled with color. Stepping up to one of the piles, I rifled through the paintings.

They were gorgeous, mostly landscapes filled with bright colors of the sky contrasting against the mirage of flowers or mountainscapes. There were a few portraits of people, but none of them I recognized. They were all so lifelike, almost as if they were photographs and not paintings.

Remembering that I needed to find the boys, I gently placed the paintings back against each other and moved further into the room.

There were a few sculptures in here as well. They were mostly of animals, though I did spy a random half-finished hunk of wood that looked like a woman's figure.

This place smelled so much like Ajax, it was like I was being wrapped in his scent. It was very relaxing.

I found the two of them in one of the corners. Ajax was working on a tree stump with a chisel while Theseus swished a brush in broad strokes against a canvas. I didn't know Theseus painted. I tilted my head to peer over his shoulder to look at the scraggly stick figure in the middle of the splotchy green field-looking thing, and came to the assumption it wasn't a hobby he indulged in often.

I cleared my throat, but Ajax didn't bother to glance up from the wood, and Theseus wouldn't hear me anyway.

I rolled my eyes and poked Ajax in the back.

"Mmm?" He hummed.

"Percy said dinner was ready."

"Mmm," he hummed again, continuing to tap on the chisel for a few moments before picking up a paintbrush on the table next to him and tossing it at Theseus without looking up.

Theseus turned around with a scowl. "I'm not getting up to get you water again, you have legs, you can do it yourself, Ajax. Oh, Atalanta."

I chuckled. "Dinner is ready."

Theseus smiled. "Okay."

He stood from his stool and strutted over to Ajax, grabbing the back of his shirt and pulling him away from his work.

"Wait. One more minute." Ajax grumbled as he reached towards his work stool while Theseus dragged him towards the door, with me following behind.

"It will be there when you get back." I smiled.

Ajax pouted. Yes, pouted. "But…"

I poked his stomach. "You need to feed your body before you can feed your work."

He nodded, yet I could still see the longing in his gaze as we walked out of the workshop.

Back inside, someone had woken Jason. Percy had set up dinner on the counter in a mini buffet style. The six of us sat around and ate the meal Percy prepared for us, like an awkward family. We didn't talk much, but there wasn't any tension that I could detect.

When we were done with dinner, Ajax told us to just leave the dishes in the sink, and he would get to them later. Percy had been right, I had really enjoyed his salmon. I wouldn't admit that my new fishy DNA was the cause. It was probably Percy's fantastic cooking. I could admit to myself, however, that I was stalling as I slowly stacked my plate on top of the others.

They would be with me, I reminded myself. There was nothing to be afraid of.

With a warm smile on his face, Jason herded me with the others towards the door and out the cabin. Ajax led us down a path through the trees which led to the ocean.

I noted again how despite the ground being covered in snow and the air having to be in the negatives, I didn't feel but a slight chill. Despite this, Hip brought my shoes and insisted I put them back on.

The water was calm, much like the first night I had moved to Argos. The tide was high, waves pulling in and slowly flowing back out, like nature's rhythmic beat. It was extremely dark out, and I could hardly see the water itself beyond the churning darkness against the slightly lighter shale sand. Yet, the guys were surefooted as we navigated around rocks and drift wood, and I wondered if they could see in the dark. My anxiety of entering the water and my concentration on not tripping kept me from asking.

As we reached the surf, the guys began to pull off their shirts. I frowned, as it was too dark to see, but just imagining all of their shirtless bodies warmed my cheeks. Then when their silhouettes began to strip down to their pants...

"What are you doing?" I squeaked.

"Do you want us to go swimming in our pants?" Hip asked, and I could just hear the grin in his tone.

"Well...no! But do you have to be completely naked?"

Their pause made me think they all shared some kind of look, but I couldn't tell.

"Wearing human clothes interferes with shifting to our tails." I heard Percy say.

I bit my lip. Right, their tails. Tails which I had yet to see. I wished in that moment it wasn't so dark out so I would be able to see their shifted forms...and not their naked forms.

"Okay, I'm going to turn around then. Just...hop in the water or something." I closed my eyes and turned away from the boys. I knew it was silly, I wasn't a white-as-the-snow virgin.

I felt someone step up close to me, their warmth seeping even through my clothes. "Does our little human feel shy?" Percy whispered wickedly.

"Like you said, I'm not human anymore." I shot back, hoping he didn't hear the hitch in my voice and see the shiver run up my spine.

"Correct, and as a Mer, you will need to get used to seeing naked bodies. Our people aren't shy." He purred, and I felt hands slide up my shoulders and gently turn me back towards the waves. I still kept my eyes closed.

"It's too dark for me to see anything, so I think I'll just keep my eyes closed and you all can go ahead and make yourselves decent in the water."

"You can't see?" Percy asked, the curiosity in his voice almost breaking that sexy as sin tone he was using.

"No, it's pitch black out. Of course I can't see!"

"It will take time for her eyes to adjust outside of the water, probably not until after she fully shifts." I heard Ajax say, much closer than where he had been standing before. I felt a second wave of heat step up to my side.

My eyes snapped open. I couldn't see much better than before, vague features amongst the silhouettes. "So you guys can see in the dark?"

"Some of us better than others. I can see perfectly." Percy crooned as he stroked my cheek with the back of my hand. Had he taken off his glasses?

"I can see well enough." I glanced over to where I felt Ajax and gasped when I saw his eyes glowing brightly in the darkness, one eye a bright amber and the other an icy blue.

Another body moved up behind me and gently gripped at my hips. "I am personally glad to be able to see your pretty lips."

My eyes grew wide at Theseus's words. The three of them were so close, and despite not being able to see, I was acutely aware that they were all shirtless, possibly naked. My own clothes felt like a measly shield against their attention.

I felt a hand grasp mine and pull me away from the intimidating mass of the three men. "Okay, you three, time to back off her."

I let out a breath and smiled up to Jason, thankful for his intervening, then blinked when I realized his eyes were glowing as well, a bright green. I looked back and saw that Percy and Theseus's eyes were now also aglow, as if the inside of eye sockets sported lightbulbs. Their freaking eyes glowed! Were mine glowing as well?

TIED TO THE SEA

Jason leaned forward and whispered into my ear. "Don't be afraid, Atalanta."

I nodded and gulped down the bubbling anxiety in my chest as he gently guided me close to the water.

"You'll want to at least take off your shoes." Hip, who was already waist deep in the water, called.

I nodded, kicking off my shoes and awkwardly tugging off my socks with one hand while Jason helped me balance with the other. The shale and sand were cold and rough against my bare feet. Tentatively, I stepped into the oncoming surf.

I sucked in a breath as I felt a surge of energy shoot up from my feet and spread into my tired limbs. I stood up straighter and looked up at Jason, a wide smile spreading across my face.

Without a thought, I ran into the ocean like a little kid experiencing their first time at the beach. The deeper into the water I went, the more energy I felt soaking into my limbs. So much of the lethargy I had felt since I woke up washing away in the salty brine.

With a giggle, I dove into the water and swam further away from the shore. Under the waves, I instinctually held my breath and kept my eyes closed. Just feeling the pleasant sensation of the cold water wrapping around me.

It was so weird, it almost felt like the water was a long lost relative that was welcoming me home after a long absence. I had never felt such warmth that was the sea's embrace.

For a long moment, I reveled in the feeling before a tap on my cheek made me open my eyes. I was pleasantly surprised when I didn't feel the familiar sting of the salt on my eyes. It was also clear, so very clear, and brighter than the surface. In the water, I could clearly see the guys as they surrounded me.

I blushed at their shirtless forms. At least they had kept their boxers on, even if it didn't leave much to the imagination. Especially when several of them were hard.

In front of me, Hip was smiling. "There's no need to hold your breath."

His voice was clear, not the garbled sounds I was expecting.

He pointed to the gills on his neck which were open. I watched as they widened and then narrowed as he breathed. I touched my own throat and felt the little slits which were my own gills. I could breathe underwater with these.

Hesitantly, I opened my mouth and inhaled.

Water rushed into my mouth and down my windpipe, making me panic. My mind screamed that this was *wrong*! I shut my mouth and rushed to the surface, my frantic mind becoming a jumbled mess.

My lungs burned, demanding oxygen, but there wasn't any, there was only water.

I felt something grab my leg.

It was keeping me from the surface, from sweet air!

TIED TO THE SEA

I kicked and thrashed.

"Atalanta, calm down. Breathe, I know it's weird, but just breathe." Someone said. I couldn't recognize the voice.

Arms grabbed at my sides and I screamed, releasing the last reserves of air that I had in my lungs. "LET ME GO!"

My lungs were on fire, and the edges of my vision were beginning to go hazy.

Someone gripped my cheeks, and I caught bright gray-blue eyes before hearing a beautifully alluring voice say, "Atalanta, open your mouth and breath normally. Trust us, it's going to be okay."

I couldn't tell if the fuzziness in my head was from the voice or my brain blacking out, but regardless, my body obliged. I opened my mouth and sucked in a lungful of water.

Chapter Five

ATALANTA

Nothing happened.

Well, not completely nothing, but I wasn't drowning. My brain, which had been blacking out, cleared. My lungs, though aching, were pleasantly happy with the water that was currently filling them.

Needless to say, I was shocked.

Exhaling, I felt the water rush out of my mouth and was surprised by the sensation of it flowing out of my gills. Cautiously, I took a deep breath in, not only feeling the water rush in through my mouth, but through the slits in the side of neck as well. It was similar to how I imagined a can of beer felt after you stabbed it in the side.

Focusing, I realized that Theseus was floating in front of me. He had been the voice which commanded me to breath. I didn't know if I should hit him for stealing my free will by using his ability on me or hug him for saving my life and keeping me from suffocating myself. I decided hugging him was the better choice, since he had only been trying to help.

"Thanks," I croaked out, my vocal cords feeling a bit strained from using water instead of air.

"Feeling better? Less panicked?" Theseus asked, trying to sound comforting.

I nodded and looked around at the other guys, feeling awkward at my freakout. Ajax, who was at the edge of the circle the guys were making around me, drifted closer and patted the top of my head.

"Same," was all he said, which I took to mean that the first time he had shifted he had panicked as well.

I gave him a weary smile, grateful for his attempt to make me feel less ridiculous. Of course I could breath underwater. I knew I had gills, but that didn't stop my once human brain from thinking water equals no breathing.

No longer panicking, I took a deep breath in and explored our surroundings. We were in open water, with not much around besides the occasional fish and the shifting sand. I spied color off in the distance and swam towards it. The webbing on my hands and feet acted like snorkeling fins, only better because it didn't feel like clunky plastic and rubber weighing me down.

Swimming much faster than I was used to, I almost zoomed right past the reef I had seen.

Coming to an awkward halt, I tumbled through the water and stared upside down in awe at the colorful swarm of fish and coral.

I had never been diving, but if this was the sight they got to see, I envied divers. The fish had their own little world down here. Multiple breeds swam in little pods or alone, weaving in and out of the coral and sea grass. I could watch them for hours.

A tiny red fish broke off from its pod and actually swam up to me, stopping in front of my face. Slowly, I righted myself and studied the fish as it studied me. I wanted to reach out and pet it, but I didn't want to break the magic that was happening.

I felt an odd sensation at the back of my head, similar to the feeling I got when someone was behind me. Swirling around, I didn't see anyone. Brow scrunching, I remembered that I was here with the boys, and scanned the water for them. I spotted them floating together on the opposite end of the reef from me.

I turned back to the tiny red fish to see it swimming back to its pod. Somewhat disheartened, I swam over the coral to meet the boys on the other side.

"This is amazing," I whispered.

They didn't say anything, but several of the boys grinned, bringing a smile to my own face.

An undercurrent came out of nowhere, shoving me towards Hip. He caught me in his arms, grinning. I almost thought he was going to kiss me, but instead he let go and actually slapped me on the ass!

"Race you!" He challenged before taking off.

I glanced at the other four before taking off after him, not giving them a chance to overtake me. A bubble of energy urged me forward. I wouldn't let Hip or any of them win this time!

I don't know how far we swam, but I came *dead last*.

I pointed at them. "Okay, but I'm new at this. Just you wait, I'll win next time."

"I'm sure you will," Hip sniggered, floating through the water, his arms behind his head like he was lounging on a couch.

Theseus gave me a comforting smile. "You still gave us a run for our money."

"I mean, I am the swim team captain. If I let you win, I could never live it down." Jason laughed, patting me on the back.

I sighed, exasperated. My body relaxed and I stopped treading water. My clothes were heavy from being waterlogged, and the moment I stopped moving I sank slowly down to the ocean's floor. The sand puffed up in big clouds as I landed against it.

I stared up at the surface above me. Now that I could see clearly, I noticed the night sky through the shifting water, and it was breathtaking. Small flickers of light from the moon peeking from behind the clouds in short spurts twinkled against the water, almost like the sparkling stars. I could only wonder what it looked like when the sky was clear, or maybe during sunset.

All of the guys — who had been watching me — began to settle beside me, with Jason close to my left and Theseus to my right.

I took the time in their silence to adjust myself, to get used to the feeling of breathing water and seeing everything in a near supernatural focus.

After a while, I popped up, feeling ready to learn.

"Okay, teach me how to grow my tail."

The guys chuckled.

I stood, my body bouncing against the sand, and I wobbled as I tried to stay upright, almost tumbling into a summersault again.

Jason chuckled and gripped my hips to center me, my feet touching down on the sand.

I looked around at their near naked bodies and a little naughtiness rose up and tampered down my shyness.

"Actually...I would love to see your tails first," I grinned devilishly.

The guys shared a look with one another before shrugging and with grins of their own began to slowly remove their boxers. I mentally strong armed myself into not turning away and committing every moment to memory. Just before any of them completely undressed, hands covered my eyes from behind, effectively blindfolding me.

"Hey!" I whined, pulling at the hands.

I felt a chest press hard against mine. "Now, now, don't ruin our chastity."

Theseus.

"That's not very fair. You undressed in front of me before." I grumbled.

He chuckled. "I hope you realize your complaining falls on deaf ears."

"I don't care if you can't hear me! I'm still going to complain!"

"I'm assuming you're still complaining so I'll just stop you right there," He said before tilting my head back and kissing me squarely on the mouth.

This was my first time kissing someone upside down and it was no less amazing as his cool lips sent tingles dancing over my body. All too quickly he pulled away, but not before licking my bottom lip.

I growled and was about to pull him back towards me when he rushed over my head, a large mass of green scales filling my vision.

Blinking rapidly, I swiveled my head to watch him kick his powerful tail and speed through the water until he was only a speck in the distance before he rushed back towards us. He was breathtaking. They all were.

Strong bodies with scales in similar patterns to mine, covering the tops of their arms, making patterns at their hairlines. Unlike me, they didn't have scales covering their whole torso, just a large diamond in the center of their chests, tapering up from their waist line and encircling their belly buttons. I guess nature felt I needed more protection

Their tails looked just like the ones I'd seen in photographs. Each one of them had their own color scheme, which was interesting as I had only ever seen Ajax's scales...no, wait, that wasn't right. They had shown me their scales when I had first woken up.

I shook my head, brushing away my confusion. I pushed off the sand and swam closer to them.

Hip was the closest and most noticeable with his bright silver scales that shimmered as he moved, almost reflecting the other colors around him. His tail fin flowed, almost looking like a thin cloth which came to two points, swaying back and forth in the water. I swam around him, seeing that he had long and wispy dorsal fin that began at his shoulder blades and ran down along his spine, tapering off near the tip of his tail. He also had two ventral fins at the points on his hips where skin became scale.

I paused for a moment and giggled to myself. I was sure they would be calling me a nerd if they heard my inner thoughts and realized I actually knew the different fins on a fish. Having a father who often masqueraded as a fisherman came with at least a little knowledge of marine life.

As my gaze moved up his tail and settled on his face, my jaw dropped. His eyes! The whites of his eyes were gone, replaced with the pure color of his irises. In this light they looked blue, but if I knew Hip they would change again the next time I looked. I glanced at the other guys to see that they all had the freaky eye thing going on— except Ajax, who's eyes still looked human beyond the eerie glow they gave off.

I marveled on this discovery for a moment before moving on to study Theseus. His scales were green, and unlike Hip's solid color, his green was static, flowing from one shade to the next, but predominately a deep emerald. His ventral fins were further down his tail.

I put my hand to my chin, mentally debating with myself before deciding his were more like pectoral fins, as unlike Hip's, Theseus' fins rounded at the tips. My eyes moved lower to study his tail fin. It was much more like the classic fin depicted in drawings and in Disney.

I snorted. "Oh my god, you're the little mermaid."

"What?"

I looked into his eyes, unable to resist smiling. "Red hair and a green tail. You're Ariel from The Little Mermaid!

His mouth fell open, his face flashing in horror. "I am not!"

"Oh, this is fantastic." Hip sniggered.

Theseus's head whipped back and forth between the guys. "Don't you dare start!"

Hip shrugged, feigning innocence. "We didn't say anything."

"Oh, I'm so sure you didn't, you little shrimp."

"Shrimp? Who you callin' a shrimp, Princess?!"

I rolled my eyes and ignored them. They were all steam. I doubted they would do anything more than bicker. I moved on to inspect Ajax. His scales were amazing to look at: jet black, shimmering with iridescence as he moved, very much like an oil slick. His tail was similar to Hip's, with black ventral fins at his hips and a wispy curtain-like tail fin.

A shimmering of gray caught my attention. The diamond of scales on his chest, right over his heart, had a patch of gray scales encased by his black ones.

My hand reached out and touched the lighter scales. I thought of my own spattering of light scales which covered the scar tissue on my body. Were these scales also covering scar tissue? If so, what could have caused such a horrible wound?

I gritted my teeth and looked into Ajax's eyes, gathering up the courage to ask him what caused his injury. I halted when I realized how sad he looked as he stared down at the spot I was touching. I pulled my hand back and hugged it to my chest. It wasn't my place to be digging into his past and I scolded myself for thinking I should.

I inhaled and moved on, not wanting to linger any longer on that sad gaze. I turned to Jason, my trouble boy, the one who had saved my life that night by turning me. His coloring was similar to my own, but his scales had more blue in them than mine. Still, the purples and near pink patches of scales I spotted were not what I expected on such a masculine guy.

I gave him a smile as I swam closer to him.

Jason reached for my hand and pulled me closer. "Are you enjoying yourself?"

"Maybe, just a little."

"We figured you would want to study us at some point. You're too curious not to. I will say, it is hard to tamper down my jealousy when I see you starting so intensely at other men like that."

I instantly felt guilty. I had been so focused on myself that I hadn't considered them. We hadn't spoken much about it since I had woken up, but it was clear they all knew about my feelings for each of them now. They had seemed to settle in around me without much of a thought. Shouldn't they be mad? Fighting with each other, or at the very least angry with me for stringing them along like this? And, oh, my God, Theseus had kissed me in front of them! They had clearly seen that, there was no way they hadn't.

What was I doing?

Whore.

Slut.

"Hey, hey," Jason gripped my chin between his fingers gently and drew my attention back to him. "I can see your mind spiraling. I know we have a lot to talk about where all of us are concerned, but one thing at a time, okay? First, we want to get you back on your feet, and then we will talk."

"But..." I glanced at the others, who were looking at us now. Though, I didn't see Percy in my line of sight.

I began to look around for him when Jason's voice drew my attention back to him. "You've been through an ordeal. Some things can wait. For now, why don't you finish checking us out and then we can see about getting you a pretty tail of your own?"

I felt the blush rise up my cheeks. "Do you need to make it awkward?"

"It is what you're doing, aren't you? Checking out our sexy bodies?" Jason teased with a wiggle of his eyebrows.

"I'm studying your—well!" I crossed my arms over my chest. "Shut up!"

I huffed and turned away from him when he and the others started laughing. I proceeded to again look around for Percy. I spotted him a ways away from our little condensed group. I kicked off and floated closer to him. He was still in his human form. He looked beautiful as his hair, which was usually tied up in a short ponytail, floated around him, and without his glasses he resembled those statues of angels, matching melancholy expression included.

"Percy, are you okay?"

"I am well, Ms. North," He said, clipped.

I cocked an eyebrow at him." If that were true, you wouldn't be over here, separated and lacking shiny scales."

"Perhaps."

"Soooo?" I prompted.

"Why don't we finish your inspection and work on controlling your shift?"

I pouted, knowing I wouldn't be getting an answer out of him. I had already decided that I shouldn't be trying to push them, anyway.

I turned back to the others and looked to Ajax. "So, how do I get more scaly?"

Hip snorted and muttered under his breath, "I like how she's not even bothering to ask us anymore."

I rolled my eyes. "Because you four are horrible teachers."

"Can't argue with you there." Hip shrugged.

Ajax swayed his powerful tail and drifted closer. The movement itself was quite small, and I bet when they really kicked with their tails they could probably move through the water just as fast as any speed boat.

"You said before that you pictured your shift like a little ball in your chest. If releasing the tension makes you more human, then…?"

I thought on it for a moment before throwing out, "Then I should picture tightening the ball?"

He nodded. "It also helps just to picture yourself growing said tail."

Okay. I could do this. I closed my eyes and once again saw that little glowing stress ball right next to my heart.

"Wait!" Hip called, causing me to lose my concentration and open my eyes.

"What?" I asked, looking around worried. "Whats wrong?"

He gestured up and down my body. "You're still wearing your clothes. You won't be able to shift like that."

I looked down at my waterlogged sweater and jeans and then back at the five guys surrounding me. "I am not taking off my clothes."

Theseus shrugged and gave me a failed attempt at an apologetic smile as his eyes sparkled with humor. "If you don't remove them, your shift will not only be painful but you'll tear right through your clothes and have to walk back to your house butt naked."

"Not that we would mind seeing you naked. In fact, we will join you in your walk of shame, if you want," Hip grinned.

I bit my lip. "There is no way I'm letting you guys see me naked. Can I at least keep my shirt on?"

"You'll end up having the same problem with your fins." Jason replied.

"Then no," I said crossing my arms.

I was sure they had seen my scars—even if they hadn't brought them up—but that didn't stop me from not wanting to expose my mangled body to them.

"Atalanta."

"No! It's not going to happen."

"We can close our eyes."

"I think it's time we head back, okay?" I looked at Jason, trying not to cry again. "Please."

Jason gave me a sad smile and nodded. "Okay. Whatever you want." He turned back to the others. "Let's go back."

The other four had a range of expressions from disappointment to worry. I squared my shoulders and swam back towards where I thought the shore was, only to be pulled in the correct direction moments later by Percy.

I felt bad for ruining the outing, but I wouldn't let myself feel bad for getting freaking naked in front of five guys I hardly knew. I decided that I would head out next time I was alone, and try shifting then.

With my hand in Percy's, we came back to standing water level. God, did it feel weird the moment that I broke the surface. My lungs pushed all of the water out like a squeeze bottle before I took in my first breaths of actual oxygen. So I guess it wasn't really possible for me to drown anymore, even if that wasn't already obvious with me breathing under the water.

We left the other four behind to change back and trekked up the sand back towards the cliff.

"You will have to let us in at some point, Atalanta," Percy whispered.

"You're one to talk." I snapped back. He was just as full of mystery as the rest of them, with an even harder face to read half the time.

"You may have a point, but this is difficult for all of us. We may have known each other for years, but it is not as if we were ever close. Having to work in this group dynamic will be a learning experience. It will be harder to get some of us to open up to each other. But it will be easier once you learn to trust us."

"I just don't understand how you guys can be okay with this. I didn't even know you all knew about..." I fidgeted with the sleeve of my sopping shirt. "About what was going on."

Percy, who still held my hand, turned my palm upwards and began to run his fingers over the lines.

"There are a few things that happened that day. One of them being an argument with Jason that brought everything to light. Once we sorted everything out and realized that none of us could let you go, we decided to try."

My mouth fell open and I turned my gaze away from him. "Oh."

I looked back at the others, who were walking up from the water. My eyes had reverted back to seeing only silhouettes so I couldn't see their faces, but I doubted they were smiling.

"And this is okay with all of you? Dating me all at once?" I asked, looking back at him.

I watched his shadow nod. "We are okay with it for now, as long as you are willing to try. As for the future, no one can know what will happen. If it makes you feel better, our kind don't all practice the human idea of monogamy. Many of our women have multiple men."

I frowned. "Why do I feel like you've said that me before?"

"Because I have. Though, that time I tried to have you believe I was speaking only of common animals."

"Oh yeah, I remember now," I lied. I didn't remember that at all, but I still felt like I'd heard it before.

Without me realizing it, we had actually come out of the water closer to my cabin. After climbing the cliff in silence, I stared at the empty building with its lights off. A shiver ran up my spine. Even with the guys there, I couldn't help but feel like all of the warmth my father, sister, and I had put into making it a home was gone.

"My place?" Ajax suggested after he and the others made it to the cliff's landing with Percy and I.

I nodded, and without a word, the five of us trudged through the woods back to Ajax's much more welcoming home.

When we got inside, I spoke up. "I shouldn't have snapped like that. I'm sorry, I know you guys are only trying to help."

"Don't worry, short stuff. We understand." Jason said with a pat on my head.

Ajax grunted in agreement.

Hip came over and kissed my forehead. "Yeah, like Jason said earlier. You've been through a lot. We'll talk about it more another day. Okay?"

"Let's get you to bed," Theseus said, putting his hand on my shoulder.

Despite my protests, Ajax gave me his bed while he insisted that he would sleep on the couch. I didn't know where the others were going to sleep, but Jason was on the floor next to me, stealing as many pillows as he could find to build himself a pillow mountain. I think Hip ran back to my cabin to grab the air mattress.

"Good night, sweet dreams."

I didn't have the courage to tell him that wouldn't be the case.

I snuck out after the guys had fallen asleep to go practice shifting. It wasn't as dark as before, which made it much easier for me to find my way through the forest path down to the cliff edge.

I was back on the beach again. The waves were much rougher than before, the wind whipping my face, causing my cheeks to sting. But still, I was determined to try. It wasn't as if I could drown now.

I dove into the water. It felt amazing as the water sent tingles over my body, giving me the energy to speed through the waves. I visited the fish of the coral reef again, several of them welcoming me, before I attempted to shift.

It took several attempts, but finally I succeeded. I had a gorgeous tail of purple and blue scales.

"You look beautiful, Atty."

I spun around, and before me was another mermaid with dark skin and gorgeous forest green eyes. Her tail was a deep charcoal red with wispy fins.

"Cal? They told me you were dead," I croaked as I studied her mermaid tail in shock and wonder.

"Oh, my dear baby sis. There's no need to worry anymore. I've got you." She wrapped her arms around me. They were so warm, and I sunk into her embrace.

"We'll always be together. Even in death."

My eyes snapped open and I looked up at her. "What?"

It wasn't my sister holding me anymore, but a rotting corpse that resembled my sister. Her flesh was no longer a warm brown, but gray and sunken in. Her eyes, nothing but hollow sockets, arms skeletal.

I screamed and shoved her away.

TIED TO THE SEA

The corpse held out her bony hands, an inhumanly wide smile gracing her face. "Together forever. That way you'll never forget me."

Heart racing, I turned tail and swam away as fast I could. That thing couldn't be my sister. She just couldn't.

"Atalanta...wake-"

Something snagged my tail. I looked back frantically, and the enraged face of my dead sister stared back at me. "What's wrong? You don't like my new form? It's your fault I look like this, Atalanta. All your fault."

"I'm sorry, Cal! I tried to save you!"

She wrapped her skeleton hands around my neck, the tips digging into my flesh. "You didn't try hard enough."

She shoved me down into the ocean's black depths.

"Atalanta! Wake up!"

My eyes snapped open. I was drenched in sweat and my heart was racing about a mile a minute. I sat up and let out a sob.

Another bad dream. What had I seen? I quickly tried to grasp the fading images but they slipped through my fingers. I needed to know.

Someone was next to me on the bed, a huge form with mismatching eyes.

"Atalanta," The man held me in his arms and crooned, trying to calm me down. "It's okay. It was just a dream."

Atalanta? Who was Atalanta? That wasn't my name, my name was Kelly...No wait, Tasha?

Which one?

Which name?

Who was I right now?

Panicked, I shoved away at the man. I didn't know him. Where was my father? My sister?

Other men came into the room. I didn't know them either. Were they Emmanuel's men? How had he found me?

I scrambled backwards until my back pressed against the headboard. The four men were staring at me, worry and concern in their eyes.

"Atalanta, calm down," said the one with gray-blue eyes. His voice rang, bell tones making my mind go fuzzy.

I shook my head, trying to throw off the feeling.

The one with golden hair stepped closer to me, his hand out.

"STAY AWAY FROM ME!" I screamed.

"Atalanta," said another voice.

My eyes snapped to the doorway and stared into familiar green eyes. Not quite my sister's, but richer. This man was important. Something told me this man was mine.

"Jason." When his name fell from my lips, it all spilled back in.

Yes, I was Atalanta North. We were in Washington.

I turned back to the man I had shoved away. He was Ajax. There were other men in the room with us. I looked at each one and slowly, their names floated to the top of my mind. Percy, Theseus, Hip.

My gaze slid back to Jason. As if he were some sort of anchor for my mind, the longer I stared into those eyes of his, the faster everything returned. My father was in the hospital, I wasn't human anymore.

Cal was dead.

The image of the corpse dragging me deeper under the water sent shivers wracking through my body. I took it back. I didn't want to know.

I curled into a tight ball, grasping my head, hoping to erase the images I kept seeing.

Jason crawled onto the bed with me and Ajax. "It's okay. It was just a dream. You're safe now."

Slowly, he scooped me into his arms and rocked me back and forth. As much as I wanted it to, it didn't make me feel better. I couldn't stop seeing those empty eyes.

You didn't try hard enough.

"What happened?" Percy demanded.

"She was scared. I tried to wake her. Bad dreams," Ajax said softly.

Percy growled in response, "Yes, I can see that, but why is she like this?"

"Shock."

"Well, do something!" Hip shouted.

"I can't just remove this from her. It's not that simple."

Remove? Is that what Ajax could do? He could remove my emotions? Could he make it all go away? Those eyes.

I looked towards him, pleading. Begging him to make it stop.

"Sweetheart, don't give me that look. Please."

My eyes shot from him to Theseus. He could do it if Ajax wouldn't. He could compel me to forget again.

"Atalanta, look at me," Jason said, pulling my attention to him.

His warm hands brushed my cheeks. "It was a dream. Whatever you saw, it wasn't real."

But he was wrong. It was real. My sister was dead, and I kept forgetting.

Chapter Six

JASON

I had been able to soothe Atalanta back into an uneasy sleep after she had woken from her nightmare, questioning Ajax softly as soon as her breathing evened out. All he had to say was that her terror had woken him up, and when he was able to shake her awake she was extremely confused.

Hip crossed his arms. "She acted like she didn't even know who we were until Mr. Perfect came in."

"I don't think she did," Theseus added, his face almost as haunted as Atalanta's had been.

"I have a bad feeling." I said quietly and turned to look at Percy. "Do you think this was just disorientation after waking from her nightmare or something worse?"

Percy, who looked deep in thought, said, "I...actually don't know. I will need to do some research."

When he began to leave the room, my stomach dropped a little. "Wait. I don't think we should be leaving her side."

I didn't want to admit that I was a little scared of not having him there.

"She will be okay, as long as you stay near her."

"Yeah, why is that?" Hip asked. "She snapped out of it the moment you showed up."

"Mates." Ajax grumbled.

My eyes shot to him. He looked disgruntled, his focus fixated on Atalanta, who was curled up in my lap.

"My parents said the same thing, but we never performed the ceremony. We can't possibly be mated."

"Technically, you are not, but you cared about her when you turned her. Assuming she had similar feelings at the time, those feelings are amplified by the connection the two of you forged by the change. It's very similar to a mated pair. You are anchors for each other, mentally and physically," Percy said.

My eyebrows shot up and I remembered how Ajax had demanded for me to stay close to her during her transition, that it would help her. This is what he must have been talking about. I looked down to Atalanta's sleeping form. Even now, my skin tingled where it met hers and I felt more centered than when I was separated from her. An anchor, huh? I kind of liked that.

"This is bullshit. So what? She'll love him more now because of some connection they have? Where does that leave us?" Hip stage whispered, his posture stiff and fists clenching and unclenching at his side.

I had hoped that we had made some progress in the last two weeks. This had just set it back about ten steps as he glared daggers at me.

"I bet she wouldn't feel the same if she remembered what you said to her that day." Theseus muttered.

I felt that one right in my gut. Guilt that I had been trying to shove down came back to the surface. He wasn't wrong. It was only by the grace of the gods that she never asked what I'd said to her that day.

My eyes widened as I studied the others. All of them were now glaring at me, including Percy. Would they tell her?

Feeling defensive, I leaned back away from them into the headboard. I gripped Atalanta tighter to me, causing her to grumble in her sleep.

Percy sighed and rubbed his face, almost pushing his glasses off his head before he straightened them. "I think we are all a little worked up at the moment. Yes, what Mr. Monroe said that day was wrong, and he will have to atone for it in the future. But right now we are all tired, and fighting about it will get us nowhere. We should try and get some rest."

After that, the guys all reluctantly acknowledged Percy's words and began to leave the room. Ajax, instead of going back to his spot on the floor next to the bed, grunted something about working and stormed off. Hip and Theseus went back to their spots in the living room, leaving me holding Atalanta alone in the room with Percy.

We were quiet for a few moments before Percy asked, "Where were you earlier?"

"I went on a walk."

"Any particular reason you went on a walk in the middle of the night?"

"I needed to clear my head." I said as I carefully moved Atalanta out of my lap and laid her down on the mattress. She immediately curled up into a tiny ball, grasping the pillow in her arms.

A small smile ghosted my lips. She was so cute.

"Do you want to talk about it?"

My flicked back to Percy at the door. "Not really."

Percy sighed and then did something that surprised me. He crawled into the bed and laid down next to Atalanta and I.

"I am here for when you want to talk."

"Percy..."

Percy removed his glasses and placed them down on the nightstand next to him. He always looked so handsome without his glasses. His sharp features softened, making him seem somewhat approachable. "Get some sleep, Jason. Tomorrow will be a long day."

I nodded and settled down on Atalanta's other side, my hand resting on her hip. Just as I was drifting off to sleep, I felt another hand land softly on top of mine.

The next morning, Atalanta was acting strangely. Since waking up, she had been distant, constantly staring off into nothing. The only one she seemed to respond to was me, which wasn't doing anything to reassure the others.

All of us except Ajax were sitting at his kitchen table eating a late breakfast. Several times, we all had tried to strike up a conversation with Atalanta but she would just stare into her bowl of Captain Crunch.

"Do you want to try to shift today?" Theseus asked, looking at Atalanta, his expression hopeful.

When she didn't answer, Theseus's gaze cut to me, turning from hopeful, to resentful, and then finally to pleading.

I nodded and turned to Atalanta. "Hey, Atalanta."

Her eyes slowly moved from the bowl to meet mine. "Mmm?"

"Theseus was wondering if you wanted to try and shift again today."

Her brow furrowed and she glanced at Theseus. "Why didn't he ask me himself?"

I didn't have the heart to tell her. "Do you want to?"

"Not really," she grumbled and went back to looking into her cereal bowl.

I looked over at Percy, Hip, and Theseus, their faces reflecting the concern I felt.

'We need to do something' Hip mouthed, gesturing desperately to Atalanta's forlorn face.

Percy nodded his head towards the living room, and slowly all of us stood and walked towards the door and out of earshot of Atalanta, who didn't even look at us as we left.

"Maybe something fun?" I suggested. "Something she likes."

"Okay, but what would that be?" Hip asked.

"Reading? Watching movies?" Percy threw out.

Theseus shook his head. "We need to get her out and about. Being stagnant won't help."

At that, an idea popped into my head. Smiling, I said. "The aquarium. The university is holding an event there today and there will be all sorts of booths set up."

Hip nodded. "She did really like that reef. It might not be the same, but I doubt we will get her back into the water just yet."

"I like the aquarium," Theseus smiled.

"Then it's settled. Percy, are you coming with?"

He shook his head. "I'm going to look into what happened last night. I want to know if her memory loss has something to do with trauma or something else."

"Okay, what about Ajax?"

"I'll go ask," Theseus said before giving Atalanta one more glance and walking out the door.

"I'm going to get started." Percy said before stealing his own glance at Atalanta and leaving.

Hip and I locked eyes.

"Listen…"

"I'm sorry."

My eyebrows shot up, surprised.

"Percy was right. I was really tired last night and I was just worried about Atalanta. I…well, I did mean what I said, but—" He stopped again, not finding the words.

I chuckled. In all of the years I had known him, it wasn't often he was at a loss for words.

I put my hand on his shoulder. "I get it, man. It might be hard, but I don't want to come between you and her. I can see she's liked you from day one. I'm still jealous, actually. But I know if I tried to keep her for myself, she would resent me. Truce?"

"Truce," He agreed and then scrunched his nose. "This whole thing is weird."

"A bit."

"And the other three are just so okay with it!" He hissed.

I mirrored his expression and nodded. "Maybe it's like they said, because they're older?"

"Whatever it is, there's no way they aren't at least a little jealous."

"Oh, I'm sure they are."

Hip was silent for a moment, looking pensive before asking, "Is it true? You know, that this is normal for our kind?"

I tilted my head and thought about it. "Any time I've been to the city, I saw several pairings like ours. So, yeah, I guess it is. My mom has only been with my dad, so I don't really know how the others do it."

"Huh," He murmured, his face contemplative.

Theseus opened the door and popped his head back in. "Ajax isn't coming. I'm going to go back over to Atalanta's to warm up the car. Get her dressed and head over, okay?"

We nodded and he shut the door. In unison we looked at each other, gave sharp nods, and stormed into the kitchen to Atalanta.

"Sweetheart," I said, poking her in the cheek.

Slowly, as if in a trance, she looked up at me. "Yes?"

"Time to get dressed."

"Can't I stay in my pajamas today?"

"Nope," I grinned.

"Listen, Jason. I'm not really up to—" she squealed when Hip came up from her other side and scooped her right out of the stool.

Hip heaved her up onto his shoulder, fireman style. "Sorry, Speedy. No isn't the correct answer."

"Put me down, Hip!"

He snorted. "Not going to happen."

"Jason! Tell him to put me down!"

"Sorry, Atalanta. I broke both my arms. I'm not capable of taking him on."

"Your arms are fine!" she shrieked.

"No, they aren't. See?" I said, shaking my shoulders and letting my arms flop around lifelessly.

She growled and then slapped Hip's ass. "Put me down, Jackass!"

"I thought your name was Hip?" I chuckled.

"Me, too." Hip grinned and then patted Atalanta's ass.

We stepped into Ajax's room, Atalanta still struggling.

"If I put you down, will you get dressed?" Hip asked.

"I'm not going to do shit!"

"Whelp, then I guess you'll be going out in public in your jammies." He purposely readjusted her and began to walk back out the door.

"Wait! Wait! Okay, I'll get dressed."

Her panicked expression was so damn cute.

Hip grinned. "I don't know. How do I know you wont just hide under the covers or something?"

"You'll just have to trust me." She huffed.

Hip immediately let her down, sliding her body down his front until she was settled on the ground. "Of course I trust you, Speedy. Remember, it's you and me against the world."

I felt a pang of jealousy in my chest watching the two of them. I was aware that there was this closeness between the two of them that I had yet to really reach with Atalanta. A part of me wanted to be angry about it, but there was a competitive flare that was sparking to life in my chest, and I chose to grab onto that.

I would succeed in becoming as close to her as Hip seemed to be.

Hip kissed her on the cheek before stepping back and following me out the door to wait in the hall for her. A few minutes later she stepped out in a familiar worn hoodie with the words "TEAM QUIN" on it.

I smiled softly and gestured to the hoodie. "I believe you were wearing this the day we met."

"Who's Quin?" Hip asked as he pointed at the words.

She huffed and crossed her arms over her chest. "Only the hottest vampire around."

"Should we be jealous?" I grinned as I placed my hand on the small of her back and guided me to the door.

"Very much so. He wouldn't have manhandled me like a caveman. He has more class than that."

Hip and I shared a look before he said, "You're right, we could never hold up against the suave sexiness of a vampire."

The moment the three of us stepped out the front door, I scooped Atalanta onto my shoulder like Hip had done, much to her displeasure.

"But I put on my clothes! Jason!" She whined.

"I am but a savage barbarian, as I don't have enough class to escort you through the woods like a lady. I'll simply carry you."

She grumbled, but didn't fight me as I quickly made my way through the path Theseus and Percy had left in the snow. It had piled up pretty high during the night and was nearly up to my knees on either side of the dents the others had left in it.

"You look like an angry kitten right now." Hip said as he trailed behind us.

"I have claws like a kitten, too, nice and sharp. Why don't you come closer, Hip, and I can show you?"

"Touchy, touchy. Don't worry, kitty, we are taking you someplace fun."

"Aren't I suppose to meet with Clint today?"

"Shit," I cursed and patted my pockets with my free hand to try and find my phone. "Hey, can you grab my phone? It's in that back pocket in front of you."

"If you need it so badly, why don't you put me down so you can get it?"

I gave her a gentle tap on her ass. "Not gonna happen."

"Don't worry, Sweet Cheeks, I got it." Hip said before I felt his hand slip into my back pocket and pull out my phone.

I suppressed a growl. I said truce, not bromance.

"Why, thank you, you're so helpful," I crooned in an overly sweet voice.

I turned my head and looked back to see him give me a wink as he handed me my phone.

I texted Percy about Clint. While waiting for a reply, I noticed several texts from Davie and Margo. They were wondering how I was feeling and if I was up to hanging out.

I had told them that I had come down with mono and had been too sick to come into school. I was sure with Hip and Atalanta also missing from school, the rumor mill was filling up with all sorts with nonsense. I had told my friends that Atalanta had been in a boating accident, but I doubted the school gossip cared about that story.

I texted them back, telling them that I was fine and taking Atalanta to the aquarium now that she was discharged from the hospital.

"Jason, Hip's teasing me!"

"You're just so teasable."

I smiled and looked down when I felt a buzz in my hand.

Percy: I'll take care of it.

Davie: She's well enough to be walking around?

Margo: Yay~!

I texted Davie back.

Me: She's able to walk around but gets tired easily.

Davie: That's good to hear. Margo will probably want to celebrate

Looking up, I saw Atalanta's cabin coming into view. Theseus was standing propped up against the hood, studying his own phone.

Margo: We will have to celebrate her release and your brave recovery ;)

I chuckled and slipped my phone back into my pocket. Focusing on getting Atalanta better was step one. I would worry about celebration parties later.

Theseus looked up from his phone when he saw us coming and cocked his eyebrow.

"She didn't want to walk through the snow."

"He's lying! Theseus, help! I'm being kidnapped!"

I tried so hard to keep a straight face when Theseus didn't react to her.

"Did you have to carry her like a sack of potatoes?" Theseus asked.

"She wanted to stare at my ass."

Theseus looked at me skeptically for a moment before rolling his eyes and getting into the car.

"He's lying! Theseus, why—Oh. Fuck! Jason, turn me around so I can tell him the truth."

Hip and I just laughed.

"Now, where's the fun in that?" I chuckled.

When I reached the car, Hip opened the door for me and I slid Atalanta off my shoulder and into the passenger seat.

She immediately tapped Theseus on the leg and whined. "They kidnapped me!"

"Well, you seem all right. And I mean, how can I be mad when they brought you right to me?" He smiled.

I snorted. Smooth.

His smile was genuine, and considering this was the first time she had looked at him all morning, I couldn't really blame him.

Hip and I hopped in the back and we were off down the road. Atalanta sat in the front seat, probably sporting a pout on her face while Hip and I were talking about the new Kingdom Hearts game that had just come out.

"Before we forget," Theseus said before reaching into the back for a bag of bandages and handing it to Atalanta. "We should make sure you're all wrapped up."

I leaned over to see her better and watched as she stared at her clawed hands, the frown on her face deepening. I had an inkling that she was sinking back into the slump we had just pulled her from.

Acting on instinct, I unbuckled my seatbelt and leaned into the front, taking the bandages from her and booping her on the nose.

She looked up from her hands to stare at me, the all too familiar shadows darkening her eyes.

"It'll be fun. Like dressing up as a mummy for Halloween," I whispered. It was the best thing I could think of.

"We passed Halloween."

"It's never too early to test out costumes." Hip threw out, catching on.

"Exactly." I pulled out one of the bandages and began to wrap it around her wrist. "See, you're way ahead of us. I normally have my costume picked out by December."

She squinted her eyes at me. "You choose your Halloween costume for next year right after halloween?"

"Of course." I said confidently.

She giggled, the sound of it lightening the weight that had settled in my chest.

TIED TO THE SEA

"You're so weird."

I stuck my tongue out at her and watched as those shadows receded. I happily helped her cover up the rest of her visible scales. Her hands were a problem though, as we didn't have the mittens she had worn yesterday. And we were just pulling into the parking lot of our destination.

She looked around, wide-eyed and curious. "An aquarium?"

"Yep," I smiled, trying not to sound worried since we couldn't let her walk in with her hands like that.

As soon as Theseus pulled into a spot, I hopped out of the car and opened the passenger door.

I took her hands into mine. "Do you think you can try relaxing that little ball in your chest?"

She gazed down at our linked hands and shook her head. "I don't know, Jason. I wish I had known so we could have brought Cal's...Cal's gloves."

Hip hummed. "Hmmm, yeah, we messed up a bit on that. But we wanted to bring you someplace fun. Get your mind off things."

"Like Ajax said, you just need to relax." I said.

"I don't think I can do it."

"Perhaps it's not about her relaxing." Hip suggested as he leaned over into the front seat and began to rub Atalanta's back.

Theseus, who had come to stand next to me, whispered, "Maybe it's about trust."

"Trust..." I echoed quietly before kneeling down in front of her. "I was born a Merman. Grew up as one my whole life."

Her face scrunched up, confused. "And? I knew that already."

"The day I saw you in the hall. The day we met, I was pretty freaked out that you had seen me drinking the salt water. It's not that I wanted to lie to you. But I've been trained since birth to keep what I am hidden, so pretending you were just imagining things was my natural response. I also thought you were cute. And I really liked the strong and confident girl who confronted me without hesitation. But I did lie to you, and I kept lying to you."

"Jason—" she started, but I held up my hand for her to stop.

"I'm just as bad as he is," Theseus piped in before I could tell her the rest. "I know I apologized for this already, but I shouldn't have pretended you were crazy. Yes, it was salt water in that bottle, and yes, my voice was what was causing your mind to go all fuzzy. But I swear I never used my abilities on you. At least not on purpose. The day we met I was singing to myself and I'm sure that effected you. It's why you probably felt so comfortable around me. It wears off, though, so I don't want you thinking that I have you under some spell."

I looked over at Hip, who was still massaging Atalanta's back. Silently prompting him to hop on this truth train I had started. He shrugged. "I never lied to her about anything."

I frowned and glanced back at Theseus, who wore the same expression as me.

A teary eyed Atalanta giggled and sniffed. "It's true. He might not have told me the truth but he never really lied to me. That's more my fault, I guess." She looked back at Hip. "You are more the type who will only answer direct questions."

Hip shrugged again. "I have no idea what you're talking about."

She rolled her eyes and smiled.

I squeezed her hands. "I want us to start trusting each other. Really trusting each other. Because I'm in this for the long haul."

Her smile fell. "There are things about me that you don't know. That I don't think I can tell you yet."

I nodded. "That's okay. You can tell us your secrets when you're ready."

"It's not okay and you know it." She scolded, her jaw clenched and fangs showing through her scowl. "We keep pushing things off. And I can't just expect you to tell me the truth and then keep my mouth shut."

I tilted my head. "Well then, how about one truth. One secret that we know, and you can share one secret you know?"

"Th-that sounds fair." she nodded.

I took a deep breath, letting it out slowly before saying, "We know about the files, Atalanta."

Chapter Seven

HIP

There. Someone had finally said it. From the moment I'd seen that file, I had been itching with the curiosity to know who Atalanta North really was. I had done some digging, trying to find any trace of her online but found nothing, and I mean nothing. There was a total of one Atalanta North in the United States and that one was an old Irish woman from Tulsa.

But when our Atalanta woke up, it was clear to even Jason that she wasn't in the right mind for us to go digging into her past. At the moment, just poking the wrong spot seem to set her off in some way. So we kept putting it off, and I was smart enough to realize that it wasn't making things better. Yet I wasn't the one brave enough to pop the unstable bubble we had formed.

"W-what? What file?" She stammered, her face going pale.

I swallowed the pit in my stomach and said into her ear, "The ones that hold your fake identities. You, your father...and your sister. I found them the night of the storm."

She twisted around to look at me. "You had no right!"

"It wasn't like I was purposefully digging for it. I found them—"

She cut me off with a growl. "You found them while going through our stuff. You may not have been looking for those files, but you were still looking for something. They weren't just laying out on the counter."

My eyes flicked to the guys, hoping for some help. Their expressions matched mine. Deer in headlights. "I was nervous. You were unconscious and I didn't know what to do with myself and before I knew it I was digging through your stuff."

"You're nosy, is what you are."

Shoving us out of the way, Atalanta hopped out of the car. I scrambled out after her, readying myself for a chase. She just paced back and forth on the snowy pavement though, shoulders tense, muttering under her breath. The three of us stood off to the side, fidgeting, not sure what to do.

My shoulder drooped. "I'm sorry, Speedy."

She stopped her pacing and studied us for several moments. "I'll take your sorry. But so you know, I'm going to be mad at you," her glare slid to the other two. "At all of you. For at least three days."

I blinked, not expecting this reaction. Usually when a girl was mad, they would throw a fit like a toddler. Waving their arms and screeching like a banshee. Actually, I had expected her to bolt and we would have had to chase her down. But instead she stood, quietly fuming, her mind running a mile a minute.

Finally, she sighed and softly said, "This isn't the first time we've been found out. It happened a few times in the early days, but it's been several years since the last incident. Usually we would be packing our bags and ditching town before you could even finish making your morning coffee. But...well, things have clearly changed."

"Why the fake names? Are you in Witness Protection or something?" I asked.

"Not technically. But I'm not really up to talking about it right now, okay?"

"Atalanta—" Theseus began.

"You need to understand," she interrupted. "The fact that I'm not burning this name and hopping on the next bus out of here is hard enough. This has been my life for almost ten years. It's going to take more than a pretty smile to get me to tell you everything."

Theseus nodded slowly. "Fair enough."

"You wanted one truth?" She crossed her arms over her chest. "I'm really scared about what's going to happen. I don't know what I'll do if my trouble ends up at your doorsteps. But something tells me that if I stick with you guys, it's going to turn out okay."

We all smiled warmly at that. It was a bit cheesy for my taste, but it still made little flutters in my stomach. When no one said anything for a solid minute, I knew I needed to break this weird mix of warm and fuzzy yet also uncomfortable atmosphere.

I snorted. "That's a boring truth. I was hoping for something like...you pick your nose when no one is looking."

She scrunched her nose. "Very mature."

I shrugged. "Just doing my job."

TIED TO THE SEA

Jason jabbed me in the ribs and I started laughing.

Theseus walked up to Atalanta and wrapped his arms around her, his nose nuzzling into her hair. "Will you forgive us for snooping?"

She tugged on his shirt collar and dragged him to face her and grumbled. "I said three days."

"Awe, come on. How can you be mad at me? Your favorite cripple." He grinned.

She scoffed and shook her head. "That's messed up and you know it."

I walked up to her other side and hugged her as well. "And you think he's the sweet one. Just you wait till you see how messed up he can be."

"You're one to talk." Jason snorted.

I glanced over at him and saw jealousy in his eyes. Keeping my gaze locked on his, I hugged Atalanta closer to me and watch that spark turn into a small flame. I basked in satisfaction before I remembered that we were supposed to be on a truce. I let go of Atalanta and backed away from her, sliding my hands into hers.

I smirked and leaned in to whisper in Atalanta's ear. "You may be mad, but it seems you trust us a bit more now."

She looked down at her now human hands, her smile widening as she slipped her hands out of mind and studied the short fingernails.

Jason came closer. "Well, would you look at that."

"We'll be able to go inside now." Theseus said.

Atalanta looked at the three of us. "I've never been to the aquarium before."

Jason took her hand and pulled her towards the large blue building in front of us. The parking lot was full of cars and there were a few people trickling in and out of the large glass doors I could see in the distance. Theseus had parked us pretty far in the back, which had played to our advantage.

Inside was relatively crowded as the atrium had booths lined up along the edges. Scanning them, I saw that they mostly were from the local college. Students running the booths were handing out pamphlets and bracelets saying things like *Save the Sea Turtles* and *Coral for the Homeless*. A few of them were selling trinkets, but most of them were just giving information on sea life and charities people could donate to.

I stopped in front of a booth that was run by the aquarium and selling stuffed animal from the gift shop. It had a large colorful banner on the front of it saying, "Adopt a Sea Buddy!". I glanced over my shoulder to see the others checking out a booth that talked about the importance of getting rid of the plastic in our ocean. I scrunched my nose as I remembered the many times I had pulled fishing line off of sea life. Turning back to the booth in front of me, I spied a turtle.

Picking it up, I liked how squishy it was. Stuffed animals nowadays were too stiff for my liking. The turtle was about as large as a basketball and covered in soft faux fur. It was cute, its green flippers hanging at its sides, making it look really cuddly. The eyes were really lopsided though, and it had a tear in one of the flippers. A factory defect on top of being damaged.

"How much?" I asked, looking up at the girl who was covering the booth.

Close to my age with curls of blond, she was staring at me with a familiar expression. Eyes glazed over, cheeks flushed with heat, mouth slightly open. I watched as her eyes moved slowly up and down my body.

I coughed to try to get her attention and smothered my grin when she snapped her mouth shut and spluttered.

"I'm sorry. I seemed to have spaced out. How can I help you?"

Yes. 'Spaced out' was a good cover word for checking me out.

"That's alright. I can't imagine you find too much excitement here on a normal day." I held up the turtle. "How much?"

She began to twirl her dirty blond locks around her finger. "Yeah, it can get pretty boring. Today isn't too bad, though. Um, that one is $34."

I winced internally as I pulled out my wallet. They wanted to charge that much for a defected toy? I reminded myself that places like this always jacked up prices.

I opened my wallet to check inside. I only had a twenty. All the cash I had saved up from the market went to the new helmet I got Atalanta.

I sighed and put down the turtle. Oh, well.

I gave my best flirtatious smile to the clerk. "Seems this buddy won't be finding a home today, at least not with me. Thank you for your time."

The clerk's smile fell into a pout and looked as if she were about to say something but I just gave her a wink and walked away.

I walked up to the others, who were still standing at the booth from before.

"Hey, find anything interesting?" Atalanta asked.

"I did, but it wasn't in the cards for me." I sighed dramatically.

She frowned. "And here I thought you were one to always be able to get what you wanted."

I smirked and a few moments later, I felt a tap on my shoulder. Turning around, I looked down at the clerk.

"Here." She held up a bag for me. "Since he's defective, no one would have bought him. Maybe he can go home with you today, after all."

I smiled wide and took the bag from her. "Thank you. I think he'll be well loved."

She leaned over and whispered in my ear. "My number's in the bag. Call me some time."

With a wink, she walked away, her body swaying with purpose.

I turned back to Atalanta, who stared at me, eyebrow cocked and lips thin.

I grinned and held up the bag. "I guess you're right."

The guys were glaring daggers at me.

"Did you just—"

"Right in front of Atalanta? Dude, not cool."

I rolled my eyes and stuck my hand into the bag, pulling out the turtle. I held it out for Atalanta. "I thought you might like him."

Her eyes widened as she slowly took the turtle from me. "Oooh, he's so cute! Oh my god, he has a torn flipper! And look at those eyes."

"You got her a broken toy?" Jason chuckled under his breath.

"I love him. I'm going to call him Salt," She crooned and cuddled him close.

I smirked at the guys. I knew Atalanta wouldn't be able to resist the turtle's cuteness, especially with it being a broken toy.

She tugged on my shirt to draw my attention. "Don't think for one second that I'm going to let you get away with flirting with another girl just to get out of paying for my present."

I pouted. "I didn't flirt with her."

"I'm so sure you didn't."

"It was for a good cause?"

She sighed and gave me a kiss on the cheek. "Thank you. I love him. But next time, don't flirt with the clerks."

I raised three fingers. "Scout's honor."

"I doubt you were ever a scout," She snorted.

"I was. For like a year."

"Oh? Then what happened?"

"I got kicked out for making all the other kids do my work for me."

"You're incorrigible," She giggled and then snuggled Salt closer to her.

Jason look dumfounded. "You…you don't mind that he just manipulated some poor girl? She's going to be waiting for his call."

Atalanta shrugged. "He didn't really hurt anyone. I'm sure she'll be upset when he doesn't call but it's also her fault for thinking she could buy a guy's affection. I mean, she didn't even know your name, did she?"

I shook my head. "Nope."

"Then it's just as much her fault as it is his for using his looks to his advantage."

"Speaking of," I slipped my hand into the bag and pulled out the paper with her number on it. "I don't want her getting huffy and trying to storm over here to take it back. So I'm going to give her a nice smile and slip this into my back pocket if thats okay with you."

She nodded. "As long as I get to tear it up as soon as we are out of eyesight."

I did as I said by flashing the girl a flirtatious smile and pulled out her number and slipped it into my back pocket, the girl giving me an inviting smile and a wink back.

"You two are horrible people," Jason groaned.

I slung my arm over his shoulder. "Perhaps, but you still like us."

"Jason." A voice called off to our left.

An older couple was striding up to us, curiosity on their faces. I sensed they were Mer right off, putting me on high alert. I let go of Jason's shoulder and slowly positioned myself in front of Atalanta.

"Mom. Dad. I didn't know you were doing this event."

Ah. That's why they looked familiar.

"It wasn't planned, but the other professors canceled at the last minute so we volunteered to come help out."

The woman looked at our group before settling her eyes on Theseus. "Aren't you the boy who works at the community center with Doris?"

"Yes, the name's Theseus."

There was something there for a moment, a look that passed between Jason's mother and our ginger friend. A small shake of the head and widening eyes. As if he was cautioning her of something.

Oh, something I would definitely be looking into later.

"Oh, yes. I remember now. My apologies, we've been so busy with the college these days, my brain's been a little scattered," her gaze slid to me. "I remember you, though..."

The father leaned in and whispered into her ear. "He's the boy the Clarks found on the beach. You know, the one the elders—"

"Oh," she breathed.

My advanced hearing allowed for me to hear him just fine, and I cringed at the flood of sympathy I saw in her gray eyes. I looked away, pretending to be interested in the booth that we had been standing next to. The student running the booth was absorbed in his phone, not paying attention to diddily squat.

I made eye contact with Atalanta, who was now standing to my right, still out of their direct eyesight. She was staring at me with that curious eye of hers. I wish she didn't have to wear the bandage, but on the off chance someone from Argos showed up to the aquarium today, we didn't want them asking too many questions about her eye color.

I gave her a millimeter shake of my head. Please, don't ask me. Not here.

Her face hardened and told me she would definitely be questioning me later.

"Jason, it's good to see you. It's been far too long," came a third voice.

My eyes snapped away from Atalanta to see a suave looking gentleman walking up to us, wearing a tailored three piece suit. He had auburn hair and gray eyes just like Jason's mother. If I had to guess, he was her brother. Jason's uncle.

My suspicions were confirmed a moment later. Jason's shoulders stiffened when he spotted the man, his fists clenching at his side. "Uncle Calder."

Reaching back, I took one of Atalanta's hands into my own and squeezed.

"What are you doing here?" Jason asked, his voice sickly sweet.

"I felt that it had been far too long since I came to the surface and saw my favorite nephew."

"I'm so grateful you came all this way to see me. Though, I made a promise to hang out with my friends today. If you don't mind, I'll rain check with you?"

Calder's eyes cut to Theseus and I, disgust evident on his face. "Of course. I'll let you go."

Jason nodded and smiled at his parents. "I'll see you guys back at the house."

Taking that as our cue, I walked forward, Theseus coming up behind us to shield Atalanta as we passed.

At the sound of Atalanta's yelling, I went on full alert and spun to see her being pulled back by Calder's hand on her wrist. Her eyes were wide and full of fear.

I saw red.

"Now, now. You don't think I'd let you run off without introducing me to your little female, now do you, Jason?" He tugged Atalanta against his chest and breathed deeply into the crook of her neck. "You're a Mer, and judging by the bandage across your eye, you were made."

I could see Atalanta shaking and struggling against Calder's grip. His inhuman strength way too much for her. I think the only thing preventing her from making even more of a scene was that we were surrounded by people.

I was about to cold-cock the guy if he didn't let go of her. In fact, it was only Theseus's hand on my shoulder that kept me from pulling her back into my arms. My eyes sliced to Jason, whose face was deceptively calm. His spine was as stiff as a board and his smile looked painted on.

"Uncle Calder. I'm sure you're scaring my friend. Please, let her go." Jason cautioned, stepping forward.

"Oh, young nephew. Are you trying to give me orders?" His eyes lifted and they were glowing a bright silver.

Jason lowered his eyes. "No, sir, I just thought—"

"You're not supposed to think." He warned.

"Calder," Jason's mother hissed. "Not in front of the humans."

"Of course, baby sister." He let Atalanta go and she stumbled into Jason's arms. "You know you have to document any made Mer with the council."

"She isn't made, she's… um—"

"My cousin." Theseus interrupted. "From the Guinea Gulf."

Calder's eyes widened. "I see. And her bandages?"

"She was in an accident. Got caught in a fisher's net. My aunt thought it would be a good idea to come here for a few months."

"Hmm," he murmured before looking at Jason's parents. "Just be sure our young Jason doesn't become too attached. We don't want *more* tainted blood ruining the bloodline."

I watched as Jason's father curtly nodded and his mother just stared at her feet. Who was this man that had complete control over them?

"We better get going." Jason mumbled, his voice hoarse.

Calder looked back to us and damn if his gaze didn't send a shiver down my spine. "Run along, then. I don't want to interrupt your time with your...friends."

"Thank you, sir. I hope you have a good day."

With Atalanta in his arms, Jason hurried off further into the aquarium. Theseus and I followed behind them.

Our pace brisk, we didn't halt until we were far into the building, in a dark corner surrounded on all sides by fish tanks.

Jason let out a heavy sigh. Turning to Atalanta, he said, "I'm so sorry about that. Are you okay? Did he hurt you?"

"No, he didn't. Creeped me out more than anything." She let go of his hands and hugged herself. "Was that jackass really your uncle?"

Jason clenched and unclenched his fists, his nostrils flaring as he breathed heavily. "Unfortunately."

"What kind of hold does he have on you guys?" Atalanta asked as she began to absently rub her wrists.

Jason gritted his teeth and stared at her. It was obvious he didn't want to talk about it. His eyes flicked around the area, at me, at Theseus, at anything else but her. He began to study one of the fish tanks as if the little fish were the most interesting things in the world.

"Hey," She put her hand on his cheek. "Just tell me one truth."

He inhaled deeply. "I hate him, but I was taught to respect him. It's complicated, but right now... I hate that he touched you and I'm so sorry you had to see that."

She reached up and wrapped her arms around his neck, standing on her tip toes while he leaned over slightly. It almost looked cute, with her hand still grasping the stuffed turtle.

"Let's just hope it doesn't happen again." There was something in the way she said it that lead me to believe if it did happen again, she wouldn't be the helpless damsel twice. Especially with knowing what she did to those girls.

She looked back at Theseus and I. "There are a few things I want to talk to the two of you about, but for now, can we just have fun? Go look at some fish? I'm tired of drama for the moment."

Theseus approached them as Atalanta let go of Jason's neck and practically picked her up in a large hug.

"Yeah, let's go look at the fish."

I kept quiet as the four of us wandered through the aquarium, dancing around the topic of Jason's family. Atalanta loved seeing all of the fish. She crooned at the guppies and excitedly pointing out random species that she recognized. Most of the tanks had a little button on the side which played a recording of a woman's voice informing us about the species inside the tank. We never pushed the buttons though, as Atalanta would simply point out the plaques with the same information to Theseus. I watched Theseus roll his eyes every time she did it. But instead of reminding her that his eyesight was perfectly fine, he just shook his head and smiled at her.

I felt bad as I watched him stare at her mouth, eyes furrowed in concentration as she spoke animatedly about something but then would completely miss when Jason had something to add. I obviously didn't understand the difficulties of reading someone's lips, but I guessed that sign language wouldn't be as demanding when we were in groups like this. Yet, Theseus was really good at pretending to be able to hear, and I assumed that was why the others seemed to forget simple things like getting his attention when they spoke, or not talking over each other. Atalanta did well to remember it most of the time, at least.

"The sign says they have a turtle sanctuary. You guys want to go check it out?" Atalanta asked, gesturing to the sign with the hand clutching her stuffed turtle's fin.

"Sure." Theseus nodded.

When we go to the doors of the sanctuary, the attendant told us that only so many people are let in at a time to see the turtles and we needed to wait a few minutes before entering.

"I wasn't aware that turtles migrated this far north." I pondered as I studied the board which had information on all of the turtles currently staying with them.

The attendant smiled. "They typically don't. All of our turtles here were transported from the south. The doctors here are experts and can help even the worst cases."

Jason leaned in and whispered into my ear. "A few of the doctors here are our kind. Let's just say they have a knack for healing sea life."

I chuckled. With all of the powers our kind seemed to display, healing wasn't too farfetched.

Atalanta struck up a conversation with Theseus about choosing a last name for the stuffed turtle. He kept throwing out silly names like Billy Bob and Juan Bon Bon. Seeing the smile on her face warmed my heart.

I glanced at Jason, who was also staring at her, his smile matching mine.

I took a deep breath and walked in front of him, cutting off his view. "You know…I've always been jealous of you. Knowing who your family is. Where you came from."

He blinked, taken aback by my sudden confession, and then started laughing.

I scowled. "What?! Don't laugh! You're all Mr. Perfect, with the perfect family, perfect grades, you're the captain of the swim team and the damn student council president."

"I'm sorry," he said between snorts of laughter. "I suppose it does look like that from the outside."

"Yeah, your uncle..."

"My mother's side of the family can be a bit...controlling."

I raised an eyebrow at him. "A bit?"

He shot me a warning look that told me not to dig too deeply. I held up my hands in an attempt to placate him.

"All I'm trying to say is that I was wrong. Your uncle seemed like a dick, and if he's anything to base your family on...well then, I guess you've had a rough time of it and I'm sorry."

"Well, I would be lying to myself if I didn't admit that I wasn't somewhat jealous of you. Your family doesn't seem to dump expectations on you. You have a lot of freedom to be who you want."

"Of course they dump expectations on me. My abuela always wants me to study harder and become a doctor and my grandfather wants me to take over his farm. But I don't let their wishes stop me from being me. They might be disappointed if I don't do what they want with my life, but it is my life and I only get one."

He nodded slowly, his eyes glazed over in thought.

I placed my hand on his shoulder. A silent gesture of support. I couldn't promise that we wouldn't bicker anymore —it was just too fun to piss him off— but I made a promise to myself that I would stop judging him.

"What are you two talking about over here all serious looking? I thought we decided today would be fun."

"Sorry, Speedy. I was just declaring my undying love to Jasey-bear. Unfortunately, he doesn't return my affection." I pouted and gave her my best puppy dog eyes. "My heart is broken."

She smirked and looked at Jason. "He's not your type?"

"I'm not into blondes," he replied smoothly.

I clutched my chest in mock hurt. "You wound me."

I slid my arm across Atalanta's shoulder and turned her towards the door to the turtle room. The attendant held the door open for us to walk in.

"Come on, Atalanta." I harrumphed. "I bet the cute turtles can mend my broken heart."

Chapter Eight

ATALANTA

I was hungry. Well, more like starving. But I didn't want to interrupt our time at the aquarium. We had just left the turtle sanctuary and were heading towards a door that had a cartoon dolphin painted on it. The turtles had been so cute, but I felt a pang of sadness seeing their injuries and scars. One of the turtle's plaques said that he was too injured and adapted to human care to ever be released back into the wild. I felt for him, being separated from his family and the world he knew.

Noticing the unshed tears in my eyes, Jason had placed his hand on the small of my back and hurried me through the sanctuary, waving to a few of the doctors who were working with a turtle who had a huge gash in its shell.

I gripped the plush turtle that Hip had gotten for me closer to my chest as we walked through the dolphin doors. Once inside, I halted, wondering how we had transported to Florida, but then realized that the giant room was only made to look like we were outside. Vaulted glass ceilings kept out the cold while the walls and floor were painted to look like we were on a tropical island. Right past the doors was a ramp that led down to a sandy area and a massive pool that was blocked off by a short wall.

I could see a trainer standing on a platform in the middle of the pool, working with the dolphins.

Coming down the ramp I watched, fascinated, as the woman got the dolphins to jump high in the air and through a hoop. She had a mic on and was talking through speakers to tell the people in the room about the dolphins they had in their care. She was putting on a show, making jokes and talking with the dolphins as if they could understand her.

When the four of us approached the short wall, the two dolphins—which had been watching the trainer as she held a small fish in her hands—turned and looked in our direction. With trills and clicks, they left the woman on the platform and swam towards us.

Since reaching the aquarium, I had felt this odd little buzzing in the back of my head. I had thought it was a tension migraine since it would fluctuate as we walked through the building. Yet, as these dolphins approached us, that little buzzing turned into soft static that seemed to bounce through my skull, only growing louder as they came closer.

I winced and pressed the palms of my hands into my ears, hoping to block out the noise.

"Are you okay, Atalanta?"

My eyes snapped to Theseus who was staring down at me with concern. I tried to think of how to describe what I was feeling when the dolphins reached us. They clicked and wiggled around excitedly, pulling our attention.

"Uhhh," The trainer spluttered before catching herself and falling back into her performance. "It seems Donny and Nila have taken interest in some of you! Dolphins, like most animals, have a great sense of people. If you hold your palm out, they might even let you pet them."

The people around us crowded closer, a few children bouncing on their toes, hoping to get a chance to pet the dolphins.

My brows furrowed as I stared at them, that static in my brain still raging. Was it them? Was this some sort of Merperson thing?

I looked at Jason and Hip. "Can you two hear that?"

They looked at each other and then back at me, shaking their heads.

My eyes slid to Theseus, who was still staring at me with concern. "Do you feel anything?"

He shook his head slowly, reaching out to put his hand on my shoulder. "What are you hearing?"

So it wasn't some weird Mer thing. Maybe I was overthinking things and it was a migraine after all. It had been a long time since breakfast. I was probably just suffering from low blood sugar or something. Or maybe I was crazy.

"It's nothing. My head feels weird, I think I need to eat." I glanced back at the small crowd of people and the dolphins. "Let's get out of here."

Theseus didn't look convinced, and now Jason and Hip shared that same concerned expression.

I gave them my best smile and walked away from the dolphin pool, exiting the room. I tried to ignore how the sensation faded the further I got from the dolphins. Maybe it was a fluke. Some sort of newly made Mer thing. I'd ask Ajax about it later, and if it happened again, I would tell the other guys about it.

"Do you want to eat at the cafe here, or go somewhere else?"

"The food here is probably overpriced and not that good. Are there any good places around here that you guys know of?"

"I think there's a Chili's nearby." Jason suggested.

"They've gone downhill in the last several years." Hip said, shoving his hands into his pockets. "Pick something else."

Jason sighed and pulled out his phone to look for places to eat. "Fridays?"

"Nah."

"Ruby Tuesday's?"

"Nope."

Jason scowled at him. "Well, then, why don't you pick?"

Hip shrugged. "I've never been in this area."

Jason tilted his head, brow furrowing. "I thought you came up here for the local market?"

Hip looked taken aback as if he was confused how Jason knew about this market. I, too, was curious. What market?

"That's the next town over…" Hip hesitated before saying, "Um, there is a place I know of over there, if you guys are up for the drive."

I nodded, curious to see what type of food Hip liked. We agreed and made our way to the car. I was thankful not to see Jason's uncle again. I did spy Jason's parents, who were busy with one of the student booths, and the girl from the gift shop booth. She smiled widely at Hip as we passed, but when her eyes landed on me, that smile turned into a glare. She was not happy that I got Salt.

Too bad. He was mine.

I took Hip's hand and grinned back at the girl triumphantly. This one was mine, too.

Hip glanced down at our conjoined hands, over at the girl, and then chuckled softly.

He gripped my hand tighter, pulling me closer. "Don't worry, Kitten. I'm all yours."

"Stop calling me Kitten."

"Okay, Speedy."

I grumbled, which only made him laugh.

Thirty minutes later, Theseus pulled into a parking lot that Hip had directed him too. It was a small plaza with a Walgreens, a liquor store, and at the end was a small place called *Griasol*.

Hip lead us to *Griasol*, which turned out to be a restaurant. It was tiny, with no more than three booths and a four person table. Next to a large counter with a register was a case filled with baked goods. My stomach growled as I practically drooled over them.

"Buenos días, Tía. Tiene algo de buena cocina?" Hip called into the empty restaurant.

My eyebrows shot up. Hip spoke Spanish?

A short, plump woman came shuffling out from an opening behind the counter that I assumed led to the kitchen. When she spotted Hip, her face grew warm and welcoming. "Hijo mío. ¿cómo estás? ¿Son tus amigos?" She gasped when her eyes landed on me. "¿es tu novia? ¿Qué le pasó?"

Hip nodded. "Sí, estos son mis amigos, y ella se metió en un accidente."

She came rushing around the counter and gave me a big hug. "Don't worry, sweet girl. I'll fix you up some good food. You'll feel much better."

I blinked. What had Hip said to her? All I caught was the word accident. I wish I spoke Spanish.

"Um. Thank you?"

"No worries, little one. We will fill that belly. You are too skinny." She looked at Jason and Theseus who stood in the door behind me. "My, you two are handsome. Tramposo, you be sure not to lose her to them."

Hip actually blushed. "Tía."

"Don't *Tía* me. Now, why don't you go sit and I'll bring you the special?"

Hip huffed and walked over to the last booth, gesturing for us to sit down. I made eye contact with Jason and Theseus, their curious expressions matching my own. We cautiously moved further into the restaurant and sat down on the inside with Hip next to me, while Jason and Theseus sat across from us.

"Did she just call you a tramp?" I whispered leaning over the table closer to Hip.

Pink tinted the arch of Hip's cheeks. "She called me trickster. It's less of an insult and more a term of endearment."

"So, she's your aunt? You don't look Hispanic."

The three of them shared a look. What was up with the silent conversation thing they kept doing? I thought that was only a book thing.

I squinted my eyes at them and then stared down Hip. "Jason's father mentioned...Hip, are you adopted?"

He wouldn't meet my eyes. "Yeah. I'm adopted."

"Are your parents...are they human?"

"Yes."

"Do they know? That you're...um, well...not."

He nodded. "It wasn't really something I could hide from them when I was little. When they realized they hadn't found a normal baby on the beach, the town's elders brought them in and told them about us."

Hip's aunt came back out with four plates and placed them down in front of us. I found it funny that she didn't even bother giving us menus or taking our order, just taking it upon herself to bring us food. I only recognized the rice and black beans, and some sort of chicken dish. The chicken was cut into large chunks and coated in a creamy sauce.

I moaned as I shoveled a bite into my mouth. And then another, and another. Before I knew it, my plate was empty. With a pout, I glanced at the plate next to me which still had some food on it. Without hesitation, I swapped that plate with mine.

"Not even going to ask, really?" Jason groused.

I shrugged and met his narrowed eyes with my own puppy dog pout. After a few moments, he sighed, reached across the table and snatched the boys plates and scrapped their food onto the plate that was once his.

"Hey!" Theseus and Hip shouted in unison.

I grinned and took another bite of food. Deciding to distract them from my food thieving, I returned to our earlier conversation. "You guys have mentioned them before. These town elders. Are they like what books say they are? Just a council of old people?"

Jason tilted his head. "Basically."

"I never liked town elders or elder councils or whatever. In every book I've read, they've done more harm then good."

"I don't disagree with that." Hip grumbled. Jason and Theseus looked uncomfortable, so I changed the subject.

"The aquarium seemed pretty busy today. I'm surprised I didn't think to ask this, but what day is it?"

Being unconscious for two weeks, one tended to lose track of time.

"It's Saturday," Hip said as he tried to sneak back some of his food.

I slapped his hand away. "Saturday *what*?"

"February 13th."

My eyes widened. "That means tomorrow is February 14th."

Wow. The past year flew by so fast. And Cal and my father weren't going to be here to celebrate it with me. A cold knife sliced right through my heart. I clenched my jaw, trying not to let the emotions show on my face. I glanced down at my hands and watched in horror as scales began to ripple underneath my skin.

My eyes snapped back up to the boys. Smile. Everything was okay. Breathe.

"Yep, that means tomorrow is Valentine's Day," Theseus said, not having noticed my underlying panic. It didn't seem the other guys noticed either, but a pregnant pause fell over us.

And then all of their eyes snapped wide.

Jason whipped out his phone, looking at the screen as if to double check the date. "Fuck!"

"Shit." Theseus spat.

Hip stood. "Tía, we're leaving!"

Jason and Theseus stood as well and began to herd me towards the door.

His aunt poked her head out from behind the kitchen door. "Leaving so soon! What's the hurry?"

"Tomorrow's Valentine's Day!"

"Don't tell me you forgot?!" She chastised him.

Hip didn't answer her as the door closed behind us. Before I knew it, we were all back in the car and on the road.

"We royally messed this one up, guys." Theseus said, his eyes shooting to the rearview mirror.

I craned my neck back to look at Jason and Hip, who had their eyes glued to their phones. Their eyebrows were angled down in similar expressions of concentration as their fingers flew across the small screens.

I bit my lip, wondering if they were really freaking out because it was Valentine's Day or… they knew. I doubted it, but I needed to check, anyway.

"Guys, I don't see what the big deal is. It's just Valentine's Day."

"Of course you don't, because you're beautifully different," Jason said, not looking up from his phone.

"But you're still a girl. And I'm your—" Hip's eyes snapped up and shot to Jason, and then Theseus. "We are your boyfriends and we can't not make a big deal out of it."

I raised an eyebrow at him. "So is that what we're doing now? Are we making it official?"

Hip's eyes widened. "I—um, I mean…if you want to."

"How am I possibly going to update my relationship status on Facebook?"

"They have an 'It's complicated' option, don't they?"

We all burst out laughing at that. Theseus glanced away from the road, meeting my eyes with a look of confusion. I smiled at him and began to mouth that I would tell him later when I remembered that I had spotted a large notepad in the back seat with a pen attached to it. Reaching back, I fumbled around for the notepad until Jason handed it to me.

I scribbled onto the notepad and held it out for Theseus to read. He quickly pulled off to the side of the road and read the words I had written on the page.

The two stooges said they are making a big deal because I'm apparently their girlfriend. Since you are freaking out about this valentines thing too are you my third stooge?

Theseus began to laugh before leaning across the console to give me a kiss on the lips. "Sweetheart, I'm no stooge. I'm your freaking prince."

I blinked and my cheeks began to heat. I glanced nervously to the other two in the back. I couldn't tell what they were thinking, which was strange. Their faces still had the matching frowns they had when they were concentrating. I thought I saw a spark of jealousy, but it was gone too swiftly for me to tell.

"Wait, she called us stooges?" Jason asked, leaning forward to read the notepad." Darling, I'm just as much of a prince as he is."

"Yeah, what he said!" Hip seconded.

I couldn't tell if they were actually upset or joking. Hoping to keep the tone light, I smiled. "I don't know,

Hip. I feel like you're less of a prince and more of a devilish rogue."

Hip grinned. "Does that mean I get to be the one to steal the maiden's heart from the princes?"

My jaw fell open and my eyes flicked between Jason and Theseus who had turned his head back to see the others. Jason slapped Hip on the knee while Theseus growled. "I dare you, Shrimp. I doubt you could steal shells from the ocean, let alone her heart from me."

"Is that a challenge?" Hip asked, giving Theseus a feral grin.

I settled back into my seat and listened to the three of them bicker about who would win in a contest for my heart. They weren't actually hostile, and I didn't think they were serious. It seemed more like they were measuring dicks. Regardless, I didn't feel like getting in the middle of it. After a few minutes, Theseus turned back to driving, a smirk on his face.

"Cheater," Hip grumbled. "Just because you can't hear me doesn't mean you won, you know!"

I smiled and closed my eyes. My mind wandered, thinking about the guys and everything that was going on. I still didn't know how to feel about all of this. It almost seemed too good to be true that these amazing guys actually wanted to be with me…as a group. It was weird, to be honest. I wondered if their acceptance of this was all an act. I know Percy said that it was normal for their kind, but would there come a point where they would want me to choose? Could I choose?

My selfish side told me not to choose at all, and the side that was trained to run told me that I needed to get as far away from all of them as I could. They were too close now and my heart told me I couldn't leave, but I also couldn't pull them into something they wouldn't want. I would need to try to get each of them alone and talk to them individually.

Pushing my romance clusterfuck aside, there was also the issue with my new lack of humanity, my dad and Cal, and then Clint being here. My head hurt thinking about all of it. There was so much going on, I honestly didn't know how to feel at any given moment.

I opened my unobscured eye and looked over at Theseus. At least for now, while they were trying out this weird plan, I had a distraction. Like Jason said, one thing at a time.

Awhile later, Theseus slowed to a stop. Opening my eyes, I was surprised to find us at the library and not Ajax's house.

I looked over at Theseus and back to Jason, who were both hopping out of the car and rushing to my door. There was a cute fumble with who would get to open my door before I rolled my eyes and opened it myself.

I frowned when Jason kissed me on the cheek and got into the seat that I had vacated but not before handing me my turtle. "You guys aren't coming with?"

Theseus, who was next to me, answered. "Sorry, Atalanta. We have some major Valentine's planning to do and can't have you knowing what we're up to."

Hip rolled down his window and poked his head out. "Yeah. If we have you tagging along, you'll figure out our plans and ruin all of the fun."

I scrunched my nose. "So you're having Percy babysit me?"

"Of course not. You're going to be babysitting him." He turned me towards the library's doors and patted my ass to encourage me forward. "I warn you. He's temperamental before he gets his bottle and nap."

I rolled my eyes and walked towards the door of the library. I turned to wave at the boys as they drove away and noticed the colorful wall of the community center. Ajax had painted a lot more onto the mural while I was out. Now there was this section with a large raven sitting on top of a pedestal, wearing a broken crown. The raven stared up at another bird. I couldn't really tell what kind of bird it was, but it was black like the raven and much smaller. The smaller bird sat on top of an open book, staring down at the words on the page. As I looked towards the back of the building, a forest sprouted up and he had painted small creatures among the green leaves.

The color popped against the gray and white of the snow around us. The raven and small bird were my favorite, though. He made them so lifelike, and the way the raven stared up at the smaller bird…there was something about it.

"Ms. North. Are you going to continue to admire his work or do you want to come out of the cold?"

I turned to see Percy poking his head out of the library's doors. Theseus was right, he did look grumpier than usual. There were shadows under his eyes and his expression looked like it had been set to a frown for quite a while. His usual neatly contained hair was out of its ponytail and sticking up on one side as if he had just woken up.

I smiled. Well, the guys had been able to cheer me up some. It was my turn to try and infect Percy with the happy bug.

"Good morning to you too," I said as I walked passed him into the library.

As per usual for a Saturday, there were several students from the nearby college studying at the various tables throughout the library. There was an older woman who waited at the counter for Percy, and he walked past me to help her. I saw that my favorite chair near the counter was open and quickly took it. Settling in, I watched Percy as he spoke with the old woman and then walked away to find a book, I assumed.

While he was gone, I studied the other people. There was a group who sat at one of the tables together. One of them was a woman who looked to be around my age. She was pretty, with long blond locks that curled down to her mid back. I watched as she smiled and flirted with the guy next to her, her fingers twirling her long hair.

Slowly, I reached up and ran my hands through my hair. I hadn't had much time to linger on it, but my once coarse, short, tresses were much softer and had begun to reach past my shoulder. I stared at the dark strands. It was nice to finally have hair that was more like Cal's, easily managed, but it wasn't mine and would take some time getting used to.

As I stared at my hair, I realized that my hands were shifted. Panicked, I shoved one hand into my hoodie pocket and made sure that the other was neatly hidden underneath the stuffed turtle.

Moments later, Percy came back. I looked up at him with a smile. Some of the hair I had been studying had fallen in front of my eyes so I tried blowing it out of my face and failed.

Percy gave me one of those millimeter smiles and gently tucked the stray locks behind my ears. "It's gotten quite long."

"Yeah, I was just looking at it. How come it's growing so fast? Hair does not grow that quickly in two weeks."

"Our kind produce more keratin than humans. Therefore our hair is softer and grows much faster. Especially our women." Percy looked down at the stuffed animal I was still holding." And who is that?"

"This is Salt. He is a brave turtle rogue and friend to the Mer." I held him up for Percy to inspect. "Despite his looks, he's an intelligent creature who solves problems with his brain rather than his strength. He saved a whole flock of krill once, you know."

"That is quite the backstory. Hello, Salt. That's a rather unfortunate name you've got there." Percy shook the turtle's fin.

I don't know how he was doing that while keeping a straight face. I couldn't stop from laughing.

"His names Salt because if anyone complains about it being a stupid name, I can say, 'well you don't have to be so salty about it!'"

Percy cocked a brow at me. "You've been spending too much time with Theseus."

I fell into another fit of giggles at that.

Percy let go of Salt's fin and held out the same hand for me to take. Nervously, I revealed the clawed hand from my hoodie and placed it in his palm. Without hesitation, Percy helped me stand and wrapped his large hand around mine so that it was curled into a fist and hidden. With long strides, he pulled me towards his office.

I had never been inside the room before. When I first entered it was so dark, but Percy didn't move to turn on any lights. When my eyes adjusted, I could see that there was a lamp sitting atop a desk which seemed to be the only light source at the moment. Slowly, I studied the room as my eyes revealed more to me.

"Percy. You're a bit of a hoarder, aren't you?"

"I am not a hoarder."

"No, you're right. I would call you closer to being a slob."

He growled. "I get enough of that from Jason. I do not need it from you as well."

"But look at this!" I maneuvered towards where the lamp sat. "There is a desk here, right? Because all I see is paper."

I pointed to one of the many piles of books and then to the shelves of the empty book case. "And I'm pretty sure those books have perfectly fine homes right there, yet you leave them laying here as if you're creating a fort."

Percy was in front of me in a flash and pulled me in for a kiss. His lips were rough as they dominated mine and when his tongue dove into my mouth, my legs wobbled slightly and a shiver escaped me. I felt as Percy's hands came up behind me and grabbed my ass, holding me firmly in place.

It felt far too soon when Percy pulled away from me, but not before licking my bottom lip. "Hush now."

I gaped, my jaw working but no words coming out for several moments until I successfully stuttered, "But...it... it's still messy in here."

Percy's eyes narrowed. "Fine. I'll clean it."

Disappointingly, Percy let go of my ass and picked up one of piles of books and began to put them back on the shelves.

Looking around, I spotted a large comfy chair. I placed Salt down in it, took the bandage that covered my eye off, and picked up a stack of books as well to help Percy. I had to be doubly careful as a lot of these books seemed very old and I was afraid my claws would tear right through them.

For several minutes we worked side by side as we bickered with each other over the best way to organize the books. He was insisting on sorting them by age, color, and size while I argued for the much more reasonable alphabetical order by the author's last name. He eventually broke, and I won. The fact that he had scooped me off the ground and plopped me into a chair with the orders to 'sit there and stop trying to help' were just the way he showed his appreciation.

"You're being unreasonable," I grumbled and tried to stand.

Percy gave me a hard look which commanded me to settle back down in the chair. "Half of these books are so old the author's name is too faded. My way makes it easier."

"You could simply look up the author based on the books content and relabel the books," I replied, glaring back at him.

He ignored my glare and picked up more books. "That is far too much work."

I rolled my eyes at him. He simply scowled and gave me a kiss on the lips. "Just do as I say, please."

"Well, I mean, if you're going to ask nicely." I settled into the chair and played around with Salt for a few minutes before the boredom got to me. Leaning back over the arm rest, I watched from my upside down view as Percy move through the room and sorted books. He was in a crisp white button down with the sleeves rolled up to his elbows, accompanied with a black vest slacks, and he looked really good. His hair was out of its usual ponytail and a mess though, constantly getting into his face as he picked up books. I spotted a rubber band around his wrist.

"Percy." I called. "Come here."

His brows scrunched but he didn't move closer to me. I smiled. "Come on."

He put down the books he was holding and approached me cautiously, as if I were a lion waiting to pounce on my prey. "Yes?"

I sat back up and patted the floor in front of me. "Sit."

He didn't cock his eyebrow at me like I expected him too. He just sat down in front of me like I asked, trusting without a thought. But he was facing me, so with a smile I put my hand on his shoulder and shoved him until he got the picture and turned away from me. "Your hair's a mess, I'm going to fix it for you."

Without a word, he settled back and let me run my fingers through his tangled hair. He was right about Mer and soft hair, because the strands between my fingers felt like silk. I wanted to just continued to stroke his hair, but it was now untangled and I knew sitting on this floor probably wasn't the most comfortable. Reaching down, I slipped the rubber band off of his wrist and slid it onto mine. Gathering up all of his hair, I began to braid it.

"So, Jason told me that you know that we know."

I stiffened but didn't stop braiding. "I'm assuming you're talking about the files?"

"Yes."

I bit my lip and took a deep breath. "So, listen. I told this to them already, but I'm not ready yet. And I know you enough to know that you're just as curious as I am and have probably figured everything out but it's not what you think, or maybe it is, and, um—"

"Atalanta. You are rambling."

"Sorry." I finished his braid and tied it off with the rubber band.

When I tapped his shoulder he leaned back into my legs and tilted his head back to look up at me. "To be honest, yes, I am curious. But at the moment, I really just want to know one thing about it, if that's okay."

I stared down at him, trying to keep my expression calm while I mentally freaked out. "...what's that?"

"How many names have you had?"

My eyebrows rose. "Really? I was expecting you to ask me what my real name was."

"To me, you are the girl who dumped a bunch of books into my lap and convinced me to read trashy romance. Ultimately, who you were in the past does not matter, but I know how much having to pretend to be someone you are not can affect you."

Oh. I studied him, staring into those brown eyes, wondering when he had to put on a mask and pretend to be someone he wasn't. With his blunt personality, it was hard to imagine.

As he continued to stare up at me, his head now resting in my lap, I knew answering his question wouldn't be so bad. He wasn't asking why we had to use fake identities, only how many times.

I bit my lip and broke eye contact with him. "Thirty-seven."

I saw him blink several times out of the corner of my eye, looking surprised by the number. I had to admit, it was a little satisfying to see the intelligent librarian actually look surprised.

Sitting up, he reached over and pulled a familiar book out of a box. "The girl with no name. When I first read it, I thought it might be some adolescent crisis of identity...but it was because you haven't really felt that you've been able to have an identity for so long, wasn't it?"

He held out the book to me. It was one of my favorites, the cover severely worn from all of the years I had handled it. It was the first book I had ever gotten signed.

I took the book from his hand and gently ran my hands over the cover. "This is from when we lived in Boston. My name was Elly Nolle. There was an author's convention going on in the hotel next to where we had been living. I was really depressed and my father had literally dragged me out of the house to try to cheer me up. I hadn't even read the book before but the cover looked nice and the author was really kind."

I opened the book and showed him the writing that I knew he had already read. "When she asked my name, I sort of blanked. It was really embarrassing, just standing there awkwardly and not answering her. But Jamie Addams, she just gave me this look like she had seen right through me and wrote that. And it spoke to me, you know? After that, it became my go-to whenever I got the chance to go to a convention."

Percy turned back towards the shelves. "Thirty-seven times is a lot to change ones identity."

"Yeah," I chuckled. "I was twelve and Cal was almost fourteen when it all started. We were pretty messed up, so keeping our real identities a secret was basically impossible for longer than a month or two. In those first three years alone we had to burn our names 16 times. By that point, we were basically living only in hotels and out of backpacks. Our father didn't know what to do."

"What changed?" He asked.

My heart pounded at the question. Was I ready? No, I wasn't, and I didn't believe I ever would be, but I tried to remind myself that they had already seen. And Percy had yet to judge me so far.

I leaned forward so that my head was on his shoulder and I held out my left arm in front of us. Slowly, I slid the sleeve of my hoodie up my arm. The scales covered most of them but you could still see some of the hideous scaring. "I tried to kill myself. Ended up in the hospital, and then in a mental health facility."

He studied the scars for several moments before gently reaching up and running his fingers over them. I shivered at the foreign touch over the sensitive skin. Surprisingly I liked it and wanted him to touch me more.

"These were why you didn't want to shift last night?"

I nodded and pulled my sleeve back down. "I know you guys know about them. But it's hard."

He leaned his head against mine. "I understand."

"You do?" From what I saw of his body, he didn't have any scars. His skin didn't carry a single blemish. But I did remember how he wouldn't shift last night either.

He lifted his hand and stared at it. "I'm different from the others."

I snorted. "Thats a bit cliché, don't you think?"

"And calling me cliché when I'm trying to open up is rude, don't you think?"

"Touché. Sorry." I wrapped my other arm over his shoulder and brought him in close for an awkward hug. "Please, continue."

"I am from a different race of Merfolk called Deep Sea Mer. A little self explanatory, but my kind hale from the deepest depths of the ocean. From places so dark and cold that it is almost a wonder how anything could live there. We are a warrior race that are often considered savage and less intelligent than the other races."

I watched as his hand shifted. Black scales surfaced and the skin around it looked so much paler, it was almost a light blue. The claws he sported were much longer than my own, and what I had seen on the other guys as well. It looked like the hand of some sort of demon.

TIED TO THE SEA

"My true form is nothing like the others. We are a race that others fear. I…"

"Were you too afraid for me to see what you looked like?"

"Not afraid."

"No, of course not. Percy, listen," I reached out and took his clawed hand in mine. "Yes, *you and other mer* might believe that your form is scary, or even downright ugly, but I still know it's you. And I like you. We all have our ugly side. You just saw mine. Some people are just lucky that they can easily hide that part of themselves. And while this might sound cheesy, those kid's movies had it right: it's what inside that matters."

Percy's hand squeezed mine and he relaxed against me. We sat like that for a few moments, a blissful silence full of acceptance.

I inhaled and slowly murmured. "Besides, I think it will be good to have a merman who hales from a warrior race on my side."

Percy stiffened. "Why? Did something happen?"

My mind flashed to Calder and the shiver that ran up my spine when he had touched me. And let's not mention…him. If I wasn't careful, I'd have that asshole knocking on my door. And this time, I couldn't just run.

I shook my head. "No, nothing happened, but you never know."

His hand squeezed mine. "Remember what I told you. I will protect you. You are safe with me."

I smiled, closing my eyes and resting myself against him. "Thank you."

Chapter Nine

ATALANTA

I stayed with Percy for the rest of the day and helped him close the library down at ten. At first I stayed in his office reading, but once I noticed Percy frequently had to stop cleaning to help someone at the counter, I convinced him to let me man the counter while he cleaned. He agreed with the condition that I shift my hands back to normal, as he unfortunately didn't have any gloves with him. I was silently proud of myself when I discovered that it was much easier this time. I was even able to get my feet shifted back to normal.

Once he showed me the basics of how to work the computer and check out books, he left me to my own devices, only checking in on me occasionally.

After ushering out the last person and locking the doors, I helped him tidy up. We even made a competition out of who could put books back the fastest. The two of us moved swiftly through the isles, putting back misplaced and returned books. Percy won.

I think I was finally getting the hang of his micro-expressions, because he seemed smug about winning to me despite his face not looking all that much different.

"Do you want to try going out and shifting again?" Percy asked as he locked up.

I thought about it for a moment. I had shown him my scars earlier and felt pretty comfortable with it. I was also curious to see if he would show me what his shift looked like.

"Okay, sure," I nodded.

"All right. Let me just tell the others," He said, taking his phone out of his pocket.

"No," I held my hand out to stop him. "I mean, you can tell them. But—um…can we try it alone? Like, maybe have them join us later or something? I don't want to hurt their feelings, it's just…"

I wasn't ready for all of them to see. One at a time felt a little more comfortable at the moment.

Percy studied me for a moment before slowly nodding and texting the others. He held up the phone to show me the group text he was going to send.

I am taking Ms. North out for a swim. We won't be long. I want to see if she will feel more comfortable shifting with just one of us around.

My brows rose. I was surprised that he willingly showed me his text and that he had understood exactly how I was feeling.

"Yes, that's good." I bit my lip. "You don't think they'll be mad? Or jealous?"

"Let's find out." He hit send.

Mere seconds later, the phone buzzed with life. I leaned over to see the replies.

Jason: Keep her safe

Mr. Clark: Good, we aren't ready. Keep her away as long as possible. and what Jason said.

Dawson: let us know if she succeeds

"Who's Dawson?" I asked as I read the names over each text.

"Theseus. His current last name is Dawson."

"Current?"

"You are not the only one who needs to change their name. But that is something to discuss another time. Come on." He took my hand and began to lead me around the building.

I wondered about Ajax's response but didn't need to wait long when Percy's phone buzzed again, this time with a phone call.

He answered. "Ajax."

Then, without another word, he handed the phone over to me. I took it and put it to my ear. "Hello?"

"You okay?" Ajax asked gruffly.

"Yes?" I chuckled.

"You're too far out of my range."

I frowned. Out of range? "Oh, you mean your empath ability thing can't reach this far?"

"Yes. I don't like not being able to feel you."

I smiled at that. "Well, I'm okay, Ajax. Just thought I'd try shifting."

"And you don't want us there?"

"No, it's not that, it's just…" I bit my lip.

"I understand. Be safe, little bird."

My mind flashed to the painting he created of the raven and the smaller bird. "Okay, Ajax. I'll see you soon."

He hummed on the other line before hanging up on me. I handed the phone back to Percy. He took the phone and then smoothly slipped his palm into mine and guided me through the dark woods towards a cove.

In the dark, I could see Percy leading us to a small box propped right on top of a rock far away from the water.

"You can put any of the clothes you don't want to get wet in here," He told me as he let go of my hand and began to unbutton his vest and shirt.

I mentally slapped my cheeks to pump myself up and began to remove my clothes and the bandages on my face. It was just Percy.

No one else was here to see my body.

Just Percy.

I slowly removed my hoodie and my long sleeved shirt, folded them up and put them in the box with Percy's clothes.

Just as I was hooking my fingers into my pants, I paused and glanced over at Percy. He was already undressed, and judging by the silhouetted junk I could see dangling in the breeze, he wasn't going to be modest this time. As I continued to stare, my eyes locked on his cock. I could see it getting larger. I gulped and turned away from him.

I heard him chuckling behind me.

Bastard. He was not going to get me again with this shit.

Inhaling, I turned back around and made contact with his now glowing amber gaze and shoved my pants down, taking the underwear with it.

Keeping eye contact with him, I folded up the pants and panties and tossed them into the box.

I put my hands on my bare hips. There. I did it.

That challenging gaze flicked down to my breasts and back up to my eyes.

Fuck. I was still wearing my bra.

Gritting my teeth, I reached back to unhook my bra. I slipped it off slowly and dangled the garment in front of me before dropping it into the box as well.

I was completely nude now. I could feel the cool breeze caress my skin. In the back of my mind, I noted that it was snowing again, but I wasn't freezing like I should have been.

I watched as Percy slowly swept his eyes along my body. I felt a little triumphant when he growled. His cock certainly couldn't hide the attraction he felt towards me as it was currently standing at a full salute.

With a sway in my hips, I turned and walked towards the water.

Oh, yeah. I was totally the one in control at the moment.

Suddenly, I felt a sharp sting on my butt and the sound of flesh hitting flesh. Blinking in shock, I watched Percy's bare ass run past me.

"Did you just slap my ass!?"

He looked back at me over his shoulder. "What are you going to do about it?"

"Why—you!" I shouted and chased after him.

With the grace of an olympic swimmer, Percy dove into the waves with me following behind him, not as graceful.

Just like the night before, as soon as the water washed over me, I felt an amazing boost of energy. Much slower than Percy, I followed behind into deeper water until I lost him.

I halted and looked around, worried that I didn't see his pale form in the darkness. When I felt large hands gently grasp my hips, I gasped, inhaling ocean water.

I twisted my head around to see Percy's grinning face. He came alive just as much as me when the ocean surrounded us. It was nice. Different from his usual calmness and nothing like Hip or Jason with their boyish attitudes, but still nice.

He nuzzled into my neck. "You were holding your breath again."

I took a deep breath in, letting the water rush through my nose and gills. "I hadn't noticed."

"It will take some time for you to get used to."

As he continued to nuzzle my neck, I couldn't help but be painfully aware that his body was flush against my back. One of his arms slowly wrapped across my stomach while the other came up between my breasts, his hand lightly gripping my shoulder.

"Percy," I breathed.

"Mmm?" He hummed in reply.

"We're naked."

"I am very much aware of that."

God, his deep chuckle was not helping my quickly fogging mind.

"Did we come here to teach me how to shift or to fool around?"

"Perhaps a bit of both." He nipped a spot on my neck just below my ear, sending a pleasurable shiver to run down my body. "Getting you riled up will make it easier for you to shift.

I couldn't really argue with that logic. Reaching behind me, I wrapped my hand around his shaft. Percy growled low in my ear, the hand he had innocently resting at my shoulder moving down and cupping my breast.

Sporting my own wicked grin, I began to stroke my hand up and down his cock. As I suspected the night before, he was well endowed.

Percy continued to nip and lick my neck while his hand skillfully massaged my breast before pinching my nipple, making me gasp and buck back into my own hand. The hand that he had on my stomach lowered, leaving a trail of fire on my skin.

I looked down, watching the hand move slowly closer to my crotch, and nearly got distracted by the scales on my body. They were rippling as if I kept sinking in and out of my shift.

Percy brought back my attention with a caress to my other breast. I tilted my head back, eyes closing. He thrust into my hand, reminding me that I had a mission of trying to drive him just as crazy as he was starting to drive me.

I began to stroke him again. It was awkward at this angle, but I managed to cup the head and run my thumb over it. This elicited a low groan from him and a rewarding stroke from his hand, which had cupped my core.

Wanting his mouth on mine, I let go of his cock and reached up tug his mouth from my neck. He took the hint and kissed me hard, like he had in his office. His teeth bit my bottom lip before licking away the sting and diving his tongue into my mouth, demanding.

When he pulled away, he growled. "Who said you could stop touching my cock?"

I giggled. "You're blocking my other arm, and I wanted a kiss."

He grumbled and loosened his grip on me to turn me around and encouraged me to wrap my legs around his waist.

There we were, suspended in the water with my bare folds pressed up against Percy's cock. Would I have ever thought this could happen? Of course not. Did I complain? Hell, no.

Placing my hands on his jaw, I brought Percy back in for a kiss. He accepted me, letting me lead while one of his hands ran up and down my spine, the other massaging my ass.

I moaned and rubbed myself against him, enjoying the sparks of warmth as his cock grazed across my clit. I wanted more. My body craved to have him inside of me, but I knew I wasn't ready for that just yet. Instead, I brought one of my hands down to stroke the other side of his cock in time with my own gyrations.

Percy broke away from my mouth. "Good girl. Don't forget to pay attention to the head."

I panted, enjoying his direction, and moved my hand up to cup the head of his shaft. Percy leaned forward and took one of my nipples into his mouth, suckling. I moaned and rubbed myself against him harder.

I could quickly feel the orgasm rising within me as we continued. I don't know when it happened, but at some point Percy had seized control from me and thrust against me. His hand, which had been on my back, came over and joined my hand that was stroking his cock.

I let go of him, allowing him to take over, and pulled his head back up from my breasts to kiss him desperately. My other hand clawed into his shoulder as my orgasm quickly rushed up and slammed into me like the ocean's waves. I moaned into his kiss as I felt him cum along with me.

Our kiss slowed, less desperate, until we separated, panting. We floated in silence for several minutes, still wrapped around each other, the evidence of what we had done washing away.

"Your eyes are glowing." Percy said, his voice low and gruff.

I smiled, giddy. "So are yours."

Actually, his eyes had shifted like I had seen before, the color encompassing everything. It was wicked cool.

"They are beautiful, your eyes. You are stunning, but your eyes…" He trailed off.

I blushed, not really knowing how to take the compliment.

"Thank you?" I squeaked.

Percy chuckled and slowly, painfully, separated us. My body felt chilled without his touch.

It was then that I noticed that he was partially shifted. Pitch-black scales ran from the top of his shoulders down to the clawed hands that he had showed me earlier. The scales continued down his sides and in interesting patterns across his chest. I noticed deep claw marks on one of his collar bones. I looked down at my own hand to notice that I had partially shifted as well.

"Shit, Percy. I'm sorry. I didn't mean to hurt you."

He took my hand and kissed my scaled knuckles. "No need to apologize. The pain is an arousing reminder of what we just did."

I blinked, again not knowing how to respond to that.

TIED TO THE SEA

"You Deep Sea Mer were always masochists." Came a malicious voice behind Percy. "I never quite understood it. But I guess one can never truly understand beasts."

On high alert, Percy spun around to face the voice, his hand still holding mine forcing me behind him, blocking me from the intruder's view.

"Calder," Percy hissed his name. "What are you doing here?"

My stomach sank at the sound of his name. *Shit. Shit. Shit.*

"I'm simply out for a swim. I smelled your...copulation...from a mile off, and came to investigate."

Percy growled, menacing. "You should know better than to come near a male and his claim."

"I was simply curious, my friend. When I caught your scent, I had to know who the great Percival would take to bed with him. This scent with you is very familiar. You know, earlier today I ran into my little nephew. He had a female with him with this exact scent."

I continued to hide behind Percy, wanting to make myself as small as possible. His tone, the sheer desire to cause pain and suffering behind it, was something all too familiar to me. It turned me into a coward, as feeble as I was all those years ago.

The guys clearly didn't want Calder to know that I was once human. I couldn't let him see my eyes.

"Leave." Percy demanded.

Calder ignored him. "Why don't you show me your female, Percy?"

Percy inhaled slowly, his muscles bulking up as he tensed, making him seem so much larger. "I don't need to show you shit, Calder. You do not own me. Now leave, before I make you."

"You're right. Your…kind…is particularly immune to the syren's call. But that doesn't mean she is. Why don't you come out from behind him, Darling?"

His voice washed over me and a familiar feeling of cotton being stuffed into my head clouded my thoughts. Before I could even stop myself, I drifted out from behind Percy. I caught a glimpse of deep red scales right before Percy tugged me back behind him, breaking the control Calder had over me.

"My, my. I never would have thought my nephew would be able to successfully turn someone."

"I gave you your chance." Percy spat.

And he started to shift.

His black as night scales flared, multiplying. It happened in nearly two blinks worth of time but I watched as his legs fused, scales spread, and he formed a long, powerful tail. Huge spines sprouted from his back and his claws were even longer than before. He looked like the predator I knew he was.

He lunged for Calder so fast, the other Mer didn't even have the chance to raise his hands.

Percy slashed his claws to force Calder backwards. I watched as Percy utilized his powerful tail by slamming it into Calder's middle. I realized then that

Percy wasn't even trying to hurt him, just pushing him further away from me. I wanted to cheer, seeing that Percy definitely had the upper hand. That was, until Calder pulled a spear from some sort of holster on his back.

I felt helpless, like a dear in headlights as I just sat there. Watching as the tables quickly turned, and Percy was being the one pushed back as he dodged Calder's jabs and slashes with the weapon.

Somehow Percy was able to get in close and tackle him to the ground. The two of them tumbled across the sand, black and red scales flashing. Percy was hissing things at him in a language I couldn't understand.

Red scales.

I screamed when suddenly Calder flung Percy off of him with the spear and slashed Percy across his stomach. Blood flowed out into the ocean, dirtying the clean water with its metallic smell. I dove, wanting to do something to stop him. But I only made things worse when my movement caused Percy to become distracted and Calder struck him again.

With a grunt of pain, Percy pushed Calder off of him, causing the other Mer to fly backwards a few feet. Taking the opportunity, Percy rushed towards me.

"Atalanta, run!" he shouted, bleeding from the wound in his stomach and now his shoulder.

Calder laughed maniacally as he righted himself. "Look at the little newborn, trying to protect the all mighty Percival." He spit blood out of his mouth. "Well, it looks like she didn't try hard enough."

Didn't try hard enough.

Red scales.

Red.

Red.

So much blood.

You didn't try hard enough.

Those eyes.

Darkness rushed up around me.

Chapter Ten

PERCY

Kill.

I turned when I heard Calder mock Atalanta for her brave attempt to protect me. He had ignored my warnings, and despite me showing my superior strength, still refused to leave.

I would kill the threat before he could harm what was mine. Calder may have been skilled with that spear of his, but he relied too heavily on it. Just like he relied on his Syren voice and seat on the council to ignore consequences. But I had also acted recklessly, my shoulder and stomach throbbing as proof of that.

I inhaled, calming my mind and kicked off, rushing forward. *Get in close*, my father would say. *Spears are useless when you can't swing them properly.* I jerked to the side, dodging Calder's jab. I miscalculated when the blade nicked the skin right above my hip before it bounced off my scales.

Rusty.

Weak.

I wouldn't let it happen again.

Past the spear's blade, I grabbed the wooden shaft between Calder's grip and pulled, attempting to snatch the damn thing from him, but he had a tight grip. In a split second, I switched tactics and pushed the shaft into him. He may have had a solid hold on the weapon, but the weak noble couldn't compete with me on physical strength.

I shoved the spear down, pinning the shaft to his chest.

"Let...go..." Calder wheezed. I wasn't sure if he was trying to use his syren voice or simply commanding me, thinking the power of a councilman would sway me.

He had a lot to learn.

I shoved further down, wondering if I could crush his ribs and stop that feeble heart of his.

Calder's eyes were wild, beginning to look panicked as he failed to push the spear off his chest. Good. He should have known better than to come anywhere near a mating pair unless he was part of the pod.

My eyes glanced up to Atalanta to check if she was okay. She wasn't where I had last seen her. I thought perhaps that she had run like I had told her, until I saw the pop of color from her scales through the clouds of sand Calder and I were kicking up. She was on the ground, curled up into a ball. Motionless.

"Atalanta!" I called, hoping she would respond.

She didn't.

I cursed. *Not again*.

In my distracted state, Calder was able to build one good shove and I tumbled off of him. Before I could right myself, I felt the chilling burn of that stupid spear slice across my back.

I gasped and gritted my teeth. I needed to get that damn thing away from him.

Feigning immobility from the pain, I peeked back and watched as the cocky bastard raised the spear above me with one hand. Intending to stab me through the heart, no doubt.

As the spear came down, I bucked and slammed my tail hard into Calder's hand, knocking the spear clean out of his hold. It tumbled a distance away, and while Calder clenched his empty hand in shock I lunged for him, fists closed. My hit landed squared in his solar plexus.

Calder doubled over, spluttering. Not wasting a second, I smashed my other fist into his head, knocking him out.

I shouldn't have given him the chance to walk away in the first place, and if he had been anyone else, I probably wouldn't have. It was unfortunate that I couldn't slit his gut open and revel in his dying screams, as I had other things to worry about.

Keeping an eye on Calder, I swam over to Atalanta. She was curled up like she had done the other day, hands grasping her head, which was between her knees. I didn't think she was conscious. Her breathing was too even, too slow. Gently, I ran my fingers through her hair, hoping to rouse her. After a few moments, she didn't wake up, which confirmed my theory.

Calder was still unconscious, but I doubted it would be for long. Swiftly, yet as delicately as possible, I scooped up Atalanta into my arms and began my swim back to shore, snatching up Calder's spear along the way.

I could be petty.

With my tail, it only took a minute to reach the shore. Without a thought, I shifted back to my two-legged form and hugged Atalanta closer to me. I worried when the gravity of the surface hit, it would be difficult to carry both Atalanta and the spear, but she was so light I could easily hold her limp form with one arm.

I made a mental note to start feeding her more.

Trudging through the wet sand, I debated over trying to put all of our clothes back on, but decided it would be more of a hindrance with my wounded state. My blood was getting all over her. Blood, scales, and wet sand were a combination that would easily ruin those clothes.

I did, however, grab my phone from the box after an awkward fumble between Atalanta and the spear before deciding to just shove the spear into the sand. I didn't leave it though, despite knowing it would be easier than now holding it, Atalanta, and the phone. I opted to stick the phone between my teeth and began making my way up a different path than we came.

I made my way through the forest as fast as I could, not wanting to spend all night out here, possibly ringing the dinner bell for all of the hungry animals that weren't hibernating with the blood I was dripping everywhere.

I was grateful when the small two-story apartment complex came into view.

Why did you choose the second floor, you dick? I grumbled internally as I stomped up the stairs, groaning when I reached the top. I tried to remind myself of the circumstances, and that I wasn't *that* out of shape.

If the others saw me this undignified, I wouldn't know what to do with myself.

Reaching the door of 2A, I propped the spear up before ringing the doorbell. After waiting a couple of minutes, I rang the bell again. I knew it was working because I could see the lights flickering through the small kitchen window next to the door.

Figuring he was either not home or asleep, I grasped the handle and attempted to open the door. Of course, it was locked. No one locked their doors in Argos! Grumbling more and rolling my eyes, I twisted the knob and broke the lock. I would buy him a new one later.

I had never seen the inside of his apartment before, but it was clean and well furnished. The kitchen to the right of the entry had all new appliances, and the carpet looked almost brand new, different from the apartments I had seen in the past which often were run down. There were advantages to owning the building, I supposed.

After placing the spear onto the small table in his living room, I carried Atalanta down the short hallway into what I assumed to be the bedroom. Kicking the ajar door open, I flicked on the light.

Theseus was sprawled across his mattress, legs hanging off the side, still fully dressed as if he had just come in and passed out.

He didn't even flinch when the bright overhead light turned on. Knowing I was more hostile than needed, I stormed over to the lump and kicked the mattress next to his head.

With a yelp, Theseus was awake and tumbling off the bed. I gave him at least some credit when he bounced back rather quickly, taking a defensive position before realized who had woken him.

"Jesus fucking *Christ,* PERCY! What the—wait, what happened?" He rushed forward at seeing the blood-covered Atalanta in my arms.

Reluctantly, I released her to him to look over. As soon as my hands were free, I signed. "She isn't injured. All of the blood is mine."

"That doesn't tell me what happened." He grumbled as he placed Atalanta gently on his bed and dragged over what looked to be a medical bag.

He pulled out a flashlight and opened her lids to check her pupils. "Well, she's responsive. But she's out cold."

"No shit, Sherlock." I grumbled before tapping on his shoulder and signing, "she passed out, but I think she's just asleep now."

"Why did she pass out? Did she hit her head? Did she see something? What happened?"

I huffed. "Give me a moment."

TIED TO THE SEA

I sat down in a rather expensive looking computer chair, not caring that I was probably ruining it. I signed out the story to him, telling him about Calder showing up and how I had to defend Atalanta and myself, ending with Atalanta falling unconscious.

When I was done, Theseus stared down at Atalanta for a minute before saying, "she probably was triggered by something in the fight. Maybe the blood or something. It's been clear that she has PTSD from whatever happened in her past."

I waited for him to look back to me before signing. "But why wouldn't she have woken up by now? She doesn't look catatonic."

"I think she just fell asleep, to be honest. Most likely, once her body was down, it felt like staying down once her brain recovered. We need to remember that her body is still pretty strained from the change. She's bound to take random naps."

I pursed my lips, still worried about the fainting. "You think she fainted because she was overwhelmed by something?" I asked.

Theseus nodded. "More than likely. She's proven to be vulnerable to anxiety attacks. With how much stress she's been under, I'm surprised she's only conking out on us now."

I frowned. "She was prone to panic attacks before the change, as well. Mr. Clark mentioned to me that he once had to sit with her in the woman's bathroom while she had one."

"His name is Hip, Percy. Stop being so damn formal. And while we're at it, use more conjunctions, you sound weird."

I ignored his comment and signed, "we should figure out her triggers. That way we can better avoid them and help work her through them."

He sighed. "Agreed. Let's get you two cleaned up. Luckily, I have two bathrooms. Take a shower so I can take a look at your wounds."

He stood and picked Atalanta up to carry her into his bathroom. "Try not to pass out while you're in there!"

I tampered down the jealousy of him seeing hold her so lovingly. After everything that had just happened, my possessiveness was rather high, but I logically knew that it was simply instinct that made me want to punch Theseus and take Atalanta back into my own arms.

When I stood, the dried blood made my skin stick to the back of his chair and it peeled away rather weirdly. Yes, I was certain he would have me buy him a new chair as well.

Chapter Eleven

THESEUS

Honestly, when I got back home an hour ago and fell asleep, exhausted, I did not expect to be kicked back into the waking world by a naked and bloody Percy holding a naked and unconscious Atalanta.

I looked down at the beautiful woman in my arms as I carefully stepped into the shower that I had turned on. She was fine. Her pulse and breathing felt normal, and her pupils were responsive. I couldn't help the anxiousness over not being able to pull out the never-before-used stethoscope from my medical bag and actually hear her heartbeat and lungs. But Percy wouldn't have brought her to me if he thought she was in any real danger. Would he?

No, she was fine. Just really tired.

I got that. I was pretty tired myself, hardly able to keep my eyes open as I held Atalanta up with one arm and snagged the bar of soap to try to clean her up.

I yawned as I scrubbed off the sand and grime from her back, arms, and chest. Well, not all of me was half-asleep, as my dick was at full attention and poking her ass.

"Sorry, buddy. You're just going to have to suffer." I muttered as I shifted her against me so I could lean down and get her legs.

Sleeping Beauty was as limp as a doll. Just about as heavy as one too.

She didn't really eat much lunch, and I doubted Percy got her dinner. I should feed her more. I might not be able to sculpt her a statue in her honor or quote some of the surface's greatest love poems, but if there was one thing I thought I might be able to impress her with, it would be my skill with a knife and skillet. When I came to the surface all those years ago, I could admit that my cooking skills were something to be desired. But living on my own gave me a lot of time to practice.

I finished up our shower and carefully stepped out. She had stirred a couple of times, but didn't wake up. My heart skipped when she nuzzled her face into the crook of my neck.

"I got you, sweetheart. Let's get you to bed," I said softly as I wrapped a clean towel around her.

A touch on my shoulder had me jumping and turning to see Percy standing behind me. I had actually forgotten he was here. He was still naked but all of the sand and most of the blood was cleaned off of him. The wounds he'd gotten from his fight with Calder were pretty bad and hadn't fully clotted.

"Come on. Let me take a look at those wounds."

'They will fully close up soon.' He signed.

"Don't be stubborn. Let me put her down." I grumbled, moving past him back into my room.

Placing Atalanta gently down on the mattress, I smiled when she curled up, grabbed the nearest pillow and wrapped herself around it without even opening her eyes.

TIED TO THE SEA

Turning, I gestured for Percy to sit back down in the chair that I would now need to replace, thanks to him. When he complied without complaint, I snatched my medical bag from next to the bed and brought it closer to the chair. Rifling through it, I pulled out some butterfly bandages, disinfectant, and a small bag of unopened disposable cloths.

I glanced back at the still bleeding gash across his stomach and added gauze and wraps to the building pile.

"Calder did a number on you," I muttered as I began to work on the wounds.

What looked to be a stab wound in his shoulder was almost fully sealed, but I wiped it down with the disinfectant and attached the butterfly bandages. "Luckily, you won't need stitches. Well, technically you do, but these will heal too quickly for that, so the bandages will work just fine to help the process along. This is going to hurt." I looked up at Percy, making eye contact with him before pressing the cloth into his stomach.

Though I felt his body tense under my touch, Percy's face didn't even flinch. I often wondered why he was born with such warm brown eyes when they really should have been the color of cold steel.

"You should have killed him," I snarled.

'Killing him would have brought more trouble than was worth.'

"If I had to guess what you two were doing out there, then it was your right to take his life. Remember,

179

our laws aren't like the humans. You would have gotten more than a slap on the wrist, but now he knows about her, and by morning, so will others."

'We wouldn't have been able to keep her secret forever. Not everyone in town is loyal to you. The council's spies are everywhere. Killing Calder wouldn't have just affected us, but brought the council's wrath fully down on her. I might not have gotten in trouble, but that doesn't mean they wouldn't try to take her away from us.'

I growled and pulled Percy to standing and, using his shoulders, forced him to face away from me. "They are going to come for her, anyway."

If he replied, I was glad I couldn't hear it.

The wound on his back was the worst. It had hardly closed and had cut deep into the muscle. Luckily his scales had protected his spine, as I could see where the slice suddenly cut off and picked back up again.

"Now this one might actually need stitches. It should have healed by now."

Percy twisted back towards me and signed. "It stings much more than the others. It really hasn't healed?"

It only stings? Fuck, man.

I shook my head.

Percy's brow furrowed and he stormed out of the room to come back moments later holding a spear.

I laughed. "You took his precious spear?"

'The fucker owed me payment for the trouble. I took what was rightfully mine.'

My brow furrowed, wondering if I had read his lips correctly. Did he really steal the spear as payment? Was that a Deep Sea thing? I know I wasn't taught anything like that. Similar to the human expression of 'an eye for an eye', perhaps?

Percy leaned closer and studied the spear. He mumbled something but I couldn't really see it.

After a few moments, he turned back to me. 'The blade is the usual Damascus steel. It shouldn't be causing this reaction.'

I tilted my head to the side and crossed my arms, thinking about it. "Maybe it's coated in something? Stonefish venom would cause this kind of reaction. But that wouldn't make sense, since your other wounds are healing."

'I don't know.' He passed over the spear. 'What do you make of it?'

I took the spear and examined the weapon. It was a gorgeous piece of work. The shaft was thick and carved with intricate patterns and different sea life: a shark, a whale. The blade was fastened to the hilt with a thick gold band, which I found odd. With how thick the hunk of metal was, the balance would be off.

I confirmed it when I attempted to balance the staff in my hand and the blade tilted and thunked to the floor. Bringing the spear closer, I studied the band.

"There are ridges here." I gently ran my thumb over them. They gave way beneath my touch and a small hole opened up right over the spine of the blade.

Leaning forward I sniffed and proceeded to gag. "Yep, that's stonefish venom. That shit is illegal."

I propped the spear against the wall and looked over at Percy. "You're lucky you're not human, or you would be in way worse shape. The best we can do for you now is to stitch it up and wait for your body to push the poison out of your system."

It looked like Percy huffed, his shoulders slumping a tad before he signed for me to get on with it and turned away. Pulling out my small suture kit from the medical bag, I got to work. Ten minutes later, he was all stitched up and the cuts were clean.

"All right, you're all done." I patted him on the shoulder and began to stick everything back in the bag.

I was exhausted.

I glanced over at Atalanta, still sleeping soundly.

That bed looked so inviting at the moment.

Percy waved, grabbing my attention and signed. "I will go lay on the couch."

"No," I sighed and heaved my medical bag back to its usual place. "If she wakes up and doesn't see you, she'll probably flip. I'll go sleep on the couch."

"And you need to stay here to keep her calm if something goes wrong."

I snort. "Isn't that Jason's job? He's the one who's her mate and all. Actually, I'm surprised he isn't rushing over here, breaking into my apartment like you."

TIED TO THE SEA

Percy cocked an eyebrow at me. "I told him she was safe and sound. All tuckered out from the swim. I'm hoping to give him a good night's sleep. Though, I don't know how much he will get with her not being in arm's reach."

"He has been looking like a sack of crap, hasn't he?"

I actually caught a spark of anger on Percy's face when he signed. "It's in his instincts to worry about her. We haven't been much better."

My eyes slid to Atalanta's sleeping form. He wasn't wrong. Those two weeks had been torture, and now that she was awake, I found it difficult to leave her side...but seeing how she only responded to Jason this morning, it had shattered any confidence I had.

Were we doing the right thing? I had been so sure before, but...

I looked back at Percy, who, for once, I could read. He was just as insecure about pursuing this relationship as I was. Maybe that was why he had really taken her out tonight. To reassure himself that she wanted him as well.

Slowly, Percy began to sign. "Listen. Jason may be connected to her in a literal sense, but that does not diminish the connection you have to her. Of all of us, she trusted you the most to take the first leap. She showed you her scars."

My gut clenched up as I remembered the first time I had seen the scars on her legs. "It was an accident."

Percy shook his head. "She's too smart for her own good. She would have known the risks of doing anything with you. Whether she realized it or not, a part of her trusted you with that bit of herself. Don't let your fear chase you away from this. We need you just as much as she does."

Was that true?

I sighed. Whether it was true or not, thinking about it when sleep weighed on me was pointless. As my father had taught me, *thinking on important things when you're tired easily leads to mistakes, and mistakes can end up making things worse than they were.*

"Let's talk about this later, okay? I'm tired," I signed as I walked over to my dresser, pulled out some boxers and tossed them to Percy. "Bed time."

Taking off the boots and jacket that I still had on, I slowly moved Atalanta into the middle of the bed. Settling down beside her, I finally relaxed.

When Percy settled down on the other side of Atalanta, I tensed for a split second before brushing all of my anger and guilt aside. If someone had told me two months ago that I would be sharing a bed with Percival, I would have laughed in their face. He was an arrogant coward, whom before recently, could hardly stand to look at me without guilt leaking out of every pore.

My mind flashed back to a little over a week ago when I had cornered Percy and asked when he had learned American Sign Language. When I had first learned the language, I figured it would make my life easier. That was until I realized I was the only one in the town that knew it. It hadn't been a complete waste of time though, as I remembered when Atalanta had first apologized to me using it. I had felt so touched.

Percy, on the other hand, in all the years we had been on the surface, had never once hinted at knowing it. Then he had the gall to try to brush it off, claiming that he found the human language to be interesting and had learned it out of pure curiosity along with several others. I called bullshit, but the fucker was a locked box so I just convinced myself he would never reveal the truth and I dropped it.

If it wasn't for Atalanta, I would be trying to ignore him like I always did. Being near him was too awkward.

Yet...what he said a few minutes ago. Did he mean it?

I hadn't been needed in years.

Coming to the surface had meant stripping away everything that made me who I was. The leader who was no longer needed to lead. It had been the hardest thing I ever had to do.

I sat up, my mind snapping out of its dozing state when I felt the bed shaking. "What's going on? Are you laughing?"

Percy looked up at me, a grin on his face, and signed. "Atalanta is singing in her sleep again."

Oh. I peeked down at her prone form. Her mouth was open and it was clear that she was mumbling softly, though I didn't know what. When she was out during those two weeks, I had seen her do this a few times. It was really only when at least two of us were sleeping on either side of her.

I made eye contact with Percy. Embarrassed, I asked, "What does she sound like?"

He settled back and stared up at the ceiling for a few moments, his expression pensive. Eventually, he reached over and snagged my closest hand and guided it to rest at the base of Atalanta's throat.

My eyebrows rose as I felt the vibrations of her singing. If I really concentrated, it was like when I went to concerts and felt the vibrations of the music. I could just make out the different notes she made.

A smile spread across my lips as I looked back over at Percy, who had let go of my hand and began to sign. "Do you remember the sound of my mother's apprentice, Emilee? She often performed for your family during events."

My mind reached back, recalling the older girl who had sung for us on numerous occasions. She was pretty and an extremely talented singer, though I often wondered why it was her performing and not Percy's mother, who was a close friend and my own personal tutor as well.

I nodded. "Yes. Her voice sounded like bells."

"Atalanta sounds a bit like that. But softer." Percy signed before turning his back towards me.

I felt my smile wobble as my gaze moved back to the singing sleeping beauty. I stayed like that for a while, my hand resting lightly against her throat as I imagined what she sounded like as I finally drifted off to sleep.

Chapter Twelve

ATALANTA

I was so warm.

It was like I was wrapped up in a blanket cocoon.

Sleep…

No, wait…I was supposed to be doing something, wasn't I?

I stretched, working the kinks out of my muscles. The sheets beneath me were so soft. My cocoon, though, was hard. I wiggled against it but it wouldn't budge.

My brain was filled with cobwebs.

A feeling I was really tired of. Taking mental stock, I wasn't surprised when I couldn't remember crawling into bed last night.

I needed to get up, so I continued to wiggle, thinking that the blankets would loosen.

"Atalanta," Someone groaned, causing me to freeze.

"Percy?" I mumbled.

I inhaled, smelling a mix of books and lemons. Had Percy been cleaning? Slowly, I pried open my eyes. I was staring at a naked chest. Turning away from the sculpted muscle, I saw Percy's brown eyes staring at me over my shoulder.

But if he was behind me…

My eyes snapped back to see Theseus's sleeping face looking back at me. My cocoon was the two of them, their arms and legs wrapped around me in double snuggle.

Now, I certainly would have remembered climbing into bed with the two of them last night. At least, I hoped I would.

"Percy?" I asked again, this time with worry evident in my tone.

"You are safe, Atalanta."

"How did I get here?"

Percy slowly untangled himself from around me. "What's the last thing you remember?"

I shifted so I could face him, unable to free myself from Theseus's grasp as he only snuggled closer when I tried. I smiled and brought my hand up and slid it into Theseus's limp one, squeezing his fingers. I thought back to my last memory.

"My last solid memory is us at the library," I bit my lip as the flush filled my cheeks. "Though, it's a little fuzzy after that…I remember the beach and then—wait, did you and I…um?"

Percy shook his head. "We did not have sex."

I couldn't say I wasn't a tad disappointed.

"You did, however, rub yourself against my cock quite enticingly," He growled and leaned forward to give me a searing peck on the lips.

"Oh."

"Oh? Is that all you can say?" Percy smirked as he reached up to brush a few stray strands of hair behind my ear.

I gulped. "And then what? Did I orgasm myself into passing out?"

I really hoped that was the real reason for my missing memory.

He chuckled. "Unfortunately, no. That's not to say you didn't cum for me, in fact you returned the favor."

Well, damn. I felt bad that I didn't remember any of that.

His face fell, becoming serious. "But that isn't everything that happened last night. Jason's uncle appeared, breaking one of our sacred laws, and basically challenged me while I was being intimate with you. I fended him off but you had collapsed during the fight. I brought you back here to get cleaned up and have Theseus check you over."

"Wow. I missed all of that? It must have been good not-sex-sex," I laughed nervously, my eyes shifting away to stare at the wall over Percy's shoulder.

"Atalanta. It's okay to be scared," He took my free hand and squeezed it reassuringly. "And it's okay to show me your fear. I'm here to help."

"I...Percy, I am scared. I don't know what's happening. I keep forgetting things. And not just last night, but other things. When I had that nightmare, I didn't even know who you were, or the others. I couldn't remember what name I was using. I can't remember my favorite color or if I had a favorite cereal. I keep forgetting Cal." My voice cracked at her name.

Tears were beginning to stream down my cheeks and I blubbered, "There are so many things I can't seem to remember, and I don't realize it until it's staring me in the face. When I made my bowl of cereal this morning it wasn't until I ate it that I remembered that I don't even like Captain Crunch, and then when Jason made me get dressed I wondered why all the clothes in my bag were black and gray. Was it because they were favorite colors? I didn't know!"

How much of my life was being forgotten?

Percy wiped away the tears so tenderly before bringing me in for a hug.

"I know, we're scared too." He said quietly.

At my look of confusion, he continued. "Believe me, we noticed something was not right with your memory when you first woke up. It was wrong of us not to bring attention to it, but I didn't want to worry you. I am looking into it. Don't worry for now, okay? One thing at a time."

Jason had said that too, but how long before there were too many things and not enough time? We kept pushing everything aside. Were there more 'things', and I was just forgetting them? I needed to make a list. Yes, that's what I needed to do. Make a list of everything I could remember, because how long would it be before I forgot everything?

I shook as I tried to hold in the tears. It hurt, but I couldn't cry anymore. I wouldn't cry. I wouldn't cry.

It was wishful thinking.

"Atalanta, my sleeping beauty, don't cry. We've got you." Theseus muttered. His voice, which was rough from sleep, snapped me out of my head as he sat up and nuzzled my neck.

I laughed through the tears as his soft three-day-old scruff tickled my neck.

"There we go, there's that smile." Theseus tickled my sides, making me laugh more. "It's Valentine's Day. No girl should cry on Valentine's Day. Especially not my girl."

I giggled as he unwrapped himself from me and stood.

"Our girl," Percy reminded before looking me in the eyes and saying, "There *is* a lot going on, but it won't always be this way. This, too, shall pass."

Leaning back, Theseus gave me a peck on the cheek. "It's going to be okay, Atalanta. Whatever is wrong, we'll fix it."

Theseus didn't even know why I was crying, but he was comforting me regardless. When you combined Percy's form of comfort, stemming from logic, to Theseus and his sweet words and gestures, the two were an effective pair. The heaviness that had been building in my chest dissipated.

Sitting up on the bed, I hugged my knees close to me. "We should at least tackle one of the things. Like Clint. We can't keep brainwashing him to push off talking to us. Won't that break him or something?"

"I mean, right now he's a non-issue. I could also just tell him to leave," Theseus mumbled.

I snorted. "We can't do that. It might bring more trouble than it's worth."

Percy rolled his eyes. "Fine. Tomorrow, then. In the morning we will go meet him at the inn."

"Wait, isn't tomorrow Monday?"

"Yes."

"Then I need to be at school. It will have to be after."

"Atalanta...I don't think that's such a good idea," Theseus said

"Why?" I asked, brow furrowed.

"For one thing, you are still struggling to control your shifts," Percy said as his eyes roamed over my body.

I looked down to see that I was not only naked aside from a towel draped across my lap, but also completely scaled up again.

God damn it.

Okay.

I took a deep breath in and did what the others had shown me yesterday. I thought about the boys, the safety they brought me, and loosened that little ball in my mind. I watched as almost all the scales on my legs and hands receded, leaving my limbs looking mostly normal.

I touched my face, expecting the scales that were usually on my cheekbones, and smiled when I only felt smooth skin.

"I got it handled, see?" I grinned up at Percy.

Percy rolled his eyes. "If you insist on going, we are not going to stop you. Though, I will be arranging precautions."

"Understandable." I nodded.

Theseus clapped his hands with a boyish smile. "Good, now that's settled. Are you ready for a day of fun? Or did you want to sleep some more?"

"No, I think I've slept enough." I hopped out of bed and stretched. "Do you guys have something planned? You, Hip and Jason were pretty freaked out yesterday."

His smile grew wider. "I'm glad you asked. We've prepared a day of pampering for you."

I cocked my eyebrow at him.

"What is with that look?" Percy asked, a mischievous twinkle in his eye. "Are you skeptical that we would want to pamper you? Is this not the day for lovers?"

There was a small flame that lit inside of me when I watched Percy and Theseus's eyes move over me slowly. Remembering that I was naked, I quickly grabbed the sheet off the bed and covered myself.

The guys chuckled, but their eyes continued to roam.

"No, th-that's not it," I stammered, feeling like a sheep cornered by hungry wolves.

TIED TO THE SEA

Percy tilted his head. "What, then? No, wait. I'm guessing you feel that you don't deserve to be spoiled by us. Perhaps because you feel that you are a burden or just don't see that we actually care enough to try. You would be wrong in both cases."

"Hey! It's my thing to psychoanalyze people. Don't steal it."

"You don't own the monopoly on it, Ms. North. Besides, I believe I am owed some payback for our first meeting."

"I only guessed your favorite book genre."

"And I'm only guessing the reasoning behind your skepticisms."

Theseus cleared his throat. "If you two are done with your weird foreplay, I believe it's time for my turn with Atalanta."

Percy stepped back, and while I could still see some heat in his gaze, the rest of his face fell to its usual neutral.

"I will see you later," Percy whispered before leaning in again and giving me a kiss on the forehead.

He sauntered smoothly out of the apartment. I frowned when he picked up a familiar looking spear and I wondered where he had gotten it. He was out the door and gone before I had the chance to ask.

The moment the door closed, Theseus came closer and gave me the sweetest of kisses, slow and loving as he stroked my cheek.

He pulled away and whispered, "Now, let's get to pampering you."

I smiled and stood up on my tippy toes to kiss him again. "So what would that entail?"

"Well, first," Theseus hummed and nipped at my bottom lip. "I'm going to make you breakfast. You're welcome to take a shower while you wait."

I looked down at my body and realized that I was pretty clean for having had a tumble with Percy at the beach.

"Um, did I already take a shower?"

"I might have…um…washed you off last night, after Percy brought you here." Theseus mumbled as pink tinted his freckled cheeks.

I blinked, wondering how I should feel about that and then was surprised that I felt nothing but thankful. Theseus and the other guys had been nothing but chivalrous since I had met them.

"It bothers you. I can tell. I'm sorry, it's just that I didn't think you would be comfortable sleeping in dried sea water and sand." Theseus interrupted my pondering. His cheeks were a deep red now and he looked rather flustered.

I grinned. "It's okay, it actually doesn't bother me. But if you feel the need to make it up to me, how about some breakfast?"

"I'll get right on that, then," He sighed as a small grin returned to his face.

He walked away, leaving me alone in his bedroom. Shyly, I looked around the room. It was tidy, but felt eerily empty. There weren't many personal items that I could see. The desk had a small stack of video games and a large computer, but nothing else. There weren't any posters on the walls or knick knacks on the small nightstand next to the bed. The only personal thing I saw was a giant medical bag that was next to the bed.

"*Meow*"

I paused in my studies and looked around for the source of the noise and meowed back. "Mew?"

I crouched down and peered under the bed, but the cat wasn't there.

"*Meow*" came the cat again, but this time from behind me.

"Theseus?" I called as I popped back up and spun around. "Do you have a cat?"

But of course he didn't answer. Not seeing the cat, I clutched the sheet closer to me and poked my head into the open closet.

No cat in there.

I gave up for the moment when I spotted the shirts hanging in the closet. Looking down at the sheet, I shrugged and dropped it to the floor before perusing through the shirts. Most of them were nerdy shirts with comic book characters or funny sayings. I decided on a dark blue one with the words 'Of course I'm talking to myself, sometimes I need expert advice.' and pulled it over my head.

Now, if only I could find some pants.

As I rifled through his closet, looking for a pair of sweatpants or something, I heard someone walk up behind me. Looking over my shoulder, I saw Theseus standing in the doorway with his jaw hanging open, eyes focused on my bare ass.

I couldn't help but wiggling my butt before waving to get his attention. "Can I help you with something?"

His eyes stayed focused on my ass. I grinned, rolled my eyes and stood.

Theseus blinked and looked back up. "I'm sorry, did you say something?"

"Nope." I fingered the shirt. "Can I borrow this?"

"Yeah, sure. But only that."

I cocked an eyebrow at him. "Sooo, I can't borrow any pants?"

"No."

I snorted and snagged the pair of sweatpants I found and began to put them on.

"That's stealing," Theseus growled and placed his hands on my hips, pulling me closer.

"Well then, I'm a dirty, dirty, thief. What are you going to do with me?"

"I could cuff you and torture you with my tongue."

A shiver ran down my spine at the thought. "I think I like the sound of that."

He came in and gave me a slow sweet kiss before pulling away and saying, "It's just too bad that I need to feed you."

"What! But...but...tease!" I spluttered.

"Yes, I am. Now, come on," He squeezed my ass and smacked it playfully. "Time for food."

I grumbled as I followed Theseus out of the closet and stopped when I spotted a cat on the bed. He was huge, with a beautiful, long coat with varying shades of browns and grays, with a darker brown strip going down along his back. He met my gaze with intelligent green eyes.

"Why, hello, fluffy. Are you the one who was meowing at me?"

Theseus shook his head. "Not likely. This is Twitch. Who you heard was probably Bubba. He's a talker, but prefers to stay hidden around strangers."

I looked at him and grinned. "Two cats? I wasn't aware you were a crazy cat lady."

"Two cats hardly justifies crazy cat lady status." He snorted.

I shrugged and approached the kitty on the bed. "You're such a pretty fella."

"I would be careful..." he warned, but it was too late. I already had the kitty in my arms.

My eyes widened. "What? Does he not like being held?"

"Normally, no...at least not by strangers." He replied, extremely confused.

I looked at the cat, who I had propped against my shoulder like a baby. He seemed content as he purred and nuzzled against my cheek.

"I think he likes me." I cooed.

"I think he does," He chuckled and ran his fingers through his hair. "Little shit doesn't even let me hold him most of the time."

"If he doesn't like you, why adopt him?"

"I didn't, Bubba did. Came home one day with that one," He pointed at Twitch, "Grasped in his teeth and hardly a few days old."

I nuzzled the cat and stroked his fur. "Aww, were you an orphan kitten? You poor baby."

"Poor baby, my ass. I spoil the shit out of that cat," he grumbled.

"That attitude is why he attacks you." I grinned.

Twitch let out a mew and I scratched his ear, thinking he wanted more attention than I was already giving him.

When Twitch began to squirm in my arms I took the hint, put him down, and followed Theseus into the kitchen, where he had made me some pancakes.

"Holy crap, these look delicious!"

Theseus pulled a couple plates from a cabinet and piled some pancakes on a plate for me along with a few spoonfuls of chopped fruit. Taking the plate, I sat down at the little nook table, smothered everything in syrup, and took a bite. Yep, they were as yummy as they looked.

"Unfortunately, these are from a box. I would have made it from scratch but I don't have any flour."

I shoveled several bites into my mouth before asking, "You normally make pancakes from scratch?"

"Normally no. To impress you? Yes"

Well damn, he was cute.

From a box or not, he could at least cook better than I could. The few times I had made pancakes they somehow always ended up becoming as flat as chips and burnt to a crisp.

After we finished breakfast, Theseus swept me into his living room where he sat me down in a chair that he had placed between the couch and television.

I craned my neck back to look up at him. "What now?"

"Now, I'm going to cut your hair."

"My hair?" I plucked at the strands, realizing that they had grown at least another inch since the day before.

I vaguely remembered Percy telling me something about the keratin, but those damn cobwebs made it hard to grasp the memory. I shuddered and shook it off.

Feigning a smile, I focused back on Theseus and said, "Can you shave it all off?"

"Ha-ha. Not going to happen. I will, however, cut it up nice and cute."

At my worried expression, he booped the tip of my nose before bending down to kiss me. "You'll like it. Don't worry."

With my back stiff, I leaned back and tried to remind myself that even if it turned out horrible, my hair seemed to grow rather quickly nowadays.

Theseus turned on the TV, to a romantic comedy of all things, and began to run his fingers through my hair.

"That feels amazing," I groaned, hoping he would just do that for eternity.

Surprisingly, Theseus made quick work of my hair. He pulled out a little kit with scissors, a comb, and a folded up smock, which he placed over me and fastened at my neck. With skilled hands, he combed back my hair and began to clip away.

Twenty minutes later, my head felt a lot lighter. Theseus picked up a small mirror and showed me his work. My shoulders relaxed as I took in my new haircut, which actually looked cute. He had cut it in a layered bob, the ends brushing right up against my jawline.

I tilted my head back at him. "You're actually good at this!"

"Don't sound so surprised. You didn't think I would have come anywhere near your head with scissors if I didn't know what I was doing, did you?" He chuckled.

I shrugged in reply and stood up, brushing all of the little hairs from the smock before taking it off and handing it to him.

When I saw Theseus glance at his watch, I asked, "What now?"

"It's a surprise," He took my hands and walked backwards, pulling me towards the door. "Come on."

"Wait, I'm hardly dressed! And what about cleaning up?"

"I'll get it later! We'll be late if we don't leave now."

Quickly, Theseus pulled me outside and rushed us down the stairs. He didn't even lock the door!

Off we went, driving to the next town over. It was awkwardly quiet at first until Theseus fumbled with the radio, mumbling something about forgetting. I didn't have the heart to tell him he had it sitting on static. It was okay, I kind of liked the white noise.

When we got into town, Theseus pulled out his phone and checked it for directions before pulling in front of a small clothing shop.

Theseus hopped out of the car and opened my door for me. "Let's go, pretty girl."

"A clothing store?"

"Yep. I thought you could use a new outfit."

I frowned and then looked down at the shirt and sweats.

"I don't have my wallet on me."

Honestly, even if I did, I wouldn't have been able to get new clothes anyway. But I wasn't going to mention that part to him.

Theseus snorted. "As If I would let you pay for your own clothes."

I crossed my arms and scowled up at him, he really was very tall.

"Please," He puppy dog pouted, "It's my day to spoil you and I would love to buy you some new clothes. Don't take offense, Atalanta, but most of your clothes are rather worn. I know you've been in Washington for a while, but over here it's pretty cold all year round. I want you to always be warm and snuggly."

He wasn't wrong, but...still.

"Fine! But I *will* be paying you back."

Theseus rolled his eyes and held out his hand for me to take and we made our way into the store.

Looking at the clothes, I realized I wasn't sure what my size was.

My nose scrunched as I picked up a pair of jeans and put it against my hips. They looked too big, but I couldn't tell. Was I supposed to measure it to my hips or to the side of my butt? I wished Cal was here. She was the one who usually helped me pick out clothes.

I paused, knowing there was something I was forgetting again.

Knowing nothing would come of worrying about it, I tried my best to shrug off the cold feeling inside and continued to peruse the clothes. Theseus helped me pick out some clothes that looked good me. A tight pair of jeans, calf high boots, and a really cute jacket that was similar to my father's, with faux fur in the hood.

I felt so uncomfortable when we went to check out. I was wearing the clothes and Theseus just placed the tags down on the counter so the older clerk could ring up the items. When Theseus gave me a kiss on the cheek and pulled his wallet out of his pocket, I didn't know whether to pinch him or kiss him back. The old woman didn't make it better when she looked over at me and winked.

I played with the cuffs of my new jacket while Theseus led me out of the store.

"We don't have much time, but luckily we will make it."

"Make it where?" I laughed as we passed by his car and jogged down the street.

He didn't answer, but I found out only two minutes later when we came upon a large brick building with an enormous tan sign that sported black lettering.

I tugged on Theseus's sleeve. "A movie theatre?"

"Yep, and we're just in time."

Theseus took my hand and walked inside the theater. It was small, as expected for a tiny town, but I was pleasantly surprised to see that it wasn't run down. We walked up to the service counter where Theseus got us tickets and asked for something I didn't quite catch.

The ticket clerk smiled and nodded before picking out something from behind the counter and handing it to him. Coming closer, I could see that they were large bulky 3D goggles.

As we walked to Theater 4, I pointed to the goggles. "What are those?"

"These babies are called Closed Caption Glasses. They help me watch the movie."

"Closed caption?" I took the glasses and held them up in front of my face. "So that's what they mean when a theater advertises closed caption?"

He nodded. "You see this button here? Thats the *on* button, and when the movie starts, subtitles will be projected onto the glasses."

I frowned and pressed the button. Words flashed in front of my eyes but it was really uncomfortable. I passed the glasses back over to him and asked. "Wouldn't it be easier to just put the subtitles on the screen?"

He opened the door for me and we walked into the dark corridor. "It would be, but a lot of people complain that it's too distracting from the movie."

"That's stupid. I think subtitles add to the experience—" I paused when I watched Theseus's eyes begin to glow. "Uh-um, your eyes are doing the glowy thing."

He chuckled. "It helps me see. If I can't see, how will I know what you're saying?"

"Oh... but won't having light brights for eyes draw attention?"

"Good point," he said as the glow in his eyes faded. "If you need to tell me anything, just text it to me, okay? And to answer your other statement: yeah, it can be stupid and unfair. But it's better to let people live their own lives."

"That's not right! If they have such a problem with it, then maybe make separate times, at least? Like some of the show times have subtitles and some don't?" I hissed.

He couldn't answer though, as the previews had started and it was even darker than in the hall. Looking around, I could see there were several other people in the theater, but it wasn't packed. I think there were a few couples there all snuggled up close. Something was odd. Squinting, I realized that the seats weren't standard theater seats, but giant love seats for two.

I followed Theseus up some steps to one of the love seats.

This was so cool!

I flopped down into the seat. The bottom part was wide enough for me to spread my legs out and the cushion was a soft leather. I had heard about seats like this before, but had never seen one myself. With how nice they were, I wondered if the tickets were expensive.

Theseus settled down next to me and surprised me when he wrapped his arm around my waist and pulled me in close to him. The warm and fuzzy feeling that burst to life in my chest fizzled out when he had to put those clunky glasses on. I wondered if there was something I could do to help him.

I pondered on this while the movie began. I didn't actually know what we were even seeing, but when the Marvel logo flashed across the screen, I shouldn't have been surprised. I couldn't help but smile as I settled in and rested my head against Theseus's shoulder.

The movie itself was rather boring. Visually entertaining, yes, but way too easy to predict. Glancing over at Theseus and his big clunky glasses, he looked so absorbed in the movie. His face lit up like an excited little boy when one of the characters did a sick flip over a car.

I chuckled and settled into him. This was nice.

About halfway through the movie, I noticed the shadow of someone walking into the theater. I tensed as the form moved swiftly up the steps and towards where Theseus and I were sitting.

I felt Theseus shift and look down at me. "What's wrong?"

My eyes quickly flicked to meet Theseus's and then to the form that was now only so many feet away. He tensed alongside me for a split second before he sighed.

"Jason, the movie's not over yet."

I frowned and studied the form more closely. It was familiar. Jason crouched down in front of our seat.

"I've come to get you, my princess."

"What? But the movie…"

"Jason, it's not your turn yet!" Theseus hissed loudly.

There were mutters and half hearted complaints to be quiet. I bit my lip and turned to Theseus, gesturing for him to lower his voice. He wasn't paying any attention to me, though. He was pouting at Jason, his eyes glowing.

"Just a few more minutes, man."

"You've had her all morning, Theseus. Sharing is caring."

"But the movie's almost over," Theseus whined back.

"Then you wouldn't mind if I come sit with you, would you?"

"Um, well..."

"Great, scoot over." Jason patted my leg and squeezed himself into the seat on the other side.

I covered my mouth to muffle my snort when I heard Theseus groan. We scooted over to make room for him, Theseus grumbling next to me, making me snicker harder.

"It's nice to hear your laughter," Jason whispered in my ear.

"Isn't it a bit rude to interrupt a date?" I asked, my smile wide.

I felt him shrug. "It's not like I'm cock-blocking him or anything."

"Will you shut the fuck up!" someone in the theater shouted.

"Sorry," I stage whispered back and sunk into my seat.

I felt Jason chuckle beside me. Scowling, I poked him in the side. It was his fault we got yelled at. How did he know we were here, anyway? And what did Theseus mean when—

Oh, my, God! THE BASTARD POKED ME BACK!

I gasped and pulled my eyes from the screen to glare at Jason. I could see he was grinning like a fool.

This meant war.

I took my time, not reacting at all to his attack. Waiting for him to settle and lose his focus to the movie before I struck, poking him right in the stomach. His retaliation was quick as he poked me right back in the side. And on our battle went! The strikes were fast and lethal, but I was surviving. Until I was betrayed!

"What are you two doing?" Theseus whispered rather poorly.

I had just finished my retaliation on Jason and in all of the excitement I twisted around and poked Theseus right on the cheek.

He blinked, his eyes going wide behind the glasses. "Did you just...?"

I clasped my hand over my mouth trying to stifle my giggles and gasped when Theseus poked my arm.

The two of them began double teaming me from both sides until it was no longer just poking, but full on tickling. Completely aware of our surroundings, I tried really hard to contain my fits of laughter, but clearly I didn't do well enough because the next thing I knew, an attendant came up next to us.

"Excuse me. There have been complaints about noise. I'm going to have to ask you to either quiet down or leave," The young man whispered sternly.

I was too busy laughing to answer but Jason stood up abruptly. "My apologies, my man. I'll fix the problem right away."

The attended look so confused until Jason leaned down, scooped me up and slung me over his shoulder like a sack of potatoes.

"Jason!" I squeaked.

"Time to go, Princess. Bye, Theseus!" And Jason booked it out of the theater with me over his shoulder.

I could see Theseus palming his face and turning to apologize to the attendant before we turned the corner and out the doors.

I couldn't believe what was happening. Jason jogged all the way out of the building with me over his shoulder, laughing like a maniac.

When we finally reached his car, Jason put me down and gave me a kiss on the cheek. "Hello, Atalanta. I like your new hair cut."

I smiled up into those deep green eyes. "Hello, Jason. Thank you."

"I have something for you," he opened the back door and rummaged for something. "Since it is Valentine's Day, I thought it only appropriate to give into to the trend and get you the cliche stuff. Give you the full experience."

He reappeared in front of me holding a bouquet of flowers, a box of chocolates, and... "Is that an elephant?"

"You're too special for a teddy bear, and he looked cute. Happy Valentine's day, Atalanta."

"He is cute." I took the bouquet. "And these are beautiful, Jason. Thank you."

"You're welcome, Princess. Now let's get to pampering you."

"Ugh, there's more?"

He chuckled and gave me a kiss. "There's always more."

Chapter Thirteen

ATALANTA

As it turned out, Jason's idea of pampering came right out of a movie. He brought us back to Ajax's cabin, where he had set up a spa in the living room. Soft pillows spread across the floor like a bed were surrounded by candlelight. Jason gave me a back massage and a manicure. He even pulled out his phone and played relaxing piano music.

"Now, time for a pedicure," Jason said after he finished painting my fingers a bright blue.

"Don't I get the chance to pamper you?"

He smirked and tilted his head. "What, like give me a manicure?"

"Yeah, why not?"

Jason shrugged then looked around at the little pile of stuff he had accumulated next to him, including several different nail polish bottles he had bought. Picking up a purple one, he held it out to me.

"You want purple nails?"

"I mean, if I'm going to do it, I should do it right."

"If that's your plan, then shouldn't they be pink?"

He held up his hand. "But then they wouldn't match my scales as well."

I giggled. "Okay, fine. Hold out your hand and stay still."

He held out his hand and I grabbed the clippers, beginning to shape his nails. "If you want them to match your scales, I can try to do a mix of the blue and purple."

"That would be perfect."

We sat in comfortable silence while I clipped, filed, polished, and painted Jason's nails. Between each nail, I studied Jason's face. His smile was wide, but he looked…tired. His usually tamed mousy brown hair stuck up at odd angles, and there were dark circles under his eyes. He also looked like he'd lost a few pounds.

"Jason, are you okay?" I asked, pausing in my painting.

"I'm perfect. I mean, who wouldn't be when their nails are being painted?"

"You look tired."

Jason hummed. "Yeah, maybe a bit."

"Come on. Tell the truth," I grumbled. "You haven't been sleeping, have you? Do you want to talk about it?"

He sighed and sat back, staring at the hand I had finished painting. "If I'm being honest, I haven't been able to sleep well because I'm worried."

"…about?" I prompted.

"About you."

"Me?"

"Listen…there's something I need to tell you."

My stomach sank. Oh, great. Was he going to tell me I was part dragon now, too? I mean, being part dragon would be pretty cool. I bet I could breath fire and shit.

"It's nothing bad, necessarily. It's about us. I don't know if you've felt it." He took my hand and that pleasant hum started up.

I nodded. "Yeah, that warm tingle whenever we touch."

"Me changing you, it formed a connection. My parents told me that it's akin to a mating bond." He said slowly, his expression telling me he was rather worried about my reaction.

But...something inside of me told me that what he said was right. Jason was mine, he was my mate.

"So, what does that entail exactly?"

"You believe me?"

"Of course. Why wouldn't I?"

"Most wouldn't." He let go of my hand and stared down at his palm. "To answer your question, it means being apart from one another for long periods is rather difficult. The feeling isn't as intense for you, because your instincts aren't as strong, but for me—"

He paused and clenched his hand into a fist. Without a thought, I reached out and placed my hand over his.

"Let's just say it's intense. When you were unconscious, sleeping was impossible. My instincts drove me to always watch and make sure you were okay. It hasn't changed much since you've woken up.

When I went to go see my parents, I was running a fever. I felt sick and achy, almost like—"

"Withdrawal." I said knowingly. Even if he was right and my feelings weren't as intense, I still felt it.

"Yeah, just like that."

I pulled Jason from where he sat right next to me and laid my head on his shoulder. "And last night, when I was with Percy and Theseus...you didn't sleep at all, did you?"

He snuggled into me, his limbs wrapping around mine. "No. I couldn't."

"Why didn't you tell me before? If us being apart causes you so much pain, then why leave me with Percy all night?" No wonder he interrupted my date with Theseus.

"It's not like you can be with me all the time. I've already wrecked your life enough. I didn't need to make you feel guilty about basically being chained to me."

I sighed. "I thought we were past this. You didn't wreck my life, Jason. You saved it."

He began to pull away from me, but I tensed up, keeping him still.

"It is my fault, though. If I hadn't called you a slut, you wouldn't have run off into that storm in the first place!"

I dropped my grip on him and leaned back, eyes wide. "You called me a *what*?!"

He dragged his hand over his face. "We got into a fight. You were...I was...I fucked up. You found me sleeping at the bottom of the pool and dove in to save me. I freaked out because my stupidity put you in danger and I was so angry. The others were there and... I just...I'm sorry."

I blinked and stared at the frazzled man. Then, slowly, I got up and walked into the kitchen. Silently reaching into the freezer, I grasped a handful of ice. As I walked back into the room, Jason was staring at me, befuddled. Looking directly into his eyes, I snagged my fingers around the elastic of his pants and boxers and dumped the big handful of ice down his pants.

"Shhiiittt!!" Jason swore as he gripped his crotch.

To add salt to the wound, I smacked him upside the head. Hard. "Jason, you were an asshole. But..."

I waited until he had pulled the ice out of his pants and focused back on me.

"You have suffered enough for your mistake." I stepped closer to him and cupped his cheek. "And you've more than made up for it. Even if I don't remember what happened that day, you calling me a slut wouldn't have pushed me onto that boat. That decision was mine, and mine alone. Now, come."

I took his hand and led him over to the couch.

"What are we doing?" he asked, stumbling over a few of the pillows on the floor.

"*You* are going to sleep."

"But I still haven't made you lunch! And I promised you a pedicure." Jason protested as I shoved him onto the couch.

"I can fend for myself, and the pedicure can wait."

"But—"

"Nope." I pushed him until he was laying down. "Close your eyes and count backwards from twenty. That's an order."

He sighed and closed his eyes. "Twenty, nineteen, eighteen."

As he counted, I stroked his hair and began to softly sing a lullaby.

> I love you, a bushel and a peck,
> A bushel and a peck and a hug around the neck,

"What kind of song is that?" He mumbled.

"Hush." I shushed him and began to sing again.

> A hug around the neck and a barrel and a heap,
> A barrel and a heap and I'm talkin' in my sleep,
> About you, about you...

Jason didn't even make it to ten before he drifted off.

"Idiot." I whispered softly before standing.

"My turn?"

I jumped and turned to find Ajax standing at the edge of the room. He looked good. For once, his wild bear appearance was tamed. His usually scruffy beard was trimmed, his hair combed, not covered in paint. It was hot.

I creeped away from Jason. "Jason mentioned something about taking turns before. Did you guys draw straws or something?"

"Yes."

"And it's your turn?"

He nodded with a grin.

I looked back over to the sleeping Jason and remembered what he had said about needing me near him. Looking back to Ajax I asked, "We won't go far, will we?"

He shook his head.

"Okay, so what are we doing?"

"Food first."

He ushered me towards the kitchen and gestured for me to sit at the table. For a large man, he moved around and prepared us lunch with such quiet grace, I would have akin him to a ballet dancer. It was nice to just sit and watch him as his hands moved swiftly, chopping up lettuce, peppers and onions. Pulling ground beef out of the fridge, he fried it up and added spices. I wondered what he was making until he pulled out a familiar box.

"I love tacos," I whispered excitedly.

"Same," he replied.

As Ajax cooked, I checked in on Jason. He was out like a light, snoring loudly on the couch.

I thought about what he had said before. Mates. I wondered what that meant for us now. In books, it was similar to marriage, yet deeper, on a more physical level, and not just a promise to each other and a title. But beyond the tingling sensation, I didn't feel anything like what Jason felt. Certainly not constantly thinking about him and feeling physical discomfort when he wasn't nearby.

What he was going through was almost scary.

Is what he felt for me due to the connection?

"Jason genuinely cares about you."

I flinched and looked up at Ajax, who was standing next to me with a plate of tacos. "Did I say that out loud?"

He shook his head. "No."

My brows furrowed. "Are you sure you can't read minds?"

"I'm sure."

"Then how could you have possibly known what I was thinking?"

"I felt it," he tapped his head. "Empath."

"Yeah, but empaths only feel emotions, right? Like when I'm angry or sad?"

"Practice. You felt worried, then unsure as you stared at Jason. From what I overheard, I connected the dots."

"I don't get you." I scrunched my nose up at him. "You either emote like a caveman or spew out impossible knowledge."

He shrugged. "I'm complicated."

"I'm sorry, I just realized that was rather bitchy of me to say." I whispered, my shoulders slumping. He didn't deserve me saying that.

"But you weren't wrong." He grinned and put the plate down in front of me.

"It was still rude, so I'm sorry."

Ajax sat down in the chair next to me and gave me a pat on the head. "You're quick to rudeness when you feel cornered. At least you're kind enough to apologize."

Tongue-tied, I shoved a taco in my mouth, the heat rising in my cheeks when Ajax smirked and began to eat his own taco.

After a few bites, I changed the subject. "So, it seems that everyone has their own plan for me for today. What's yours?"

"Paint or wood?"

Was that a question?

"Umm...wood?"

"Good choice." He shoved the last bite of food into his mouth and then held out a hand for me.

I took it and followed him as he guided me out of the cabin and over to his workshop. Inside, he brought me over to a workbench with a hunk of wood. There was a chainsaw propped up against the bench.

"Pick a piece of wood, and I'll teach you to carve it."

"Sweet! Can I use the chainsaw?" I asked excitedly as I poked the giant tool.

"No. Not today."

"Aw, why not?"

Ajax reached over and picked up the chainsaw, heaving it over his shoulder. "Too big for you."

"Well, at least you're not saying it's because I'm a girl and it's too dangerous."

"It is too dangerous, you're so tiny. I'll find a smaller chainsaw next time."

I smiled wide, excited by the idea of hacking a wood with a power chainsaw. "I'll hold you to that."

I studied the piles of lumber he had and chose a pretty large hunk. With ease, Ajax picked it up out of the pile and propped it on top of his work bench.

"Okay, now what?" I asked.

"What do you want?"

"Like, what do I want to carve the wood into?"

"Yes."

I turned to the piece of wood and studied it, my fingers on my chin. I wondered if I should just pick something or do that thing that artists do where they see into the wood and sculpt what they see. Squinting at it, I tried to peer deep into the bark, waiting for the wood to tell me what it wanted to be. When that didn't fucking work I shrugged and said the first thing that popped into my head.

"How about a sleeping dragon?"

Ajax looked at the wood and nodded. "Yeah, that could work."

TIED TO THE SEA

Reaching over, he tossed me protective goggles. From there, Ajax took the chainsaw and revved it to life. It was amazing watching him slice through the wood like extremely messy butter. Wood chips flew everywhere and I understood the purpose of the goggles.

Ajax cut the wood into a sort of dome shape before switching off the chainsaw.

I lifted the sawdust-covered goggles. "That was so cool! You're definitely showing me how to do that."

"With a smaller chainsaw, you could even carve small details."

"Then you definitely need one." I walked up and pat the wood dome. "What now?"

Ajax put down the chainsaw and walked over to the workbench and rifled through the tools, pulling out a marker. He drew a sketch of the dragon onto the wood then pulled out some more tools.

"Now we carve."

Taking my hands, Ajax showed me how to use the chisels to carve chunks out of the wood. After a while when I felt confident, Ajax left me to carve on my own while he worked next to me.

Looking up from the wood, I glanced over to Ajax, who was working on an easel. "Whatcha painting?"

"You." He answered without looking away from the canvas.

"Oh, are you doing one of those still life paintings?"

223

"Yes. It's unfortunate you're not naked like the usual models."

"Wait, so that's not just a movie thing?" I asked, my voice squeaking as I rushed over to look at the painting. "The models are actually naked?"

On the canvas was a rough sketch of me bent over the workbench, fully clothed, thankfully. I was surprised. For a rough sketch, it looked quite good.

"Sometimes." Ajax looked up from his painting meeting my eyes. His stare was intense and heated me from the inside.

I gulped, my mouth suddenly dry. "How many people have you painted naked?"

"A few."

"Thats pretty neat." I bit my lip and moved back over to my dragon and continued chipping at the wood. I felt Ajax get up from his chair and approach me, his warmth radiating against my back.

"You're jealous." He said, his voice a low rumble.

"Not really." I chipped away at a piece of the dragons tail, focused.

He poked my cheek. "You're a horrible liar."

"Am not. You just cheat with your freaky mind reading thing."

"Empath. I'm an empath," he grumbled.

I rolled my eyes. "Yeah, sure. I'm not buying that that's your only ability."

There was no way a regular empath could be so accurate with predicting thoughts like he was.

"Well, I can also alter emotions."

I paused as I actually remembered something. "You mentioned, before, that you could take away my sadness."

"I can take. But I can also give."

I felt his fingers run up the back of my neck and from there It felt like lightning had struck me and suddenly I felt extremely aroused. Surprised, I dropped the chisel and braced myself against the workbench. My breath was coming out in short gasps.

"Cheat."

"Resourceful." He said as he replaced his fingers with his mouth, kissing the back of my neck leisurely.

I took in a deep breath to try and calm my racing heart. "Is this the point that I'm supposed to warn you not to touch a woman like that? What ever happened to being scared of you?"

"You still should be."

"Yeah, sure," I let out a nervous chuckle, "you big teddy bear."

Ajax growled and spun me around, his multicolored eyes glowing. They really weren't hiding themselves now.

I thought he was going to kiss me but instead he lifted my hand, his fingers tangled in mine and kissed my palm. His mouth moved down to my wrist where he nipped right at my pulse. It was like he was trailing fire along with his mouth. I was helpless, my body quivering as he spiked me with pleasure.

I moaned when he moved his mouth to the crook of my neck. "Ajax."

My free hand came up to clasp his shoulder.

"Atalanta," he rasped.

When he lifted away from my neck and stared into my eyes I knew he would kiss me then.

The sound of a throat being cleared shattered the moment, and our attention turned to the person who made the sound. Hip was standing there with that smile. The fake one I had seen him use so many times.

"Sorry for interrupting, but I believe it's my turn."

My stomach sunk. "Hip…"

"I'll just wait outside," He said, that smile still in place as he turned and left.

I looked up at Ajax. "I need to—um…"

He nodded in understanding. "Go."

I leaned back up to kiss him on the cheek but hesitated. Perhaps it wasn't the time for that. Settling back down on my feet, I dashed out the door after Hip. He stood right outside, leaning against the building. I had practically run a good three yards looking for him before realizing where he was standing.

"Hey," I breathed.

"Hi, Speedy, where you running off to?"

"I was coming after you, of course." I said, taking a step closer to him.

He tilted his head towards where I had come from. "What about finishing up getting some nookie from Tall, Dark, and Silent?"

"You said it was your turn with me. As it seems, you guys are taking some sort of shifts today."

"I would have waited." His face still, like a mask.

I hated that fucking smile.

"I'm sure you would have. Doesn't make it okay." I tried to take his hand but he pulled away. "Hip, are you okay?"

"I'm fine. Why do you ask?"

I scowled and poked his cheek, right over that fake ass dimple. "Because of that. You may have everyone else fooled, but you can't fool me. I know what acting looks like."

His happy demeanor burned down, leaving behind hurt and worry. His youthfulness seemed to drain away, revealing someone who saw too much in the world. I understood that feeling.

"I'm sorry. It will take some time getting used to the idea of this...dynamic we're building. Talking about it is one thing, but seeing it is another. And I just...I need a minute to process it."

I tugged at the sleeves of my jacket. "I kind of know how you feel."

"No offense, Atalanta, but how exactly do you know how I feel?" Hip scoffed.

I wrapped my arms around my middle, hugging myself. "Well, if I had to guess, seeing Ajax and I just now left you feeling jealous? Maybe worried and scared that I would somehow like any of the others more than you?"

His eyes went wide and his lips parted in surprise. "Y-yeah. How did you?"

"Because it's something I can't stop thinking about. Since the moment I woke up, it's like all of you had somehow decided, 'whelp, she can't choose, so clearly we all get to share her' and have been acting like you're okay with it. But there's just no way. Beyond feeling extremely guilty about not having the ability to choose one of you, I'm constantly worried about what each one of you must think of all of this."

He laughed. "You're the most observant person I have ever met. And the most selfless. It may suck, but if it means I get to stay by your side dealing with all of these emotions for a while, it will be worth it."

"But why? I seriously can not be worth all of the trouble. And we haven't even known each other that long! A month? Maybe two?"

"A person may get to choose their own self worth, but they have no control of their worth to others." Hip said, looking up at the sky.

My brows furrowed. "Huh?"

"You say you're not worth all of the trouble? Well, I say you're worth all of it and more. I can't speak for the others, but you're the first person beyond my own parents who've ever been able to see past my bullshit. And not only that, but you called me out on it. That first day we met, when you cornered me in the hall and told me that acting like an idiot wouldn't get me any real friends? I was a goner that day, even if I didn't realize it."

He put his hands on my shoulder, his expression excited. "I mean, you know how crazy it is to meet someone who can match me wit for wit? It's like seeing color for the first time. You're like a bright golden apple amongst a dreary orchard of gray. So, as long as you'll have me, I'm going to keep you. Now, come on, I have a gift for you."

I let out a nervous laugh as I held back the tears that wanted to push to the surface. "I'm pretty sure that was a good enough gift."

"Maybe, but a girl deserves nice things on Valentine's Day." Hip took my hand and gave me a kiss on the knuckles.

We walked into Ajax's cabin to see Jason was awake and arguing with Theseus, while Percy stood off to the side looking bored. When he noticed us come in, Percy's expression brightened, if his micro-shifts were anything to go by.

"It seems to be my turn now."

Hip scoffed. "What? No, it's not. It's my turn."

"But Jason told me that I would get her after sunset," Percy said.

"And I was supposed to have her before then, but I only just got her from Ajax." Hip pointed out.

"Do you have any idea how annoying it was trying to explain to the cops that you didn't actually kidnap

229

her?! Seriously, Jason. Not cool." Theseus shouted, drawing my attention away from Percy and Hip.

Cops had seriously shown up after we left?

"It was my turn!" Jason shouted back. "Besides, I thought it was hilarious."

"It might have been to you, but I'm the one who got left behind to clean up the mess."

Jason shrugged. "We will just have to schedule it better next time."

"Jason," Hip interrupted, drawing my attention back to the two of them. "Can we push Percy's time? I haven't even started what I had planned."

And of course Ajax chose that moment to walk through the door. He stopped and stared at the rest of us. "Loud."

I leaned into him and whispered, "It seems the cocks are in a chicken fight."

"And you're the hen?"

"Basically."

Ajax grunted. "I'm hungry."

"Yeah, me too." I clapped my hands. "That's enough, boys. It's time for dinner."

"But—"

"Nope. I'm hungry."

Hip and Percy then quickly strode towards the kitchen and said at the same time, "I've got it."

They glared at each other before practically racing to see who would get to cook.

I sighed. I needed a moment to myself.

Mumbling about needing to use the restroom, I left the squabbling chicken coop and locked myself in the bathroom.

I slumped to the floor, my back against the door. My brain felt full with everything the guys had dumped on me today. Like another brick added to this bucket that was dangling over my head.

I chuckled as I heard the sound of something breaking and shouting.

Still. At least their antics had almost made this day feel normal. Distracted me. I didn't feel as alone as I would have thought.

"Happy birthday to me." I whispered softly.

> *Come on, sweetie. They may want to take away our special day, but that doesn't mean we have to let them.*

"Happy birthday to me."

> *Another year older, my silly little monkey.*

"I'm twenty-two now, Dad," I whispered to the bathroom tile.

> *Yeah, but you'll always be my baby girl. Now go show your mom the present you got.*

I couldn't remember the sound of my mother's voice. But did that matter? I could at least remember Dad and Cal singing to me. Dad couldn't sing for shit, but Cal's voice was golden. She would always add a silly name on to the last lines just because it annoyed me.

> "Happy birthday, Dear Mrs. Figgleston Causerhouser the Thiiirrrd. Happy birthday to you!"

I let out a sad chuckle. "Fuck you, Cal."

I felt and heard the knock at my back. "Atalanta, are you okay in there?"

It was Hip. I must have been gone longer than I realized. Lost in my memories.

I took a deep breath before answering. "Yeah, I'm all right. I'll be right out!"

Okay. It was time to stop my pity party.

Chapter Fourteen

HIP

I stepped back when Atalanta came out of the bathroom. It was clear she had been crying and now I knew why. At least she stood with her shoulders held high. She was getting there. Slowly getting back to that little light I'd seen a few times before all this shit happened.

I wiped away the tears on her cheeks. "You should wash your face with some cold water before you head in to the other room for dinner."

She stiffened and touched her cheeks.

"What is it they say? Never let them see you sweat? Brave face, my little kitty cat." I winked and walked away, giving her a moment alone to compose herself.

I sauntered back into the kitchen where Percy stood at the stove, preparing a basic pasta sauce. When I came in, he looked up and met my eyes with a glare. It wasn't completely my fault he just so happened to drop the only jar of sauce. It was a good thing I also happened to pick up the ingredients on the way over. Homemade was so much better, anyway. It was a lucky happenstance, really.

I crouched down and peered into the oven's glass door. The garlic bread looked almost done.

"Smells good," Atalanta said as she came into view, looking much more refreshed.

"It still has a while before it's done. Why not settle down with Jason and Theseus? The two idiots are still fighting."

She studied me before saying, "It's my time with the two of you right? I think I'll stay here. Maybe I can help, if you want?"

I laughed. "Didn't you tell me you can't cook? I think it's better if you just sat right here."

With ease, I lifted her by the hips and propped her up on the counter. "You can be our beautiful culinary muse."

She may have rolled her eyes but she couldn't hide her smile. "That was cheesy."

"And from what I hear, you like cheese."

"Did someone say cheese?" Jason asked poking his head into the kitchen.

"Sorry to disappoint, it's just Hip."

"Hip is made of cheese?"

I rolled my eyes and pulled the bread out of the oven. "I would like to think I'm made of the finest quality of milk products."

Atalanta inhaled deeply. "Is that garlic bread?"

"It sure is." I placed the tray on the opposite counter of Atalanta, next to Percy. "I made it my—"

"Hand it over." Atalanta demanded, holding out her hands.

I poked her nose. "It's still hot."

"I'll wait till it cools, just give it!"

How could I resist that smile? Cutting off a bit of bread, I put it on a paper towel and handed it to her. I couldn't help but laugh as she was practically drooling.

"That looks really good." Jason said as he intently watched the slice in Atalanta's hands.

"Mine!" She growled.

"I wasn't going to steal it," He pouted.

"I see your eyes. It's mine."

"It is far too crowded in here. Monroe, Clark, please leave." Percy said as he stirred his sauce.

I scowled. "I'm cooking too, you know."

"Yes, and your bread is done."

I rolled my eyes at him before kissing Atalanta on the cheek and sitting over at the kitchen table with Jason. He was tapping away on his phone, probably texting those human friends of his. Which reminded me that I needed to call Anita. Theseus was sprawled across the couch, seemingly taking a nap. I wonder where Ajax had scampered off to?

"Oh my fucking God, this bread is delicious!" Atalanta moaned over on the counter as she devoured the rest of the slice I gave her. "What brand is it?"

"Mr. Clark's" I grinned coyly.

Jason looked up from his phone. "Wait, you made this? As in, you bought a loaf and put garlic butter on it? My mom used to do that."

I shook my head. "No, as in, I made the bread from scratch. I did put garlic butter on top but I also mixed sliced garlic and herbs into the dough."

Atalanta's face lit up with wonder. "Whoa, you really made this from scratch? Hip, that's so cool! Can you bake other things? Like muffins? Or cakes? Can you make brownies!?"

"Yes, I can in fact make those things."

"Good. Then I say you'll have to make them for us. I think brownies would be a great dessert, don't you think?" Jason asked.

I gave him a wicked grin. "I will only bake for my kitten."

"Okay, then." Without hesitation, Jason smiled and looked over to Atalanta. "Sweetheart, ask Hip to make us some brownies!"

"While I don't want to manipulate Hip for your gain, Jason, I do really love brownies." She turned her attention to me, a pout ready on her lips. "Pretty please, make us brownies."

"Atalanta, you should know better. If you want to manipulate me, you can't blatantly point it out like that."

"Please," She said again, giving me the puppy dog eyes.

"No."

"But it's Valentine's Day. Shouldn't a girl get chocolate on valentines day?"

"Jason gave you chocolate earlier." I pointed out.

"But you haven't given me any chocolate. Brownies would be perfect."

I growled and glared at Jason. Standing up, I grunted. "Fine. But you're cleaning up, and I'll make sure I make a nice big mess."

He gave me a shit-eating grin and shot a wink in Atalanta's direction.

Luckily, Ajax had most of the ingredients I needed. All that was missing was the fresh chocolate, which I decided to steal from the extra box of chocolate I knew Jason had bought for himself yesterday.

Percy finished up dinner while I swiftly measured out and mixed together the batter. As they sat down to dinner I popped the tray into the oven and set a timer on my phone. When I noticed that Ajax was still missing, I set out to find him while everyone else sat down and began eating.

It wasn't hard to find him, back in that workshop of his. I wondered if he ever took a break.

I poked my head in through the door. "Dinner's ready!"

"Coming."

I waited patiently for a solid minute before rolling my eyes and walking in. I found Ajax sitting on a stool behind a medium sized canvas, his face tight with concentration.

"Hey, Ajax. Dinner."

"Uh-huh."

"Don't make me douse you in water," I threatened.

"I'd like to see you try," He grunted, not bothering to even look at me.

I raised an eyebrow. "Are you okay?"

"Yeah."

God, this was awkward.

I sighed. "Alright, silent giant. What's up? If you were just being your usual reclusive self, you'd still be in there laughing at Atalanta manipulating me to make brownies."

He glanced up and cocked an eyebrow at me. "She manipulated you?"

"Well, I guess it's not manipulation when it's blatantly obvious, but she gave me the puppy dog eyes. What was I supposed to do?"

He snorted and turned back towards his painting. I walked around to see what he was so focused on. It was a painting of Atalanta. She was sitting on her father's air mattress, reading a book. There was something about the painting. The colors he was using. It wasn't like he was doing a still life because her skin tone wasn't right and neither was the room. Instead of an alluring brown, the color of her skin was almost blue with hints of yellow. The room around her was a light yellow and blue as well, and it almost looked like that yellow was bleeding into her figure. Did the paint smudge?

"Is there a reason the colors are all funky?" I asked.

"Yes, it's—" He began, but I interrupted him.

TIED TO THE SEA

"No, wait, don't tell me." I scrunched my nose, thinking on it for a moment before throwing out, "They're the emotions of the moment, right?"

"That's correct," he said, looking astonished.

"Sorry," I said. "I wanted to try and guess. Knowing your abilities and all, it wasn't super hard, but I'm glad I'm right."

"You and Atalanta have that in common. Knowing things about others." He said, his eyes sad.

"You're pretty good at it too, you know."

He shook his head. "I cheat. Before I was turned, I was very blind to others and how they felt. You and her, and even Percival sometimes, you're all able to do it without powers."

I shrugged. "It's no great ability to read a person. You just need to pay attention."

"Many of us see, and we hear, but don't actually pay attention to others."

Well, shit, wasn't he the philosopher? I don't think I had ever spoken this much to him.

"I guess you're right about that. So do all of your paintings capture the emotions? What was she feeling here?"

"Not all," Ajax hovered his fingers just over the wet paint. "The book she was reading had some pretty funny scenes in it. The yellow was the small moments of laugher she felt."

"And the blue is literally that. She was feeling blue?"

"It's almost always how she feels now."

"She's depressed." I stated.

He nodded. "And scared."

"Do you have any idea how we should fix that?"

Atalanta had been depressed since the day I had met her. Like a dark cloud hung over her head. It was why I loved when she let herself go and showed us that fire inside.

He circled the yellow color that was around the figure of Atalanta in the painting. "Us. Our light and positivity helps, even if just a little. She'll get better as long as we stick by her, as her support system."

"In due time and all that shit." I looked around, spying another painting of Atalanta, this one only a rough sketch of her chiseling on a piece of wood, of all things. "We haven't talked about it, how do you feel about all this?"

He looked away from his painting and at me skeptically.

"What? I actually want to know your motivations behind doing all this. You, Percy, and Theseus are this large question mark. You particularly are the hardest to read."

"I'm for it."

"But why? I sort of get Percy and Theseus. You guys were saying that its normal in Mer culture but…you were human, weren't you?"

"I was."

"So like, polyamory was normal where you came from, or…?"

He was slow to answer, his gaze so far away as he stared into what I suspected to be a rather long past. "I lost my humanity a long time ago. You eventually stop caring about social expectations."

"How long?"

His answer was simply a glare.

"Okay, fine. As long as you don't decide to just drop and leave."

"You're a nosy one, Trickster." He pulled a small box out of his back pocket. "I finished your gift."

I took the box from him gently and fiddled with it between my fingers. "Thank you. Ajax…I hope my prying didn't upset you."

"And I apologize that me kissing Atalanta upset you."

"It didn't—" I began to deny but paused and sighed. "You felt it. I'll get used to it."

"Everything in due time." He echoed my words.

"Thank you again for this." I said, holding up the box.

I turned around and began to walk out before pausing. "Ajax."

"Yes?"

Should I tell him what I learned?

I grit my teeth and then relaxed. "It's time for dinner. Let's go."

Dinner was a fun affair, similar to how it was at home. Plenty of banter to fill the empty space between shoveling food into our mouths. It was good to see Atalanta eating with such gusto. I was especially pleased with how much she liked the bread I'd baked; she ate half a loaf on her own! I told myself that I would certainly bake more bread for her in the future.

"How is it that you can eat so much and be so tiny?" Jason asked with a chuckle as Atalanta scarfed down her third helping of pasta.

Atalanta shrugged. "Fast metabolism?"

I knew it was more than that. At school, she would never bring food from home nor would she spend any money to buy lunch. I had assumed she struggled financially and was all too eager to share some of my food with her. After seeing the inside of her home, it wasn't so much a struggle as that the poor family was destitute. Her slim form was from a lack of proper nourishment. Being in a coma for two weeks certainly wouldn't have helped things. Weren't those who were in witness protection provided with government funds to help get them by? Or was that something they provided on their own?

I knew asking her would probably get me nowhere at the moment. She might have begun to finally trust us, but asking her intricate questions wouldn't work.

She was certainly doing better about opening up to us, at least.

I held out the bread basket to her. She took another slice with a shy smile.

After finishing dinner, Percy and I played rock paper scissors to decide who would get to take Atalanta out first. At which point Atalanta had scolded both of us about treating her like a toy and not a woman.

"You're right. We should let her decide, shouldn't we, Percy?" I grinned.

"You are right. I believe in letting Ms. North decide who she should be with next."

"Well...um, I—uhhh..." she stuttered.

"It seems you're having difficulty deciding." I slid over to Atalanta's side and placed my hand on her hip. "Maybe you would like to share Percy and I?"

Percy joined me on her other side. "Yes, would sharing be more to your liking?"

My eyes skimmed over the others in the room. All three of them were watching with varying degrees of heat in their gaze. I was surprised when seeing their own arousal sparked something in me. A hunger to touch Atalanta, while they watched.

I wanted it.

She wanted it, too. I could see it in her slightly parted lips, and the tinge of red that was just visible on her dark cheeks. Though, when I looked into her eyes, I wondered if perhaps it was only curiosity and unwanted reaction from her body. Because that shadow of hesitation and fear were hidden behind the lust. She wasn't ready for this.

I leaned in and kissed her cheek. "We're joking, my little kitten."

Stepping back, I did a mock bow. "I concede. Percy, please do show our girl a good time."

"Wait, where are you going?" Jason asked.

"Preparing for my turn, of course."

"Hip..." Atalanta said.

"Have fun," I said as I strolled out of the cabin.

There was much to prepare.

It was late into the night when I returned. Having always been a night owl, I wasn't disappointed to find everyone already asleep, save one. Percy sat in a chair reading from a book.

When I entered, he looked up. "You were gone for quite a while."

"It took more time rearranging things than I would have thought...did she have a good time?" I asked.

"She was pretty bummed after you left. Of course she wouldn't have admitted it."

"Is..." I tilted my head and studied him. "Did you paint your nails?"

He nodded and held up his hands, looking at his colored nails. "Atalanta. Jason started it with his date idea, and after you left she insisted on painting everyone's."

I didn't know if I should be grateful for having escaped the painting or sad for missing out.

"Orange isn't your color."

"Perhaps," Percy said noncommittally as he turned his attention back to the book in his hands.

As quietly as I could, I crept over to Ajax's bedroom. It was different from the other night. Instead of the others sleeping on the couches or on the floor next to her, Atalanta was in the middle of a man sandwich. Ajax on one side while Jason on the other, Theseus, the goddamn tallest of all of us, somehow squeezed himself at the head of the bed between the others, curled up.

"He's like a cat," I mumbled under my breath.

I tilted my head and studied the group, wondering how I was going to get Atalanta out from between them without waking the others. Like a math problem, I walked around and looked at it from all angles before just saying 'fuck it,' and going with the first thing that popped into my head.

Walking up to the foot of the bed, I ran my fingers up Atalanta's leg, which had been sticking out from underneath the blanket. She began to squirm under my tickling, compelling me to continue tickling until she grumbled and sat up.

Rubbing the sleep from her eyes, she looked at me. "Hip?"

"Hello my little speedster. Up and at 'em." I whispered.

"You're late."

I tilted my head. "Am I? I thought I was right on time."

"I was sleeping. Doesn't that mean the day is over, when you fall asleep?"

"No, because then you enter the dream world. Wonderful dreams can extend your days."

She deadpanned. "I have chronic nightmares."

"Well, there you go. I was right on time to stop you from having a nightmare like the White Knight I am. Besides, it's not midnight yet, so I believe the day isn't technically over."

With her hand in mine, I swept her out of the cabin and onto my motorcycle. I drove it deep into the woods on a path that only locals would know. The air was crisp and the path was black as pitch, but being inhuman had its benefits. Unconcerned about visibility when the path got thinner, I easily weaved through the trees before halting right before our destination. Putting down the kickstand, I hopped off and helped Atalanta.

"Sooo, your idea of a romantic Valentine's Day is to bring me to the middle of the dark woods to...kill me?" She asked, looking around with a worried expression.

I chuckled. "Hey, I believe the statistic is that about 30% of murders are crimes of passion."

She laughed it off, but I could see her shoulders stiffening.

"I'm sorry, Atalanta. I didn't mean to scare you. It was only a joke." I said, rubbing her shoulders.

TIED TO THE SEA

"I know. It's not your fault I'm, well, not weird...I suppose damaged would be the right word?"

Slowly, I took her arm and lifted it, kissing her wrist over where I knew her scars started. "We're all damaged in some way or another. Like fine china being slowly swept across the ocean floor. Some of us simply get scratched up by the sand. While some of us get smashed against rocks. That's life, and you shouldn't judge yourself for it."

"Has anyone ever told you that you would make an amazing poet?"

"People have called me an intelligent prick, but not a poet, no."

"Well, they don't give you enough credit." She said as she slipped her arm from my grasp to take my hand in hers. "Granted, I don't think you give yourself enough credit either. Now, are you going to kill me or show me a good time?"

I wiggled my eyebrows. "Have you ever heard of being killed from a good time?"

"Hah hah, so funny. But seriously, what are we doing?"

"Can you see?" I asked.

She shook her head. "Not a damn thing, but based on the fact that your eyes are glowing I can assume you can."

"Yes, I can." I said, guiding her around a tree stump.

"Something I hope I learn in the future."

"I'm sure you will. For now, I'll use it to my advantage," Halting just at the tree line where I set up everything, I pulled my hand from hers. "Okay, this will only take a second."

"Is that water? Are we near the ocean?" She asked looking around.

"Shhh, questions will only spoil the surprise."

Reaching into the bag I brought with us, I pulled out what I needed, quickly snapped them, and dropped them at my feet. They landed into the water with a splash.

"What was that?"

"So jumpy, kitten." I tisked.

Closing my eyes, I concentrated on the mass of water in front of me, willing it to wrap around the objects I dropped.

I could do this.

With a smooth breath, I opened my eyes and lifted six glowing orbs out of the lake. The balls of water were each no bigger than a baseball, but they shined brightly against the darkness in varying colors. The balls hovered in the air around my head for a few moments before I held out my hand and made them float over to Atalanta.

"Holy shit," She jumped back as the balls approached her. "What the fuck are those?"

It was at this moment that I realized I never told her about my abilities. Well, that might put a bit of a damper on this.

I laughed it off. "It's okay. It's just water."

She squinted at one of the balls as it hovered closer. "And glow sticks?"

"Yep."

"Oh, thank god." She let out a sigh of relief. "I thought you were about to tell me that they were some sort of water fairy or something."

"That would be way cooler, I think."

"I don't know. Hip, when were you going to tell me that you could control freaking water!?" She poked one of the orbs, her finger going right through it.

I walked back over to Atalanta's position at the tree line. "I'm sorry. I suppose with everything that's going on, I completely forgot."

"So...Ajax is an empath and you can control water. Wait, can everyone control water?" She asked, her eyes wide with excitement.

I shrugged. "I'm pretty sure I'm not the only one, but no, I don't think the others can do this. It's sort of my talent."

"Your talent?"

"Whether you want to admit it, we are magical beings, and magical beings can do magic. We all have talents." I scratched the back of my head. "I'm not really the person to talk about it, though. I really don't know much."

"Because...you were adopted?" she asked hesitantly.

"Yeah, because of that."

She looked away from me and stared up at the floating water in wonder. "Well, I think this is pretty amazing."

"The evening isn't over yet. Come, our little fairy friends are going to be our guides."

I walked next to her as I pushed the orbs ahead as guiding lights through the trees. We didn't go far. Lifting the orbs higher, I used their light to illuminate a plush blanket I laid out in a clearing.

"Oh, Hip..." she breathed out as she squinted in the dim light to see the blanket.

"Stargazing by fairy light sounds like a good idea, don't you think?" I sent the orbs up and deposited the water into bottles I had hung in trees around the clearing.

Their glow was soft as I lead her over to the blanket. "I even have snacks."

She sighed happily and flopped down, her arms spread wide. "This is amazing."

I smiled and joined her. "I'm glad you approve."

She snuggled close into me as we stared up at the stars through the trees. I was lucky that it was a clear night and the stars shone brightly through the trees. I knew I couldn't afford to buy her nice clothes or fancy chocolates, but honestly, I was okay with that. Her face looked so content in this moment.

"Aren't you supposed to be watching the stars?" She asked me after several minutes.

"You are my stars."

TIED TO THE SEA

"Oh my god. Stop, you cheese!" She slapped my arm playfully.

I chuckled. "You can't blame a guy for trying."

"I swear, your romance levels are off the charts. All of you, today, every day since I've woken up. It's almost too much." She said, her gaze turning away from me to look back up at the sky.

"Yeah, I hear men are like that sometimes. Too much."

"It's almost scary."

I was quiet for a minute before saying, "That's what love is like, Atalanta. Overwhelming, scary."

Her eyes snapped back to mine.

"You can't be serious. You can't all love me. We hardly know each other." She said shaking her head.

"You're not wrong, but I can be serious. Do I love you? Perhaps. I don't know, but how I feel about you, how drawn I am to you, it is overwhelming. As for the others, I don't know, but I guess we will have to see, won't we?" I sat up. "As for getting to know each other better."

I reached into the basket I brought and pulled out a white box and a smaller black box. I willed the water back out of one of the bottles and brought it down to light up the boxes I held out to her. Staring at it, Atalanta also sat up, and under the orb's glow she opened the white box. I knew she could read the inscription on the small cake inside the box when she started to tremble.

"You heard me."

"I did. Happy Birthday, Atalanta."

Chapter Fifteen

ATALANTA

I shuddered as I stared at the beautifully written words inscribed onto what was clearly a birthday cake.

He had heard me. He knew. Of everything, that was one of the most important things no one was supposed to know. If they knew your birthday, it was easier to trace you, find out your real identity, know who you really were. Track you down.

Did it matter? They already knew so much. They themselves were entrusting me with their secrets.

But if this got out, they could be in danger. He would come. Yet, this was also the sweetest thing any human being had ever done for me. Well, I suppose Hip's lack of humanity held a factor in that.

The warring emotions in me pushed the tears to the surface. I covered my mouth as if it could somehow hold the emotions in.

"Why?"

"Because everyone should celebrate their birthday." He whispered.

"Today isn't my birthday, Hip. It hasn't been in a long time. Atalanta North's birthday is in November."

"No, that file said your birthday is in November. Your birthday is today."

"No! Hip, no one can know!" I clasped his jacket hard and looked up into his eyes. "Hip, no one can know it's my real birthday. Something like that...it could...just, please don't tell anyone!"

"Atalanta, look around. You and I are the only ones here, you don't have to hide. Not from me and not from the others. We aren't going to go around and spill your secrets."

"Why is this so important to you?"

"Beyond the fact that you're supposed to be learning to trust us?" I winced at that but he continued. "I don't know my real birthday, Atalanta. Yeah, every year my parents bring out a cake and there's singing and birthday wishes, but deep down, I know it's not really my birthday. It's a lie. Celebrating a fake day? I know what that's like."

He poked my chest near my heart. "I know that it hurts. So I'm doing something about it. We don't need to tell the others right now, though you should consider it, but for now, you and I are going to celebrate your birthday like we should have been doing."

He pulled out a lighter from his pocket and lit a candle that he placed in the birthday cake and began to sing happy birthday to me. It was really sweet, but I broke into a fit of giggles. My golden boy was a horrible singer. I blew out the candle all the same, though.

"Sooo, what did you wish for?" He asked as he pulled out forks for us.

"Not telling. You're not supposed to tell your wishes."

Just before I was about to scoop up a bite of cake, he held it out of my reach. "Well, that's not fair. I brought the cake."

"And it's my wish!"

He scoffed and held the cake further away. Pulling out the lighter, he quickly relit the candle before blowing it out again. "I wished for you to tell me your wish. So now you have to tell me or it won't come true."

"Telling me your wish makes the wish null and void." Lunging forward, I successfully sunk my fork into the cake and pulled away a huge bite.

Quickly, I shoved the bite into my mouth. My cheeks puffed out like a chipmunk as I chewed the giant piece of cake. It was delicious. Not just plain vanilla or chocolate. Was that raspberry?

Swallowing, I looked over to Hip, who was watching me with a heated gaze. "Did you make this?"

"Not this time." His hand came up and used his thumb to wipe away some chocolate off my cheek.

I watched as he stuck his finger into his mouth and licked it clean. I watched in fascination as he slowly pulled his finger out of his mouth and used his own fork to get a bite of cake. He ate it before scooping another bite and holding the fork out for me. Leaning forward, I slowly took it into my mouth and savored the sweet chocolate and raspberry flavor before pulling back. Keeping his eyes locked on me, he licked the fork clean before putting it down. The wicked grin he was giving me sent shivers over my entire body.

"Now, time to open your birthday present." He held out the little black box that I had forgotten about.

Taking it, I slowly opened it, the glowing orbs once again floating in close so that my eyes could clearly see its contents.

"Is that a snow drop?" I asked pulling out the necklace.

It was a pendant, a flower encased in resin and polished until it shined. It was beautiful.

Hip nodded. "Ajax helped me make it. So, technically, it's a gift from him as well."

"How could you have made this so quickly?"

"I asked him to do it after our first date."

Our first date? The one where he took me up to see one of his family's orchards after that fight? The memory was fuzzy, but I did remember the little patch of snowdrops.

I stared at the necklace. Hip knew they were my favorite flower and had this made for me. Slowly I hooked it around my neck and stared lovingly at the little flower which would now be preserved, frozen in time for eternity.

"I love it." I said, looking back up at Hip.

"I'm glad." His smile was so genuine, the rare golden article.

Standing, Hip held his hand out to me. I took it and he pulled me swiftly to my feet and flush against his body. I stared into those blazing eyes of his that looked a silver blue in this light.

TIED TO THE SEA

Kiss me.

Damn it, Hip, kiss me.

He didn't, though. Instead, he pulled his phone out of his pocket and began to play music. The two of us swayed slowly together. His hands on my hips, mine placed firmly on his chest. The singer spoke of dancing with his lover in the dark and how perfect she looked, despite her being a mess. Hip's eyes told me that he believed the same thing.

He made me feel so cherished. They all had.

"Today was more than I could hope for. Actually, considering I've never been in an actual relationship, it's hard to imagine that this is real." I said, laying my head against his chest.

"Now who's being the cheesy one?" He whispered.

I grinned. "I can have my moments too, you know."

"I'm glad I could be here to witness it," His chest rumbled with a chuckle as he took my hand and guided me into a twirl before bringing me close to him again.

God, his laugh was so sexy. Was he just going to dance with me?

I would have expected him to make some sort of move by now. No, I scolded myself. Hip wasn't like that. He came off as carefree and a bit of a goof, but he was probably the most romantic of all five of the men that I was slowly giving my heart too. He wouldn't make a move unless I gave him permission.

Before I could give it a second thought, I lifted myself up to close those few inches between us and brushed my lips against his. Just a small peck, an invitation, one that for a moment I thought he might not take when he went still and sighed. My heart soared when his hand came up to meet my cheek and pulled me closer, sliding his lips tentatively against mine.

It was the sweetest kiss I'd ever had.

My attention was pulled away when I heard a splashing sound and the clearing grew darker. Breaking our kiss, I saw that the amazing fairy balls that Hip had made float around us as we danced fell apart, falling to the ground with a splash, reduced to puddles of water and glow sticks once again. Before I could comment, Hip pulled my mouth back to his, more heated than before.

Desperate to touch him, I ran my fingers through his hair, which was like the softest silk. A part of me wanted to tug his hair, demand for him to unleash the tension I felt building in his body, to turn this sweet romantic kiss into a frantic one. I was curious to see what Hip would do when he lost control. As if the universe sensed my plans, Hip's phone began to ring, causing him to break our kiss again too soon and pull away.

Pulling his phone out of his back pocket, he answered. "Ye-llow?"

"Hey, I know Percy said she was fine with you, but it's past midnight. Can you bring Atalanta back? She has school in the morning."

It was Jason. I smiled. He was so cute with his worry. Remembering what he told me before, I took the phone from Hip and whispered calmly, "Hey Fishy Fish."

"Are you okay? You sound a little winded."

I smiled up at Hip. "Yeah, I'm fine. We'll head back soon, okay?"

"Okay. And tell Hip he should have just woken us up and told us he was taking you. Waking up with you gone was... unpleasant."

"I'm sorry, Jason." I frowned, feeling bad that I hadn't told him myself.

"Not your fault. I'll see you when you get in."

"You sound like my Dad," I said.

"Ew." Jason gagged over the phone. "Would your dad threaten you with eating your chocolate?"

I raised and eyebrow. "Is that a euphemism for my body?"

"No, it means he's literally eating the chocolate he got you." Percy called from somewhere in the background.

"Yeah. That's totally what I meant." Jason said, sounding sarcastic.

"Leave my chocolate alone, you dick!" I hung up on him and turned back to Hip. "Okay, Hip. Let's go before he eats all of it."

Hip grumbled something under his breath. He brought me back in for a quick kiss before taking my hand and walking me back through the forest towards the cabin.

His body, flush against mine on the motorcycle, was so warm in the cool evening.

The rest of the night was utter chaos as Hip and Jason had decided that playing board games and staying up till dawn was the best way to spend our time. Damn, were those two competitive; the monopoly board got knocked over more times than I could count. Percy sat quietly in the corner reading his book, but Theseus and Ajax joined in on a few of the games, getting swept up in the yelling and merriment. I ended up falling asleep in Ajax's lap just before the sun rose.

"Hey, Sleeping Beauty, it's time to wake up."

"Go suck on a nut," I grumbled as I snuggled into the warm bed.

"Come, little one. You are the one who insisted on going to school today." My bed said as it too tried to nudge me awake.

I growled. "That was before Tweedle Dee and Tweedle Dum demanded for us to play monopoly for the 3rd time."

"Name calling is rude, Atalanta."

I cracked open my eyes to see Jason and Hip eating at the kitchen table, already dressed and ready for school. Had they slept at all?

I was still in Ajax's lap on the couch while Theseus stood in front of us with a welcoming smile. I didn't see Percy.

"Yeah, you could have simply said no," Hip said as he bit into his toast.

"I was on a winning streak," I pouted.

"You were not!" Both Hip and Jason shouted.

I pressed my cheek into Ajax's chest. "Ugh, no loud noises before food."

"Percy made you a breakfast sandwich before he left. He also wished you the best of luck at school today." Theseus said as he held out a wrapped sandwich.

I took it, grateful to have something to fill my empty stomach and scarfed it down.

"Are you sure you want to go, Atalanta?" Jason walked over and crouched in front of me. "If I'm being honest, there is going to be a lot of staring and people asking questions. Especially with Hip and I being gone, Davie and Margo are saying there are a ton of rumors flying around."

"The curse of small towns, I suppose," I mused, putting on a brave face despite the shiver that ran up my spine.

Ajax pet the top of my head.

"What are some of the rumors?" Hip asked as he cleaned up their breakfast.

Jason pulled out his phone and stared at the screen. "Margo said that it's mostly that either one of us had eloped with her, and the other is too embarrassed to show their face. Davie said he heard one that said Hip and I fought over you and after winning, one of us ran off with you after burning the other's body."

"That's stupid." I rolled my eyes. "People really don't have anything better to do with their lives?"

"It's funny, the things humans come up with," Theseus snorted as he looked over Jason's shoulder at the text messages.

"It's getting late." Ajax poked me in the side, encouraging me to get up.

"Right. Get dressed, we need to get going."

Jason and Hip played rock paper scissors to decide who took me to class. Jason won. I wondered if the guys were just going to make all their decisions based off of rock paper scissors.

Ajax helped put the bandages on my eye and hands. We had decided that for now I would wear them until I could control my shifts completely and look into colored contacts. Until then, we would keep with the story that I had been in a boating accident.

A half hour later, Hip, Jason, and I were pulling into the school's parking lot. Students were hanging out next to their cars, chatting before the bell rang. I could already see several of them staring as they realized whose car it was.

"Ready?" Jason asked me.

I could do this. It was just school.

I nodded, grabbed my backpack, and stepped out of the car. Hip, who had ridden behind us on his bike, winked at me and held out his hand.

Just before I was about to take it, however, Jason stopped me, his hand against my risen one.

I gave him a questioning look and he explained. "They think that the two of us are dating. Holding his hand will cause more rumors to spread."

My frown deepened and I quickly glanced around. The number of students blatantly staring had risen, and my heightened hearing picked up on several conversations about us.

'Look, they're all back. What happened to Atalanta?'

'Did you see? She was about to hold his hand. Are they dating? I thought she was with Jason.'

'I thought for sure Monroe had killed Clark.'

'It looks more like Atalanta got in the middle of their fight.'

'She looks terrible.'

I looked at my free hand. I did look pretty bad with all of these bandages on, but at least the tips of my fingers looked like normal human nails.

I smiled. "Let's go inside."

The guys nodded, and with my hand in Jason's, we walked to the other side of the lot and through the front doors.

I tried to keep myself from pressing into Jason's side as I felt so many eyes on me. God, I hated school. Why was I here again? Dad. That's right. He wants me to graduate. It should be considered illegal for a now twenty-two year old to be in fucking high school.

I took a deep breath and muttered, "Atalanta North, age 17."

"Atalanta. We can go home if you want." Hip said, looking concerned.

I shook my head. "No. I need to do this. I'll be okay."

"If you say so." Hip didn't look convinced, and neither did Jason.

"Can we go see my father after school?" I asked, steering the conversation in a different direction.

"Percy said you said you wanted to go see Clint, remember?" Jason reminded me.

"Oh, yeah."

"Atalanta! Jason!" Someone called. Looking up, I saw two familiar faces coming towards us.

"Davie. Margo."

"Holy shit, Atalanta. You look terrible. Are you okay?" Davie asked. "Jason told us you had gotten into an accident, but we never figured it would be that bad."

"He's right." Margo said as she gently placed her hand on my shoulder. "Are you sure you're okay to be up and walking right now?"

I clenched my jaw and clutched Jason's hand harder. "Yeah, I'm okay. They have me on some pretty good pain meds."

"Ah, good ol' drugs." Davie chuckled.

"Will you be okay getting from class to class? I can help you. Most of our classes are next to each other." Margo offered.

Were they? I never noticed. Or perhaps I forgot.

"It's okay, Margo. I am her official crutch until she gets better." Jason said.

Margo crossed her arms and cocked a brow. "You only just got out of bed yourself, Jason. We wouldn't want her getting sick."

"Well, if he can't do it, then I suppose that job now belongs to me!" Hip grinned and took my arm.

"Seriously?" Margo scoffed. "People will talk more than they already are. Atalanta, please just let me help."

I gaped like a fish, honestly not knowing what to say.

More rumors really wouldn't be ideal, but having Margo escort me...

I looked up at Jason. Why couldn't he do it, exactly? Because he had been sick? I never did ask what he told people about why he had been away.

Jason smiled down at me. "It's okay, Margo. I'm not going to get her sick. Besides, if she does need help walking, I'll be able to support her. I've already got special permission to sit in with her classes anyway."

What? Was that true? Why was I only just hearing about this?

The bell for first period rang.

"It seems that is our cue to go." Davie said, placing a hand on Margo's shoulder. "We'll see you guys at lunch."

Looking back at Davie and Margo, I couldn't help but feel bad at seeing their dejected expressions. I had been taking up a lot of Jason's time, but he was their best friend.

"We should hang out with Davie and Margo tomorrow. Go get some food or something," I whispered to Jason.

"Are you sure?" He asked, eyebrows raised.

"Of course!"

"It's a bit obvious that they make you uncomfortable, or at least Margo does," Hip muttered.

I fiddled with my jacket sleeve. "I like Margo! She's extremely funny and sweet."

"But she still makes you uncomfortable." Jason said.

"Did you really get permission to sit in on my classes? What about your own?" I asked, changing the subject.

He nodded. "For a couple of days. Just to make sure nothing happens. My grades can handle a few more days."

"The senior student council president should set a good example." Hip grinned.

"Exactly, by helping out our newer student, who's now injured, around school." Jason shot back.

"I doubt that's what he meant." I commented.

"Would the fact that the injured student is your girlfriend show favoritism?" Hip pointed out.

Jason growled at him. "Shouldn't you be getting to your own class?"

Hip hummed but continued walking with us. Our pace felt extremely slow, but all too soon we came upon the classroom. My history class was on the smaller side and the 14 pairs of eyes drilled into my skull, just like the first days of entering this school.

I hated so much attention. At least the teacher had yet to arrive and begin the barrage of questions.

With Jason's hand still in mine, I made a point to slowly hobble to the desk. Flopping down into the seat, I looked back up at Jason and Hip, who were standing there watching me as if I were going to suddenly sprout a third eye. I understood their reluctance to leave me alone in public, but I wasn't an invalid.

"You two should get to your own classes."

"But I already made arrangements to sit in with you."

"And I'm...well I don't have an excuse at the moment, but I'm sure I'll come up with something when the teacher asks why I'm here." Hip shrugged.

"I'll be fine." I insisted.

Jason and Hip sported mirrored pouts, which was pretty cute if I was being honest. They didn't understand that I wasn't an invalid. I knew that Jason could easily handle being away from me an hour or so at a time. I had to wonder why I didn't feel the separation as badly as he did.

"Please," I whispered, giving them a pout of my own.

Hip stared at me for a long moment before sighing and putting his hand on Jason's shoulder. "Let's go."

"But—"

"Coach will make us do extra strength training if we miss roll call."

They had the same first period? What sort of class did strength training?

Finally, as the two of them left, the teacher entered. It was an older woman with pursed lips and beady eyes. She reminded me a lot of my math teacher, actually. I wondered if they were possibly siblings. If it were true, Mrs. Write was far kinder, if just stern. When she saw me, she asked if I was well enough to focus on her lesson.

After telling her I was, she nodded and simply said. "If that changes, don't bother raising your hand, simply go to the nurse's office. Much less paperwork for me if you collapse there."

My first couple of classes went by at a snail's pace. The only bright side was seeing the boys between classes, showing up at the classroom door just as the bell rang to escort me to my next class. Margo and Davie were there as well, adding to the ever entertaining banter that Jason and Hip provided.

Now in third period study hall, I was able to relax a tad as surprisingly all the other students were so focused on studying for the SAT and ACT that they didn't bombard me with tons of questions.

I disregarded my giant pile of make-up work and skimmed my eyes over the crowd, wondering exactly how many of them were Mer. How many were there in Argos?

One thing that certainly didn't go unnoticed by me were those damn water bottles. Finally, the mystery of why so many carried around large jugs of water was revealed. Jason hadn't been carrying one around today that I had noticed, and neither had Hip. If I remembered correctly, they told me that it...

I sat up in my seat, my mental musings halted as I refocused on the notebook in front of me.

The water bottles. Why was it that they needed the bottles?

I knew someone had told me, but I couldn't remember what they had said.

I gripped my head and tried to focus, force myself to remember, but it was a blur.

This was stupid!

What else was I forgetting? When you forget something, it's not like you know you forgot it. It was just poof, gone, and you don't realize the information you wanted isn't stored in your head anymore until you actually needed it!

At this point, my faulty memory was getting more frustrating than anything else.

I wrote a note down in my notebook about the water bottles and hopefully, I would remember to ask Jason at lunch.

At the sound of a throat being cleared, I glanced up from my notebook and met the eyes of the girl in front of me.

"Are you okay?" she whispered.

I nodded.

"It's just that you looked pretty constipated. Do you need me to help you to the bathroom?"

"No, that's kind of you to offer though. Just a hard math problem." I said, going with the first thing that popped into my head.

"Okay. If you need anything, I'd be happy to help."

"Thanks, um...?" I reached, wondering if this girl had always sat next to me in study hall.

"Kayla!" She exclaimed, offering me her hand.

Slowly, I took her hand to shake then quickly let go. "Thanks, Kayla. I'm Atalanta."

She giggled. "I know, you've been the talk of the school for a while now."

"Oh."

"Are you healing up okay?" She asked. "I heard you got into an accident."

I blinked, taken aback by the genuine question whereas all of the other students so far had been much more shallow in their line of questioning. Had I really tried to elope with one of the guys? Was I dating Hip or Jason? Was it true my sister was dead? It was nice to know they weren't all self-centered teenagers.

I smiled. "It was an accident, but despite the bandages I'm healing up quite alright."

"That's good to hear."

I studied the girl. I believe she was in my gym class as well, which means she had more than likely seen what I had done to those girls several weeks ago. She didn't appear scared, though. I wasn't surprised we'd never spoken before, as it was easier to stay inconspicuous when I didn't make any close connections. I had failed pretty miserably at that this time around.

Could this be my chance to actually make a friend?

I was not going anywhere any time soon, but...no, even if I couldn't leave, that didn't mean that *he* wasn't still out there looking for us.

I gave Kayla a muttered thanks and went back to pretending to do homework.

Chapter Sixteen

JASON

Just two more minutes. That's, like, ten seconds twelve times? Easy peasy.

I couldn't stand another second listening to Mr. Stevens ramble on. What did they call it? Senioritis? I suppose I could blame my distracted mind on that, but the obvious answer was being separated from Atalanta was deeply affecting me. It had only been forty minutes, and already I had been starting to feel too hot and my muscles were beginning to feel achy. A feeling that had been my constant companion for the last few days.

I could admit to myself that leaving her with Percy and then Theseus was somehow easier than leaving her completely alone at school, but it seemed there was only so much my instincts could handle yesterday. Before I knew it I was driving over to where I knew Theseus had taken Atalanta on her date. Did I feel bad about interrupting them? Maybe, but by the point I was walking into that theater, the pain, the need to be near her was crippling.

It wasn't like I could push her to be around me all the time, though. Atalanta was her own person and I couldn't very well be her shadow for the rest of her life.

I would just have to learn how to deal.

A minute, twenty-four seconds.

Train myself to deal with the pain.

Tapping my pencil on the desk, I glanced over to Hip, who had his nose in a D & D manual through the whole lesson. Completely ignoring Mr. Stevens when he would berate him. I doubted the book was that interesting as he hadn't changed the page at all, his eyes glazed over. I had caught him glancing up at the clock several times.

Did he feel the same thing I did?

I'd have to ask him about it when I got a moment.

At the glorious sound of the bell, I sprang out of my seat and tried my best not to full out run for the door. Hip was right with me. The two of us were out the door in seconds and heading down the hall to the room we knew Atalanta was in.

My shoulders relaxed when she came through the doorway, a small smile on her face.

Giving her my own smile, I held out my hand for her to take. When her skin touched mine, it was like a hit of my favorite drug, all my muscles releasing tension as a tingle raced up my arm.

I noticed that her own shoulders fell and her smile grew wider as she stared up at us.

She turned that smile to Hip and I tightened my lips so the slight disappointment that bubbled up in my chest didn't show on my face. It was getting a bit easier, I guess, and maybe one day I'd be okay with sharing that smile.

The three of us met up with Davie and Margo and made our way to our usual spot, Hip breaking off as he usually did to go buy food from the cafeteria. Before my ass hit the bench I realized that Atalanta and I hadn't brought lunch either.

I stood back up. "I forgot to pack lunch, I'll be right back."

I looked to Atalanta, silently asking if she wanted me to get her anything. Her eyes flicked over to Margo and Davie, who were swapping their lunches, and back to mine before giving the smallest of nods. I mouthed 'Do you want to come?' and was surprised when she shook her head, sporting a smile.

Looking closely, I could see she was fidgeting with the sleeves of her jacket but otherwise she looked confident. My brave girl.

I would need to find out what about Margo made her nervous. Well, there were a lot of things about Atalanta North that I still had to discover, like her real name for example. As curious as I was, it wasn't smart to push her on it. Luckily we had all the time in the world now.

I didn't venture into the cafeteria often; it was crowded and the eyes on me were numerous.

Smile, just smile.

I waved to some of the guys who were on the swim team.

"Hey, Monroe! Come over and sit with us!"

I shook my head. "Sorry, Brett, I'm just popping in for some food."

Getting in line, I looked over at Hip who was a few people ahead of me. "Seems we all forgot to pack something."

He shrugged and gave up his spot to stand next to me. "I usually just buy."

"Wouldn't it be cheaper to just bring something from home?"

"Too much of a hassle. There's usually a ton of chores I have to do in the morning. Besides," he actually broke eye contact with me. "I'm on the school's meal plan."

I frowned. I knew he wasn't super well off, but to be on a meal plan? Those were also pretty restrictive, on top of the fact that he had been giving Atalanta lunches before. Knowing him, he was probably charming the lunch lady, but still.

"You want me to get us all lunch today?" I offered.

Hip glared at me, going on the defensive. "I think I'm good."

"I just know it would be easier on you. I don't mind, seriously."

He stepped forward, moving with the line and grabbing a tray. "What's your angle, Jason?"

"No angle, seriously. Think of it as an olive branch. You were right the other day, we've spent years at each other's throats, for what? Because we didn't know the other's life?"

"But also because you're an asshole."

I chuckled. "You're not much better. You're just good at making it seem innocent. I know what you had Theseus do to those girls who hurt Atalanta, and remember that girl you manipulated into giving you the turtle? That was a pretty dick move."

"Those *girls* deserved it, and did you see Atalanta's face? She loved that turtle." He rolled his eyes and grabbed a carton of chicken tenders.

I gritted my teeth, thinking back to the attack on Atalanta.

"You aren't wrong about that." I admitted, grabbing my own carton of chicken tenders as well as a burger. "But you can't deny that leading on that girl just to get a stuffed animal was a dick move. I may have my moments, but it's never to screw with someone intentionally like you do.

Hip halted the line and turned to me. "Listen, you're right."

I blinked, surprised at his sudden admission.

He continued, "Will I stop being who I am to please you? Hell no. However, I can see you're trying to be better for Atalanta's sake, and for that, I accept your olive branch.

With a shit eating grin, Hip took everything that had been on his food tray and placed it on mine before stepping out of the line and walking away.

"Well, that was odd." I mumbled and then looked around, realizing that every person in the line had listened to our entire conversation.

"Eavesdropping is rude." I said to no one in particular.

I grabbed three bottles of juice, two cookies, a brownie, and a third helping of chicken tenders. With the tray overloaded with food, I quickly paid for everything and met up with Hip. I smiled at Brett and the swim team guys, avoiding the eyes of a group of freshmen girls who were ogling the two of us.

Several people tried to stop us by starting up conversations, but I just smiled and brushed them off as politely as possible.

Atalanta was laughing at something Davie had said when we came up with the food. I placed the heavy tray down and distributed the food between the three of us, then handed the two cookies over to Davie.

Davie took the cookies and looked at the giant chocolate chunks in it with reverence. "Bless your soul."

"You really shouldn't feed his sweet tooth," Margo chastised.

"Sugar is the gift of the gods, Margo. How could I deprive him of their blessing?" I asked.

"Easily," she snatched the cookies out of Davies hand.

The puppy pout Davie gave her was pathetic, but it certainly worked as she gave him back one cookie. Seeing the smile on Atalanta's face as she watched the two of them bicker was like seeing a flicker of light in a dark cave, and it was contagious as my cheeks tightened from my own genuine smile.

Lunch was...nice. I had missed my friends, they always made me feel grounded. They were human with normal human problems. Most of the time I envied that, but it was also pleasant, pretending that the most important thing in my life right now was supposed to be my grades, and prom.

Or Atalanta stealing my brownie.

I looked at her in horror as she shoved the last of *my* brownie into her mouth. "Hey!"

"You left it unattended, therefore it was up for grabs."

"You little sneak," I lunged for her and began to tickle her sides.

Oh, God, her snorts were adorable, but she squirmed like an eel. With all her jerking, the two of us ended up tumbling off the bench in a fit of giggles.

"Jason!" Margo shouted in alarm as she rushed around the bench towards Atalanta. "You could have hurt her!"

Atalanta froze next to me at Margo's quick approach. It was subtle and I probably wouldn't have noticed it if I hadn't been holding her, as within a split second she relaxed and grinned up at Margo.

"I'm okay. Remember, they gave me some very nice drugs." Atalanta reassured her.

"He should still be careful with you." Margo held out her hand for Atalanta to take.

She hesitated, staring at Margo's hand, and I made the quick decision to distract from that hesitation by taking the outstretched hand for myself.

Hopping to my feet, I leaned down to scoop Atalanta into my arms. "You're right, Margo. I must take care of my princess. Or better yet, a king must always see to his queen."

"Oh, so now you've moved up the ladder of self-importance," Hip snickered.

"Jason, I'm fine." Atalanta insisted as she squirmed, trying to get out of my hold.

"Oh, I know you are," I leaned in to whisper into her ear. "But let me do this, to appease Margo?"

She did a quick glance over to Margo who was staring back at us, clearly worried before looking back to me and rolling her eyes. "Fine. For Margo."

"Thank you."

We decided to head to class before the lunch bell rang to avoid the rush of students, me carrying my precious cargo the whole way. Atalanta surprised me by asking Margo and Davie directly about hanging out the next day. They agreed and Margo began to gush excitedly.

At the door to English class, Davie gave Margo a sweet kiss before leaving us for his own class but Hip lingered, his eyes locked onto Atalanta, no doubt not wanting to leave her once again.

"Can you get the door for us and help me get her into her seat?" I said.

He perked up a bit and opened the door for us. Walking into the classroom, it was empty as I expected beyond someone standing in front of the white board. A familiar someone who wasn't Damon.

I nearly dropped Atalanta as my body froze, stomach sinking. "Uncle Calder."

Calder turned from the white board, giving me a cheshiresque grin. "Why, Jason. I wasn't aware that you would be in one of my classes."

"What? Y-your classes? Where's Damon?" I stammered.

"On sick leave. It's a good thing I was in town to act as his substitute. No one knows the English language better than I."

His gray eyes slithered over our group before landing on Atalanta.

Immediately, a shiver wracked Atalanta's body. I looked down at her, her gaze locked onto my uncle. Her face slack, eyes haunted.

"Red..." She rasped out.

"Atalanta?" Hip said, his hand reaching out to stroke her cheek.

She blinked, light filtering back in as she shook her head as if dislodging cobwebs. "Yes? Sorry, I spaced out for a second."

Looking back over to my uncle, Atalanta cautiously said, "It's good to see you again, sir."

"Likewise, child. How are you feeling?"

"I'm doing all right."

"That is good, I assumed with the way my nephew was holding you, you might be having some trouble with your injury." His eyes slid up to meet mine.

"Just a precaution. But I'm okay." She tapped my shoulder, asking for me to put her down.

No.

I refused to put her down. Breaking eye contact with my uncle, I carried her over to her seat, waiting for Hip to pull out the chair before placing her into it and moving to a position that would block her from Calder's burning gaze.

He couldn't know.

She was Theseus's cousin.

She had been in a boating accident and was here to recover.

I looked over to Hip and gave him a stern glare. That was the story we would be sticking with.

As the bell that signaled the end of first lunch rang, Hip looked even more reluctant to leave than before. He actually began to slide into a seat as if he belonged in the class.

Calder strolled over to his desk and lifted a clipboard. "I don't believe you're in this period, Mr. Clark. I wouldn't want you to miss your own class."

"I just thought —" Hip began, but Calder interrupted him.

"Run along, Mr. Clark."

There was a push in my uncle's words, power that forced Hip out of the chair and quickly walking out the door, his muscles tensed.

I glanced over at Margo, who looked a little confused but otherwise wasn't saying anything about the tense aura that was hanging in the air. Atalanta's body was locked up as she sat in her seat, watching my uncle.

Calder didn't say anything else as the rest of the students shuffled in. On the board he had written in big letters:

MR. MONROE

I had to stop myself from rolling my eyes. I wondered what Calder was getting at, taking on the human name of my father. Was it to laugh at me? I would have thought it would have disgusted him to do such a thing.

Margo leaned over and whispered. "Is that the uncle that your family has you go visit every summer?"

I nodded.

Every summer since I had been born, the elders and council deemed it necessary that I left behind the human world to visit the Mer city of Anthans. The city that my mother was from. As it was only right to cleanse me of the filth of the humans and teach me the ways of the Mer. It was only the right of maternal progeny that allowed my mother to keep me up on the surface while human school was in session.

I wasn't the only kid who'd been forced to visit the city, and because of...reasons...my parents weren't allowed to come with. As the next of kin, Calder had been the one to watch over me in those months.

I felt a hand slide into mine, the warmth and tingles comforting. I looked away from Calder towards Atalanta, who looked just as nervous as I felt.

What was Calder doing here, and what had he done with my cousin?

As soon as the bell rang to begin class, Calder introduced himself as the substitute and then without letting in any room for question, immediately began a lesson on *Memento Mori* by Jonathan Nolan.

"A fascinating story about a man named Earl, who's hunting down the person who killed his wife. You might think this would be a standard detective story, however, Earl has a very interesting form of amnesia that was caused by the attack. Earl can't remember more than a few minutes of information at a time. He remembers all of his life up until the attack, but from there, he must leave notes for himself. Like things he had done that day or people he had met."

"Like the guy from that Adam Sandler movie. Ten Second Tom." One of the students commented.

"Exactly," Calder puts the book down and looks at the class. "Now, like with all literature, there is hidden meaning, but before we speculate, what does the story show us? As it is told all from the perspective of a person who must write down notes to remember if he had even brushed his teeth that morning."

As per usual in any classroom, there was a deadening silence before someone slowly rose their hand, that someone being Atalanta.

"Yes, Ms..." He prompted for her name.

"...North."

"Yes, Ms. North."

"The story brings into question the reliability of the narrator." She answered.

"Exactly, please explain for the class."

"Um, well the narrator is our gateway into a story, be it in first, second or third person, we trust the narrator to navigate the story for us, show us what happens, but when you have a story where the narrator is proven to have some sort of condition, like perhaps mental illness or..." She hesitated and I could see her skin pale. "Memory loss. How can we, the readers, trust that we are seeing the story as a whole, with the real events? While it might be true from the narrator's perspective, there could be parts of the story that are distorted or missing."

Calder nodded. "That is correct. In this instance, if Earl leaves notes for himself, who's to say that someone can't slip in and write whatever they wished? How can we trust anything that Earl tells us about his story? A lesson to keep in mind for more than just literature, dear students. Believe what you will when people tell you things, but always look at things from multiple angles so you can gain your own truth."

He locked eyes with me. "Because you never know if the person telling you things is as reliable as they seem."

I clenched my fist.

Chapter Seventeen

ATALANTA

There was something, *something* nagging at the back of my mind. The stupid fog was so heavy, but I had a vague memory. Something Percy had said. Had he said that Calder had come to see us that night on the beach?

No.

I think he had said he...interrupted us.

I couldn't fucking remember, though. So frustrating.

And it only became worse at Calder's question on the story. Was I no different from Earl? Did Calder know about what was going on?

Too many questions with no answers. I hated when I couldn't get answers.

I did know one thing, at least. I couldn't trust Calder. He reminded me of a snake who was just waiting for the right opportunity to strike. His eyes on me made my skin crawl, and it was clear by Jason's reaction that Calder wasn't the world's best uncle.

This class couldn't end soon enough.

Calder has us go down the line and read a passage from the story before we opened up into a discussion about what we thought. I kept silent, watching Calder as he charmed the students. By the end of the lesson, the students—especially the girls—were putty in his hands, happily accepting the homework he assigned.

Nothing like the disrespect that students so often showed substitutes.

When the bell rang, I snagged my bag and stood to file out with the rest of the students.

"Jason, I would like a word." Calder said.

I froze and looked back at Jason, who was still in his seat and sitting so still that he could have been a statue. When I moved to sit back down to wait for him, he shot me a look and then nodded towards the door.

He didn't want me to wait, but I didn't want to leave him behind.

Sitting back down in my chair, I gave Jason a defiant glare and crossed my arms over my chest. He sighed in response, his head drooping down before standing and facing his uncle.

"How can I help you, Uncle Calder?"

"I simply wanted to speak to my nephew. Catch up and all that." Calder approached Jason and gave him a hug so awkward that it could have rivaled Lord Voldemort's.

Jason gave him a tight smile and hugged him back. "I have to get to my next class. Perhaps we can do this another time?"

Calder rolled his eyes and stepped back. "I've never understood your desire for this, human education. It's not as if you learn anything of value. So I must wonder why it is more important than catching up with your family."

To my surprise, Jason didn't respond to this. He simply gave a small bow. "Forgive me, Uncle. I would be happy to spend time with you."

Calder's eyes slid to me. "Will you be staying, child?"

"She will not." Jason said before I could respond.

"You should let her answer. As royalty, she is above you." Calder said.

Royalty?! The fuck did he mean by royalty? There wasn't a royal bone in my body, though Cal would have thought herself a queen. Did this have something to do with us telling Calder I was Theseus's cousin?

I looked over to Jason, who met my gaze, giving such a minimal shake of his head that I could have imagined it. He didn't want me to reveal anything, but that didn't mean I couldn't try to take advantage of what I just learned.

I took a deep breath and straightened my shoulders.

"Jason was right, we should head to our next class. Besides," I tilted my head towards the door. "Students will be coming in for your next lesson."

Calder's smile fell and his jaw clenched. "Of course. I shouldn't keep you."

"Thank you, sir."

"I'll see you soon, Uncle."

Together, Jason and I hurried out of the room.

"Do you know why he's here, Jason?"

"No idea." He turned to me and clasped my shoulders. "Are you okay? You seemed pretty freaked out earlier."

I bit my lip. "Your uncle showed up the other night when I went for my swim."

His eyes went wide before he straightened, looked around and then dragged me off away from the students and into the men's restroom. There were several guys in there, but Jason gave them all a friendly smile.

"Finish up and get out." He said simply.

I felt the anger and power behind the words, compelling all the humans to leave. And they did, doing a little jump, zipping up, and walking out with blank looks on their faces, no questions asked.

One guy simply rolled his eyes and took his time finishing up before swaggering out. "You could have said please."

Taken aback by that, I quickly studied the guy as he walked past, and noticed barely visible gils on the side of his neck. He was also a Mer. I was curious if there was another way I could tell if a person wasn't human. Maybe like an internal antenna or something that pinged me when I was looking at one.

Jason pulled my attention from the guy when he quickly shut the door behind him and locked it.

"Why didn't you tell me about this? What happen?" He hissed.

I hugged myself. "I...I don't remember. Percy only told me when I woke up the next morning. I thought he would have told you. He didn't give me the all of the details, just that Calder showed up and they had some sort of altercation."

Jason paced and ruffled his hair before slamming his fist into one of the stall doors, causing it to slam so hard that the hinges cracked.

I jumped, stepping back until my back was flush against the wall. "Jason!"

He froze and turned to me. His eyes had phased, the dark green spread. Scales rippled across his arms and hands which were tipped with claws. I knew if I wasn't wearing bandages, my own scales would probably be doing the same, my panic responding to his anger.

Jason's body tensed up before he took a deep breath in and exhaled slowly. His features partly shifting back to human, his eyes still alien looking.

"I'm sorry," he whispered, stepping closer and brushing his thumb over my cheek. "I'll text Percy and find out what he knows. For now, try to stay away from my uncle. If he shows up and one of us aren't around, then leave. Call me, or Percy, or one of the others." He ran his hands up and down my arms, as if he were trying to chase away some cold.

I wasn't shaking, was I?

"I get that your uncle's a little…creepy…with issues on personal space, but you make it sound like he's some sort of serial killer or something."

He sighed. "My uncle's complicated, but he can't know that you're a made Mer, and especially not that I was the one turned you."

"Why? It's not forbidden or anything, right? Ajax and your dad were once human." I pointed out.

"Yes, but you're different. You're female." He inhaled and let out a huff. trying to clearly keep calm.

"And?" I pushed.

"And there are several reasons why they would not only want to take you, but also me."

"They?" I frowned. "The pronoun game, Jason. It helps no one."

"The council. Not like the elders of the council here in town, but the council that resides in the nearest Mer city and capital of the northern pacific kingdom of Attica."

I gulped, trying to process the information. "Okay, and the reasons why they would want us?"

"You are not good at just accepting the simple answer, are you?" He chuckled. His smile pulled away some of the apprehension I felt.

I crossed my arms. "I'm a determined woman who likes answers."

His grin grew wider before falling quickly. "When you turn someone, there's a pretty low percentage of successful transition. Most of the time, it just kills the human. That percentage is even lower for females, and considering your circumstances, the fact that you're standing in front of me right now is a miracle, which means you're strong."

"Males of our kind outnumber the females about seven to one, so, women are coveted in our culture. Not only are you female, but a turned female. They will want to collect you, be sure that they can put you within a harem of high breed—of *their* choosing. Pop out the next great generation of Mer. Gods forbid they find out the whole story, they will probably want to lock you up for safe keeping."

Holy fucking crap, really? That can not happen, there was no way I would let some weird medieval council drag me into some dungeon and make me fuck some strangers and pop out babies to grow their population.

"And why would they want you?" I asked, afraid to really know the answer.

He looked away from me and rubbed his shoulder. "For several more reasons. The biggest one being that not only has my mother successfully turned someone, but now that I have as well, they will want—"

"To use you for essentially the same thing. Make more Mer babies, or whatever."

"Basically." He nodded, looking dejected.

I scoffed. "That's pretty sick."

"In their defense, it's a different culture." He mumbled.

"That doesn't excuse turning us into baby machines." I put my hands on my hips and stood on my toes, getting in his face. "We aren't cattle!"

He shook his head and held up is hands in placation. "I'm not trying to excuse it, but not only is their culture different, they are a different species all together."

I leaned back, studying him. "You speak as if you aren't a Mer."

His eyes fell and he pulled away from me. "We should get to class."

I crossed my arms and bit the inside of my cheek, holding back the urge to push him on that. It wasn't really my business, was it? I mean, I guess it should be, since we were in some sort of relationship. But if I made him tell me about himself, I would need to return in kind, right? Everything inside of me rebelled against that idea. Fuck, this was complicated. Were relationships usually this complicated?

I watched Jason's back as he walked away from me towards his next class, his shoulders tense. I wish Cal had prepared me for this somehow. Despite our circumstances, she had never been afraid to date. She would have known what to do in this situation.

The rest of the day carried the feeling of a crackling storm that was just waiting on the edge of a mountain range. Even with the boys' constant presence between classes, the stares and whispered questions from the other students were extremely grating on my nerves. Small towns were always terrible when it came to rumors and muttering stares, but Argos had to be the worst. Or perhaps it was simply because I had been drawing so much more attention to myself.

Hip almost went ballistic when we told him about the incident with Calder after class and what I recalled Percy telling me about what happened the day before yesterday. Hip then told me the same thing Jason had. "Stay away from the creepy uncle". Which didn't help my stress at the thought that Calder could be around any corner. By the end of the day, I understood why people took to alcohol.

The last bell had rung and Jason and I were waiting at his car for Hip. Originally, the plan was for Jason to take me straight to Clint after school, but that was before we realized that Hip's last class of the day was English Lit. So there we were, on our toes, waiting for something.

"He's late." I whispered.

"Just give him one more minute, and we can go in."

Luckily, Hip came storming out right after the words left Jason's lips, looking agitated. "The fucker held me up after class. Wanted to know if I understood the lecture. Utter bullshit. I'm surprised he even knows human literature. I would have taken him for a xenophobe."

"Are you okay?" Jason asked.

Hip wrapped his arms around me and hummed. "I am now."

I chuckled and hugged him back. We were snuggled close for a few moments before Jason joined. Walking up behind me, he wrapped his arms around the both of us.

Hip growled. "This isn't a group hug, Monroe."

"It is, now."

Hip grumbled something under his breath but I couldn't hear it smooshed between the two of them.

"Think of it as payback, Clark. You have to learn how to share." Jason teased.

"Dick."

Jason's chest vibrated with laughter before he finally let go. "Alright, Princess. I believe it's time to hop in your chariot and allow me to wish you off to meet one of your soldiers."

Hip, who was still holding me, looked down and pouted. "But I wanna drive you."

"It's going to start raining soon. She shouldn't be on the back of your bike in the cold rain."

"I have a jacket for her. Besides, I think a bike ride is exactly what she needs."

I rolled my eyes. "What is it with you men and talking around women? Hip, I would love to ride your bike if you've got a jacket. Jason's right, it might start raining soon."

"Not might, it will. In about two minutes."

I glanced over to Jason, who wasn't even looking at the sky. "That's a pretty accurate prediction."

"Didn't we tell you? Jason is a weatherman," Hip said, his tone mocking.

I cocked a brow. "Like, you study the weather?"

"I can sense it. It's my special skill."

I tried not to snort, as he didn't seem all that proud of his skill. Remembering Hip's ability with water, I told myself to ask them in detail about what it meant to have special skills.

"Well, that's a pretty useful gift," I smiled before walking up to quickly kiss his cheek. "If you're always right, we better get going, then. I'll meet you there."

Jason pouted at me before giving Hip a stern look. "Ride safe. We are heading to the inn where he's staying."

Hip rolled his eyes, pulled a brand new green leather jacket out of his backpack and held it out to me. I swapped it out for the one that Theseus had got me yesterday, handing that one and my bag over to Jason to take with him. The long sleeved under armor I was wearing cooled instantly in the air, but it felt nice. Not having to wear so many layers to stay warm was extremely convenient. Today I had only wore the new jacket and the under armor, whereas normally I'd have on a good four layers.

Hopping on the back of the bike, I hugged Hip tight around the middle and squealed as we took off.

Jason had been correct; roughly two minutes into our ride to the inn, it had started raining, just a light drizzle. The jacket Hip had gotten me had kept my torso nice and dry.

I wondered where he had gotten the money for it. I had guessed he wasn't too much better off than I had been. I hope he wasn't wasting his savings on me. I'd have to talk to him about it later; maybe he would let me pay him back. If I remembered.

Luckily, it didn't take us long to reach our destination. Hip had been right, the ride helped ease away some of my tension.

The building, like most of the town, was on the disheveled side. The wood looked as if it had seen better days. The parking lot cement was cracked and there were several pot holes littering the pavement. There was a sign out front advertising that they would be remodeling soon, thanks to the new town 'face lift'. Whatever that meant. I guess I had noticed that some of the other buildings around town had begun to look nicer since I had arrived. Though, it wasn't tourist season, so I wondered where they were getting the money.

The inside of the inn was really cozy and quite nice looking as compared to the outside. In what looked like the lobby area, a bright fire had been lit in the corner of the room and there were several large, cozy chairs that surrounded it in a half circle. The floor and walls were made of wood, similar to the outside of the building, but the wood in here looked new and gleamed in the fire's flickering light. It was welcoming and comforting. The front desk attendant even offered us cookies.

I had other things to focus on. I took a deep breath and walked with Jason and Hip into the inn and followed them towards a door that was labeled 221B.

I looked over my shoulder at the other two. "I think I should do this alone."

"I don't like the idea of leaving you alone with this guy." Jason said and Hip nodded in agreement.

"He's...well, he's sort of our handler. He's just as uncomfortable with your presence. Wait back downstairs and I'll call you if I need you."

The two of them reluctantly turned and walked back down the stairs to sit with the front desk attendant and her cookies.

Once they were out of my line of vision, I knocked on the door.

Thanks to my new heightened hearing, I heard Clint in the bathroom, and at the sound of the knock he cursed and fumbled for his pants before tip-toeing into the room.

Ew, he didn't flush the toilet. Wait, did he just grab a gun?

"Clint," I called. "It's me."

"Chocolate," He called back.

"Rainbows," I replied.

Clint opened the door, shirtless, his slacks hanging loose around his waist. There was a smell on him that I had never noticed before. Ajax had mentioned to me that Clint had a strong scent of gun powder, I wondered if that was what I was smelling. I hadn't noticed it last time, but I supposed my senses had gotten stronger the longer I'd been awake.

"Atty, come in." He backed away from the door, letting me pass before he leaned forward to check the hall and quickly shut the door.

I noticed how he kept his hand on the gun that he held behind his back.

Once he shut the door, he turned and looked me over, his expression intense as always. "How are you feeling?"

"I'm doing much better today, thank you."

"You look better. Sorry we haven't met sooner, but...you know."

I nodded, pretending I knew what Theseus had told him.

"Food poisoning is a bitch," He sighed.

I bit my lip to keep from smiling. Food poisoning?

"Please, sit down." He gestured to the bed next to me while he sat down in a chair.

I precariously perched myself on the edge of the bed and waited for Clint to say something. My father had always been the one to really handle the Bureau directly. While I had talked to our handlers plenty of times, I had never been the one in charge.

"So, what's your next move?" Clint started.

"I honestly have no idea." My shoulders slumped. "I can't do much with Dad in a coma. Has...has my cover been blown?"

He raised a brow. "You tell me."

He was talking about the guys, or at least the people in the town. *Lie, I had to lie.* "They don't suspect anything. To the people here, I am just Atalanta North, a normal girl who was in an accident. And I haven't heard from...him."

"That's good. As for my end, our informants haven't heard any news, though Emmanuel has always kept his..." he paused as he tried to look for the words, trying to keep tactful. "Side project...of finding you close to his chest. Only his top lieutenants know anything about it. But there are always ripples in the grape vine when he's found a lead, so we believe you're safe for now."

I shivered hearing his name and hugged my arms around myself, making sure my sleeves were pulled down. "I really wish he would just give up. I'm not worth all the trouble he's gone through to try and find me."

"You know exactly why he won't give up," he said, giving me a pointed look.

Now that was one thing I was sure I would never forget. The smell of another person's blood mixing with my own. A sickly metallic scent coupled with the sound of a gasping gurgle as a person's lungs filled with fluid. Breaths short as the bullet in the woman's chest did its work. Of course, Emmanuel wouldn't let me go.

I had killed his sister, after all.

Chapter Eighteen

AJAX

"Please, Ajax, tell me you're finished with Mr. Yagermejensen's sign. He keeps emailing me that people aren't going to be able to find his inn if there is no sign. As if you wouldn't be able to figure it out from the fact that it's the only inn in this damn town."

I sighed and looked down from my perch on my ladder at Argos' mayor, Leto. She emanated irritation *constantly*. Like a high grade sand paper that was slowly rubbing back and forth across my skin. She was a beautiful woman of asian decent, with jet black hair and alabaster skin, but as with most beautiful woman in power, she had a bit of an attitude. At least with me, for some reason. With others, she was actually genuinely kind. Perhaps it was because I refused to sleep with her.

"It is." I affirmed.

Her irritation flared. "And when you were you planning on delivering that?"

"When I'm done." I gestured to one of the many other signs she had commissioned for me to do, including the one for Edith's craft store.

She rolled her eyes. "As long as it gets done."

She finally walked away, thank the gods, letting me get back to work. I just had to remember that the pay for the town restoration job would be really good. Plus, seeing the faces of the other town's people as I showed them their signs and the artwork they asked for was all worth the headache from Leto.

Pulling out my level, I made sure that the sign was straight before tightening that last screw. I climbed down my ladder and was careful to move it and hook it back to the side of my truck without hitting anyone. Edith came out the front door of her shop when she saw that I was done.

"Oh, Ajax, my dear. It is wonderful." The old woman stared up at the sign in wonder before turning to me with tears in her eyes. "You're doing a good job, hun. It's just what I've always wanted."

I looked back up at my work, a giant paint brush crossed with scissors that snipped the end of a string of yarn, which spelled out "Imagine That Art Supplies". Making these creative signs were fun. The warmth of Edith's joy felt wonderful in the aftermath of Athena. However, when the old woman hugged me, suddenly all of her emotions sank into me. A flash of stress over a phone call I knew she'd had earlier, annoyance at a complaining customer that had just left, her discomfort at my awkwardly standing there.

I slowly hugged her back as I built back up my walls, until all of it became a dull hum over my skin.

After a moment, I separated from her, plastering a smile on my face. "I'm glad you like it."

"Like it? Oh, darling, I love it! You have some skilled hands there, mister. You know, I have a granddaughter who's looking for a mate of her own. I could give you her number."

TIED TO THE SEA

"No," I blurted out, a bit panicked. "I'm okay."

Her face fell, and I felt the slick feeling of her pity roll over my shoulders. "Ajax. I know it's difficult, but you can't be alone for the rest of your life. Now, I know it's not my place, but you're a strong male, any woman would be happy to have you as a mate. Despite what you might think of yourself."

I shook my head. "I'm fine."

"If you insist." She gave me a sad smile, radiating that motherly warmth.

I always liked Edith, but she knew far too much about everyone in town. At least she didn't use it to her advantage, outside of when she tried to play matchmaker.

I tried to turn down the generous tip Edith slipped into my hands, only to blush when she scowled and slipped it into my back pocket before patting my ass and shooing me away.

Rolling my eyes, I hopped into my truck and drove over to Mr. Yagermejensen's Inn. I had a few more jobs to do today before I could head home. I wondered if everyone would be staying at my cabin again tonight. It was interesting having all the company after so many years alone. I did feel bad that most of us were either on the floor or one of the couches. Maybe I could build another room if this kept up. It would be a fun project, as I hadn't done any major construction in a while, mostly just focusing on my art.

My chest filled with pride as I realized how much of my artwork was dawning the town. Most of the shops had new signs that I had crafted, several of them had requested me to paint some sort of mural on their walls outside. Turning the once sea-darkened wood into bright and colorful paintings. Not to mention all of the mermaid sculptures I had put up all over the town. It was a bit like I was finally putting my mark on the world, a very interesting feeling after so many years of being the closet artist who was shut off from the world.

When I pulled up to the inn, I noticed a familiar motorcycle in one of the parking spaces and remembered Atalanta's meeting with that man. I didn't mind him too much, beyond his obvious attraction to Atalanta.

With a new spring in my step, I walked into the building. Mimi was minding the counter, and while she gave me a pleasant enough smile, she radiated annoyance. I couldn't really tell the cause, but the way her eyes kept sliding over to Jason and Hip sitting in the lounge chairs, I could at least guess.

I waved and walked up to them.

"Ajax, perfect timing. You'll be able to settle a dispute with us!" Hip shouted.

I grunted and crossed my arms, waiting to hear what they were bickering about this time.

Jason rolled his eyes. "Oh, sure, run to Ajax. Just acknowledge you're wrong and move on."

"You're the one who's wrong!"

These two were so stupid. Tuning out their bickering, I concentrated, trying to locate Atalanta's signature.

There it was.

What?

"Kill," I growled out before storming off to where I felt her.

The sickening churn in my stomach was fed by an ocean of negative emotions. Whatever that piece of shit human said to Atalanta didn't matter if he was six feet under and couldn't ever say it again.

I could hear Hip and Jason call after me as I stomped up the stairs, over to the door that emitted all of the horror and guilt.

Rearing back, I kicked in the door.

BAM!

Aaaand now I had a gun in my face.

BANG!

Guns are only as fast as the person pulling the trigger, and this person wasn't fast enough.

Dodging the bullet by millimeters, I grabbed the slide of the barrel, preventing him from firing again before slamming the human's wrist while jerking the gun from his grasp. Pressing the magazine release, I ejected the clip and tossed it behind me, then emptied the chamber.

"What in the ever loving fuck?!" The man shouted.

I followed the voice to see Atalanta. On. The. *BED.* And the human was shirtless. Twelve feet underground then, possibly spread across thirty countries. They would never find all the parts.

I focused my attention back on the human who looked like he was ready to attack me. His feelings of confusion and anger were brimming, but there was something else there too. When he swiftly moved to step between me and Atalanta, I knew that he was feeling protective.

I sighed. Fine, I supposed I wouldn't kill the human. But that didn't mean I wouldn't kick him a few times in that pretty-boy face of his.

"Ajax! Dude, calm down!"

Before I could take a full step towards the man, I felt hands wrap around me and pull me back.

"Ajax, you need to take a chill pill. What has you so raging bull?"

"She's upset," I ground out. "His. Fault."

"Oh, Ajax." Atalanta tried to get up from the bed, but Curt? Clint? Kile? Snot.

Snot used his body and backed her back onto the bed. "Stay down, Atalanta."

"He's not going to hurt me, Clint." She shoved around Snot and came to stand in front of me. "Ajax, I'm fine. Please calm down. You're bleeding."

I snorted. A small cut on my ear from the bullet. It would heal soon.

Taking in a deep breath, I raised the Snot's gun. Everyone in the room tensed before I tossed it to the ground, far out of everyone's reach.

"Use both hands next time." I grunted before shaking off Jason and Hip.

"Someone would have heard the gunshot and called the police." Atalanta said before shoving the man aside and hurrying past all of us to the door. "We can't be here when they show up."

"Atalanta," Snot called.

"No, Clint. *You* can explain to them why you discharged your weapon. You know procedure, and I can't be here when they start asking those questions."

I watched her as she walked out of the room. Beyond nervously rubbing her shoulder, she outwardly look fine, confident even, but I could feel her anxiety and terror. Him firing his gun freaked her out considerably. I followed after her, needing for her to be okay.

The other two followed while Snot stayed behind. He radiated anger and jealousy, sprinkled with worry. I wondered if he was worried about himself or Atalanta. Considering he was about to face down Mathews and Jefferson, the town sheriffs, I could only smile at the hell they would bring down on him.

Atalanta stormed down the steps at a brisk pace. Mimi was missing and no other patrons were in sight.

Jason rushed forward and ever so gently took Atalanta's hand. "We need to go out the back entrance."

Without looking at him, she nodded and changed directions, letting Jason lead her to the back towards the emergency exit. Luckily, the door didn't have an alarm on it and no one was lingering out back. The four of us hurried around the side of the building, with me taking the lead, crouching low.

Just as I rounded the side of the building, I stopped short and held up my fist, signaling the others to stop. The cops had just arrived. I waited until Mathews and Jefferson hopped out of their patrol car and rushed into the building, guns drawn. I lowered my hand and stood straight, calmly and casually walking towards my car.

"Where do we go from here?" Jason asked.

I looked back to him as he continued to hold Atalanta's hand. Atalanta's eyes kept flicking around, to our surroundings and back to the ground. Her free hand still rubbing that spot on her shoulder, the one I knew bore a large scar from a bullet.

"Library," I said, holding out my hand for Atalanta to take.

Her eyes met mine for a moment before moving to Jason's. With a nod, he let go of her hand, allowing it to take mine. Yet instead, she walked past me and hopped into my truck.

A little hurt, I looked to the other two. "Meet you there."

They nodded and I hopped into my truck and pulled away.

Atalanta sat quietly in her seat, pulling at her sleeves and rubbing her shoulder. Feeling her maelstrom of emotions was torment. I held in the bile that rose in my throat.

Reaching over, I held out my hand to her. Offering my help, praying to the gods she would take it so that I could relieve her. But she didn't.

"I know you want to make me feel better, but taking away my emotions won't solve the problem, Ajax."

"I just want to help."

She gave a curt nod. "I know. And knowing you're here for me helps enough."

I nodded and retreated my hand. There was a part of me that feared that she would never let me touch her when she was upset, even if it was just to comfort her in the human way. Perhaps I would need to make my intentions clear in the future as my own hurt twisted in my chest.

We made it to the library a few minutes later. Without a word. Atalanta got out of the truck and hurried to the library's doors.

Jason and Hip showed up moments later and the three of us followed after her. Percival was sitting at his desk, reading one of those young adult books Atalanta got him hooked on. When he saw us enter, he quickly closed the book and tried to hide it from our sight, that calm look of his morphing to concern as he read our expressions.

"What happened?"

"Ajax here attacked Atalanta's ...um...cousin? Friend? Clint. He attacked Clint and Clint shot at us." Hip said, pointing at me accusingly.

Percival's eyes cut to mine. "And why would you do such a thing?"

"She was upset."

I noticed more than a few eye rolls.

"We can not go attacking humans every time she gets upset." Percival scolded.

I clenched my fist. "This wasn't…it wasn't—"

"Please don't be mad at him." Atalanta interjected, her eyes meeting with the floor. "Knowing how I felt in that room. I don't blame him for feeling protective of me."

"What did Clint do to you?"

"He only reminded me of…he reminded me that there are things I need to tell you."

I felt her fear and anxiety spike. It was so abrupt that I staggered on my feet, and when she met my eyes, I saw very familiar flashes.

A little girl's screams.

Searing pain.

"Ajax, put your barriers back up," Someone said, pulling me out of it.

I jerked my eyes away from Atalanta's and dove straight into the nearest trashcan to hurl up my lunch.

"Ajax, I'm so sorry!" Atalanta's regret brushed against me, this time more gently as I put up a wall around my mind.

"Not," Hurl. "your fault."

Percival sighed. "I have some chocolate in my office."

Shakily, I stood up straight. Jason patted my back and handed me a bottle of water.

"Is there a reason our silent giant just hurled up a storm?" Hip asked.

"Ajax's empath abilities are exceptionally strong." Percival came back and handed me the bar of chocolate. "Sometimes if the emotions come on too intensely, too quickly, it can make him sick."

Percival, like Edith, was nosy and knew way too much about other's personal lives. Granted, most of the Mer town knew that little fact about my abilities, so I shoved down my annoyance.

Taking a bite of chocolate, I studied Atalanta, who didn't look well. Her dark features were ashen and her uncovered eye was red from unshed tears. Reaching forward, I carefully removed the bandage from her bright green eye.

"Please, tell us."

She shook her head and backed up from me. "No, not if you're going to be sick."

I kept my expression neutral, not wanting to show my anger at her using my illness as an excuse. It was time for her to be the brave girl I knew she could be.

"I'll be fine."

We stared each other down in a contest of will. She was strong, but I wasn't giving in. Not this time.

She sighed and pulled out her phone. "I'll text Theseus, he should be here for this too."

A few minutes later, I felt the dark aura of Theseus approach. His happy-go-lucky expression quickly morphed into one of worry when he spotted Atalanta, and he picked up his pace to be by her side.

Taking her hand, Theseus asked, "What's wrong? What's going on?"

"There are some things I need to tell you guys. The truth, though." She looked around. "I'd prefer if we had some privacy."

Surveying the room, I could see that there were several people in the library milling around, reading, browsing, or studying. Percival noticed it too.

Walking back around his counter, he picked up the phone and pressed a button. His voice came up over the com system. "Attention, the library will be closing early tonight. Please make your way to the front to check out now. Again, the library is now closing, so please make your way to the front."

He put the phone down with a loud CLA-TCK on the speakers.

"We could have gone into the back or to Ajax's or something. No need to kick them all out," Atalanta said.

Percy just shrugged in reply and sat down, waiting at his computer for people to come up. We stood around awkwardly for a couple minutes as a few of the patrons came up and checked out, but the majority those in the library were blatantly ignoring Percy's announcement.

When it became clear that those people weren't leaving anytime soon, Percival stood up from his seat and shouted, "EVERYONE EITHER COME CHECK OUT YOUR BOOK OR GET THE FUCK OUT!"

Wow. Who knew the deep-sea Mer could be so loud?

Our little group stared wide-eyed as the last of the stragglers came to the front and begrudgingly checked out their books. Percival's steely glare was probably what kept all the people from complaining.

Once the last pair of patrons left, Jason locked the doors behind them. Turning back to Atalanta, who had positioned herself against a wall, Jason walked up to her and took her hand.

"You can start when you're ready. We take this at your pace."

The four of us nodded in agreement.

Atalanta tilted her head towards her favorite lounge chair. Continuing to hold Jason's hand, she slumped into the chair. Not wanting to crowd her, Theseus, Hip, Percy, and I pulled up chairs and sat across from her while Percy brought up a seat for Jason to sit in.

I watched the two of them. Feeling how Jason's touch physically soothed Atalanta's nerves.

I missed that feeling.

"Well," She exhaled. "Where to begin?"

Jason gave a soft smile. "How about starting from the worst part?"

She squeezed his hand, her anxiety spiking. Along with this feeling, an odd emotion that I had felt before but could never place. A sort of hollow horror. It felt familiar somehow, and I wish I could remember why.

"When I was twelve years old, I killed four people."

Oh, that's why.

TIED TO THE SEA

Chapter Nineteen

ATALANTA

Yep, those were the looks I expected. The four men before me showed me the usual series of emotions. Shock, disbelief, and finally settling on horror. From there, people typically tended to break off. Some moving to pity, others disgust, perhaps being bland and sticking with horror, and sometimes, a rare few showed understanding.

In this instance, Ajax and Percy had been of that rare few. I had to wonder what had happened in their lives before they had met me. Jason and Hip fell into that pity category, and Theseus, he sort of just looked sad. Like what I had said made him feel the weight of his own past. Was he like Ajax and Percy? Did he understand?

"Now, please, start from the beginning." Jason said, his voice a little croaky.

My chest felt hollow as I entered a familiar headspace. It had been a long time since I had repeated this story aloud to anyone. Starting was always the hardest part, so I supposed Jason's method made it a smidge easier to just blurt out most of it.

"I'll save you from the gruesome details. My mother was a drug addict. Had been one on and off for years. One night, when I was stuck at home with a fever, my father had taken Cal out to the movies while our mother stayed home to watch me."

Broken pieces of the night flashed in my mind. I had been so jealous. They knew I wanted to go see the new Disney movie, but there I was, stuck in bed, all covered in sweat and snot.

"My father never realized how deep in debt my mom had been with her dealer. Nor did he know that it wasn't just some street thug that sold the stuff to her. That night, they came to collect."

The *BANG! BANG! BANG!* at the door met with my mother's muffled curses, when I assumed she realized who was on the other side.

"Four guys and a woman came busting into our home. Demanding all sorts of things."

You's owes us over ten G's, Mary! You's better pay up now or it will be your body.

"They got ahold of my mother and I. At the time, I honestly didn't understand what was going on, or what two of the guys were doing with my mother in the next room. All I knew was when the woman and one of her goons came storming into my room and dragged me out of bed, I was afraid."

The woman's breath on my face was disgusting as she held me up by my hair. *Look what we've got here, Tony. An unripe bitch! We could use this one at the warehouse if she doesn't fill out enough to be used on the streets.*

"They wanted to make me some sort of worker in their operation if I didn't work out for them as a prostitute," I take a deep breath, not looking into any of their eyes. Not wanting to see the pity. "I struggled, of course. It didn't get me much of anything beyond a few good punches to the face and a bullet hole in my shoulder." I rubbed the shoulder as the memories made it ache.

My mind was nothing but panic at first, but that screaming force telling me to live surfaced, pushing through all the pain in my shoulder and making me take action.

"My father was a federal agent, and the way he raised us, Cal and I knew how to hold a gun. Knew how to fire one, too. I fought the gun away from the woman, and in the struggle, I shot her."

Stay alive.

Gotta keep living, gotta protect momma.

Stay alive.

I touched my malformed hip. "Her guy got me pretty bad in the leg, but honestly, by that point, it was all a blur. A twelve year old sick girl with a gun in her hands, and terrifying men who were trying to kill her."

What's going on in here? Another man entered the room and I screamed, firing the gun again, and again, and again. Until two more bodies laid at my feet.

"One of the guys that had been in the room with my mother freaked when he heard all the gunshots and bailed out the window. And that's how my father and Cal found me, ten minutes later. Bloody and beaten, surrounded by dead bodies."

I paused, let out a shaky breath, and took the chance to watch the guys' reactions. They were all kind of stuck between shock and horror. Not gonna lie, it was kind of funny. Despite not being human, their reactions perfectly matched the face of every jury member and judge that had handled my case after I told my account.

"Well, fuck." Hip sat back and stared up at the ceiling.

"I knew something horrible had to have happened," Percy rubbed his face before whispering, "I had hoped it wasn't something like this."

"You were so young." Theseus murmured thoughtfully.

"Tragedy doesn't have age restrictions. It could have been worse. I could have been too young to actually defend myself."

His eyes cut away. "You're right, but still."

"What happened next? Why witness protection?" Jason choked out, his grip on my hand like a vice. He was quivering so violently as tears streamed down his cheeks.

I reached up and wiped a few away. "I was in the hospital for a while, then on trial to testify my account. It was hardly ever a question of if I were to be locked up for killing those people, but more if I should be kept safe from the remaining members of the gang. The woman I had killed, she was the sister of Emmanuel Milos, a drug cartel general with an extremely large following."

"A man like that would not take the death of his sister lightly." Percy muttered, more to himself.

"Not at all. For the last seven years, Emmanuel Milos has been the shadow that has haunted my sleep. He and his crew have been hunting me and my family for years. Any time he got too close, or Dad felt our cover was blown, we would pack up and leave town. New names, new home, no life."

"Seven? But you said you were twelve?" Hip asked.

I looked at him. He would be the one to notice the gap in time. "Emmanuel didn't surface until after the trial. With everything that was going down, his face was all over the news. Thanks to him and his crew pushing drugs, a little girl had to kill four people. The public was out for his blood."

Ajax shifted in his chair, looking uncomfortable. "I vaguely remember hearing about this. The news never released your name, but there was a wonder if you were going to survive."

I gave a wry smile. "Ta-da."

They didn't seem to think that was funny.

I inhaled slowly. "The details of everything after that is a little complicated. I don't think I can explain all of it now, but to make a long story short, we were in witness protection and then we sort of jumped the tracks. My father, having worked in witsec for years, knew the system, and he knew its flaws. He also made a *lot* of connections. Using those connections, he went through unofficial channels to set us up with new identities and new homes. His superiors weren't happy with him, but it's not like they could really find him after the fact."

"What about Clint? Who is he, exactly, if you aren't under official witness protection?"

"I don't know all the details. Eventually, my dad struck some sort of deal with the higher ups. My dad could do things his way, and in turn he would hunt down every dirty cop in Emmanuel's organization. Clint is one of the few people in on it. Acting as a pseudo-handler in turn with passing information. But I honestly don't know that side of things, never wanted to. Cal was actually the detective."

I sat back and closed my eyes, trying to calm the jitters in my stomach. I believed I deserved some hot chocolate for my dry mouth and a nice cozy blanket for a nap.

"What should we do?" Theseus asked softly.

"What do you mean?" Jason replied.

"Well, we can't just let this human live. He's clearly still a threat to her."

I cracked open an eye and peeked at Theseus. It was a surprise to hear such hostility from my sweet boy.

Hip was staring at Theseus in horror. "We can't just go all 'avenging warrior' and kill the guy!"

"Then *what*?" he growled. "Wait for him to come to us? Let him get close to her again? Fuck no."

"I actually agree with Theseus. It would be better in the long run to rid ourselves of this human." Percy said and signed.

My spine snapped straight. "You can't just walk in and kill Emmanuel. He's not some old man who runs a book shop and does crosswords on Sunday. He has literal generals and drug soldiers that we would need to get through, not to mention we would then be on the run from the moment he was dead."

Percy pushed up his glasses and leaned forward. "What would you have us do? Atalanta, if this man shows up here, your life would be in danger. That's not acceptable to any of us."

"I didn't tell you the truth so that you all would go White Knight and save me from the big bad villain of my story! I told you so I wouldn't have to keep lying to all of you."

Jason spoke up. "I agree with Atalanta. Picking a fight would be more dangerous than just holding down the fort and being careful."

"I agree with Jason," Hip said, much to everyone's surprise.

There was a pregnant pause as everyone stared at him before the room exploded as everyone began to shout at each other. Lines were being drawn while I watched in horror as the hostility grew.

"I say we kill him." Ajax grunted.

"Of course you would say that! You attacked a human for just upsetting her!" Hip snapped at him.

"SHE WOULD BE SAFER IF HE WAS GONE!" Theseus shouted, far louder than everyone else.

Jason let go my hand and pointed at Theseus. "She would be safer if we *didn't* attack a drug lord and his fucking *army*!"

"He will find her here eventually, and when he does, not only will she be in danger, but the whole town would be at risk." Theseus shot back.

Hip snorted. "As if a town full of supernatural beings couldn't handle a bunch of dudes with guns."

"Not everyone has your abilities, Mr. Clark. And not everyone in this town is a trained warrior."

"It seems that there's a problem with a very simple solution." Came a new and chilling voice.

While we had all been so focused on arguing, Calder had taken it upon himself to stroll on in.

"That door was locked for a reason," Percy growled.

All of the guys shifted in front of me, blocking my view of Jason's uncle.

"I didn't realize it was locked. I just thought the knob was rusty."

"The door doesn't have a knob," Ajax muttered.

"May I ask what you're doing here, Uncle Calder?" Jason, even in such a tense situation, kept with a respectful tone.

They trained him well, it seemed.

"I came to this public institution to read some good old American literature, and happened to overhear your little squabble."

"And?" Theseus asked.

"Well, you have a Mer who's in need of protection from some low life human. What better place to protect a Mer than with her own kind?"

"What are you saying, Calder?" Percy demanded.

"I am saying that we should bring Miss Atalanta back to the city."

"That's a good idea." Theseus mumbled.

"Hell no," Hip cursed.

Jason slowly shook his head. "Uncle, she can't."

"I disagree. She would be safest there." Percy replied.

Ajax simply grunted.

The city? As in, what, the Mer city?

I peeked from around the broad shoulders of Ajax at Calder. His eyes narrowed, face turned up as if we were the gum under his shoe.

Red.

A shiver went up my spine and again I hid behind the guys, who had begun to argue amongst themselves once more.

"Percy, we can't send her there. You know what will happen." Jason tried to reason.

It was Theseus who answered. "She would be perfectly safe in the city. No one would dare harm her there."

Jason's head whipped around to look at Theseus. "It's not all starfish and rainbows down there, Theseus. Don't be an idiot."

Percy looked pensive for a few moments, his mind clearly racing a mile a minute before answering. "It may not be ideal, but she would be safer from the human."

"Percy." Jason's face had fallen into one of betrayal.

I could only guess that Percy knew what would happen to both of us if we went to the city.

My stomach coiled. I didn't want to be a breeding machine any more than Jason did.

I fidgeted with my sleeves. "I can't leave."

"With all due respect, you don't really have a choice." Calder said.

"Of course she has a choice," Hip snapped at him.

"*She*," Calder spat out the word like one spat out shit, "is an undocumented changed female. As is our law, she must go before the council, to be documented and paired with a mate."

I gulped. Well, I guess the cat was out of the bag.

"She has a mate." Ajax finally spoke up.

Calder scoffed. "I may care for my nephew deeply, but no one here, especially you, would be fit for mating."

Ajax growled and took a menacing step towards Calder. The others attempted to hold him back, and Ajax's muscles bulged as he fought against their grip.

Theseus grunted with the effort of holding Ajax. "Calder, please. I ask that we discuss the topic of Atalanta's mating at another time."

Was it my imagination, or did Calder actually look nervous? I was tempted to let the situation play out, but with all the airs he put on, I had a feeling that beating the crap out of him would be more trouble than it was worth.

I stifled a snicker as I put my hand on Ajax's shoulder. "We don't want to get blood on any of the books."

"I'll buy new ones."

This time, I couldn't hide my laughter. "Ajax."

"Fine." Ajax stopped trying to attack Calder and shrugged off the others.

Taking a deep breath in, I stepped around the guys and faced down Calder.

"Alight, you've got us. I'm a changed Mer, but I don't care about your laws. My father is laying in a hospital bed, unconscious, with no idea about what has happened to me or that my sister is gone. I won't just leave him."

Calder's face morphed into something akin to horror with a mix of disgust before his eyes snapped to Jason. "You changed her while she still had ties to the human world? What reckless...completely idiotic...*foolish!*" Calder spluttered, and his pale face flared red.

"There were extenuating circumstances, Uncle."

"I don't care for your extenuating circumstances. We have these laws for a reason!" He pointed his long, skeletal finger at me. "You have 24 hours to get your affairs in order."

Meeting each of the guys eyes, Calder said slowly, "Tomorrow, you will bring her to the docks for transport. I shouldn't have to tell you what will happen if you don't."

Calder spun around and stormed out of the library, the sound of the door slamming behind him echoing over the high ceilings.

There was a deadening awkward silence between all of us. And I just stood there, staring at the door, my heart beating like a jackhammer in my chest. What did Calder mean? What would happen if I didn't go with him tomorrow? Honestly, it was easy to assume what might happen, but I didn't want to hear them say it aloud. I didn't really want to know, because I couldn't leave Dad.

I *wouldn't* leave him.

He could wake up any day now, and the idea of him waking up alone in that hospital bed, not knowing what happened to me or Cal…

My hands shook with the effort stay still. In. Out. Breathe, stay under control. One thing at a time.

In an attempt to distract my racing mind, I asked a different question, one that I thought might be harmless. "I understand wanting to keep the whole mermaid thing a secret, but why exactly would I need to cut all ties to the human world? I mean, half of this town is Mer, right?"

All of the boys except Theseus turned to look at me, his focus still on the door. Percy tapped his shoulder to get his attention and then signed to him what I assumed was a repeat of what I had just said.

Theseus's jaw tightened and he took a breath before meeting my eyes. "Because eventually, they would notice that you had stopped aging."

I blinked, trying to move the cogs in my brain to process what he had said. "Stopped? Wait...are you saying that I'm like an eternal vampire now? Wait, okay. No...what!?"

"Mer age differently than humans." Theseus rubbed the back of his neck. "Born Mer age at a rate of their choosing—"

"Made Mer stop aging all together," Ajax said, looking down at his feet.

My face went slack as I studied the men in front of me.

Hip, who was clearly just as surprised as I was, stared at the others, eyes wide, mouth hanging open. Jason and Percy looked guilty while Ajax looked a little haunted. Theseus just gave me a strained smile.

My hands shot up and I turned towards the door. "Alright, I'm done. My weird limit just shot through the roof, and I need a nap."

"Atalanta," Jason whispered, reaching for my hand.

I pulled away from his touch. "I'm sorry, today has been...hard. I would really like to go home and rest. Process everything."

He nodded, looking a little hurt by my rejection.

Hugging myself, I left the library, the guys following behind me. The sky was gloomy and the ground was wet. The perpetual drizzle of Washington was the perfect reflection of my mood. That sadness that always lingered in the back of my mind. Today had honestly sucked.

I wished Cal was here. Her smile was infectious.

"Atalanta, before we go, I have one final question for you," Percy said, giving everyone in the group pause.

"What's that?"

"Your real name, what is it?"

I blinked and gave him a slow smile. "Every girl has a right to her secrets. I think I'll keep this one for now."

***

"This isn't the way to the house," I mumbled as I stared out the window.

"I thought we could make one stop before heading back."

"Jason, please. I just want to rest." I curled up in the seat, hugging my knees to my chest.

I saw him look at me out of the corner of my eye. "I think you need this."

I sighed and closed my eyes.

My head was pounding and my stomach churned. I hoped this little side trip was quick and painless.

The car pulled to a slow stop. "We're here."

Cracking an eye open, I saw that we had pulled up in front of the hospital. I sat up and looked at Jason. He gazed back at me with a soft smile before hopping out to rush around and open my door. Taking my hand, he led me into the hospital.

Dad looked exactly like how I had left him. Small and quiet on the uncomfortable looking hospital bed.

"Hi, Daddy. I missed you."

Slowly, I trudged into the room and ever so carefully laid down next to my father. Curled up and careful to avoid the wires and his I.V., I listened to the sound of his heart.

"I went back to school today." I whispered as I laid my head on his chest. "Hopefully I'll finally be able to get that stupid piece of paper you were so determined for me to get."

BaBump...BaBump...

I inhaled slowly, the sound of my father's beating heart lulling me to sleep. "Listen...the boys that were here with me last time? They know."

"We can trust them," I yawned. "All they want is to protect us."

BaBump...BaBump...

"I know what you would say. 'My baby girl, the only ones you should trust in this life are the ones you know are willing to let down their lives for you'. Well—"

"We would," Jason whispered confidently.

I looked over my shoulder at Jason, who had been sitting quietly in the guest chair.

"Yeah, what he said. So you don't need to worry, Dad. I'm okay."

I laid my head back down on his chest. I knew I was probably imagining it, but my father's heartbeat felt stronger than before.

Chapter Twenty

PERCY

Thunk-thwack!

I clearly needed a new lock on my door.

Thunk-thwack!

Because despite having locked the door, when I came out of the shower, I found the last man I wanted to see tossing a tennis ball at my wall.

"Calder. I can assume that telling you that you need to reevaluate your idea of personal boundaries would be equivalent to trying to tell humans dolphins aren't actually all that intelligent." I walk towards him, cautious, naked as the day I was born.

He tilted his head and gave me a slow smile. "I don't know what you mean, Percival. I'm simply stopping by my old friend's home."

"We are not friends," I said cooly. I reached for the sword that I had hidden behind my dresser, gripping it and pulling it out of its sheath before swinging it around to point at Calder. "Leave."

"Now, *this* is a surprise. Despite your upbringing, I was under the impression that you didn't know a sword from a *mop*." Calder said calmly as he stared down the point of the sword.

"As I said, we are not friends." I slowly pressed the sword to his chest.

He slowly raised his hands, one still clutching a tennis ball, placating. "Touchy, touchy. Fine. I came here to discuss the young made Mer that you have been hiding. I want to make sure that you convince her to come to the city."

"I will not make her do anything. If she wants to go with you tomorrow, it will be her choice." I growled.

"Even though you want her to go? Even though you know what will happen if she doesn't...?" He trailed off.

Ah, yes. The conundrum. Atalanta would be safer from her tormentor if she stayed hidden in a Mer city for the next fifty or so years. However, given our traditions and laws, there was a very good chance that most of us, Ajax, Hip, Theseus, and I included, would never see her again. Jason, at least, would have a chance.

At first, it was an easy choice. Protecting her from a mere human and his little army would be simple enough. We could keep her safe.

Yet...

I knew Calder was aware of her presence and what would come if he forced the issue. Then he just had to show up today.

If Atalanta didn't go with Calder tomorrow, it was likely a group of guards would be there to force her. Or even worse, they would hunt down her ties to the human world and cut them. Effectively making her more pliable to their wishes.

There was no way I would allow that to happen.

Thus, the conundrum.

We could make a run for it. I know Jason at least would follow if we were to flee into the night, staying far away from all of the threats until everything mulled over. But Atalanta would never leave her father behind. I could always arrange for him to be transferred to a hospital far from any coastline...

"I can see your mind turning, you know. Playing every piece on the board and trying to predict where the game would lead. It's quite intriguing actually. Though," he shoved the tennis ball onto the tip of my sword, and in one swift move tore the weapon out of my hand. "A warrior, you are not."

I growled and lunged forward, landing a punch to his jaw. Clearly, Calder wasn't as steady on land as he was in the water. He fell to the ground in a satisfying heap, with a split lip.

He spit out blood and set his blazing glare on me. "Do you have any idea what you have done!? Attacking me while protecting your claim was one thing, but this was unwarranted, and I could have you strung to a post and whipped for this."

"Oh, shut up," I drawled. "You are in my territory and were asked to leave. By our laws—and even some human ones—I have full grounds to kill you right now."

Calder hissed at me, his human guise failing as red scales rippled across his skin.

I chuckled and walked to my front door, opening it for him. "I may be more of a scholar than a warrior,

Calder, but I still can, as they say today, kick your fucking ass."

"You will regret this."

I rolled my eyes. "And you sound like a cliche villain."

For a moment, it looked like he would attack me. Nostrils flared, face beet-red, but it faded. He composed himself and stood, straightening his clothes and leaving without another word.

As he slammed the door behind him, I sighed.

This would come back to bite me, I knew it.

My eyes slid to the clock by my bedside. 10:09 p.m. Not too late, I supposed I could either go for a swim or find the others and discuss what to do.

10:12 p.m.

"Swimming, it is."

Not bothering to put on any clothes, I left my home, a quaint building attached to the back of the library, and into the familiar forest trail which led to the beach.

Diving into the waves I pushed the shift over me. My gills opening fully was akin to taking a breath of fresh air.

The waves were calm and the taste of salt on my mouth was all soothing as I closed my eyes and drifted along with the currents.

If Atalanta went to the city tomorrow, I wondered if I should follow. I did miss my old home. Beautiful in its own way, and what the humans would consider an amazing feat of architecture.

I did not belong there anymore.

And yet, I couldn't help but picture Atalanta's face. The haunted look I always saw hiding within the shadow of her eyes pulled to the forefront as she finally revealed how she became The Girl With No Name.

I wanted to stop seeing that look, and I'm sure the others felt the same. And for that to happen I needed to be there with her every step of the way.

"Percy?"

I jerked and spun around to see — "Jason. Why aren't you with Ms. North?"

I quickly let go of my shift, taking on my less monstrous guise. Teeth and claws receded to the average length, glowing tail and spines retracting.

"I really needed a swim, so I texted Ajax to watch over her while she stayed at the hospital with her father."

"Oh..." I relaxed, knowing that she was under some form of protection.

"Are you okay?" He asked, studying me.

"Calder showed up at my house, not long ago." I grumbled.

"What!? Are you okay?" He shot forward and ran his hands over my shoulders, checking me over.

I gave him a reassuring smile. "I am fine. Actually, more than fine."

He tilted his head in that cute way he did when he was confused.

"I may have punched your uncle in the face."

"Oh, shit!" He burst out laughing.

"He deserved it for breaking into my home and practically demanding for me to force Atalanta to the city." I crossed my arms.

Jason's laughter skittered to a halt. "What?"

"I told him no, that it was ultimately her decision if she goes."

"You want her to go, though." I could see the hurt and betrayal on his face which acted as a lance through my heart. I didn't like the idea of hurting him like this.

"I feel that it will be the safest place for her right now."

"That's bullshit and you know it." He snapped.

I sighed. "Jason."

"No," he pointed furiously at me. "No, you understand exactly what's at stake for her *and* us once the council has a hold of us."

"Does she?" I asked.

He nodded. "Yes. I told her all about it today, in fact."

"And that is why I am leaving the decision up to her. In the morning we give her all of the information and let her choose."

"But—"

I interrupted him. "Jason, we already forced too much on her. We can't keep taking away her choice."

"We haven't forced anything on her." He sneered as if the idea disgusted him.

I looked at him skeptically. "Really? A little more than a month ago, that girl walked into town, human, closed off, someone so committed to her role as the average American girl we would sooner uncover the secret to Stonehenge than get her to break her persona. Yet, here we are."

"She trusts us!" He insisted.

"She does, I just worry it has happened far too quickly." I said, looking up at the shifting waves.

"We aren't much different." He waved his hands around, animated. "I mean, look at us. Two months ago if you had told me that I would be willing to go against my family for a girl, Hip and I would be on speaking terms, Ajax would be forming full sentences, and you and Theseus...well."

I nodded. "You have a point."

"If there's anything I've learned by watching my parents, it's that we shouldn't be judging things by human standards." Jason hugged himself, pouting. He was so cute when he pouted.

I relaxed as my tension seeped back into the ocean floor.

"When did you get so wise?" I asked, sinking down to sit on the sand.

He smiled before joining me. "I had a good role model."

We were silent for a while, laying across the sand, staring up at the light reflecting across the shifting waves. It was uncomfortable to be sitting here in my half shifted form. I was getting sand in places where sand shouldn't be.

Jason cleared his throat and when I turned my gaze to him I saw that his cheeks were dusted pink. "With all that's happened, I haven't had the chance to ask."

"Hmm?"

"What gave it away? That I...you, um..." He broke eye contact and began to swirl his finger through the sand.

I chuckled. "What if I told you that a long time ago, I had realized that you found it very easy to flirt, smile, and be the perfect jock around everyone. Everyone except the people you were actually interested in. Like Ashley Foote in the fifth grade, or whenever Atalanta was around."

His gaze snapped back to mine, eyebrows raised. "I didn't realize you watched me so closely."

I shrugged. "You are also terrible at hiding your boners whenever you stare at me too long. It was easy to put two and two together."

"And here I was hoping I was a man of mystery." He said, attempting to be suave and utterly failing.

"Maybe to an outsider, but to me, you're an open book."

Jason flopped over onto his side, his gaze focused on me with a distinct intensity. "Percy, what am I to you?"

I stood. "We should be going."

"You're not even going to bother answering my question?"

"I shouldn't have to tell you something you should already know." I said, staring out into the water.

"But I don't fucking know!" He stood and swam to block my path. "Am I your assistant, your friend, or am I just the guy with a one-sided crush?"

I clenched my fist. "Jason. You are my Jason."

He chuckled sadly. "I certainly shouldn't have expected you to be able to emote properly."

I cocked a brow. "Emote?"

He turned back towards the shore and waved me off. "Forget about it. Let's head back."

I watched as his powerful tail pushed him swiftly back to land. His dark blue and purple scales almost acting as a sort of camouflage in the darkness of the ocean. I felt terrible for causing him so much pain, but his question was just one I was not prepared to answer. Yet.

Letting my own shift overtake me, I followed after him.

Getting back to the shore, I pulled my phone out of my pants pocket and sent a group text out to all of the others.

We need to talk about what to do tomorrow.

Chapter Twenty-One

THESEUS

This was it. The sun had set on our time.

Jason and I sat at the dock, quietly watching the sun sink below the ocean waves, setting the horizon ablaze with its light. Calder would arrive any minute now, more than likely accompanied by a squad of capital guards.

Part of me hoped that everything could be resolved peacefully, but we all had our roles to play in what was about to happen.

In the distance, I spotted a shift in the waves, a shimmer of scales and tails.

"It's time." I stood, straightening my spine and squaring off my shoulders.

As we suspected, Calder and six heavily armored Mer exploded from the water in their human forms and landed on the wooden dock. The fact that they would expose themselves on land like that spoke volumes of their arrogance.

I stormed forward to meet them, Jason following behind. Calder didn't look all that surprised that Atalanta wasn't here, but he did look annoyed.

'I take it our little made Mer decided to make things difficult?' Calder said, looking relaxed in his suspiciously dry three piece suit. I'm betting one of his guards was a water manipulator.

I took a deep breath, then firmly said, "She has chosen to stay here, within the protection of Argos."

'The laws say she must come before the court council and be evaluated. Matching her with the perfect mates is of the utmost importance.'

"I am aware of the laws, Calder. My family wrote them." I hissed.

At my words, it looked like whispers started up amongst the guards that Calder brought with him. I couldn't tell what they were saying, but based on the way they were looking at me, I could take a guess.

One Mer stepped forward and kneeled. After a few awkward moments, the guard looked up at me expectantly.

Jason nudged my arm to get my attention. 'He apologized for not recognizing you.'

I looked back down at the soldier. "It's fine, it's been several years since I stepped foot in the city, let alone made a public appearance."

His face fell. 'Forgive me, Sire. I had forgotten about your condition.'

At least he was courteous about it. His comrades, however, stared at me with disdain. "It's alright."

Jason nudged me again and nodded towards his uncle.

'If we can get back to the matter at hand,' Calder said, looking impatient.

I sighed and crossed my arms, readying myself for the dance that was about to begin. I hated politics.

"First, matching her with possible mates is irrelevant. She currently has five mates vying for her hand. The council must allow a period of six months before presenting her with a new set of mates in the case of her current matches not working out."

Unmasked and obvious disdain showed on Calder's face. I wasn't surprised. Most probably wouldn't believe the five of us were viable mates. Something that was on a list of pros and cons the five of us discussed last night. All I wanted was to keep her safe, and the city would be safest for her, but I hadn't considered the consequences. The others were right, if we wanted to keep Atalanta, we wanted to avoid the council.

'There is still a matter of her evaluation.' Calder brought up.

I couldn't show my hand just yet. "If you remember, there is a two month waiting period before a newly made Mer has to be evaluated, and her two months hasn't passed."

'The girl is in danger. A human is hunting her, and as a member of the council, I feel that it is my duty to present the girl with a safe haven.' He placed his hand on his chest, trying to look fucking noble. The prick could shove the knightly sword up his ass.

I rolled my eyes. "Yet she does not wish to *go with you*. If she visits the city at any point, it will be her own choice. Her two months hasn't passed, and you have no right to try and take her from our protection if she doesn't want to go. So I ask that you and your guards leave."

'I would prefer to hear those words from Atalanta. For all I know, you're simply trying to keep the girl to yourself. And as a concerned member of the council, I have all right to want the girl safe.'

This piece of shit was relentless and repetitive. Why was he so insistent on taking Atalanta away from us? What was his game?

I glanced at Jason, who was studying his uncle, and caught him saying something, '—her? What about Atalanta is making you push so hard on this, but not my father?'

My eyes flicked back to Calder to try and catch his response. 'I'm simply doing my best to assure our continued survival. Atalanta is female, and she must be protected."

Something was just off, though, and Jason clearly felt it too. He was shifting from one foot to the other and fidgeting with something in his pocket. Probably his phone. Calder, however, seemed to be calmer the longer time passed. His posture had eased, and his annoyed frown had slowly morphed into a downright villainous smile.

"Listen, Calder. I'll see if Atalanta will talk to you." I pulled my phone out of my pocket. "I can't promise anything."

There it was. This flicker of worry crossed over Calder's face. Jason spotted it too as he quickly pulled out his own phone and put it to his ear.

'What have you done, Uncle?'

Assuming Jason was calling Atalanta, I dialed the FaceTime on Hip's cell. It went to voicemail moments later. I tried the others and nothing.

Calder watched us, his face having settled back into that creepy smile of his.

"What did you do, Calder?" I asked, putting power behind it.

Calder's lips pulled up in a snarl. 'How dare you try and push me?'

"What did you do?" I pushed harder.

He stumbled but didn't budge.

I looked at the guard who had kneeled to me before and he shook his head vigorously.

"This meeting is over." I glared daggers at Calder and the guards who stood so cockily behind them. "If she or her father have a single injury, I will make sure you suffer immensely before your deaths."

Chapter Twenty-Two

ATALANTA

"Is it just me, or do all hospitals have really shitty coffee? Like it's some sort of requirement along with their subpar food," I chuckled as I took a sip of the hot liquid.

"Should we be concerned that you'd been at enough hospitals to draw up this analysis?" Hip asked, looking concerned.

"I plead the fifth." I grinned and put the cup to my lips, trying to look innocent.

The four of us sat in the hospital's cafeteria. When I woke up that afternoon, Jason and Hip had swapped places. I could say I was rather annoyed at them. Not only letting me fall asleep in my father's hospital bed, but not waking me up in time for school. Hip assured me that he pulled some strings. Did I want to know what that meant? Not really, but as long as I got my diploma, I supposed there was no real harm done.

Eventually, Ajax and Percy showed up to keep us company.

It was almost surreal. An important part of my life was spent in hospitals, and sitting in one with the guys was an interesting experience.

After a couple of hours sitting in my father's room, Hip got antsy and wanted to explore. The two of us got up and roamed all of the areas of the small hospital that we were permitted to see. I was nervous walking around in the open with my eye uncovered, but no one seemed to take notice, all the nurses and doctors distracted with their work and families wrapped up in each other. It was nice.

I hadn't checked yet, but I was sure that some of the scales on my forearms and legs were still there.

Eventually, Ajax and Percy found us secluded in the corner of the cafeteria, Hip practically shoving food down my throat.

"If I can guess which card you picked, you have to eat another bite of pasta," Hip said, shuffling the deck of cards he had been using to get me to do stuff all day.

My jaw dropped. "This is highway robbery."

"I believe you are using that idiom incorrectly." Percy took a sip of my coffee and scowled, he and Ajax sitting down across from me and Hip at the table.

I snorted. "That's only because you haven't played a single round with him today. He cheats."

Hip gasped, putting a hand to his chest. "I take affront to that statement."

"He cheats," Ajax confirmed after taking a large bite of one of the sandwiches Hip had gotten for me.

"Then I'll just take my punishment." I shoved some of the bland pasta in my mouth.

Hip grinned and shuffled the deck of cards. "Good girl."

"So, Theseus and Jason are meeting with Calder?" I said around a bite of food.

Percy checked his watch. "They should be talking with him right about now."

"And the reason the three of you are here is...?"

"We like you," Ajax grunted.

I giggled. "I think I know that, but seriously."

"We want to make sure you stay safe. Calder isn't above underhanded tricks to get what he wants."

"You seemed to know him well."

Percy readjusted his glasses and scowled. "We were acquainted when I used to live in Anthans."

I frowned. "Anthans?"

"Oh, right, we never told you the name. Anthans is the Mer city nearest to Argos. Capital city of the Kingdom of Attica, one of the twelve Mer kingdoms." Percy said.

"Twelve? Jeez. Okay, when things settle, I demand some sort of class on all the things I don't know."

Were there other mythical creatures? How may Mer people walked among us? If Mer were basically immortal, how old were the guys? Really, questions I should have asked before.

Percy gave a genuine smile. "Sure."

"Our kind seem to like the letter A," Hip mumbled.

I snorted. "No wonder you all flocked to me."

Hip opened his mouth to make a comeback when he was interrupted by a loud click and a woman's voice coming over on the loud speaker.

"Security call to north wing. We have a Code White. Code White in the north wing."

I shot up, my chair clattering to the floor behind me. "She just said Code White?"

The guys all stood up too. Their eyes wide, alert.

"I believe so." Percy said.

I looked at my guys, concerned. "Code White means there's danger."

"Your father!" Hip gasped.

I took off down the hallway back towards the north wing and my father's room. If the guys followed behind me, I didn't notice.

Please, be okay.

A group of people were gathered at the entrance to the north wing. A couple of security guards were trying to block anyone from getting into the wing.

When the guard stopped me as well, I begged. "Please, let me through. My father is down this hall."

"Miss, please stay back." The guard said blocking my way.

With tears in my eyes, I tried again. "Let me through."

The guard's eyes glazed over and he began to move aside before his partner glared at me and shook the guy's shoulder. He blinked and looked back down at me. Had I just syren voiced a man?

"It's for your safety." The second guard said.

This was BULLSHIT!

The guys caught up behind me.

Percy walked up next to me and said with authority, "Her father is down that hallway. What's going on?"

The man, who I suspected to be a Mer, straightened when he looked at Percy. "Sir, there is a hostile."

"What kind of hostile?" Hip asked.

The guard nervously looked around at the other people in the hall before coming forward and whispering in his ear. "Councilman Calder has sent guards, and they are looking for you, miss."

My eyes widened.

The guard looked over at me. "It would be best if you left out the south entrance. We are keeping them to this wing right now. Telling them that they will scare the patients."

I was taken aback by the fact that this stranger was trying to protect me.

"My father is in this wing." I told him.

The guard looked back over his shoulder, worried, before turning to look back at me. "We will make sure no harm comes to him. Please, hurry."

I looked back towards the way we came. Rule #10: Always prioritize your safety first. He used to say 'Your father can take care of himself'. Well, my father was laying unconscious in a hospital bed.

No...

This wasn't Emmanuel. These were goddamn motherfucking *fish people*!

349

I took a deep breath and straightened my shoulders. "I'm sorry, I can't leave him behind. No offense to you."

The guard smiled and stepped aside. "I understand. I wouldn't leave my kin behind either."

Just as I was about to step forward into the hall, Ajax's warm hand engulfed mine. "Atalanta."

I looked back at him and the others, apprehension reflected across all of their faces. I understood, they wanted to protect me as well, but I couldn't just be the damsel.

"Back me up." I said, firmly.

They all nodded, if hesitantly.

I hurried down the hall towards my father's room. It was quieter than before. There were no patients wandering the halls, no nurses at their posts. I doubted the guards would harm them, but I'm glad they were staying out of sight. I would hate for anyone to get hurt because of me.

Turning the corner to my father's hall, there were two average looking humans. Well, as average as Mer could get with their tendency to be extremely attractive. I don't know why I expected them to be in full armor and scales, but the two men before us were dressed in sweaters and jeans. Leaning against the wall on either side of my father's door and chatting nonchalantly.

"Can we help you, gentlemen?" I asked, keeping my tone even.

They straightened and looked at me in surprise. The one on the right, a tall blond, spoke. "Calder wasn't lying. You're female."

I cocked a brow. "Yes, I'm female."

"It's been a really long time since we've seen a made female." Blondie gave me a short bow. "It's an honor."

The Mer on the left, a redhead with killer dimples, said, "If your maker hasn't told you, turning females is pretty hard. Most don't survive. Councilman Calder sent us to come get you. He said it wasn't safe for you on land."

"I'm sorry, but I'm not coming with you. I have people here that I must protect." I said, standing straight, hands fisted at my side.

Their friendly smiles fell, eyes growing cold. A lump of lead formed in my gut at those stares. At once, my guys stepped closer, taking up defensive position on either side of me while my own body tensed up, ready for a fight.

Blondie spoke first. "He told us you won't leave because of your human father."

"We've been ordered to rectify the situation." Redhead tilted his head towards my father's door.

A third Mer, a tan man with dark hair, stepped into view, holding a knife to my unconscious father's throat.

"DAD!" I screamed and lunged forward, only to be pulled back by one of my guys. "LET HIM GO!"

The Mer holding my father sneered. "This is why it's necessary to cut ties with humans before being turned. It creates needless bloodshed."

"That makes no sense! You're the ones causing this!" Hip growled.

"We are simply following orders." Blondie said.

I didn't take my eyes off my father. It had to be the Mer's great strength that allowed for him to hold up my father's slumped form with one arm. He was still hooked up to his I.V. and heart monitors, and I could hear the machine in his room beep, slow and steady despite the intensity of what was going on.

I tensed as I met the eyes of the Mer holding him. He was enjoying this. His eyes were practically twinkling as he watched me, pressing the knife closer to my father's throat.

"Please, no, leave him alone!" I shot forward only to be pulled back by a strong grip on my shirt sleeve. I looked back to see Percy, shaking his head at me.

"We must approach this calmly," He whispered.

"There is no negotiating this. We were instructed to bring you with us, by any means necessary." The Mer pressed the knife deeper to my father's throat, drawing blood.

Blood.

A roaring began in my ears.

"Dad!!"

I felt a tugging at my clothes, then the sound of tearing cloth making it through the roaring.

Blood. Red.

Red.

I bit my tongue.

Not the time, have to focus!

The blond was an easy target. He underestimated me; he was the most relaxed, but still large. But I had claws, now. Claws to tear through flesh, to draw blood myself. I was strong.

"Atalanta, stop!"

I kicked the man's legs, right at the knees, and shoved my elbow into his chest. He went down easily, and using his momentum, I shoved his head with my other hand so hard into the ground that it bounced.

Out like a light.

I pulled the knocked out blond up by his red stained hair and pressed my claws to his neck. Now I mirrored the man who had my father.

"Rule #11: If you can't run, fight." I pressed my claws deeper into his neck. "And fight to kill. Let my father *go*!"

Everyone was frozen, surprise blaring across all of their faces. Each heartbeat of the stare-down between me and the man who held my father felt like an eternity, but I was still, calm for the first time since I had woken up to find I had lost my humanity. Adrenaline and bloodlust were powerful things.

I wanted to tear out all of their throats, rip them limb from limb the moment my father was free and safe.

"Atalanta..." Ajax said, slowly stepping closer to me.

He sounded worried. He felt it. Felt my calm. Why should it worry him?

I heard the bang of a door slamming open and the sound of hurried footsteps coming our way. I tensed.

Reinforcements?

"Atalanta!"

I relaxed some. Jason, and probably Theseus, were here. We now outnumbered the enemy.

Out of the corner of my eye, I saw the two come into view and halt.

"I don't care how many of you there are, this doesn't change my orders. Let Kile go and come with us, and I won't have to kill your father," the dark man said.

I clenched my hostage's hair tighter. "How about you let my father go, and you and your friends walk out of this alive?"

His eyes narrowed. "You don't have it in you."

"You don't know me," I hissed, barring my fangs.

I knew I had gone full shift the moment I had seen the Mer holding my father. I could feel the scales rippling across my body, and my eyes were probably glowing just like everyone else's.

"Atalanta," Jason whispered in the same tone one would use on a feral animal.

What was their problem? I was handling this.

"It seemed we have ourselves a Mexican standoff." Came a new and unwelcome voice.

I rolled my eyes. "Calder, has anyone told you that you make entrances like a subpar Disney villain?"

Jason's uncle stood in the hall, flanked by four other guards. Now *they* were more what I expected, standing tall and holding spears. Their armor definitely wasn't metal, because it didn't clink or shimmer as they moved. Perhaps leather? Their approach was so silent.

I shifted my position so that I kept Calder in my sights while still watching the man who held my father out of the corner of my eye.

"Subpar? My dear, I don't do anything subpar."

"We can tell by your overzealous hit squad. Call them off!" Percy commanded.

Hip growled. "We won't let you dipshits take her."

Calder looked exasperated. "I clearly underestimated your tenacity, but I won't be reigned by children. The girl is coming with us."

Brandishing their spears, three of the four guards rushed forward and backed the guys against a wall.

"STOP!" I screamed.

Chaos broke out in the hall. Fast as lightning, Ajax grabbed a spear and yanked, pulling one guard forward to smash his face. Percy did the same to another guard, grabbing the spear and using it against him.

I felt hopeful. Hopeful that we would make it out of this crazy situation. Hopeful that no one would get hurt.

But of course, I had hoped too soon.

Percy screamed, "JASON!"

Blood.

Everyone paused for that split second as Jason stared down at the spear blade that was wedged right into his gut. His face was blank, the surprise and pain not yet catching up to him. Then time sped up again as blood began to bloom around the wound.

"That's enough!" I heard Calder call.

But I didn't listen as I dropped my hostage and raced at the culprit who had hurt what was mine. Launching myself onto his back, I slammed my hands into his ears.

"Ah, *fuck*!" the bastard shouted. Disoriented, he dropped the spear that was still wedged in Jason's stomach and fell to the ground with my weight on him.

Underneath his body, I snaked around him, locking his arms with my legs and wrapping my arms around his head, cutting off his air supply. He bucked against me, trying to free himself, but I had the upper hand.

That was when one of the first goons jumped into the action, tugging at my arms and yelling for me to let go of his brother. Well, his brother stabbed my boyfriend, so I'm going to go with fuck no!

Another guard was on me, tugging at my body and trying to get me to let go of my prey.

He was struggling less, now. I wasn't going to kill him, just incapacitate him.

I bit at a hand that wrapped around my arm.

"Let go of her!"

"I said that's *enough*!"

"Let go of my brother!"

More hands were on me and I was beginning to get overwhelmed. The guys were shoving the remaining guards, going back and forth above me, and so much weight was pressing down on me. It was like the giant pile ups you see in football.

"STOP!"

It felt like a wave washing over me, halting my body and ripping away my free will. Everyone else around me stopped moving as well.

Syren voice, I realized moments later. Both Calder and Theseus had shouted together.

"Break it up."

"Move away."

A breath of fresh air as all of the bodies got off of me. I was still unable to move for several moments before the Syren's voice released me and I let go of the now out-cold guard.

Looking up, I met Theseus's beautiful, worried gray-blue eyes.

"Are you okay?" He asked.

"I'm fine. Jason…"

Jumping up, I rushed over to Jason, who was slumped against the wall, the spear still sticking out of his stomach. There was blood everywhere and he looked so pale.

"Jason, hang in there." I said, my hands flying frantically but not doing anything. I didn't know what to do!

He grunted and looked up at me. "Tis' but a flesh wound."

"Is this the time to be quoting Monty Python?" I scolded.

"There's always time for Monty." He chuckled and winced.

I made a quick glance to where my father had been. The man was no longer holding him. He was in Ajax's arms. Safe.

Hip took off down the hall. "I'll go get a doctor!"

Theseus came over and put pressure onto Jason's wound at the base of the spearhead.

Turning back to Jason, I gave a wobbly smile. "Yeah, you'll be fine. I mean, we're in a hospital."

But there was just so much blood. Too much, considering the spear was still in there.

"Don't cry."

"I'm not crying."

Jason gave a weak smile then tilted his head, gesturing to my right. Looking over my shoulder, I saw Percy. My calm, steady man was crying. Tears fell down his cheeks in steady streams, but it was the slight wobble of his lower lip and shaking of his hands that broke me.

Percy fell down to his knees next to me. "I'm so sorry."

"Percy, I'll be fine. Like Atalanta said, I'm in a hospital. It's not like I'm going to die." He shuddered violently. "I'm just really cold. Not something I'm used to."

Carefully, I inched forward and slid up beside him. He was shaking so badly, I was worried he would make his wound worse as the spear swayed. As gently as I could, I reached over and steadied the spear. With my free hand, I grasped his tightly. I felt that relaxing happy tingle race through my body, warming me from the inside. I only hoped it was doing the same for him.

Percy kneeled there, his body shaking as much as Jason's as he stared at the blood that was soaking into his shirt.

"Percy..."

His eyes snapped to mine. They were glowing the brightest amber, and the color was seeping. I would have thought he was a wolf shifter if I didn't know better. He was also partially shifted. Actually, as I took a moment to look around the room, all of my guys were partly shifted. Eyes glowing and scales glinting in the light.

Suddenly, Percy lunged forward and slammed his lips to Jason's in an extremely passionate kiss.

I blinked and leaned back. Jason looked just as shocked as I felt for a split second, before losing himself in the kiss. Pushing back against Percy. Demanding, pleading. Tilting his head, he reached up with his free hand and ran it through Percy's hair and tugged.

Oh, this was hot.

Until Jason winced and pulled away with a pained groan.

Percy's face, for that one second, looked so beautiful and full of wild passion before it turned stony and full of anger.

Standing up, Percy turned towards Calder, shaking. "This is *your fault!*"

I studied Calder. His confidence was cracked. I could tell he was worried about Jason as his eyes kept flicking our way, brows scrunched, but his pride was what was probably keeping him from doing something.

"It's a regrettable outcome." He said, hesitance in his voice.

"Regrettable!? If he dies, I will torture you within an inch of your life, until you beg for death. I will keep you alive for centuries, torturing you until your mind is so broken, you will be but a shell of a man."

Calder gulped and took a step back. "You don't have it in you. You're just a scholar."

"*Try me.*"

I looked back at Jason, who met my gaze with an expression that said the same thing I was thinking. *That was really hot.*

TIED TO THE SEA

Finally, a doctor and several nurses arrived, immediately getting to work on Jason. Shooing us away, two of the nurses carefully laid him flat while another pulled up a crash cart. I felt so stupid having sat there doing nothing when I had known there were carts like that one all over the place. This was not the time for a memory lapse.

I watched as they assessed his wound and made the decision to pull the spear out.

"Shiiit!!" Jason gasped, and jolted forward before his eyes rolled back and he passed out.

I glared at Calder and gave the guard who stabbed Jason a good kick in the ribs.

Before packing the wound, the nurses poured a pitcher of clear liquid all over Jason's body. That, I could recall, was not normal medical procedure. "What was that?"

"Salt water." One of the nurses said.

They worked quickly. Rolling Jason onto his side, they slid him onto a sheet and lifted him into a bed.

"We will take him into surgery now." The doctor looked over at Calder and nodded stiffly. "Councilman."

They started pulling Jason away and I was torn. Literally, it felt like a part of me was tearing up inside as I watched them take him away, but I had to settle this.

"As soon as he's stable, we will be transporting him to Attica." Calder spoke to the nurse that remained behind.

"What?" Percy and I said.

He looked at us. "It's what's best for him. He'll mend more quickly in the water and we have some extremely skilled healers."

Okay, I was fucking done.

Storming up to Calder, I reared back and punched him square in the nose. He stumbled backwards, holding his nose as it began to leak blood.

"Percy is right! This is all your fault, and you can't just take him! He doesn't want to go back to the city and become one of your experiments. You may be his uncle, but you're not his parent, and this is his decision."

Calder straightened, and in that moment I realized that he had held something back. He wasn't any taller, but I felt so much smaller in his presence. "What about this whole incident haven't you understood, little girl? I hold the power here. I have jurisdiction over this whole town, and if I want something done, it will be done. Your resisting my orders is what caused this in the first place, and if you continue to resist, more people, including your father, will get hurt."

I stumbled backwards as I felt the push of his power.

He was wrong, right?

This wasn't my fault...was it?

My eyes bounced from the blood on the floor to the two guards I had knocked unconscious.

This *was* my fault.

A palm at my back jolted me out of my head. Looking over my shoulder, I saw Ajax standing there, clear worry on his face. Hip, Percy, and Theseus stood behind me as well. They were here for me, my support.

But...

"Calder, give us a moment alone, and then I'll come with you."

He nodded, pulled out his phone and walked down the hallway.

Turning to the guys, I said, "Calder may have been using mind voodoo on me, but he wasn't wrong. If I keep resisting him, he will continue to make this worse. Next time, we might not be so lucky."

"Atalanta, this is a bad idea." Percy said.

"It probably is, but I can't risk my father. And I can't see another one of you hurt."

"We can handle them!" Hip shouted.

Ajax nodded, his body tense, ready to go down fighting.

Theseus took my hand. "No one else will get hurt, Atalanta. Not on my watch."

He sounded so powerful and so angry that I could hardly see the sweet man who I had come to know. This was the side of himself that he always kept hidden.

I shook my head. "No, Theseus, not on mine. I go with Calder now, this will end. Emmanuel can't get to me and Calder won't get to my father, or all of you."

"Atalanta, if you go to the city, we can't guarantee you'll come back." Theseus sneered as if the idea disgusted him.

I squeezed his hand and ran my thumb across the back of it. "I know, but I have faith."

I looked over to Percy, who was so quiet. I could see his mind moving a mile a minute as he tried to figure a way out of this. I could tell the moment he realized that going with Calder was the right choice, his eyes flicking to the guards and knowing that right now we were outgunned and outmanned. Then they shot back to me, his shoulders slumping.

Out of all of us, I knew he would be the one to come up with a plan. I just had to trust in that fact.

"We go with her." Percy said, his eyes snapping up to look at all of us. "We stand trial with her and ensure the council gives us a stay of judgment. What Calder's doing is going against several laws. If we play that to our advantage then we can give ourselves time."

"Promise me," I said. I didn't know what I wanted them to promise. To make sure I wasn't going to be stuck in the city to become a baby making slave? To not give up on me? To stay? I didn't know, but I needed to hear them say it.

"I promise."

Chapter Twenty-Three

ATALANTA

The car ride down to the dock felt like I was in chains, being dragged to my doom. Anxiety prickled in my chest and I knew I was shaking. The adrenaline of the last hour was wearing off and the bravery going with it.

Calder was in the car in front of us with Percy, Hip, and the two guards I had knocked unconscious. Leaving me with the second guard I had choked out, who was driving, and the guards that never joined in on the fight. Ajax and Theseus sat on either side of me.

The other guards that Calder had brought with him were still at the hospital, waiting on Jason to come out of surgery, and they would be transporting him themselves. We had debated with Calder for over an hour on this decision. In the end, he pulled his "I am the boss" card, shutting us up.

This entire situation was a dumpster fire, and I really wished that I could just jump out of the car right now and take off. I hadn't even gotten a chance to tell Clint what was going on, or have Theseus do some mind voodoo on him, so who knows what would have happened when he realized that I was gone?

So, to list the current problems, my father was still in a coma, Cal was dead, Jason was stabbed, and a small team of government officials would probably be blowing a gasket any moment now. And I was being dragged off to an underwater city for a trial/evaluation thing.

Giant dumpster, filled with dog shit. And on fire.

Ajax's hand engulfed mine. His expression told me he wanted to reassure me.

"It's okay, big guy, I'm not going to chicken out." I tried my best to smile, but it was hard.

"I wish you would." He grunted.

"Can I ask you something?"

He nodded.

"Before, you seemed okay with me going to the city. Why?" I asked.

He was pensive for a second before replying. "It's what was safest for you."

"What changed?"

"Jason. He told me about the whole…" He waved his hand, not able to find the words.

I sighed. "Yeah."

"I want to keep you."

That got a chuckle from me. "I want to keep you, too."

"I'm feeling a little left out. Can I be kept too?" Theseus pouted.

I turned towards him so he would stop having to crane his neck to keep up with the conversation. "That's sexist."

His pout turned into a slow smile. "Is it? I would call it equality."

The guard I had not beaten up turned around and looked at us. "He's got you there."

The man had sharp features, like a model, but combined with his near albino appearance, and rather pointy teeth from the 100 watt smile he was sending my way, he was pretty intimidating.

The guard's smile fell and he turned away like I had somehow hurt his feelings. There was a part of me that felt bad that I had somehow hurt this unknown guard's feelings, yet there was another part of me that wondered why I should even care. He was part of the group dragging me away from Argos but he also hadn't taken part in the attack at the hospital.

Ugh. So confusing.

Shaking off the weird moment, I looked back at Theseus. "Consider yourself a kept man."

While Ajax and Theseus's presence helped sooth me some, my heartbeat jumped like a jackrabbit when the car pulled to a stop. The guards hopped out of the front and opened our doors.

I noted how the albino one gave Theseus a low bow as he got out. When the guard reached into the car for me, I flinched and leaned back into Ajax.

"No need to be afraid, miss. I'm not going to hurt you," he said, his all too pointy teeth flashing me.

I snorted. That's what they all said before they locked you in their basement and broke your fingers one by one till they moved to your toes.

"That's a tad specific," he mumbled, looking surprised and a bit concerned.

I blinked. Did he just read my mind?

His sexy wink gave me my answer.

That was cool.

I tentatively took his hand and he helped me out of the car. It wasn't like I could hide from a mind reader, anyway.

"No, not really," he whispered.

Hip and Percy looked thoroughly annoyed and were shooting daggers over to Calder, who was walking to the edge of the dock.

"Does she know how to fully shift yet?" He called.

We all stayed silent.

"I'll take that as a no. Callum will carry her, then." He nodded to the cute mind reader.

"No," My guys all growled at once.

Calder rolled his eyes. "This will be a lot quicker if one of us carried her, and I'm not allowing any of you to do it, lest you take off with her."

I looked over to Callum, who was already staring at me with an apologetic expression. I don't think he was any more comfortable in this situation than we were. He seemed to be giving Theseus a sort of special attention, and he hadn't joined the other guards in their attack earlier. I wondered what his deal was.

I nodded. "Fine."

The guys all groaned and grumbled. They sounded like a bunch of disgruntled teenagers who had just been given detention. I couldn't blame them, they all looked as exhausted as I felt.

I wanted to reassure them somehow, remind them that this wasn't permanent, but with Calder's guards watching our every move, and now mister mind reader, it wasn't worth the risk of another one of us getting stabbed.

"No more stalling. As the humans say, let's get this show on the road." Calder said, and jumped off the dock, clothes and all.

I had expected the guards to follow after him, but they continued to watch us, their weapons at the ready. Particularly, the two dicks I had attacked were studying me with twin sneers on their faces.

"Let's go, miss." Callum said gently, and with his hand barely touching the small of my back, he ushered me towards the ocean.

At the edge of the dock, I halted, staring into the waves, apprehension rising in my stomach. The others stood behind me and the guards behind them.

Theseus stepped up to my other side and took my hand. "Together."

I nodded and took a deep breath before diving off the dock into the water.

Just like with my previous experiences in the ocean since the change, the water below was so clear and bright it was like I was viewing it in the middle of the day instead of in the dark of night. I looked down at my webbed feet before kicking forward with great speed. For a moment, I was filled with joy as I felt the water rush over my clothed body. A sense of freedom loosening the chains around my soul.

Looking to my right, I realized that I still held Theseus's hand. His presence was very comforting.

"Atalanta, breathe." I heard Percy call.

Theseus made the motion of taking a deep breath in.

Okay, I could do this. I had gills.

Slowly I exhaled the breath I was holding, then, preparing for a jump to the surface, I inhaled the salt water. I felt the water wash into my lungs and the gills on the side of my neck open up, filtering oxygen from the water.

I sighed. "I don't know if I'll ever get used to that."

"Took me several years." Ajax said.

Looking over to him, I saw that he and the others were pulling off their clothes. I didn't pull my eyes away this time. Nope, I deserved some eye candy after all this bull. Man, I was not disappointed.

Watching them change was mesmerizing as scales and fins bloomed from their skin. Watching their legs fuse together was freaky, but strangely satisfying. It all happened so fast that I almost wished I could rewind and play it back in slow motion.

Percy hadn't fully shifted, though. Staying in a half shifted form, he looked uncomfortable.

Swimming over to him I said, "Percy, you can't keep hiding from me."

"I'm not hiding." He grumbled, not meeting my eyes.

I cocked an eyebrow with him.

His shoulders fell, and after shooting quick, nervous glances over at the others, he let the rest of his shift overtake him. His skin took on an almost bluish tint and his scales, which I already knew were black as the midnight sky, were so beautiful.

Percy wasn't terrifying, but his shift was something that some might consider nightmarish. With the long spines on his back, extremely long and pointed rows of teeth that protruded from his mouth, and luminescence running down his tail, he reminded me of a creature that a deep sea anglerfish and a lion fish had given birth to, before being thrown into a radioactive bath.

But underneath it all, he was still my sweet, thoughtful, judgmental librarian.

Tentatively, I swam closer and gave him a kiss on the cheek. "There, doesn't that feel more comfortable?"

His amber eyes slid over to the rest of our group. "Not really."

I placed my hand on his chest. "It's a step. Be proud of who you are, Percy, because at least you know who that is."

He looked like he was about to say something, but Calder interrupted. "Enough. I'm tired of waiting. Let's get going."

I joined the guys in their grumbling this time and turned around to try and find my 'ride', Callum.

He was waiting several feet away and ho-ly SHIT! "You're a shark!"

"Well, that's a little rude. Don't you think?"

"But you look like a shark!"

He didn't look like any of my guys. His pale skin didn't look like it was marked with scales, but splotched with gray skin, as was his tail, which came to thick vertical facing points. Starting at his stomach was a more cream-like patch that tapered all the way down where his feet would be, and I bet on his back was the classic triangular dorsal fin.

"Now you're just making me feel self conscious. And I have scales! They are just smaller than the others."

Swimming closer, I could see he was right, his 'skin' shimmered in the light like the rest of ours. Didn't really change the fact that he definitely was more sharklike than the others.

"I'm sorry, I didn't mean to make you feel self conscious. It just surprised me."

He sighed and didn't answer for a while. Awkwardly, I hooked my arms around his shoulder and hung on tight as our whole group took off. Cutting through the water at speeds faster than a speed boat. I was surprised I could keep my eyes open, or that the force pummeling against my skin wasn't painful, but I supposed my body was acclimated to things like this, now.

Callum and I were in the center of our entourage. The guys were closest to me with Hip and Theseus ahead, Ajax and Percy behind, and the other guards surrounding us, with Calder leading the group.

"Like you humans, Mer come in all sorts of colors, shapes, and sizes." Callum finally said several minutes into our trip.

"Are you also prejudiced against those who are different?"

I hadn't thought much about it until now, but most of the Mer I had met, despite the beautiful rainbow of their scales, were all pretty pale skinned. I was probably going to stand out like a sore thumb, but I wasn't a stranger to being a minority.

"Not really. At least not those of the Attica kingdom. We are a…how would you say it? A crockpot culture. Like your America, it was formed from many different Mer coming together from all over to form a collective."

"Doesn't mean that prejudice doesn't exist."

"You're right." He tilted his head and appeared to be looking in Theseus's direction. "It just probably isn't what you're used to."

He was silent for a while after that, so I took the moment to marvel at our surroundings. Humanity had hardly explored 20% of our own oceans, and as we zoomed past reefs, rocks, sand, and giant plummeting gorges, I was really feeling how vast our oceans were. I bet it was a similar feeling to when astronauts stared in the emptiness of space. I felt so small, yet strangely centered.

It was also very quiet. Closer to the shore, there was the crashing sound of the waves acting as white noise, but now, so deep, it was still and silent. Until it wasn't. Whenever we passed by schools of fish or larger sea life for a brief moment, that static-like noise would flare up in my mind, like what happened back at the aquarium.

At least now I knew I wasn't crazy, it had to do with the sea creatures. Perhaps something to do with what Hip had talked about, my talent.

"If your talent is what I think it might be, it's a pretty cool one." Callum said, quietly.

'Eavesdropping is rude.' I thought pointedly at him.

"Hmmm, perhaps," he hummed.

'So, what do you think my talent is?' I asked.

"I believe I'll let you figure that one out on your own. Just trust your mates and know you're not insane."

'Thank you. You're pretty nice, for one of Calder's flunkies.'

"I'll have you know I'm not a flunky. I'm simply a guard of the kingdom. My commander was the one who put me on this mission."

'Oh, I see.' He was just following orders. I felt bad for him.

We stayed silent for a while after that, I knew Callum could hear me, but I pondered over what was to come and worried over Jason's condition. I had to remember that we had literally been in the hospital. Jason would be fine. We would all be fine.

My stomach was flopping around like a fish thrown out of water.

TIED TO THE SEA

"Hey, hey. It's going to be okay." Callum reassured me, his hands rubbing at my arms wrapped around him.

I snorted. "Easy for you to say."

"True, but your mates are here." He crooned, in a comforting tone. "They have clearly bonded to you and that means they would never let anything bad happen to you. Mermen are extremely protective of their mates. In fact, this whole time, they have been mentally plotting how they would whoop the tar out of me the moment I'm out of your sight for nearly touching you."

"Really?" I couldn't hold back my grin.

He nodded. "The blond one in particular is very vindictive."

That got a chuckle out of me.

"Thanks, Callum." I squeezed my arms in a hug.

"Don't thank me yet. We're almost there."

My head snapped up, and at first I only saw flat ocean floor in front of me. But then the ground dipped down into what at first appeared to be another trench, but was actually a crater-like slope. There, far up ahead, was a glowing mass. It looked huge, and if it was this big from so far away, it had to be massive.

As we swam closer, I was reminded of the photos I had once seen of the great barrier reef. Bright colored coral, swarmed by hundreds of different types of colorful fish. But as we got closer, I realized how massive some of these structures were. It wasn't just a simple reef, it was, in fact, its own city. A city made from coral, rows of jagged buildings spiraled upwards.

375

Mer were *everywhere*, their scales shimmering in the city's lights.

"Wait, we're under water. How are there lights?"

"The Mer who are skilled at fire manipulation power all the lights in the city." Callum answered.

"Fire manipulation?" I looked back over my shoulder at Hip. "Like how you control water?"

He shrugged, not tearing his eyes away from the city in front of him. "Must be."

Hip was adopted by humans. Was it possible this was the first time he had ever seen Attica?

As we got closer, the immense size of this city almost overwhelmed me. From our vantage point, I could see over the coral buildings to the cityscape, but I couldn't see the other side. The tallest structures looked almost as big as the empire state building!

Theseus drifted back to swim next to us. He looked at me. "Magnificent, isn't it?"

"Insane, is what it is." I continued to stare at the city as it came closer, elation swelling in my chest. "How is it that humans have never found this place?"

He pointed upwards. "You're not realizing how deep we are. No human could ever swim this deep down without killing themselves."

"But we—they have machines that can."

Theseus had a mischievous smile on his face. "But we have magic defenses for those."

"Magic?" I squeaked.

"Yeah, magic," Callum twisted his head to try and look at me. "Are you telling me that you were turned into a mermaid and didn't think magic was real?"

Something tickled at the back of my mind, a distorted memory of Hip saying something similar. Another lost memory.

Callum was looking at me with concern now.

I shook my head and focused back on the looming city.

Calder called from up ahead, "Our destination is the Imperium Tower."

"Oh, you're getting some nice digs. The Imperium Tower is used for visiting diplomats." Callum said.

"That seriously doesn't make me feel better." I mumbled.

We reached the edge of the city, where much smaller buildings speckled the land. I was right in that most of their structures were made from magnificently large hunks of coral, which looked to be beautifully hollowed out with windows and doorways and everything. They must have used some sort of magic to do it, because there was no way that was natural. Something I would love to look into later.

I noticed we were following some kind of pathway, the sand shimmering with blues and pinks. With us now going at a much slower pace, I reached down and scooped up the sand. It was super small shells, the texture looked rough and sharp, but it just flowed through my fingers like silk. As we came further into the city the buildings became more densely packed and the path was then lit with floating lanterns.

Callum was right, the Mer here came in *many* shapes and colors. Men, women, and children paused in whatever they were doing as we passed. Their scales were all different colors of the rainbow and their tail types varied greatly. I spotted a woman who had a tail that resembled a clownfish with orange and white stripes. I noticed a lot more men than women, but there was just this quiet humanity to everything I was seeing.

Two women floated along down the path, holding children and chatting about their day over at the 'Scaler', whatever that was. Three men and a woman sat at a table outside of what seemed to be a restaurant, eating lunch. On one corner, there was this man playing an instrument. I had no idea what it was, but the sound was similar to that of a trumpet, just more bulbous.

It honestly felt like any city I had been to in the past, until you realized that everyone was underwater, covered in scales, with tails, and mostly naked. Oh, and of course, a giant whale had just casually passed overhead, minding its own business.

Our group was getting plenty of attention, something I definitely didn't like. It almost felt like the hair on the back of my neck was standing on end.

"Miss, your nails are digging into my skin." Callum said through his teeth.

Whoops. I loosened my grip. "Sorry, I don't do well being the center of attention."

"I had guessed that. We're almost there."

We turned down several streets before our little caravan came to a halt up ahead. In front of us was one of those extremely large coral buildings. Red and blue, wider than two football fields, and at least fifty stories tall by human standards. The door looked to be made from two giant clam shells, laden with gold. There were words in another language carved into the archway.

Up ahead, I could see Calder and Theseus talking to the men who were stationed in front of the door, decked out in armor. After a few moments, the two men bowed deeply before opening the doors, gesturing for us to be ushered though.

"I think it's okay for you to get off my back."

"Oh, yeah." I hesitated. There was something about Callum that was comforting, like a big brother vibe.

A hand touched my shoulder, pulling my attention. Hip floated next to me in his silvery half naked glory. His eyes were dark thunderclouds in that moment, and his expression told me that he needed me. Needed my support for what lay ahead, just like I needed his.

Sliding off Callum's back, I took Hip's hand. Percy and Ajax joined us, crowding me in a protective circle.

I noticed how they were glaring daggers at Callum, who just winked and said, "Told you," before he swam into the building ahead of us.

"Let's go." I said, kicking my legs forward.

Following the rest of our group into the building, I got my first glimpse of the inside of Mer architecture. It was lit up with a warm golden glow emitted by two lanterns, which were affixed to the walls, and a giant hunk of crystal that was placed in the center of the room. The walls looked like the inside of a smoothed out stone cavern, the only hint to its coral outer structure being the blue and red swirl of colors. The ceiling pitched up all the way to the top where I could actually see a small hole leading outside.

There was actually furniture! Couches, tables, and chairs were scattered about. Looking closer I could see where the legs melded with the floor as if the stone floor had been carved down around the furniture itself. I imagine it would be helpful when keeping the furniture from flooring away but a nightmare when I considered that stuff like the chairs could never be moved.

"Wow," Hip and I whispered in awe at the same time.

I met his eyes and we both giggled.

Swimming around the giant crystal, I could see a desk at the far end of what was essentially a hotel lobby. There was a Mer waiting behind the desk, speaking to Calder and Theseus.

"Your rooms will be on level twelve. Rooms 2 to 8." The clerk passed over something to Calder.

"Thank you." Turning to us, Calder said. "You'll be staying here. Tomorrow, you are to meet with the council. I suggest resting up."

"What about Jason?" Percy said, "You said he would be transferred here once he was stable."

"My guards have orders to bring him here."

The clerk lit up. "I can send someone up to tell you when your companion has arrived."

"Thank you very much," I said.

The clerks eyes landed on me and widened. "My goodness."

"That will be all," Calder shifted in front of me, as did the other guys.

Theseus usurped me away from the desk. I took a glimpse back at the clerk, who was watching my every movement. What was his problem? I thought made Mer were normal here.

Calder handed over small slates of rock. Taking mine, I noticed more Mer language etched onto it. Was it some sort of room key? I turned the stone over to study it, but it was bare.

"Callum, you will be posted here along with Trevor. Make sure none of them leave the hotel." Calder slowly met each of our eyes, his gaze full of threat.

Callum stood up straight. "Yes, sir."

Calder nodded at us before leaving, taking a huge, oppressive weight with him.

I sighed. "Well, this has been an interesting night. And since I can't leave the hotel, I think I'll be going to bed."

Looking around, I tried to find an elevator, or perhaps a staircase that I could use to get to my room.

Callum laughed. "I love mades, they're such newbies."

Between Ajax, Percy, and Hip's combination of growls and death glares, Callum stopped laughing. Clearing his throat, he pointed upward. "There is no need for stairs or...wait, what's an elevator?"

I blinked, my tired brain taking a moment to process what he was saying. Then Theseus grabbed my free hand and tugged me upward, our feet leaving the stone ground.

Oh.

Hip let go of my hand and darted up ahead of us before flipping upside down and staring down at me. "What is gravity, am I right?"

I laughed, a childish joy bubbling up in my chest. I had finally reached that point in exhaustion where you just feel bubbly and everything is funny. I had nothing to giggle at. Nothing about this situation was funny. Yet once I started, it was hard to stop.

Hip extended his hand. "Come on, Speedy."

I looked at Theseus, who had been so quiet. He smiled and let go of my hand.

"You know, astronauts use water to train for space. So if you really think about it, we are totally in space right now."

I snorted. "That's pretty silly."

"You could use some silly right now. Come on, sleepy girl." He moved back the hair that was floating at the side of my face, obstructing my vision. I think it had grown another inch since he had cut it the other day.

Theseus shoved me forward up into the cone shaped ceiling of the building, towards Hip, who caught me in his arms and flipped us into a tumble. We were weightless, floating in the water untethered.

Hip grabbed my hands and swung me around several times before letting go, using the momentum to push me upward, rocketing me up. I now realized the purpose of the open ceiling.

I did a back flip and nearly hit the wall, but was caught by large, tan arms. Ajax.

"Having fun?"

"I'm what some might called 'tired loopy'. So...yes."

Ajax guided me over to one of the open floors and to the door with the symbol that matched the slate in my hand. Taking the slate, Ajax held it up to the door, causing the symbol on the door to glow for a moment before swinging open.

The room inside wasn't very large, but it didn't need to be. There wasn't a bed, or a desk, or even some sort of side table. The only things in the room were a mirror hanging on the wall, a stone-looking cabinet, and what appeared to be a hammock.

I stared at the room for a few more moments before looking back up a Theseus. "So...this is the life of luxury in this great Mer city?"

"I have a feeling you were given one of the servant's quarters." He replied.

"Well, make the best of it, right?" I said, attempting to be positive.

I drifted further into the room and studied the hammock, which looked like a giant, rolled up leaf. I guess I should...unroll it? Looking over to the others, who were right outside the door, I asked, "Do I get a pillow?"

"Mer don't need pillows, but trust me, this will be the most comfortable "bed" you have ever slept in." Theseus replied, coming into the room and brushing his hand across the leaf hammock.

Where his fingers touched, the leaf shimmered and the tight roll bloomed open like a flower. "It's a leaf of the Kalkapta flower. A deep sea carnivorous plant which lures fish in with a sweet smell, and once in range, its leaves wrap around its meal."

I scowled. "That sounds...nice."

Percy chuckled. "It's not dangerous once it's separated from its flower, but it will still cocoon you. Morph to your body and prevent you from floating away in your sleep."

"Ah," I hadn't considered that.

"You all better get to your rooms for the night to rest. Councilman Calder will be back in the morning to come get you." I heard one of the guards say through the barricade of my guys.

All of their faces held the same disgruntlement, besides Theseus, who was continuing to look at me with a sad smile.

"The guard wants you to leave."

He frowned. "I can do what I please, and I want to stay with you."

TIED TO THE SEA

My brow furrowed. "And why is that?"

"What?" He blinked.

"Why is it that you can do as you please?" I asked.

"Uh...you know, he's right. I better go."

I grabbed his arm. "Theseus. We talked about this. No more secrets."

He wouldn't meet my eyes. "Tomorrow, okay? I promise you'll know tomorrow. For now, I want you to just keep seeing me as me."

"All I will ever see is the man in front of me."

"And that's all I'll ever want." He kissed my forehead. "Goodnight, my Sleeping Beauty."

One by one, the guys kissed me goodnight and left the room, the door closing behind them.

Without the light streaming through the doorway, the room was much darker. The dim light coming from a small lantern in the corner was the only comfort I had in this darkness. Thinking about it, I wondered how they could tell when it was morning? So deep down, the light from the surface never had hope to reach this city.

I looked over at the deadly leaf hammock. Might as well try to sleep.

Running my hand over it like Theseus had, the leaf glowed and opened up for me. Awkwardly, I half climbed, half floated into its embrace. Once inside, the leaf closed around the lower half of my body like a blanket cocoon. He had been right, it was comfortable.

It was so dark.

And for the first time since I had woken up…

I was alone.

Chapter Twenty-Four

JASON

Gods damn it.

Where was I?

Opening my eyes, I had expected to find myself in a hospital bed, or perhaps in my own room, but no. At least what I saw was familiar. I was cocooned in a Kalkapata leaf, and if I had to guess, I was being pulled along through the water. I was naked and fully shifted, something I must have done in my sleep.

Wiggling around, I popped my head out from the top of the leaf. "Hello?"

"Good, you're awake. We're almost there," said one of the mer who was carrying me.

Two mer were carrying my ass through the water.

"What's going on? Where are my companions? Where's Atalanta?"

"The made and the rest of them are in Attica. They went ahead of you, and we had instructions to escort you as soon as you were stable." Replied my other escort.

Why? Why was she in the city? What had they done to her?

I wanted to scream and fight my way through. Taking a deep breath, I knew that would be pointless. They would take me to the city and I could find out for myself. That, and I honestly doubted I could escape the group of guards that were carrying me in my condition. Fuck, who would have guessed that getting stabbed would hurt like a bitch?

So I just laid back and let them drag me along.

What was I going to do? If they learned everything, my life with my parents, with Margo and Davie, my entire life on land was over. At least, the life I had would be. They would drag human after human in front of me, telling me to turn them, and when I wasn't doing that, they would probably match me with a strong female of their choosing and I'd have to fuck her. Get her pregnant as many times as I could.

They were escorting me as a prisoner.

To top it off, my whole body ached from my stab wound and from withdrawal. I had been away from Atalanta for several hours, if I had to guess, and my body was raging against me for it. It was almost too much.

"Sir,"

I blinked. We had already arrived to the city. Craning my neck, I recognized the Imperium Tower. I brushed my hands along the outside of the Kalkapata leaf, making it release its hold on me. Tumbling out, I tried to right myself, only to almost slam my face into the ground.

"It's good to see you up and about."

Looking up, I saw the guard who hadn't joined in on the fight, the one who had kneeled to Theseus at the docks.

"The name's Callum." He held out his hand for me to shake. "And you must be Jason. Your girl was quite worried about you."

"Is she okay?"

"The last I saw her, she just looked real tired, but otherwise okay. Councilman Calder put her and the rest of your…uh…gang…up in some rooms."

He came over and slung my arm over his shoulder, supporting me, and helped me into the building. I had been here several times in the past with Uncle Calder, shaking hands, faking smiles, you know, greeting dignitaries. Being put on display as 'the next in line to inherit the family name'. Like a dancing monkey.

"I was supposed to go tell your companions when you arrived, but since I have to wake them up in about an hour anyway, and I wasn't given *explicit* orders, why don't I just take you up to the young lady's room? That way you can have some alone time with your mate… before you have to meet with the council."

I stared to Callum skeptically. What was his deal?

His face fell. "Atalanta is really nice, but she seemed…off."

"She's been through a lot. She's had a hard life, and it hasn't gotten any easier since she was turned."

He nodded knowingly, which only made me even more suspicious of him.

"You need to learn to be more trusting," he reassured me. "Lets go, she's on one of the higher floors."

After Callum dragged me up to Atalanta's floor, he lightly knocked on the door a few times. Inside, I could hear her jolt awake and struggle around in her hammock before finally freeing herself.

"Coming!" She said quickly, before mumbling, "after I figure out how to open this door."

A few moments later, the door swung open, giving way to the most beautiful yet concerning sight. Her hair, which had grown at least an inch or two since Theseus cut it a couple days ago, was sticking up at odd angles. Her beautiful dark skin looked a lot less pale than when I had last seen it. In the hospital, fighting off those men in her half shifted form, she had looked like a statue of our warrior goddess Leneatha, beautiful and powerful. Until I got a spear in the gut, quickly causing her to look so frail and afraid.

"Jason! Oh, thank God," She sprung, flinging her arms around me in a tight hug.

A sharp pain laced through my body from my wound, but it was drowned out by the pleasant buzz of our connection draining away all of the withdrawal aches I had been feeling.

"Are you okay?" We both asked at the same time.

"You two are just so cute," Callum said before he lightly shoved our bodies through the doorway Atalanta came through. "Now, get out of sight before I get in trouble for breaking the rules."

I looked over my shoulder, about to ask him to tell Percy I had arrived, but he beat me to it. "Don't worry, I'll tell the guardian his charges are safe and together."

He shut the door behind us, casting us into a near darkness.

Breaking apart from me, Atalanta began to run her hands all over my body. "They didn't hurt you, right?"

She stopped her hands right over my stab wound, where the doctors, I assumed, had stitched me up.

"That's my question, Atalanta." I put my hands on her shoulders. "What are you all doing here?"

"After you passed out, your uncle gave orders to have you transferred here. I had no choice." She looked down at her feet, fiddling with the torn sleeve of her shirt.

I shook my head in disbelief. "You should have left me. Your safety is more important."

"That's bull fucking shit and you know it!" She growled, her head snapping back up and getting in my face.

"I don't think a bull would fuck its own shit." I chuckled.

She smacked my arm again. "You know what I mean!"

I grabbed her hand before it came in for another smack and kissed her palm tenderly.

We were silent for a few moments, me holder her close, before she let out a heavy sigh. "Oh, Jason, what are we going to do?"

"We will keep being brave." I answered, pretending to be stronger than I felt at that moment. "We aren't alone in this. The others are here and they won't let us be kept here against our will. So you keep being brave, just like you were back at the hospital, which, by the way, was amazing. I never would have guessed you could fight like that."

She grinned. "My father made sure we knew how to defend ourselves after...everything."

"You were like a completely different person, an avenging goddess." I joked, wanting to lighten the mood.

She stared up at me, her eyes distant. "I've been so scared, terrified really, my entire life. There comes this point in fear, where you can either choose to let it consume you, or you get mad, get so angry that you consume it. In that moment, I was tired of being afraid. Just like I was tired of being afraid the night Emmanuel's sister invaded my home."

I kissed her forehead. "I can't lie to you, Atalanta. Being a Mer, living hundreds of years, having to hide what we are from humans. It's a hard life, and I'm so sorry I thrust it on you. I can't promise you there won't be times we will be afraid, terrified even. But know that I will always be by your side. We will do this together."

"Jason...I think I'm falling in love with you."

Twenty seconds of bravery, Monroe.

"Well, I know I love you."

For a few moments, she stared up at me, her eyes as big as saucers, then she reached up, gripping my hair, pulling me down for a kiss. Even though my body was tired, it reacted instantly, sparking to life with lust.

TIED TO THE SEA

Gripping her waterlogged jeans, I pulled her to me, pressing her body against mine and deepening the kiss.

She pulled away. "Wait, wait."

"What?"

"You're not just saying you love me because of the mate connection, right? It's not, like, clogging your mind or anything?"

I shook my head and snorted. "Hell, no. I was already falling for you before the accident. Our connection just pulled my head out of my ass."

"Good," She pulled me back to her and pulled herself up, wrapping her legs around my hips.

I dove my tongue into her mouth. She tasted so sweet, and was wearing far too much clothing. Instinctively, I gripped the back of her jeans and began to tear before she pulled away again and smacked me.

"If you want me naked, just ask. These are my only clothes and I will not be going around naked." She scolded me.

I growled. "Then you better get out of those clothes, fast."

When she hesitated, I gave pause, mentally bopping my head, remembering how insecure she'd been about us seeing her scarred up skin. This stop and go was killing me, but I could be the better man. "Hey, we don't have to do anything if you don't want."

"I'm not — I mean, I'm not a virgin, it's just..."

"I know,"

"Maybe just the pants?" she asked, looking really nervous.

"Whatever you wish," I opened my arms wide. "You're in control here."

Slowly, she began to unbutton her pants, and I was enraptured. Unable to take my eyes off her beautiful form as she slowly slid down her pants and underwear. The scales that ran down her legs glinted in the light, and *fuck* were they sexy.

Our matching scales were my claim, marking her as mine. Regardless if the council paired her with new mates. She was mine. I let out a possessive growl and immediately regretted it, afraid it would startle her.

But something amazing happened. She met my eyes, heat filling her gaze.

Straightening, she asked, "I'm in charge?"

I gulped, and bobbed my head up and down enthusiastically. "Completely."

Confidence and command filled her posture. There, *there* was the strong girl I had first met.

"Hands behind your back, Jason."

Eagerly, I locked my hands behind my back.

"Now, shift."

I nodded and gave my body back over my human form, my tail receding, and I was back on two legs, completely naked to her and hard as a rock.

She studied me, her eyes roaming up and down my body. A part of me wanted to take command, grab her and fuck her against the wall until she screamed my name, but I stayed still.

Bouncing on the balls of her feet, she floated over to me, elevated to the point where she was a couple inches taller than me. "Keep your hands behind your back until I say so."

"Yes,"

"Yes, ma'am." She corrected me.

I cocked an eyebrow at her.

"Too far?"

I slowly grinned. "No, it's hot. But I think I'm more partial to mistress."

"Hmmm, I think I like it." She ran her fingers along my jaw before grabbing me and giving me a searing kiss.

Her free hand ran down my arm and hopped over to my stomach, skimming down and causing me to involuntarily shudder. Already my body was showing my arousal as my scales rippled across my skin, surfacing and receding over and over again.

"Would you like me to touch your cock, Jason?" she asked against my lips, nipping the bottom one for good measure.

"Yes, mistress."

Pressing her full body against me, she gripped the base of my cock and slowly ran her hands up and down. When she broke off the kiss and bit into the base of my neck, I groaned.

"Oh, gods, can I please touch you now?"

She rubbed her thumb against the tip, ignoring me. Her free hand slid across my back, her claws digging into my skin and sending tingles over my body. In one fluid motion, she changed positions, gliding through the water until her face met my cock. I tensed in anticipation as she slowly brought her mouth closer to me, her tongue darting out to taste me. Just as she was about to put that mouth of hers around me, she diverted her path and kissed right at the base, her hand massaging my length instead.

"Tease," I hissed.

She chuckled in reply, keeping that mouth of hers away from my dick.

My body was twitching now. Wanting her mouth on me, but wanting to touch her in turn. I clenched my hands behind my back, reminding myself to keep them there when I just wanted to wrap my fingers in her hair and fuck her mouth.

She nipped at an area right above my cock.

"Atalanta," I groaned.

She hummed before answering. "Yes?"

"Please."

"Please, what?" She asked, pretending to be so innocent.

Wrap that pretty mouth around me? Let me touch you? Let me taste you?

Crap, what did I choose?

TIED TO THE SEA

"Oh, fuck!" She almost sent me to my knees when she suddenly shoved my dick so deep into her mouth, the head hit the back of her throat.

Her eyes looked up into mine, and if my cock wasn't in her mouth, I had no doubt she would be grinning like a cat who had caught the canary. Her eyes were glowing so brightly, one a dark amber the other an emerald green. I had no doubt that my eyes were glowing the same color, another one of my marks on her.

Mine.

I began to pull out for a thrust when she gripped my ass, keeping me where I was. I could feel her tongue rubbing against the underside of my shaft. Damn, did she know how to torture a guy.

Stay, hands. Stay.

Slowly, she worked her mouth up and down my length, using her strength to keep me from moving even an inch.

This went on for far, *far* too long, bringing me nearly to the brink before she finally released me with a satisfying pop.

I shuddered, breathing heavily and looking down at her through hooded eyes.

She licked her lips as she stared up at me. "Would you like to return the favor?"

Yes.

No. Stay calm, cool.

"You mean slowly torture you?" I asked.

"Touch me, Jason." She pleaded.

Fuck calm.

"Finally," I growled and lunged for her.

She squeaked as I lifted her up, her weightless body easy to manipulate as I pushed her up against the wall. Hooking her legs over my shoulders, I was at the perfect height to lick her glistening pussy.

My hands went up to knead her breasts as I delved my tongue into her heat. She was so wet for me, and her moans were so perfect.

"What do we have here?"

I barely pulled myself away from Atalanta to look over at the open door.

"Percy." My arousal spiked even higher under his darkening gaze as he took in the sight before him.

"Having breakfast without me?"

I noticed how when he entered he quickly shifted to his human form, his lean physique and large member all out on display.

Trying to keep it cool, I said, "I wasn't aware you would be joining us."

"I had to make sure you were okay. I see now that I should not have worried so much."

Flutters started in my stomach at hearing those words. I looked back at Atalanta, her gaze filled with such lust I knew the fact that he was here, watching us, was driving her wild.

"Now that you're here, why don't you stay?"

"Gladly." He shut the doors behind him, and for a moment, only the glow of his eyes were visible before mine readjusted to the darkness again.

He floated over to us, standing so close to my naked body, yet I could only just feel the warmth of his cold flesh. "Atalanta."

"Percy," she panted.

In a swift motion, Percy pulled her into a commanding kiss. I was definitely thinking about how my cock had been in that mouth only moments ago.

Atalanta gripped her hands into my hair, and taking that as my cue, I got back to it, devouring her cunt like it was the tastiest cake I had ever eaten. Her moans were swallowed up by Percy's kiss as he stole one of her breasts from me, working at it, caressing it while I did the same to the other.

She was writhing in our hands. Lost in the pleasure we were giving her.

She pulled away from Percy with a gasp. "Jason, I need..."

I hummed as I paid special attention to her clit.

"I need you inside of me."

I ran my tongue along her slit one more time before asking, "Are you sure?"

"Yes, I'm sure."

"Are you super duper sure?" I teased.

"Jason." She warned.

I chuckled and pulled away from her pussy, only to be grabbed by Percy, his mouth slamming into mine, his tongue delving into my mouth, searching, tasting. Just like that moment in the hospital. Hope and heat bloomed in my chest, and damn, now I was torn between kissing him and fucking Atalanta.

He made the decision for me when he broke away moments later, my mouth following his.

He chuckled and licked his lips. "That tastes divine."

I blinked and looked at Atalanta, who also stared at Percy with a shock and arousal. It was Percy who broke the moment again when he unwrapped Atalanta's legs from around my shoulders and guided her down, rewrapping them around my waist. Her heat pressed right up against me.

"Fuck her, Jason." Percy commanded before he kissed my shoulder.

I felt it then, the shift, the realization that it was no longer Atalanta or I driving this encounter, but Percy.

Readjusting myself until my tip was pressed against her entrance, I looked at her for affirmation. When she nodded, I pushed in slowly, my hands going around to cup her ass.

"Holy crap, you're so tight." I hissed.

Her hands gripped my upper arms, claws digging in. I hesitated, worried it had been too long and I was hurting her, until she growled at me and used her legs to shove herself all the way onto my shaft.

Gods, she felt incredible.

"Jason," Percy said, gripping my hips, coaxing me to pull out of Atalanta and thrust into her again, this time a little faster.

It was amazing, feeling my cock diving in and out of Atalanta's tight sheath while Percy drew himself closer, his cool body pressed against my back, his hands on my hips. His lips kissing and nipping my neck and shoulder. His hard cock wedged between my ass cheeks.

I lost it.

I pounded with no restraint into Atalanta. Our moans echoed off the coral walls of the hotel room.

As I was getting close, one of Percy's hands let go of my waist and moved around me to brush his fingers against Atalanta's clit.

"Yes!" She yelled, and I felt her tighten up around me, ready to cum.

I hadn't even noticed when Percy's other hand left my waist to stroke his own cock. We all worked each other into a frenzy before jumping off that cliff.

I came so hard, and with my body so exhausted from everything that had happened, I collapsed, leaning heavily against Atalanta and the wall behind her. I could feel Percy's hot cum on my back before the water washed it away, and Atalanta's pussy quivering around me. Sparks burst in front of my vision and I felt a snap. Our bond had just grown stronger. We were one step away from becoming full fledged mates, I could feel it. My awareness of her was so heightened I could have sworn I knew exactly what she was feeling.

And Percy had finally shown his hand. He didn't just view me as his assistant, or his friend. No, looking up into his eyes, I could tell I meant much more to him than he was willing to admit.

"Jason," Atalanta said, concern lacing her words.

"Yes?"

"I think you popped open your stitches. You're bleeding."

I chuckled. "Worth it."

In fact, I may have gone another round on savoring Atalanta's beautiful body while Percy assisted, paying his own special attention to her neck and breasts.

We were all panting heavily, with stupid grins on our faces, sprawled across one another on the floor when Callum knocked on the door.

"You nasty eel snakes better make yourselves decent. We leave in twenty!" Callum called through the door.

I groaned and rested my head back on Atalanta's stomach. "Time to face the wolves."

"More like sharks." Percy murmured.

I grinned. "Big fat sharks, who drool, and don't like cake."

She gasped and my head bounced with her laughter. "How could they be fat if they don't like cake? And what the fuck is an eel snake?"

"They fill their tummies with little children." I answered.

TIED TO THE SEA

"And eel snakes aren't real, it is just an idiom," Percy said, with his big, knowledgeable brain.

"I mean, technically we aren't real either." Atalanta said slowly, on a total sex high.

"Shit, you right." I gasped.

The three of us cracked up laughing. Percy had to have been on a sex high as well, because I had never heard him laugh so unabashedly, his deep voice warming the cold pit that had formed in my center.

"Alright, we should go." I slowly sat up and let my change overtake me. The closest version to decent I had.

Atalanta watched my change with fascination and then Percy's right after. I noticed a moment where they shared a look. I believe she was giving Percy the courage to be in his true form.

"Do you think the others will be jealous of what just happened here?" She asked as she awkwardly slipped her pants back on, stumbling sideways in the water.

I smiled and set her upright, holding her while she finished. "We can't guarantee they will be 100% happy with it, but trust me when I say they won't take it out on you."

"We, however, might lose some scales." Percy commented.

"I'm sorry!" Atalanta exclaimed, looking worried.

Percy shook his head vigorously, eyes wide. "No, I'm sorry, I was only joking. It was in bad taste."

She still looked somewhat panicked.

I rubbed her back, trying to comfort her. "We should get going."

Carefully, she exited the room, looking around before fully swimming out.

I began to follow when the twinge of pain from my wound made me flinch back and groan.

"I probably shouldn't have let you exert yourself like that." Percy hooked his arm under mine and helped me along.

"Probably, but…I mean." I smirked and tilted my head at him.

He chuckled. "Yeah."

"Do you think it was too soon?"

"It was her choice, Jason. If you keep letting your heart fill with doubt, you will only stunt the relationship you're cultivating."

I nodded, lost in my own thoughts. For years, I had been groomed to one day become the next head of the family. An agreement my parents begrudgingly agreed to after I was born. In exchange for my future, I could live out my childhood on land with my parents. My family wouldn't interfere with my life or the town which they held power over beyond teaching me.

My entire life, chained to a path I didn't choose. Meeting Atalanta, choosing her, was the first time I had ever gone against that.

We followed Atalanta and the guard, Callum, down to the floor where Hip, Theseus and Ajax were waiting.

TIED TO THE SEA

The three of them studied us. Ajax's expression remained unchanged, but the unmistakable spark of jealousy in Theseus and Hip's eyes made guilt, and something akin to pride, war in my chest.

They didn't say anything about it, though. They simply flocked around Atalanta. Asking her how she slept and if she was hungry.

Callum assured us that we would get to eat after the trial was finished. They wanted us hungry. Hunger stripped away our energy, made us more honest. Not that there was much point.

Calder arrived with several of his personal guards to escort us. As they brought us outside, Calder took my arm, pulling me away from Percy and dragging me to the side. Percy growled and moved to protest, but with a snap of Calder's fingers, several guards pulled Percy away.

"Jason. Are you well?"

I leaned against the wall of the building, supporting myself. "As well as I can be, Uncle."

"I just want you to know that I didn't want you to get hurt." He said, putting his hand on my shoulder.

He looked sincere and as someone who I had long looked up to, it made me happy to know that he actually cared, and yet...if Calder was anything, it was ambitious, and it was that ambition that caused me to be stabbed and put us in this situation.

"But it's what happened, Uncle. This was your decision to force the issue and you have to live with those consequences."

405

Turning away from him, I powered through the pain and followed after my friends.

Chapter Twenty-Five

ATALANTA

The guards were taking us through the city, and if I felt we were getting attention before, this was like I was standing one a float in the center of the city's big parade. Thousands of eyes were on us, questioning, wondering.

I tried my best to keep my mind off of them. Tugging at the sleeves of my shirt, I focused ahead, on the guards who were escorting us to wherever.

I tapped Theseus's shoulder. "So, what's the lowdown on the council?"

"The lowdown?" He chuckled.

"Yeeeaah, like what's their dealio? If I'm about to be subjected to their scrutiny, I want to know who I'm up against." And knowing my enemy would help distract me from the nerves that were beating up my stomach.

Theseus took my hand to sooth my nerves. "The council is made up of twenty Mer from all walks of life. Citizens, nobles, elders..."

"You have nobility?" I asked, surprised.

He nodded. "We have a king and queen."

"Wait, so you have a monarchy *and* a council?"

Percy popped into our conversation. "The council acts as the king's advisory, and stands judge on basic matters. Basically, they're how the King knows what goes on in the kingdom. They also meet and make decisions on how to lead, bring those decisions to him in proposals. They will judge you of your worth and inform the king. Ultimately, it is his choice on what happens to you, but the council holds a lot of sway on that decision."

"Kind of sounds similar to America's democracy set up, with the senate and the president." I said, simplifying it in my head.

"Don't compare us to your human government. We are nothing like them. The council works to the betterment of its citizens." One of our guards called from the front.

I snorted and rolled my eyes. Yeah, sure. That's what they all claimed. Blind faith.

"So will all twenty of the council members be coming to the trial?" Percy asked.

"Only nine were able to make it on such short notice. Usually, an evaluation is scheduled in advance so that all twenty may come." Callum, who was floating on my other side, shot a glance back at Calder.

Of course, he was the reason.

Callum leaned in and whispered, "Between you and me, the other members will be extremely miffed to be missing out on this trial period of the year, really."

I looked up at him. "When was the last time you had a made Mer evaluation?"

He thought about it a moment before saying, "For a male, it's been about thirty years. For a female…maybe about three hundred?"

"Three *hundred*?!"

He smiled. "You, miss, are a rare commodity around here."

"Great," I grumbled.

Theseus's hand squeezed mine reassuringly before swimming up ahead to speak with one of the guards. Ajax took his place by my side, while Hip squeezed himself between Callum and I.

The place where the council met wasn't what I suspected. Unlike the rest of the city, which appeared to be mostly made of spiraling coral that came to points, the council building was a smooth dome shape.

Swimming closer, I could see that it didn't have a door. Entering the building, we travelled through a long hallway. I squeezed in closer to my guys, Hip and Ajax holding my hands while Percy and Jason pressed in behind me. Theseus's red hair flickering like fire in the dim lighting in front of us. His shoulders were squared back and he was exuding a presence similar to Calder's.

Something was up with him.

Reaching the end of the hall, we entered a sloping crater that seem to span the entire length of the dome. It was like a closed in amphitheater with large step-like benches that ran down along the crater before it plateaued at the bottom.

The guards brought us down to that plateau and told us to stay put, leaving without further instructions and taking positions at the edge of the crater. Taking in my surroundings, I noticed statues lining the edge of the crater, staring down at us. Judging. Calder sat down on one of the benches, looking as cool as a sea cucumber.

I turned to my guys. "What's the plan?"

Jason looked me dead in the eyes, his expression so serious it sent shivers down my spine. "Don't tell them the real circumstance of your turning. We fell in love, you were smart and found out our secret, and I turned you. That's it."

Theseus shook his head. "That won't work. Kekrops can tell when you're lying."

"Shit!" Jason cursed. "I forgot. Maybe he isn't here today? Callum said only nine of the council are here."

Theseus snorted. "Unlikely, the old fool never misses a meeting."

My head snapped to Theseus. He looked so certain. Was that what was going on with him? He knew the people on the council…was he once on it?

"What do we do?" I asked Theseus.

"Atalanta, you will have to answer all of their questions honestly. Everyone else, stay quiet. Only speak when spoken to."

"Theseus," Percy said and signed.

I believe that was the first time I had seen Percy sign Theseus's name. A closed fist and a circle around the head. I had once heard that in deaf culture, a person's signed name was wholly unique to them. I didn't know if it was true or not, but I wondered what Theseus's sign meant.

No, focus.

Theseus growled. "I know what I'm doing, Percival."

"But if they find out, we'll lose her."

"We won't lose her. Have faith."

Percy breathed heavily through his nose, but shut up. I met eyes with Ajax, who simply shook his head. There was always tension between those two, just like Jason and Hip. At least *they* seemed to be getting along better. I hoped Percy and Theseus could one day work through their problems as well.

Moments later, the council entered through a door I hadn't noticed before.

Nine people. Six men and two women strode in, their backs straight, looking regal and powerful. They were wearing half cloaks that went down at their waists. Black with purple trimming. Some of the few Mer I had seen wearing clothing in the city. They floated down to sit at the same level as Calder.

"This trial of the made Mer shall now commence." An older looking gentleman with a long, gray beard said.

A woman, whose skin was dark with pink hair and a sapphire tail, smiled. "My name is Zala. Once a human, like yourself. I know all of this must feel extremely confusing, but we are simply here to help you transition well into our world. Please, tell us your story."

I stayed silent. Staring up at the nine council members before us. They were watching me like a bug under a microscope. Theseus said to be honest with their questions, yet the first one they asked was one I was not willing to answer. Especially not to these strangers.

Rule #3: become the person given to you in the file. Believe you are that person, and no one will doubt you. And one of these men could magically tell if I was lying.

I pushed myself forward, away from the guys. My name is Atalanta North.

"My name is Atalanta North. Born in Michigan, recently moved to the town of Argos, Washington with my father and sister." I paused, waiting to see if the man named Kekrops would call me out. "When I came to the town, I suspected something was up. The people there were too strange. I dug around until I figured it out."

I stopped watching for their reaction, waiting for Kekrops to call me out.

"Anything else?"

I gave a mental sigh. "What else would you like to know?"

"The purpose of this meeting is to evaluate your worth and discuss your future. We can't determine that until we know all about you, Ms. North," Calder said, the smirk on his face making me want to smack him.

I clenched my jaw, straining to keep my face neutral. "My worth is decided by only myself. My future is my own."

A male with jet black tail and a scar running up his left cheek sneered. "A feisty one."

"Aren't they all?" One with spiked up white hair and a golden tail said, making all of the men chuckle.

I watched Zala and the other female Mer roll their eyes. Clearly, there was no lost love between the genders on the council.

"So," a man, with deep red hair and silver tail, began. "You grew up in Michigan?"

I nodded. "For a time."

"And what was your life like before you came to Argos?" The woman asked again.

"Moved around some, but otherwise what one would probably consider normal. Went to school, had a few part time jobs. Nothing too exciting."

"And what of the danger?" The scarred man ask.

"Danger?"

"When I brought you here, I was under the impression your life was under threat by another human." Calder said, looking smug.

I glared at him. "You misheard."

"Lies." A really young boy with fluffy blond hair and a silver tail said. He must be Kekrops. I had expected it to be the old man.

Shit.

"It's a personal matter."

"Regardless of your personal opinions, Ms. North, you will tell this council what we need to know." The older one withe the beard said sternly.

I refused to speak anymore. They didn't earn shit.

Calder sneered. "Ms. North, we can make you speak."

I glared Calder down, daring him to use his powers on me. "And if I don't speak? Will you deem me unworthy? What happens then?"

"We kill you." The scarred one said.

"Fuck, no!" Hip shouted, and the rest of the guys surged forward from behind me.

The guards around the room shot into action, and in a split second had us all subdued. One guard wrapped his arms around my middle and squeezed.

BANG!

How does it feel, you little bitch?

Hold her still.

I was screaming. There was so much blood.

Make it stop!

"Let her go!"

Mom? No.

"She's having flashbacks. You're scaring her!"

"If she won't answer our questions, she will be considered unworthy and must be disposed of!"

"I, Theseus Attica, former crown prince of the kingdom of Attica, deem her worthy! Now let her *go*!"

The arms around me let go immediately and I dropped, gasping for air.

"Atalanta." Hands touched me and I jerked back.

I stared into pools of gray-blue. "Th-Theseus?"

"That's right, pretty girl, it's okay. Come back to us."

"Breathe," came Hip's voice from my right.

Had Theseus just said prince? He was a prince? Oh, my God! it made so much sense! All the strangeness I had seen! The guards staring at him with almost a reverent look...and respect. Why he was so quiet and secretive since we had arrived.

Holy fuck, I was dating a prince.

"What was that?" Came one of the councilmen, drawing my attention back to them.

"Don't be a fool, Tambor. The girl has clearly been through something, what do humans call it? PTRD?"

"PTSD."

"Yes, right."

Zala got up from her seat and came forward. "Dear girl, do not worry. If the prince has vouched for you, then no one here will do you harm."

I nodded, hoping desperately that I could trust what she was saying. Zala radiated warmth and comfort. Theseus and Hip helped me up and kept me from free floating. I looked back over my shoulder. Ajax, Jason and Percy were okay. Disgruntled, but okay, thank God.

"His testament should be worth nothing to this council. He may hold royal blood, but he no longer holds a title." Calder said, a couple of the other councilman murmuring in agreement.

"Regardless of the prince's testimony, this trial is still underway. Councilwoman Zala, please come back to your seat." The old man, who I had a feeling was the leader of the council, said.

Zala nodded and did as the old man told, then turned her gaze back to me. "Dear girl, we understand we have not given you a reason to trust us, and we hope with time that will change. For now, we simply have a few more questions, and then this session will come to an end."

I nodded, smug about the scowl on Calder's face.

They asked me about my family. They didn't seem happy to hear that I hadn't cut ties with them after I was turned, but too bad. I told them the things I had noticed around town. I hoped I wasn't getting the townsfolk into trouble with that one.

The next to speak was the other female. A kind looking woman with long, blond hair that cascaded down to a puddle where she sat, her tail a bright grass green.

"What about your companions? Based on the coloring of your scales, the person who turned you was Jason," she looked over to Calder. "Your nephew, Councilman."

"Yes, I'm rather proud of his accomplishment." Calder replied.

I looked over my shoulder at Jason, his expression telling me he was torn. Probably happy about his uncle saying he was proud of him, but the thing he was proud about…well.

"These men are my mates." I spoke up.

"All of them?"

"Yes," I said firmly.

"No."

My brow furrowed. "No?"

"Forgive me for saying this, but these men are not worthy to be anyone's mate." Calder pointed to my men. "A disgraced guardian, an outcast, not to mention a widowed Mer who couldn't protect his own mate, and a broken royal. My nephew is the only worthy one in the bunch."

"Calder!" several council members gasped.

"My apologies, but it's true. Atalanta would only be able to really prosper if we found her a much more suitable harem."

My mind reeled from what he had said. Looking at my men, I could see how his words had really hit them, and I wondered who he had meant for each title. Was one of them really a widow?

"And who would be in this harem?" the old man asked.

"That's still to be decided. Atalanta, from what I've seen, is an extremely strong girl with much potential," Calder smiled wickedly and stared down at me with possessiveness in his eyes. "I can think of a few candidates."

I practically gagged right then and there. That's what all this was about, he wanted me to himself! That was disgusting!

Thankfully, Calder's intention was apparent to the other council members. They didn't say it aloud, but I

417

could see the moment all of this had turned in my favor. Calder had used his power to pull a newly turned Mer away from her home and force an evaluation for his own personal gain.

"I believe it's time for the council to move to the chambers so that we may make our decision. All in favor, say aye."

There was an echo of agreement, Calder being the last to answer. Watching that dark satisfaction on his face fall was the highlight of my day. He knew he had shown his cards, and now their decision would fall out of his favor.

All at once, the council rose from their seats and swam up the pit back through the door in which they had come, leaving us a moment of peace.

The guys crowded around me. Petting my hair, touching my hands, giving me brief hugs and making sure that I was okay. With them, I didn't feel so out of control. Usually after flashes, I felt so off kilter, but with them here, I was grounded.

"What do you think?" Jason asked.

"I think we have a good chance." Percy said.

"Can we talk about how you're a god damn prince?" Hip laughed.

I snapped around to look at Theseus. "Yeah! You're a prince!"

"Former prince. I renounced my title years ago."

"Doesn't mean shit. Once a prince, always a prince. Royal blood and all that." Jason smirked.

"Not just that, he said *crown* prince." I touched his cheek. "Theseus, this was what you were going to tell me, wasn't it?"

Slowly, he nodded. "I'm sorry for not telling you. My past, it's a bit complicated. The townsfolk know who I am, but have long since accepted me as a normal Mer. I am Theseus, the community center janitor."

I chuckled. "We all have a bit of a complex past. It's what makes us who we are today. I won't judge you for it."

I turned, looking each of my men in the eyes. "As I will not judge any of you for your pasts. You may not be perfect, but you have done nothing but try to protect and provide for me. To me, you are who you are today, not who you were yesterday."

They were quiet, Percy and Theseus looking lost in their memories while Hip and Jason looked at me with so much love.

It was Ajax who moved, sweeping me into a tight hug. Emotions flooded through me. Love, regret, acceptance. When he pulled back, he palmed my cheek and pressed a delicate kiss to my lips. He was so warm in the cool water, and his beard tickled my chin.

I pulled him closer to me as more of his emotions raged through his fingertips and into my body. Heat, passion.

One of the guys cleared their throats and we broke apart.

"Thank you," Ajax whispered before letting me go.

I looked over at Percy, who gave me a sexy wink.

Hip inhaled. "I can smell your arousal from here."

"Shit, shit, shit. This isn't the time." I waved my hands through the water around me, trying to see if I could disperse the scent somehow. The guys pressed in closer to me, their half naked bodies rubbing against my clothed one, not helping matters.

"Break it up, love birds. The council will be back any minute." Callum called from somewhere in the room.

All six of us groaned, grumbled, and broke apart. I wanted them all, and I realized for the first time, it seemed they were truly beginning to accept the idea of us.

A few minutes later, the council returned. Calder's dark look both sent a shiver down my spine and gave me some semblance of hope.

Once they were all seated, the old man spoke. "The council has come to a decision."

"Seeing as this meeting was called on such short notice, and this is a delicate matter, the girl will return to the surface until an appropriate day is chosen."

"As for the matter of her 'mates', appropriate ones will be decided for her."

I was about to protest when Zala raised her hand. "Until then, you will be sent home with the five men you brought with you. Clearly, you have had a difficult life, and being turned has clearly put you in a fragile mental state. I determined that ripping you away from them will only damage you further."

TIED TO THE SEA

"You are a strong Mer, Atalanta North. When this council next meets with you, you will be even stronger."

That wasn't a statement, but a command.

"This trial has adjourned."

I sagged in relief and turned to look at my men, all of us wearing stupid grins.

We had won. We were going home.

Looking at Calder, I could tell this wasn't over.

Epilogue

JASON

Once we were escorted out of the council dome, a heavy weight had been lifted from my chest, and I could finally breathe. Uncle Calder hadn't followed us out, staying behind to, I assume, rant angrily with his fellow councilmen.

The guard, Callum, followed us however, offering to show us the city, but all Atalanta wanted to do was go home. I couldn't blame her, yet as we swam out of the city, I could see Atalanta looking back at it with a kind of longing.

"We could stay, you know. For a least a couple days," I offered.

She shook her head. "No...maybe some other time? You can show me where you spent your summers. And maybe I can meet Percy and Theseus's family?"

I smiled. "Okay."

The swim back to land was too tiring on my body, so Percy carried me on his back most of the way, while Ajax carried Atalanta. I don't know why, but Callum felt the need to guard us the whole way. I was almost worried that he was growing some kind of attachment to Atalanta, but when I asked, he assured me that he only liked her in a little sister sort of way. He had simply wanted to make sure that we got home safely.

I felt that there was something he wasn't telling me, but I didn't push. He left us with a short farewell once we reached the shore, anyway.

Where we landed wasn't too far off the track from the library or Theseus's apartment. Seeing that it was the middle of the night, the five of us trekked through the woods naked, Theseus having the honor of carrying a tired, fully clothed Atalanta.

He had won rock, paper, scissors.

Once we reached Theseus's place, we collectively slumped onto his couch, his grumbles of us getting dirt and sand everywhere pulling a few tired laughs. One by one, all of us dragged ourselves into his bathroom to take a shower, and then one by one, we collapsed, clean and naked, into a tired pile on and around the bed.

It had been a long three days, but I don't think I had ever seen Atalanta sleep so peacefully.

Early the next morning, Theseus had gotten dressed and drove over to Ajax's cabin to bring us back some clothes.

Once Atalanta was awake and had eaten breakfast, she demanded to go to the hospital to see her father.

Damn, if I had had a camera when we walked into that hospital room. All of our faces slack with shock to see Titus North sitting up, fully awake in his hospital bed. Watching Atalanta hug her father while crying tears of joy moved me so deeply, I couldn't help but cry along with her.

He was still somewhat out of it, but once he fully came to, I knew it would be difficult to explain to him what had happened to his daughters. One was dead, and the surviving one no longer human. Depending on his reaction, I was prepared to offer him the chance to become one of us as well. After speaking with the others, they also agreed. Atalanta didn't seem too excited about the idea, and I couldn't blame her. Knowing there was a chance that he wouldn't make it through the change.

We would cross that bridge when we came to it.

For now, the doctor said that they would be keeping him for another week to monitor his vitals and make sure that he didn't slip back into a coma.

It had been three days since we had returned from the trial. My parents had appropriately freaked out once I returned home. My mother vowed to never let her brother darken our doorway again. They hardly ever wanted me out of their sight, but I was an adult and I needed to be with my mate. From what I was told, Hip's parents had about the same reaction.

For now, we were all still crashing at Ajax's place, but today the guys and I had finally begun fixing up Atalanta's cabin. We had our work cut out for us, but we wanted to make sure that it was in tip top shape for when her father came home. I asked around town and was able to get plenty of furniture, and would be moving it in the day after tomorrow.

We still weren't sure how to go about telling the rest of the townspeople. While we knew there wasn't any kind of prejudice against made Mer, and we no longer needed to keep her a secret since the council knew, the situation was delicate. We didn't know when our trial was to be rescheduled. Based on the council's reactions to Atalanta, I highly doubted we would be able to keep her. Once they paired Atalanta with new sets of potential mates, they would sweep her off back to the city, and there was a chance we would never see her again. I was afraid that incorporating her into our way of life here would make it all the more difficult if she was forcibly torn away from it.

Percy had high hopes, said he was working on a plan to make sure that they could never take her away from us. I hoped he was right.

There was also the problem of Atalanta's fading memory. From what I could tell, stress seemed to be the trigger that escalated it, but it was certainly getting worse by the day. It didn't seem to be affecting her short-term memory too much, but I could still see her moments of confusion where she realized that she didn't remember something either we had told her or something about her past. But I could tell that it was scaring her and that she was trying to hide it from us.

Yesterday, I sent word with a courier out to the city asking for Zala to come visit us. She was an extremely skilled healer, and despite being a woman of the council, I knew that she would keep any secrets we told her safe, and Atalanta had seemed to connect with her during the trial.

"What's that you have in your hand?" Atalanta asked, pulling me from my thoughts.

I had been taking a break from tearing up the rotting baseboards in Atalanta's cabin, sitting on the edge of the cliff.

"It's a compass." I said, holding out the golden token my father had once given me.

She carefully sat down next to me, eyeing the raging waves below us.

"Is it a special compass?" she asked.

"Sort of. My dad gave it to me when I was little. His way of trying to guide me in the right direction." I answered.

"Ah, a symbol as old as time." She said dramatically. "Did it ever work?"

I chuckled. "No, it didn't, but I liked the sentiment."

I looked over to her. She was so beautiful. The sun was actually out today and it just made her skin look so warm and inviting to my touch. Her hair, which had grown noticeably longer, much to her annoyance, swayed in the breeze.

"You're my compass." I blurted out.

"What?"

I coughed. "I mean…since that time in my car, you encouraged me to follow my own path. For once in my life, I defied my uncle, made my own decisions. I was lost in my own shit, following along with the labels I was assigned: the town's star athlete, the perfect guy all the girls wanted to be with, the guy who would one day take his place as the head of a noble family. I wasn't happy, not really. I was just going through the motions. You were like my compass, pointing me in the right direction."

She gave me this slow, breathtaking smile. "I don't actually know what to say to that."

"You don't have to say anything," I took her hand. "Just stay with me."

I looked back over my shoulder. The others had joined us, looking out over the ocean in quiet companionship. These men were my friends and quickly becoming my brothers. Well, except Percy. We still had a lot of our own stuff to work through, but knowing that I wasn't alone, that my one-sided childhood crush was returned, it was like I could float on fucking air.

I turned back to look at the water and squeezed Atalanta's hand. "Stay with us."

She gave a soft, content smile. "Always."

....TO BE CONTINUED IN BOOK THREE

Afterword

(be prepared for much emotion and thank yous)

First and foremost, I want to say thank you to each and every one of you who have read Into The Seas embrace, reached out to me telling me how much you loved it, and have supported me over the last year. It really means a lot, and I don't think I'll ever forget your kindness.

2019 was not an easy year; my mother was in and out of the hospital, and in early January, I lost my oldest and closest friend. She did not pass away but is simply no longer in my life. It was an extremely harsh blow, and when I wasn't at the hospital with my mother, I was curled up in my bed, simply done with the world. It was with the help of a few really important people that I've slowly been able to recover.

Alas, the loss of my dear friend did not make writing this second book any easier and will probably forever change my view if not just of this series but writing in general as she was perhaps my biggest helper and supporter. Heck, Into The Sea's embrace would be a very different book if it weren't for her, as she had a hand in helping me create several of the characters(Theseus most of all) and the world they live in. So to my dearest Sherlock Holmes, I thank you and I wish you all the best in your life.

This world I created, it has meant a lot to me and gives me hope for the future. Atalanta and her guys have a long journey ahead, and it will be an honor to write it.

So now, I would like to thank the people who've helped me crawl my way out of that dark place. My mother and my spouse. If it wasn't for them physically pulling me out of bed, making sure I took care of myself and did their best to keep me hopeful, I doubt I would have been here today writing this.

Emilee, not only has she been the dedicated editor of The Nameless Syren Series, but also the loyal friend who has stuck by me through all my bull shit over the years. We may be very different people, but I hope those differences continue to make us the awesome team we are.

I would next like to thank Kat Quinn and Ashley Foote, two new friends who found me after everything and helped pull me from the rouble with their hilarious attitudes and strong personalities. Their friendship has really meant a lot to me over the past several months, and I don't think they realize just how much, so I'm hoping telling them here helps them get it. Both are brand new authors with a lot of amazing talent and potential. I will be leaving their links down below, so check them out.

Lastly, I would like to thank my beta readers and those of you in my author group. Amy, Breyana, Mary, Theresa, and Meghan, my awesome and hilarious betas, have gone above and beyond, not only trying to help me perfect this book but give me ideas for books to come. We are fast becoming a mini family, and I look forward to working with them in the future. As for my reader group, you are everything, my readers, my supporters. Without readers and supporters, what is an author but a crazy person spewing words onto a page and having it sit there?

Thank you all.

And check out my besties and word wife's works!

Ashley Foote => https://www.amazon.com/A-P-FOOTE/e/B07VKPDZX5

Kat Quinn => https://www.amazon.com/dp/B07WK95SGY/

About The Author

Avery Thorn is the Pseudonym for the Young Adult author Jennifer Natoli and it's a pretty cool fake name if I do say so myself. An artist from South Florida I've dabbled in all sorts of mediums, such as: paint, wood, clay, glass, and the classic pen and pencil. Not just visual arts either, as for many years I performed music with Tuba, the violin, and my own vocal cords. Writing and reading have always been my real passion though, and I love that I have the opportunity to get my stories in the hands of readers around the world.

You can find out more information about my other work and connect with me and other readers such as yourself through these links below:

FB: https://www.facebook.com/AverysThorns
Website: https://www.jennifernatoli.com

Email: natolibooks@hotmail.com

Thank you.

Made in the USA
Monee, IL
09 March 2025